T0182589

MR. SPENCER

T L SWAN

Arndell

Arndell

Keeperton Australia acknowledges that Aboriginal and Torres Strait Islander people are the Traditional Custodians and the first storytellers on the lands of which we live and work. We pay our respects to Elders past, present and emerging. We recognise their continuous connection to Country, water, skies and communities and honour more than 60,000 years of storytelling, culture and art.

Originally self published in 2019 by T L Swan
Copyright © 2024 by T L Swan ®

First Published by Arndell, an imprint of Keeperton
1527 New Hampshire Ave. NW
Washington, D.C. 20036

Paperback ISBN: 9781923232013

Library of Congress Control Number: 2024936679

Printed in the United States of America

Sydney | Washington D.C. | London
www.keeperton.com

ALSO BY T L SWAN

Standalone Books

The Bonus

Our Way

Play Along

Kingston Lane Series

My Temptation

The Miles High Club Series

The Stopover

The Takeover

The Casanova

The Do-over

Miles Ever After

The Mr. Series

Mr. Masters

Mr. Spencer

Mr. Garcia

Mr. Prescott (Coming 2025)

The Italian Series

The Italian

Ferrara

Valentino (To be released)

The Stanton Series

SUGGESTED READING ORDER

The Mr. Series books can all be read as standalone books. However, for the best reading experience, we suggest the following reading order:

Mr. Masters
Mr. Spencer
Mr. Garcia
Mr. Prescott (Coming 2025)

ACKNOWLEDGMENTS

There are not enough words to express my
gratitude for this life that I get to live.
To be able to write books for a living is a dream come true.
But not just any books, I get to write exactly
what I want to, the stories that I love.

To my wonderful team,
Kellie, Christine, Alina, Keeley and Abbey.
Thank you for everything that you do for me,
you are so talented and so appreciated.
You keep me sane.

To my fabulous beta readers, you make me so much better. Vicki,
Am, Rachel, Nicole, Lisa K, Lisa D and Nadia.

To my home girls in the Swan Squad, I feel like I can do anything
with you girls in my corner.
Thanks for making me laugh every day.

My beautiful Mum who reads everything I write and gives me
never-ending support. I love you Mum, thank you xo

My beloved husband and three beautiful kids, thanks for putting
up with my workaholic ways.

And to you, the best most supportive reader family
in the entire world.

Thank you for everything, you have changed my life.

All my love,
Tee xoxo

GRATITUDE

The quality of being thankful;
Readiness to show appreciation for and to return kindness.

Trust in the universe.
It always delivers.

DEDICATION

I would like to dedicate this book to the alphabet,
for those twenty- six letters have changed my life.

Within those twenty-six letters I found myself,
And now I live my dream.

Next time you say the alphabet
remember its power.

I do every day.

1

Charlotte

SAME FAKE PEOPLE. Same stupid crowd. Same uninteresting men that I've known all my life.

"Isn't it?" a voice says.

Huh?

I drag my eyes back to the man standing in front of me. For the life of me, I can't remember his name, although I'm quite sure I should know it. He always tries his very best to impress me every time I run into him at one of these family events.

Which is often.

"I'm sorry, I didn't quite hear you. What did you say?"

"I said it's great to get to know you better." He smiles and tries to turn on his charm.

I smile awkwardly. "Yes. Yes, it is." My eyes roam up and down him. He's nice enough, I suppose. Tall, dark, handsome, and has all the factors that should excite me...but don't.

I'm so utterly bored, as if I'm a stranger standing on the outskirts, looking in at all the beautiful people around me. And I know I shouldn't feel that way, because according to society, I'm one of those beautiful people.

"And then I went to Harvard to study Law and graduated with honours, of course," the dull voice drones on.

I smile on cue and gaze around the room, doing anything to escape this boring conversation. I exhale heavily as my mind wanders. The wedding reception is beautiful—straight out of a story book. It's in an exotic location, there are fairy lights everywhere, lots of stunning fashion to admire, and anyone who is anyone is here.

Why doesn't this guy interest me? Nobody seems to anymore, and I've no idea what's wrong with me.

I widen my eyes at my friend, who is standing at the other side of the hall, silently calling for help. Thankfully, she takes the hint and walks over immediately.

"Charlotte." She smiles as she kisses my cheeks. "I've been looking all over for you." She turns her smile over to the poor man in front of me. "Can I steal her for a moment, please?"

His face falls and he purses his lips, nodding begrudgingly. "Of course."

I give him a small wave and link my arm through my friend's. We walk towards the hall.

"Thank God for that," I mutter under my breath.

"One of these days I'm not going to save you. He was all kinds of cute." She tuts as she grabs two glasses of champagne from a passing tray. I smile and take my glass from her, and then we stand just out of view of the man we escaped.

Lara is one of my closest friends. Our fathers have been best friends since childhood, so we kind of inherited each other by default. She's like a sister to me. Our families mix in the same social circles and we're at a lot of functions together. I don't get to see her as much as I would like to, as she lives in Cambridge now.

Then we have Elizabeth, our other friend. Elizabeth is the complete opposite of us. We met her at school, where she attended through a scholarship. Her parents don't have money, but boy, does Elizabeth know how to have fun without it. She's wild, carefree, and has grown up without the social restraints that Lara and I have. She can date whoever she wants, nobody is after her money, and nobody judges her. To be honest, I'm not sure that anybody judges Lara or me either, but our fathers are both very wealthy men, and with that privilege comes the responsibility of upholding the family's name and reputation. Both Lara and I would give our right arm to live the life Elizabeth has. Elizabeth—or Beth, as we call her—lives in London and is hopelessly in love with the idea of being in love. Although she can't seem to find the right man, she's having a whale of a time looking.

Me, however... Well, I've never really been interested in love. After my mother died unexpectedly in a car accident when I was eighteen, grief took over. My father and two brothers suffocated me in the name of protection. I went to school, hung with my girls, and regrouped for a few years. Somehow, time slipped away so quickly, and now here I am at the ripe old age of twenty-four and I've had hardly any experience with men at all.

"Oh, he's lovely," Lara whispers from behind her wineglass.

I look over and see a tall man with dark hair standing in the corner. "Aren't you seeing someone?" I ask Lara.

"He's lovely for you, I mean. Somebody around here has to look at the men on your behalf."

I roll my eyes.

"Surely someone here interests you?"

I look around the room that is alive with chatter, then over to the dance floor that is full. "Not really." I sigh.

Lara falls into a conversation with a woman next to us, effectively dismissing me, and I look around the decadent ballroom. I look up to the ceiling and the beautiful crystal chandeliers.

I love chandeliers. In fact, I love ceilings in general. If a room has a beautiful ceiling, I'm done for. As Lara continues to talk to the lady beside her, I glance through the crowd of people, and then I freeze instantly. On the top level is a man. He's talking to another two men and a heavily pregnant woman. He's wearing a perfectly fitting navy suit and a white shirt.

I watch him for a moment as he laughs freely, and I smile to

3

myself. He looks like fun. Devilishly handsome and clearly older than me, he has fair hair that is slightly longer on the top. His jaw is square, and his cheeks are creased with dimples.

I wonder who he is.

I continue to look around the room, but my eyes keep coming back to him. He's telling a story and being all animated, using his hands to enhance his tale, and the three people he is with are all laughing loudly. A man walks past him, slaps him on the back and says something, and then they all laugh again. I sip my champagne, lost in thought.

Hmm.

I look over to the door and then glance at my watch. It's 10:40 p.m. I can't go home yet; it's too early. Honestly, I would rather have my teeth pulled than come to these events.

My eyes drift back to the interesting man, only this time I see that he's looking down my way. I snap my eyes away guiltily. I don't want him to know that I noticed him. I sip my champagne and stare back out over the crowd again, pretending to be busy.

Lara finishes her conversation and eventually turns back to me. "Who is that man over there?" I ask.

She frowns as she looks around. "Who?"

"The guy on the top level." I glance over and see he is still staring down my way. "Don't look now, because he is looking right at us," I whisper.

"Where?"

"He's up on the top level, talking to the pregnant woman."

"Oh." She smiles her sneaky smile. "That's Julian Masters. He's a judge. Damn fine specimen, isn't he? He was widowed once."

I glance up in time to see one man placing his hand on the woman's pregnant stomach before he kisses her on the cheek as she smiles lovingly up at him.

"That must be his new wife," Lara mutters, curling her lip in disgust. "Lucky bitch."

"I'm not talking about that guy. I mean the blonde man," I tell her.

4

She glances back up and her face falls. "Oh. That's…" She narrows her eyes and she thinks for a moment. "Yeah, that's Mr Spencer. Don't even bother looking at him."

"Why not?" I frown.

"Most eligible bachelor in London. An appalling rake." She raises an eyebrow. "He's loaded, from what I hear, and I don't mean his wallet is loaded."

My eyes widen. "Oh." I bite my bottom lip as my eyes find him across the crowd again. "How do you know that?" I whisper, my eyes unable to leave him.

"Page two of the gossip pages, and he's on the tip of every single woman's tongue in London. I do mean literally." She links her arm through mine. "He's a look-but-don't-touch kind of man. Don't even think about it."

"Of course," I whisper, distracted. "I wouldn't."

"He's probably seeing ten women at the moment. He dates power types. CEOs, fashion designers, models, women like that."

"Oh, I…" I shrug. "He's very good-looking, that's the only reason I asked. I'm not interested in him or anything."

"Good, because he's heartbreak dressed in a hot suit." She inhales sharply as she visually drinks him in. "He's most definitely fucking delicious, though, isn't he?"

I glance his way again and smile. Why are all the hot ones always players?

"Yep." I sigh as I drain my glass. "He sure is."

"Let's go back and talk to that nice guy. The poor man has been chasing you for months."

I glance back over at the guy and wince. "Let's not." I grab another champagne from a passing tray. "What the hell is his name, anyway?"

Spencer

"Do you want a drink, sweetheart?" he asks as he drops his hand to her pregnant stomach. "Are you okay?" he asks softly, thinking we can't hear.

Bree widens her eyes at my best friend. "I'm fine, Julian. Will you stop worrying?"

Sebastian and I exchange looks with a roll of our eyes. Good God, what has she done with my best friend, and who is this imposter standing in his place?

"I'll have a lemonade, please." Bree smiles.

"Don't leave her alone for a minute." Julian points to Seb and me before walking off through the crowd.

I roll my eyes. "Yeah, yeah. God, Bree, you must be sick to death of him. He's like a fucking rash."

Bree giggles. "He's pretty full on."

I smile at the wonderful woman in front of me. She has transformed my best friend Julian Masters' world, and I adore her for it. Julian reappears through the crowd with the drinks, and I glance down and see a woman in a pink dress. I've never seen her before.

"Who in God's name is that?" I ask as I study the perfect specimen.

"That's Lady Charlotte," Julian answers.

"Lady?" I frown. "She has a title?"

"Her father is the Earl of Nottingham."

"Really?" I reply, fascinated.

"Don't bother pursuing that one. She is well and truly out of your league, old boy." Julian takes a sip of his beer. "Her blood is too blue, even for you."

I watch the gorgeous creature talking and laughing with her friend.

"Let's go after these drinks, Mrs Masters," Julian says to his wife.

"Okay." She smiles.

I look over to my friends, annoyed. "Why do you want to go? Stay here with us."

"Because the prospect of taking my beautiful wife home and doing unspeakable things to her body is a lot more appealing than staying here with you."

I smirk at Masters. "Lucky prick." My eyes fall back to Lady Charlotte. "I need to get me some of this pregnant sex you keep talking about, Masters," I mutter.

"You'll need a willing woman for that, Spence," he replies.

My eyes go back down to the woman in the pink dress. "I do love a challenge. Maybe Lady Charlotte is dying to be impregnated tonight," I reply.

Julian rolls his eyes.

"Or simply dying to get away from you," Sebastian mutters.

I glance over to my dear friend. "I'll bet you two hundred pounds that I have a date with her by this time next week."

"Double it. Four hundred," snaps Masters. "You don't have a chance with her."

"Deal." I smile. My hands drop to Bree's pregnant stomach and I kiss her softly on the cheek. "Goodbye, darling. Enjoy your unspeakable things." I turn and head towards the woman in pink.

"Spencer!" I hear a woman call from behind me. I turn and see a brunette in a tight black dress. Sure, she's very attractive, but she's got nothing on Lady Charlotte.

"Hello." I smile.

She holds out her hand to mine. "I'm Linda." She hesitates. "We met at a Christmas party last year."

I fake a smile as I try to remember this woman. Nope, I've got nothing. "Yes, I remember," I lie. "How have you been?"

She beams instantly. "Great, although I do have a problem."

"What's that?" I frown.

"The plumbing in my room seems to have an issue."

"Really?" I smirk. There are hotel rooms at this resort, and she's obviously staying here.

"Really. I was wondering if you could come up and have a look at it after the wedding finishes."

I chuckle. Wow. That's the oldest trick in the book. "I am very good at unblocking pipes," I tease.

"I imagine you are." She giggles on cue and passes me a key. "Room 282." She smirks.

I smile down at her and stuff the key into my pocket. "If you'll excuse me, I have to see someone."

"Okay. I'll see you later." She grins.

Good grief.

I walk around the dance floor with my eyes glued to the woman in the pink dress. She's petite and curvy with the most perfect face I have ever seen. She's now talking to two men, with one on either side of her. One is older, while the other is close to my age. I sip my beer as I watch her move.

Hmm, she's fucking gorgeous and innately feminine.

She's also very different to my usual taste in women. She has a gentle air about her. I roll my lips as I watch her, and Brendan, an old school friend of mine, comes to stand next to me.

"Hey, Spence." He slaps me on the back.

"Who is that woman?" I ask, completely distracted.

He frowns. "Which one?"

"Pink dress. Charlotte."

His eyes widen, and he chuckles. "Stay away from that one, old boy. She's out of your league."

"And why would you say that?"

"Every man in the county is after her, and she won't give any of them the time of day."

I feel my skin prickle at the challenge. "Really?"

"Yes. And then you have to get past her father and brothers even if she is interested at all."

I frown. "What do you mean?"

"That's her father on the right. If I stand correct, he is the third wealthiest man in the country. He owns casinos around the world and has connections everywhere. On the left of her is her older brother Edward. Complete and utter bastard, that one."

I narrow my eyes as I watch him. "What does Edward do for a coin?"

"Guard Charlotte, from what I hear. He doesn't let her out of his sight. It's a full-time fucking job."

I raise my glass to him in a silent toast.

He shakes his head. "Not her, Spencer. She really is off-limits. Way too pure for you."

Excitement rolls over me. "The thrill of the chase is alive and well, my friend."

He chuckles. "Or the thrill of a death wish. You fuck around with her and her father will murder you without a second thought."

I smile as I turn to watch Charlotte talk to the two men. "Challenge accepted, old boy."

He laughs into his beer and shakes his head. "Next time I see you, it may be your funeral."

My eyes dance with delight. "Give me a good wrap in the eulogy, hey? I'm sure it will be worth it."

He chuckles, and with another shake of his head, he disappears through the crowd.

I stand on my own, simply watching her. She is the most beautiful thing I have seen in a very long time. At once, she glances up and her eyes fall on me, holding my gaze. I smile and raise my beer to her in a silent toast. She immediately looks away and fidgets with her hands in front of her.

I smile to myself as I watch her. Run along, boys.

I want her alone.

Charlotte

Mr Spencer smiles sexily and raises his glass in my direction. I bite my bottom lip nervously. Is he really doing that to me? He's standing alone in the crowd, a beer in one hand, his other hand tucked away in his expensive suit pocket. I snap my eyes away as my stomach flips with excitement.

Stop it! He's probably not even aiming it at me.

"Charlotte, I have someone I want you to meet," my father says.

"Dad, not now. I don't want to meet any of your boring friends." I sigh.

He rolls his eyes, and I glance back over at Mr Spencer still staring at me. I glance back up to my father. "What is it?" I ask with a huff.

"His name is Evan. I know his family, and he happens to be a lawyer."

I cringe. "Father, please," I moan. "Stop. I'm not dating one of your boring friends' sons."

My brother Edward looks at my father and scowls. "Yes, please stop. The thought makes me murderous."

I roll my eyes at my overbearing brother. "You too."

My father and Edward fall into conversation, leaving me to glance back over at Mr Spencer. As soon as our eyes connect, he crooks his finger and gestures for me to go to him.

Me?

I frown, look around, and point to my chest.

He nods with a sexy smile. I look around, instantly filled with some kind of guilt, and I subtly shake my head.

Oh my God. My stomach flips over.

He crooks his finger again, and I find myself biting my bottom lip and dropping my head to hide my smile.

"Would you like a drink, Charlotte?" my brother asks.

"Please." I smile as I concentrate on not looking Mr Spencer's way again.

My father falls into conversation with a man who walks past, and I glance around nervously. I'm not sure whether to go and talk to Mr Spencer or not. No, that's a bad idea. Perhaps I'll go and get some fresh air instead.

"I'm heading to the ladies'," I whisper to my father.

"All right, love." He smiles as I put my hand on his shoulder. I walk through the ballroom and out onto the back terrace and down the steps. Fairy lights are strewn across the garden, giving it a romantic feel. Waiters are circling the garden with trays of fancy cocktails and champagne. This wedding has been amazing, and the attention to detail has been impeccable. Every detail is perfect. I walk along the pathway down to the outdoor bathrooms. Once there, I head inside and close the door behind me.

Peace at last.

I can hear the music in the distance as I stare at my reflection in the mirror and reapply my fuchsia lipstick. My thick, shoulder-length blonde hair is down and pulled back on one side behind my ear. My pink strapless dress fits perfectly and clings to my curves. I roll my lips as I stare at my reflection. Eventually, I exhale heavily and snap my lipstick back into my silver clutch.

Most eligible bachelor in London, an appalling rake.

Great. The first man I've been attracted to in forever and he's a womaniser. Typical.

For once, I would like to meet an honourable man who is actually appealing.

Why does it have to be one or the other? Who made this godforsaken rule that any man who is a tad interesting must be a player? And why are all the good men boring as hell? God must definitely be a man.

With one last look at myself, I head back out into the garden and make my way up the path towards the party.

"Charlotte," a deep voice calls from behind me. I turn and falter, taken aback. It's him.

It's Mr Spencer.

He smiles sexily and his eyes hold mine.

"Hello." My heart rate spikes.

"H-hi." I smile nervously.

He steps towards me and takes my hand in his, and I inhale sharply. He holds my hand up in the air and nods, as if bowing.

"Forgive me for following you, but I had to come and meet the most beautiful woman in the room tonight." He kisses the back of my hand tenderly, and I raise my brows. "My name is Spencer." He smiles against my skin.

Oh, he's really quite...

I pull my hand away sharply. "I know who you are, Mr Spencer."

He smirks harder, and his mischievous eyes hold mine.

"You do?" he asks smoothly with a raise of his brow.

I clasp my hands nervously in front of me. "Your reputation precedes you."

His smirk breaks out into a broad smile. "Ah, you can't believe everything you hear, now, can you?"

His voice is deep and permeating. It somehow sinks into my bones when he speaks.

"Can I help you with something?" I ask. What the hell does he want?

"I hope so." He smiles and picks up my hand again. "Would you do me the honour of dancing with me?"

I swallow nervously, and he smiles and drops his lips to the back of my hand to kiss me softly. His sexy eyes stay fixed on mine.

Okay, hell...he's good. Really good.

"I..." I stop talking because I really can't concentrate when he's touching me.

He's so forward.

"Charlotte?" he repeats, pulling me out of my thoughts.

I shake my head in a fluster. "I don't think that's a good idea."

He turns my hand over to gently kiss the inside of my wrist. I feel his touch deep inside my stomach.

"Why not?" He gently licks my wrist, and my knees nearly buckle out from underneath me.

Oh, for the love of God!

"My father and brother..." I frown as my voice trails off. How in the hell am I supposed to string two words together when he's doing that to me?

He steps forward and takes me into his arms. "We'll dance here, then."

What?

He pulls me close to him, takes one of my hands in his, and smiles down at me as he begins to sway to the music.

"You're a wonderful dancer, Lady Charlotte." He smiles mischievously.

I smirk at his sheer audacity. "Does this routine work on every woman you meet?"

He smiles his first genuine smile, and I feel the effects of it hit me deep in my stomach. "Please don't talk about other women. I'm in the courting zone, concentrating on you and only you." He spins me around, and we both chuckle at his ridiculousness.

He lets me go and holds one hand up, and then he spins me in his arms and pulls me back to his body at force until we come face-to-face.

I stare up at him, my heart skipping a beat. "I have to go," I whisper.

"Why?" His intoxicating breath washes over my face.

"My father will be looking for me."

"How old are you, Lady Charlotte?"

"Too young for you, Mr Spencer."

He smiles softly. "I have no doubt." He bends down and softly kisses my lips.

My chest constricts.

He kisses me again, soft and tenderly, hovering his lips over mine. Unable to help it, I smile, and that's when he kisses me again but this time more urgently, his arms curling around my waist and bringing me to his body.

I've never been kissed like this.

His tongue sweeps through my open mouth and our tongues dance together.

For three whole minutes, I drink him in as we kiss like teenagers.

"Jesus fucking Christ, Charlotte," he gasps as he kisses me again.

I lose control and my hands go to his hair, and then I feel something hard up against my stomach.

Is that...?

I instantly pull out of the kiss and step back, panting for breath. He reaches for me again, but I step back farther. "Don't touch me!" I whisper sharply, holding my hand up in defence.

"What? Why?"

I shake my head. "I'm not the kind of girl you are used to, Mr Spencer."

He scowls hard. "And what kind of girl is that?"

"I'm not one of those high society sluts. Y-you should go back inside and find someone else to...entertain you," I stammer.

"I don't want anyone else!" he snaps. "If I overstepped the line, I apologise. I never... I mean..."

He's tripping over his words, confusing me.

I step back again, creating more distance. "You stepped over the line...by a lot." I glance up and I can see my father is out on the terrace, looking for me. "I have to go." I brush past Mr Spencer, walk up the path and up the stairs. My father smiles the second he sees me.

"Are you ready to leave, Charlotte?"

"Please," I say quietly. My eyes fall back down to the garden where Mr Spencer stands.

My father puts his arm around me and we walk around to the front of the house to get into the back of his Bentley. His driver shuts the door, and I peer out just in time to see Mr Spencer appearing from the shadows next to the house, watching me leave.

He smiles softly and blows me a kiss, and I drop my head at once, gripping my clutch on my lap.

"That was a great night, wasn't it?" My father smiles as the car slowly pulls out.

"It was." I force a smile. My fingertips rise to brush my lips, which still tingle from Mr Spencer's touch. I smile to myself softly.

No wonder he's the most eligible bachelor in London. He's perfect.

And he's trouble.

14

2

_____

Charlotte

THE CAR ENTERS the grounds of my father's estate. We ride down the driveway, past his expansive sandstone castle. We continue along to the lane that leads to my house on the property. The grounds are manicured to perfection. As usual, the security staff walk the perimeters morning, noon, and night. My two brothers and I each have houses on this property, including our own roads in, but we always use my father's driveway if we are with him. I smile at the thought. Dad couldn't possibly use another entrance to his house. He has to drive through the huge fancy gates to feel at home.

I love it here. My father's staff are beautiful, and I always feel safe. Although I do worry about Dad living here all alone. He's never recovered since my mother died. She was the love of his life. He had to fight hard for the right to love her, too. She was his childhood housekeeper's daughter. Our money is old money, passed down from generation to generation. Our social reputation is deeply ingrained into all of us. When he fell in love with the hired help's daughter, it didn't go down well. It seems like so much has changed since back then... And at the same time, like nothing has changed at all. I wouldn't be allowed to fall in love with the hired help, either, and all hell would break loose if I so much as tried.

The moonlight reflects off the white pebbles on the drive, and a wave of sadness rolls over me as I look around at the grand grounds. Money doesn't buy happiness. We would all hand over every penny we have in an instant if it meant we got to see our mother again.

I look out of the window with a frown, and, as if sensing my thoughts, my father reaches over and takes my hand.

"Everything all right?" he asks quietly.

I smile at him, banishing my sad thoughts. "Of course. I had a wonderful time tonight."

"What's on tomorrow, dear?"

"Nothing. Gardening with Elouise."

"You don't have to help with the gardening, you know."

"I know." I kiss the back of his hand tenderly. "I like to garden, you know that, and if I get to spend the day with Elouise, then all the better for me."

He smiles and looks out of the window, somewhat bemused. It's funny because I spend more time with the staff here than I do with anyone else. Most of them have been with my father since I was a child. Elouise is an older lady and our resident horticulturist. She's gentle, sweet, and I adore her. She lives in the village and has worked for us for about two years, forever a dear friend.

The car rolls to a stop outside my house, and I lean over and kiss my father as Wyatt opens my car door.

"Hello." Wyatt smiles and takes my hand to help me out of the car. He's clearly been waiting for my arrival, as he didn't come to the wedding.

"Hello, Wyatt." I smile in return, placing a hand on his chest before I walk past him and into the house.

"How was your evening?"

"Wonderful, thank you. How was yours?"

"Quite dull."

I smile as I walk. Wyatt is in his mid-thirties, and he's my body-guard. He usually comes with me everywhere I go. Six years ago, when my father's company began buying casinos, our world changed overnight. Suddenly, the people he did business with weren't always as reputable as we were. We needed protection from the unknown, and that's when we were each given body-guards who are to follow our every move.

My mother didn't have one with her on the day of her death, and I know my father has always questioned that if she had had one, would the car accident have happened? Would she still be here with us?

I used to hate the security, but I'm used to it now, and at least Wyatt isn't as obtrusive as my father's security team. They're hard-core. I couldn't deal with them at all.

Glancing back, I see three of them in the car behind us. They go everywhere he goes, and none of them will ever make eye contact with me. I know it's because my brother has warned them with their lives if one of them comes near me.

Wyatt is different, though. He's trusted with me. We've also become friends. Not besties or anything, as he keeps it very professional at all times, but I definitely rely on him more than I expected to.

I give my father a small wave goodbye, and then I walk up the path towards my house as the car pulls away slowly and heads back to the main house.

"Good night, Charlotte," Wyatt calls from the end of the driveway.

"Good night, Wyatt. Thank you."

After I shut the door behind me, I turn to put my bag down on the hall table, and I pick up the remote control to turn the television on. I head straight to the kitchen and flick on the kettle. I have a set routine whenever I walk into my house: television, kettle, and tea. It's like the world isn't right if one of those things doesn't happen immediately. Dead silence doesn't feel right to me. The funny thing is that I don't even watch the TV after I've put it on. I simply like the distant background noise it provides.

I grab my laptop and sit at my kitchen counter.

Who are you, Mr Spencer?

I type his name into Google, immediately frowning.

Wait. Was his first name Spencer, or was his last name Spencer?

He introduced himself as Spencer, but I thought that was his surname, hence why I called him Mr Spencer.

I think back to what Lara said about him, and I take out my phone to dial her number. She answers on the first ring.

"Hey, where are you?" she asks quickly.

"Oh, I came home."

"Why?"

I bite my bottom lip to stop myself smiling. "I was accosted by the infamous Mr Spencer."

She gasps. "Fuck off. What happened?"

I stare at my reflection in the kitchen window and find myself smiling. "He followed me to the bathroom outside, and then he kissed me."

"Are you serious?"

"I am. Remind me of his name..."

She laughs. "Did you forget to ask that while his tongue was down your throat?"

I chuckle quietly. "Yeah, kind of."

"His name is Spencer."

I hit enter on Google, and a million Spencers come up. "Is his first name Spencer or his surname Spencer? I'm confused."

"Give me a second, I'm trying to remember. Oh," she coos. "It's Spencer Jones. His first name is Spencer, surname Jones."

I type Spencer Jones into the search engine and the screen immediately fills with images of him. My smile returns. "Okay, I've got it."

"Are you Googling him?"

"Of course."

"Oh God, put the computer away. I don't think you are going to like what you read."

I cross over to the counter to make my tea. "Can you see him?" I ask her.

"Wait." I can hear the music playing as she walks through the wedding reception. "Yes. He's standing with his friend again, back on the upper level."

I press my lips together. Now I regret not staying and getting to know him a bit better. I wish I wasn't such a chicken, but I was just so shocked.

"Okay, Lars, I'll let you go."

"Charl?"

"Yes?"

"How was the kiss?"

I feel my cheeks blush. "Better than expected." That doesn't cover half of it, but I don't want to sound pathetic.

"I'll be over tomorrow for a full debrief."

"Okay, see you then." I hang up, sip my tea, and make my way over to sit back at the counter. I scroll through the images of him, my frown growing deeper. Every image is of him with a different woman.

They're all gorgeous, with the majority of the photos taken at night by the paparazzi.

Models, actresses, fame-hungry whores.

Oh...

I click on a story that goes with one of the images.

Spencer Jones and supermodel Amy Hallam leaving Vivid Nightclub.
Spencer Jones lived up to his Playboy reputation when he was spotted on Wednesday night with Amy Hallam.
Spencer was snapped earlier in the day on a yacht with Miranda Eastman, the Victoria's Secret model

I click on the link to the photographs, finding a photo of him leaving the club with Amy Hallam, the two of them holding hands and getting into a cab. She's an actress in a sitcom, and gorgeous too. In the picture, she's wearing a gold, barely there short dress. There are a few images in the set. In one, Spencer is looking down at her as they wait for the cab. In the next photo he is kissing her with his hand on her behind. He has that cheeky smile on his face, and then the next image shows them getting into a cab together.

He definitely took her home that night.

I click on the next set of images, where he is on a yacht, only this time with Miranda Eastman, a high-fashion model. She's wearing a black and gold bikini, and her long black hair is flowing down her back. She has a killer body.

There are a few shots, the first one showing him helping her onto the yacht by holding her hand. In the next image he is kissing her up against the rail, and then the one after that shows her lying on her back on a towel. He is lying next to her with his hand on her stomach, looking down at her with that same cheeky smile on his face. I frown as I look at the dates of the images.

These were taken on the same day. He was on the yacht with Miranda during the day, and then that night he went home with Amy.

I look at the expression on his face: pure mischief. It's the same look I saw on his face tonight.

Gross.

I exhale heavily and slam my computer shut in disgust.

I sip my tea and immediately get a vision of him kissing my hand and being all gorgeous. Ugh.

Thank God I ran when I did.

I could have ended up being another notch on his sleazy bedpost.

I get a flashback of his cheeky smile, and I smirk. Lara was right, he is an appalling rake...and I can see why he gets away with it. He's completely gorgeous. Of course they all line up to date him.

Oh, well, I guess that's the end of that.

I trudge up the stairs to my bathroom. I turn the shower on, making sure the water is steaming hot, and I take off my clothes as I make the solemn vow to never think of Mr Spencer again in my life.

Never ever.

I'm sitting at the dining table, staring into space. It's Sunday night, and we've just eaten dinner. My two brothers are on either side of me, while my father is at the head of the table. They're all talking, but I'm miles away.

I'm dreaming of a life where I don't have to worry about what people think of me, where my family's reputation doesn't matter, and one where my brother wouldn't have a broken heart.

It kills me to see him so hurt.

My eldest brother Edward is to take on the estate and the family empire when my father dies, because he is the oldest son. The universe clearly prepped him for his destiny before his birth too. He is strong—an alpha—and a leader. Being cold, ruthless, and domineering, he will definitely fulfil his duties well.

My other brother William is the opposite. He's pure perfection —my best friend and more like me than anyone on Earth.

William is a doctor, and our mother's death rocked him hard. I don't think he's recovered yet. Does anyone *ever* recover?

William fell desperately in love with a woman not long after our mother's death. He worshipped the ground she walked on. She was the life and soul of the party, a high-society girl, and my father knew her parents well. The wedding was an extravagant affair, on every society page, and an absolute fairy tale.

The two of them had a baby, a son named Harrison. He's four now and he's their world, making their lives perfect. That was until one day, my brother came home early from a work trip and found his wife in bed with another man. The affair had been going on for months.

It broke his heart. Ours too.

My father banished her from the house and from our lives. We only see Harrison when William brings him over now, and that's rare.

Edward, my oldest brother, hates William's ex with such a passion that I fear he would run her over in the street if he saw her. This rocked our family to its very core. How do you deal with infidelity, especially when he is still married to that person? Still with her to this day, actually.

He stayed with her because he didn't want to leave his son. He didn't want to be the one who ended the marriage, and she promised him the world if he stayed, blaming her indiscretions on him for working all the time.

But the worst part, the very worst part of it all, is that he still loves her.

He loves her so much that he would give anything to make her happy.

I see it in his eyes every time I look at him. I see how deep his hurt runs. He's dying a slow death, knowing that the woman he loves doesn't love him with the same purity as he loves her.

She never loved him, and the whole world knows it.

It's a whole new level of torture for everyone.

It was the money that she wanted—the designer lifestyle to go with her designer cocaine. She got her way too. Now they live in Switzerland in a huge mansion that she definitely doesn't deserve.

I hate her.

I hate her so much that it eats away at me day and night.

My mother would be rolling in her grave if she saw what William is living through.

It's a hell that he never deserved.

Her name is Penelope—the walking, talking devil.

I'm pulled out of my thoughts by my brother's raised voice.

"I don't know about this!" Edward snaps.

My father exhales heavily and pinches the bridge of his nose. "You know we have to go."

"Why can't you just come back here?" Edward asks William. "It's six weeks."

"Because I can't get time off. Not everyone works for Dad, you know."

"Huh?" I frown. "Hang on, what are you talking about?" I ask.

"Edward and I have to go to America for work. We'll be away for six to seven weeks while we do the tour of the casinos. We want William to come back and stay here while we're gone," Father tells me.

I look between them, confused. "Why?"

"You are not staying here alone, Charlotte," my father says.

"Wait, what?" I frown. "This is about me?" I sit back, offended. "I'm twenty-four. I can look after myself."

"No!" Edward asserts. "You'll have to come with us."

"I can't get time off, and I'm *not* leaving my job, Edward."

"For God's sake, isn't it about time you left that job and came and worked for the family business anyway? We have a family empire that you should be working on. You don't need to work in philanthropy."

"This is our mother's dream that I work on," I hit back. "You don't get to tell me what to do, Edward, or where to work. And besides, Wyatt and the staff will be here. I'm completely capable of looking after myself, you know."

"Don't tell her to leave her job. Why do you think you have the right to tell her what to do?" William snaps in my defence.

Edward turns, and I can see his anger rise to the surface. "You want to talk about leaving jobs?" He points at William. "Yes, let's do that. When the fuck are you going to live up to your responsibility to this family and come and work in the business?"

"Edward." My father sighs. "That's enough."

"I'm not," William growls. "I never will. Casinos and making money aren't life goals of mine."

I close my eyes, resting my fingers on my temples. Here we go again.

"Why is that?" Edward growls back. "Because you're hiding in fucking Switzerland with that whore."

My eyes widen. *He did not just say that.*

"Because you're too scared to bring her home in case she fucks someone else." He shakes his head in disgust. "Wake up and smell the coffee, Will. She would have fucked ten men by now. When are you going to see her for what she really is? A dirty fucking whore."

William flies out of his seat and pushes our brother hard in the chest. "Shut the fuck up."

"Admit it!" Edward screams as my father flies out of his chair to separate the two men. "She's brought nothing but shame to this family. We don't even see you anymore. It's about time you fuck her off and come home!" he yells.

They push each other and fall back. A glass gets smashed across the table as it tips over.

The staff come flying into the room, hearing the commotion. This isn't the first time my brothers have become physical over Penelope. They're always on high alert when William is home.

William pushes Edward hard in the chest and glares at him.

My heart breaks for him and his pain. "Will," I whisper.

"That's enough, Edward!" my father roars. "You will not speak to your brother like that. Do you hear me?"

"You make me fucking sick, sitting up here on your high horse. Keep your fucking nose out of my marriage. What I do with my wife is none of your concern." William turns and storms out of the room.

"William, come back here," my father calls after him, but William doesn't stop and he doesn't look back, taking the stairs two at a time. He'll be back in Switzerland by morning...like always.

I turn on Edward and lose control. "Why do you do this? Every damn time he comes home, you upset him. This is why we never see him!" I cry. "This is why he stays with her. You give him no support. None."

My father drops into his chair and puts his head in his hands.

My eyes fill with tears. "Go to Vegas, Edward, and better still, don't come back. You and your judgement make me sick," I whisper. "This isn't about you. It's about time you stand behind your brother when he needs you the most."

"I'll never stand behind him while he's married to her." He raises his chin defiantly. "You two can cower to Penelope all you want. I will not." He points at my father and me. "She will not get one fucking penny of this estate, and I'll make sure of that if it's the last thing I do. I've got solicitors tightening up our wills as we speak."

"Is that all you're worried about?" I cry. "Money means nothing, Edward!"

God, this is a no-win situation. He makes me sick. I turn and storm out of the house, slamming the door behind me.

"Charlotte?" a voice calls from behind me.

"Not now, Wyatt," I snap over my shoulder as I angrily swipe my tears away.

How many times have my father's staff heard us arguing over Penelope? God, it's just embarrassing.

"Do you want the car?" he asks softly.

"No, I'll walk. Thank you." I exhale heavily and begin to walk up the road towards my house. It's a good kilometre away, but the bright moon is out, and it's somewhat light.

I can feel Wyatt walking slowly behind me, anyway, making sure to keep his distance and give me my space.

With every step I walk farther away from the house, a little more sadness creeps in. On nights like this, when the cracks in my family are so wide, is when I miss my mother the most.

If she was here, this wouldn't be happening.

She would know just what to say to William. She would know how to quieten Edward. My father would still have his love.

If William just loved someone good and worthy of him, then everything would be different.

I wrap my arms around my waist and imagine my mother's smiling face. She gave so much love and light to all of us.

I wish you were here, Mum.

Things would be different. Things would be better.

It's Thursday, and it's turning dark when I leave work with my three colleagues. I work for the Philanthropic Society in Notting-ham. Our job is to raise money for local charities. My mother was on the board of directors, and when she passed, I wanted to continue the project she was working on at the time. I never planned on being here long-term, but somehow it worked out that way. To be honest, I think I'm here because this job makes me still feel close to Mum. Everyone who works here knew her, and she is spoken of often.

The four of us lock up the building and chatter about the day as we walk out towards the street. It's been one of those crazy days today. We were supposed to finish an hour ago. It's 6:00 p.m. now and we're only just leaving.

"Charlotte?" a deep voice calls. I turn, surprised.

"Mr Spencer." I frown.

He's leaning up against a tree by the side of the pavement, and my stomach instantly flips.

He's wearing a pair of blue jeans, which are tight in all the right places, as well as a navy sports coat over a white T-shirt. His fair hair is longer and messy on top. His big blue eyes hold mine, and with that square jaw, he looks like he should be on the cover of a magazine.

God, he's gorgeous.

He glances at my work friends, making me aware they are listening to what I'm about to say.

"I'll see you later, girls," I mumble, distracted by the beautiful man before me.

"Bye," they all call. I don't miss the way they inspect Spencer and his gorgeousness, either. I smile when I imagine the questions I'm going to be hit with tomorrow. I have a few questions myself, like *What on earth is he doing here*? My work friends eventually veer off to their cars, disappearing out of sight.

"What are you doing here?" I ask.

His eyes hold mine. "Waiting for you."

I bite my bottom lip as my heart begins to race in my chest. I've thought of nothing else but him since last Saturday. His kiss is seared into my soul, and the feel of his hard body up against mine has left an undeniable mark.

He glances at his watch. "For two hours, actually. It's fucking cold here, you know."

I smirk. "Why didn't you just knock on the door?"

"Didn't want to seem too eager." He shrugs. "I thought that tracking you down detective style, taking a day off work, and then driving two hours just to try and see you seemed eager enough."

I smile, my nerves fluttering. There's something about him. I'd wondered if I imagined it the other night.

Not at all. I can confirm that he is, in fact, a very fine specimen.

"Would you like to have dinner with me?" he asks softly.

I glance up the street, and then over to the car across the road where Wyatt is waiting for me.

"Erm..."

Spencer waits for my answer, releasing a slow, sexy smile. "Am I really that unappealing, Charlotte, that you have to think this hard?"

The way he says Charlotte is just so...

My phone rings and the name Wyatt lights up the screen. Damn it. "Sorry, just a minute." I hold up a finger. "Hello."

"Who are you talking to?" Wyatt asks.

I glance up at the gorgeous man in front of me. "A friend," I answer, annoyed that even a simple conversation warrants Wyatt to call me.

I'm sick of this nonsense.

Spencer frowns as he watches me.

"Who is he? I need a name."

"Not a word about this, please."

"A name and my lips are sealed."

Damn it, why is my life so damn complicated? He's going to run a search on him to check his criminal record, I know it.

"His name is Spencer Jones, and I'm going out to dinner with him. I won't be needing you again tonight. You may go home now," I instruct with annoyance. *If I wasn't going out with Spencer before, I sure am now just to piss you off.*

Satisfaction flashes across Spencer's face.

"You know I can't do that," Wyatt replies. "I'll be outside in the car if you need me." He hangs up.

I clench my jaw in frustration. I hate being followed all the time. I have no privacy whatsoever.

"Everything all right?" Spencer asks.

"Yes." I fake a smile as I glance over to the car. "That was my security, I'm sorry. It's very distracting, even for me."

"So, you really do have security?" Spencer glances across the road to Wyatt. "Ha, fancy that. I thought they were joking."

"What do you mean?" I ask.

"I was told at the wedding that I wouldn't be able to get near you because you were guarded. I actually thought they meant your brother."

I drop my head in embarrassment. God, everyone knows about this stuff now? I had no idea. "I'm sorry, this isn't normal, I know."

Spencer puts his hands in his pockets, and the two of us begin to walk. "Why do you need security?"

We walk towards the restaurant strip. "My father is..." I pause because I hate saying this. "Wealthy, and he's constantly concerned for my safety."

"What happens if I kiss you at dinner?"

I laugh and raise my brows. "That's very presumptuous, Mr Spencer."

"Spence," he corrects me. "My friends call me Spence."

"Spence." I smile.

"What do I call you?"

"Charlotte," I reply without hesitation.

"Like that, is it?" He links his arm through mine. "What do your friends call you?"

"Do you want to be my friend?"

"Maybe."

I smile at his ease with me. He's very familiar and seems to have no insecurities at all.

"I really did think the whole security thing was a joke," he says casually.

"I wish it was." I glance back to Wyatt sitting in the car, watching the two of us. "Does it bother you to have him watch us?"

"That depends."

"On what?"

"What actually *does* happen if I kiss you? What will he do?"

I smile. "Probably knock you out unconscious," I tease. Truthfully, I have no idea because Wyatt hasn't seen me kiss anyone before.

Spencer stops and turns me to face him. "What about if I do it in private?"

Our eyes lock.

What is it about this man? He just gets straight to the point. I've never met anyone quite like him. He's so brash.

"My private time is completely private." I smile softly up at him.

The air between us crackles.

"You're all I've thought about this week," he says.

My nerves bubble in my stomach and, unsure what to say, I turn away, relinking my arm with his. We turn the corner to the main street of town.

"Where do we go?" he asks, looking around.

I gesture up the street. "There is a restaurant up the road a little."

He takes my hand in his and picks it up to kiss the back of it.

My eyes flicker to Wyatt in the car that is following us slowly from a distance. I know he can still see us. It feels awkward being with a man while Wyatt watches.

"Don't worry about him, worry about me," Spencer says. His eyes hold mine with a tender glow, and he smiles softly down at me, clearly seeing that I'm uncomfortable with Wyatt watching on.

God, he's beautiful.

"So, this is where you live? Nottingham."

I nod. "Uh-huh."

"Beautiful."

I smile as my heart begins to beat faster. *Like you,* I think to myself.

We arrive at the restaurant, walk in, and wait at the desk.

"Table for two?" he asks a passing waiter.

"Of course, sir. Just this way." The waiter smiles.

Spencer pulls out my chair and I take a seat.

Robert, a man that I know who works here, is on his shift. He sees me and immediately smiles. "Hi, Lottie."

"Hi, Rob," I say as I flick open the menu.

Spencer opens his menu too. "Who's he?" he asks, pretending to be uninterested.

"My ex-husband."

Spencer's eyes shoot up.

"Got you."

"I didn't realise you were a comedian," he replies dryly. "He gets to call you Lottie and I don't?"

"Comedy is one of my hidden talents." I smirk as I read the menu. "And I'm Charlotte to you at this point."

His eyes hold mine and a trace of a smile crosses his face. It's as if he just accepted a silent challenge that I don't know about. "I'll add it to the list, then," he mutters.

"There's a list?"

His eyes stay glued to the menu. "There is a *big* list."

"Of what?"

"Being gorgeous and whatnot."

I bite my lip as I watch him. Lara was right, he *is* simply delicious.

Robert comes over to our table. "Can I take your order?"

Spencer peruses the menu and then looks back up at me. "How far is your house from here?"

"Not far."

"Okay, shall we have some wine?"

I nod. This feels terribly grown-up for a Thursday. "Okay."

"What's good on the menu?" He frowns, looking over the choices.

"The Aloft Cab Sav is nice," I whisper nervously. He makes me feel like a timid little girl.

"Okay, we'll have a bottle, please." He closes his drinks menu and hands it over. "We'll order our meal in a little while, please."

Robert walks away, and Spencer's eyes fall to my face.

"Why are you here, Mr Spencer?" I ask him.

He smiles softly and leans towards the table, steepling his hands under his chin. "I wanted to see you."

"Why?"

"You're on my mind."

I swallow the lump in my throat.

I like that he wanted to see me.

Our drinks arrive and we both sit in relative silence, neither of us knowing what to say.

"How old are you, Charlotte?" he asks softly.

"I think I answered that question before. Too young for you, Mr Spencer." I smile over at him.

"Well, I'm twenty-five," he says seriously. "With thirteen years' experience."

I do the maths. He's thirty-eight.

"And I'm twenty-four...with *no* experience."

His eyes twinkle with delight. Maybe he thought I was younger than that.

We sip our drinks in an uncomfortable silence once again.

"Do you have a boyfriend?"

"No."

He frowns as he tries to articulate himself. "And you're not secretly in love with your bodyguard?"

"Certainly not. You've been watching too many movies, Mr Spencer." I laugh.

He puts his hand on his chest, faking his relief. "That's good to hear. I can't compete with bodyguards and shit like that." He winks at me. "Although I do practice karate."

We both chuckle and our eyes linger on each other's. There is this mutual affection between us. For me, it's that he speaks so unguarded, as though he already knows me, but maybe it's just all his experience with women that makes him this way. He's not nervous around me like most men, and his confidence is very attractive.

I would give anything to know what's on his mind.

"What are you thinking?" I ask.

"That depends." He leans forward.

"On what?"

"I'm running a risk assessment in my mind as to whether I'm going to get beaten to a pulp if I kiss you."

I smile bashfully.

It would be worth it.

The moment is broken by the waiter returning with our bottle of wine. He pops the cork and pours a little into both our wine-glasses.

"Thank you." I take a sip. "Hmm." I eye the glass of burgundy liquid. "That's nice."

Spencer holds his glass in the air. "A toast."

"To what?" I ask.

His eyes hold mine. "Our first date."

I smile softly.

"May there be many more," he whispers darkly, clinking his glass to mine before he takes a sip. "You know, I wrote your name in my diary on Monday morning."

I smile. "Why?"

"Because when I want something, I write it down." He smirks.

I giggle. "That not at all creepy."

He chuckles.

I take a mouthful of wine and think for a moment. "Can I ask you something?"

"Anything."

"Why would you drive all the way out here to see me without calling first?"

"Because I knew if I called you, that you wouldn't want to see me."

His eyes drop to my lips and then back up to my eyes with a hunger I haven't felt before. The air between us becomes electric. God, the way he looks at me sets me on fire.

"Has someone hurt you in the past?" he asks.

I stare at him, confused. "What do you mean?"

"Physically, has someone hurt you?"

"What? No." I frown. "Why would you say that?"

"You seemed frightened of me on Saturday night."

I drop my head in embarrassment. I know he means when I felt his erection. It terrified me, if I'm honest, and I hate that he sensed it.

"I didn't know where my father's guards were," I whisper. "I don't do that sort of thing in public."

His eyes hold mine, and he reaches over the table to take my hand in his. "What about in private, Charlotte? What sort of thing do you do in private?"

We stare at each other for a moment. What can I say here without sounding promiscuous? "Private things," I whisper.

"I should like to spend time with you in private sometime."

I sit back, affronted by his gall. "Are you here simply for sex, Mr Spencer?"

He frowns. "Stop calling me that."

"It's your name, isn't it?"

"Yes, but you call me that when you are pushing me away."

"I'm merely asking you a question. There was no pushing involved."

"I'm attracted to you, yes."

"That wasn't what I asked."

"Am I here only for sex? No. Have I wondered what it would be like to have intimate relations with you? Yes."

Intimate relations.

My breath catches as I stare at him. He is the first man in my entire life who has had the guts to come on to me, and I find myself fighting a smile. "Why?"

"You're beautiful and different than most women."

"So you only pursue beautiful women?" I ask. "I'm curious as to what makes a man like you tick, that's all." I shrug, hoping that I haven't just crossed a line.

He smiles and takes my hand over the table again. "Ask me anything you want. I have nothing to hide. I'm very honest. Perhaps too honest."

"Then do you only date beautiful women?" I ask again. God, how did we get to this subject?

"I only date women that are beautiful to me." He frowns as he thinks for a moment. "Although lately, my tastes have become very eclectic."

"How so?"

"Being beautiful and nothing else doesn't do it for me anymore." He picks up my hand and kisses my fingertips. I feel the effect of it all the way to my toes.

I stare at him, lost for words, but with so much to say.

"You, for example," he continues. "The things that attracted me to you have kept me awake at night all week."

"Such as?"

"You're innately feminine. You have a confident air about you, but then..." He pauses. "When I touched you, you were frightened of me."

I stare at him, heart fluttering and words lost.

"I'm guessing you are very intelligent and articulate, but you're kept in an ivory palace by your brother so that men can't get to you, which means you definitely don't sleep around."

How does he know this?

"I believe that you will probably end up marrying someone of

34

your family's choosing who is extremely wealthy, and you'll live a life of luxury—one that is expected of you."

I sit back in my chair, appalled by his assumptions...mainly because they are true.

"This is what you've been thinking about all week?" I sip my wine. "And here I was thinking that you were imagining how to pleasure me during those intimate relations you spoke of." I roll my eyes in disgust. "You're a disappointment, Spencer Jones."

He laughs, deep and loud, and I feel it all the way through my bones. "I don't need to imagine how to please you in bed. I know how to do that, without a doubt."

Oh, I like this guy; he's so different than anyone I've ever met before.

"Well, you're wrong about one thing," I say. "If I ever choose to marry, I'm marrying for love, and my family will have nothing to do with it. And what about you, Spencer? Why are you single at the age of thirty-eight?"

He smiles and leans back in his chair. "Now, that is the million-dollar question. I could tell you some random bullshit about not finding the right girl."

"Bullshit?"

He shrugs. "I have found the right girl. Over and over, I've found the right girl."

"But?" That wasn't the answer I was expecting at all.

"I haven't found anyone who is worth fighting myself over."

"Fighting yourself?" I ask. "I don't understand."

"It's hard to explain."

I sit forward in my seat, fascinated by the man in front of me. "Try."

He smiles a slow, sexy smile, and he sips his wine, his dark eyes holding mine. "This is not the conversation I imagined us having tonight."

"Likewise." I smile. This conversation is refreshingly honest.

He sighs softly. "I love women, I love sex, and I love my independence."

I choose not to respond.

"And I am not in the business of hurting people, so I don't risk it."

"Risk it?"

"I couldn't be with someone, be in love, and then be unfaithful. It's just not who I am. Hence why I've chosen not to be with just one woman thus far."

"But you have friends with benefits?"

"Yes."

"Is that what you want with me?"

A trace of a frown crosses his face. "Surprisingly...no."

"What do you want from me, then?"

He stares at me. "That's what I'm here trying to work out."

Our meal arrives, and we begin to eat in silence. He seems comfortable, but my mind is racing. What the hell is this date about? What does he want from me? For a long time, I eat in silence as I troll through my brain for a logical answer...

And then I get it.

This is how he does it.

This is how he gets women to sleep with him with no strings attached. He's so honest and heartfelt, you want to slip straight into being one of his friends with benefits... because he assures you that there is no chance of getting hurt.

These women all know what they are signing up for and they don't care.

And right at this moment, I would give my right arm for him to take me home for some of his so-called intimate relations. I get a vision of the all the images of him with women from Google, and I cringe. Being one of those stupid girls is the last thing I need.

Stop it.

Don't fall for this crap.

He's a player...and his game is strong.

I need to change the subject. "What do you do for work, Spencer?"

"Spence," he corrects me.

"Spence." I smile around my mouthful of food.

"I am an architect and I own a steel-manufacturing company."

I frown as I chew. "How do those two things merge together?"

"I used to design skyscrapers. In the designing process, I found a niche in the market that wasn't being met, so I designed a new form of steel. I now ship to most first-world countries, and I have around four hundred staff working for me."

I smile as I watch him become all animated. He's proud of himself. I raise my glass to him and he clinks it with his. "Well done." I smile. "That's amazing."

"Thank you. It's been hard work to get where I am. What do you do for work?" he asks.

"I studied law and commerce, and then I went to work for a cause my mother loved dearly. I've been there ever since."

"You don't use your degree?"

"No, unfortunately not." I smile. "One day, hopefully, it will come in use. I have this wild idea that may come to fruition when the time is right."

He smiles and pats the corners of his mouth with his serviette.

"And your family? Tell me about them," I ask.

"I have a sister and a brother. My sister is a stay-at-home mother now, my brother a surgeon. My mother lives near London. I see them all the time."

"And your father?"

"Is a piece of shit who I wouldn't spit on," he answers coolly. "I legally changed my name to Jones on my thirteenth birthday...my mother's name."

I sit back, surprised at his venom. "You don't get on?"

"I hate him with a passion." He sips his drink. "Next subject, please."

"Oh." I sip my wine, flustered by his hatred of his own father. I wonder what that's about. I've never known anyone who despises their father.

"Tell me about your family," he says, obviously desperate to change the subject.

"Well, I live on my father's estate in my own house."

He smiles softly as he listens and continues to sip his wine.

"I have two brothers. Edward has a heart of gold but is so worried about my safety that it's almost unbearable. William, lives in Switzerland with his wife and baby."

"William doesn't work with your father?"

"No. Edward and he don't get on. Edward hates William's wife."

"Oh." He frowns. "And your mother?"

My heart drops, and before I am able to put on my brave face, my eyes fill with tears. "My mother was killed in a car accident five years ago."

His face falls.

"I miss her dearly."

He reaches over the table and takes my hand. "I'm sorry."

"Me too." I squeeze his hand, a silent thank you for being kind.

"Good Lord," he mutters almost to himself as he sits back in his seat. "I came here to try and woo you, and all I have done is make you talk about morbid things and told you I am a womanising cad who can't be trusted. My A game is most definitely slipping."

I chuckle and pick up my wine. "A very sweet cad, though."

Our eyes lock again, and the air swirls between us. He smiles softly. "You are more beautiful than I remembered, Charlotte. I'm glad I came."

"So am I," I breathe.

We eat our dinner and enjoy a dessert. I find myself genuinely surprised at how easily we get along. He's funny, witty, and not at all like I imagined.

"Sir, just to let you know the bar is closing soon. Would you like anything else?" the waiter asks.

Spencer and I look up in surprise. Where has the night gone? It feels like we just got here.

"No, we'll be leaving soon," Spencer answers.

We finish our drinks, and he pays the bill. Then he takes my hand as we walk out onto the road. I see Wyatt in the car and guilt suddenly fills me. I've never made him wait for me while I had a date before.

At least my father and Edward are away in London at a work function tonight and aren't home.

"Where is your house?" Spencer asks as we walk up the road. He presses a button on his keys and the headlights to a sporty-looking black Maserati light up.

"Just out of town." I smile as we arrive at the extremely low vehicle. "This is your car?"

"Yep." He smiles cheekily.

"I should have known that you would own a poser car."

He flashes me one of those beautiful smiles and opens my car door. I feel myself melt.

"Yeah, because the Bentley you drive around in is so understated," he hits back dryly.

I giggle as I slide into my seat. "That's not my car, it's my father's."

Spencer starts the car and pulls out onto the road.

"What do you drive, then?" he asks with interest.

I bite my bottom lip and hesitate.

He casts a quick glance my way. "Your security guard drives you around all the time in that black Mercedes wagon, doesn't he?"

I shrug, embarrassed. "Sort of."

He frowns and bites his thumbnail as he thinks, his eyes fixed on the road. "How do you stand it?"

"What?"

"The lack of freedom and their control."

I frown at him. "What do you mean?"

"They know where you are every minute of every day. How do you stand it? Don't you feel suffocated and just want to break free?"

My heart sinks. He's the first person who's ever got it. "More than you know." I sigh sadly.

He looks over at me and grins mischievously.

"What?" I smirk.

"Maybe you should run away with me and join the bad girl club." He wiggles his eyebrows. "I can teach you how to have fun in the dirtiest way possible."

I chuckle as I look out the window. If only he knew how tempting that offer is. "I'm sure you could, Mr Mischief."

He laughs and puts his hand on my thigh, like he's done it a thousand times before.

This is the weirdest thing. He's not getting romantic on me, he's not trying to be perfect or pretend to be something he's not, and it's working. Second by second, I'm feeling more comfortable with him. All this honesty has him sliding right in under my skin.

God, he plays a good game.

"This is it, up here on the left," I tell him.

We get to the large stone gates outside, and he glances over at me. "What's the code?"

My eyes flicker nervously to Wyatt in the car behind us. I'm not supposed to give anyone the code to get in. "Eleven, zero, five," I blurt out. I look at Wyatt through the passenger wing mirror and see he is getting annoyed.

Spencer pushes the code in and drives down the driveway. "This is my house here," I say.

He parks the car and looks over at me as Wyatt's headlights pull in closer behind us.

Spencer watches him in the rearview mirror. "This guy is pissing me off," he mutters almost to himself, and then he opens his door. "Come on."

I stare at him, confused. Does he think he's coming in?

"I'm walking you to the door, Charlotte." He rolls his eyes. "Fucking relax."

"Oh." I smile, feeling stupid, and I get out of the car to follow him up the six stairs to the porch and my front door.

"Can I come in...for a coffee?" he asks.

I stare up at him as we stand in the darkness. "We have nothing in common, Spencer."

"Spence," he corrects me.

"We have nothing in common, Spence."

He smiles down at me. "I don't care." He leans forward as if he's going to kiss me, and I step back.

"See?" I snap.

"See what?" He frowns.

"This is why you can't come in."

"What is?"

"This ability you have to talk women onto their backs."

He frowns and picks my hand up to kiss my fingertips. "I just want coffee, Charlotte. Why would you think I have a hidden ability?"

I watch him kiss my fingertips. "Well, it's not really hidden. It's out there for the world to see," I whisper.

He rolls his eyes and drags his hands through his hair. "Stay off Google, Charlotte." He sighs. "Nothing good will ever come from that."

"We're just not suited, Spencer." I sigh.

"Suited or not, you're attracted to me. I can tell."

"I am. I won't deny that," I admit.

He smiles softly and cups my face in his hands.

One night...just one night with him.

My heart begins to race as I imagine what it would be like to be in his bed.

He dusts his thumb over my bottom lip and watches my reaction. "I want to talk some more. I haven't had enough time with you yet."

"Talk about what?" I breathe, unable to concentrate when he touches my lip like that.

"Invite me in for coffee so we're out of sight of him." He gestures to Wyatt, who is watching with beady eyes from the parked car. Spencer drops my hands and holds his up in the air. "I'll behave, I promise."

I roll my lips to try and stop myself from smiling.

"And after coffee, if you don't want to see me again, that's fine." He raises his brows. "I'll never write your name in my diary again." He crosses his finger over his chest. "Cross my heart."

I giggle sharply, but just as quickly I remember the facts of who he really is and fall serious again. "I don't have what you're after, Mr Spencer."

His eyes hold mine, and he dusts the backs of his fingers down my cheek. "Maybe I'm sick of the afters, Charlotte. Maybe I want a before."

I feel my stomach somersault with nerves, the energy between us palpable.

"It's late," Wyatt snaps behind us, breaking our moment and forcing us both to jump.

Spencer frowns at Wyatt, who has snuck up the porch steps. "Hello," Spencer says, holding his hand out for Wyatt. I can tell he's annoyed that Wyatt has interrupted us. "Spencer Jones."

Wyatt glares at him and shakes his hand. "Wyatt. I'm Charlotte's guard."

"She's home safe, Wyatt," Spencer says flatly, glaring at Wyatt. "Why don't you run along and give us some privacy?"

My eyes widen.

"I don't think so," Wyatt replies calmly. "I think it's time *you* ran along."

Spencer smirks as if amused and puts his hands into his pockets. "Actually, I'm going in to have a coffee with my lovely date." His eyes come back to mine and he takes my hand in his, picking it up to kiss it. "Aren't I, Charlotte?"

"Yes," I whisper, wide-eyed. Oh my God, what the hell is he doing?

Wyatt's jaw clenches, and Spencer smiles and winks cheekily, clearly loving every moment of this.

"Wyatt, you-you are finished for the evening," I stammer. "Spencer and I are just going to have coffee, that's all." I open my door in a fluster. "You should go home now."

"I might see you in the morning when I leave, hey, Wyatt?"

Spencer says chirpily. "Will you be on in the morning?" he asks, acting innocent.

Wyatt radiates thermonuclear anger as he glares at my cheeky date. I have no idea what the hell Spencer is playing at.

"Spencer!" I snap. "Cut it out."

What the hell are these two idiots doing? Spencer is openly baiting him. His eyes hold Wyatt's. "You do know that she's twenty-four and perfectly capable of making her own decisions, right?"

I bite my lip to hide my smirk. He's the first person who has ever challenged anyone in my life this way. It feels good to have someone in my corner for a change.

"Wyatt, honey, go home. I'll see you tomorrow," I say softly as I walk through the doorway. "I'm fine, I promise."

Spencer walks in behind me and waves with his fingertips, giving him a big, cheesy grin. "Nighty night, Wyatt."

I close the door and widen my eyes. "What the heck are you doing, Spencer?" I snap.

"Playing with him." He smirks.

"I can see that, but why?"

"Because I won't have him dictate to me when I see you." He wraps his arms around my waist and smiles down at me. Then he leans down and kisses me. "Can we open the drapes so he can see me kissing you?"

I laugh against his lips. "Stop it, you're acting like a petulant child."

"He likes you."

"No, he doesn't."

"Why did you call him honey just now?"

I frown. "What? I didn't."

"Yeah, you did. Don't do it again." He kisses me softly.

"Why not?"

"Because I like you." His hands slide down to my behind and he pulls me against his erection. "I don't want you calling your bodyguard honey."

My heart begins to hammer in my chest, the air leaving my lungs in one long exhale.

"You...like me?" I ask nervously as I look up at him. How is a woman supposed to think with that weapon pressed up against her stomach?

Don't flinch, don't flinch, don't flinch.

"Hmm." He smiles a slow, sexy smile and pushes my hair back from my face. "I like you very much, actually."

This is the most confusing date I have ever been on. All of the men that I've dated in the past have broken their necks to impress me, and yet Spencer isn't giving a damn about what I think, and he's purposely trying to anger my bodyguard.

He lives completely in the moment.

Strangely enough, I think he may be the most appealing man I've met in a very long time. If not ever.

I imagine Edward meeting Spencer, and I drop my head to hide my smile.

"What?" He presses his finger under my chin to bring my face up to his.

"My brother would hate you."

He laughs. "Do I look like I give a fuck what your brother thinks of me?"

I smile. "No."

He leans down and his lips take mine, his tongue gently sweeping through my open mouth. My knees weaken.

"Put your arms around my neck, angel," he murmurs against my lips, knowing he has to direct me.

Angel.

I tentatively put my arms around his strong shoulders, enjoying the way he looks down at me with his big blue eyes.

You could cut the sexual tension between us with a knife. I can feel his hard erection up against my stomach, and strangely enough, I want to... I want to feel it.

This feels strangely intimate and special, even though he's just told me at dinner that it's not.

"Are you behaving, Mr Spencer?" I whisper up at him.

"God, I don't want to." He leans down and kisses me again. "You make me want to misbehave."

"What happens when you misbehave?"

"We fuck," he whispers into my mouth. "Long, deep, and hard."

My insides begin to melt as I imagine his naked body on top of mine. My arousal throbs between my legs as his lips take mine again. For a long time, we stand in the same spot, kissing like teenagers.

Our kiss turns frantic. He walks me to the couch and falls back, pulling me down and making me straddle his lap.

His hands are in my hair and our faces are pressed together as our kisses become more erotic.

His lips drop to my neck and he bites me hard.

"Maybe I should give you a huge hickey to really piss Wyatt off?" he breathes against my skin. "That'll teach him to mess with me."

"Spencer." I gasp and pull my neck away from his teeth. "Are you insane?"

His eyes find mine. "Maybe." I can feel his huge erection up against my sex, and he grinds me onto his body.

"Rock onto me, angel," he whispers. He grabs my hipbones and begins to slowly rock me back and forth over his hard erection. My body responds, quivering with pleasure.

Oh God, he feels good.

My hands are in his hair, and we stare at each as a perfect moment of clarity runs between us.

We continue to kiss, my body slowly rocking over his, and without any warning, my body begins to shudder. Spencer hisses in approval.

"Let's go to bed and fuck," he whispers hoarsely.

I pant, a myriad of emotions running through me. "What?" I whisper as my arousal fog instantly disappears.

"Let's fuck," he mumbles against my neck.

"You want to fuck me?" I whisper, shocked at his candour.

"God, *yes*." He growls as he kisses me again. "Tell me you want to fuck me too." He moans against my breasts.

Suddenly, I have this out-of-body experience watching him in his aroused state. "Spencer?" I say.

"Spence," he corrects me, and his teeth bite my nipple through my blouse.

"I've never..."

His kiss turns frantic, and he drags me across his hard cock.

"I'm a virgin," I whimper.

He pulls back to look at me, his hair all messed up and his lips swollen.

"You're a *what*?" He frowns.

3
_____

Spencer

"I haven't had sex before."

"Never?"

She shakes her head.

I watch her, my breathing ragged. *Is she fucking joking?*

"Tonight with you would be my first night."

My eyes widen in horror. "What the fuck?" I push her off my lap and stand immediately. "Are you kidding me?"

"No, I'm not!" she snaps, annoyed by my reaction. "I'm offering you my virginity. Do you want it or not?"

Her virginity.

I stare at her, my mouth hanging open. "Of course I fucking want it." I run my hands through my hair and begin to pace. "I... I mean." I stop and look back at her. "Never?" I mouth.

She shakes her head, and I wince.

A virgin. A virgin. A fucking virgin. I'll split her in fucking half. I have no idea how to fuck gently.

"This isn't exactly the reaction I was expecting," she whispers.

I look over at her and my face softens. "God, Charlotte." I lean down and tenderly kiss her beautiful big lips, holding her face in my hands. "You're the perfect woman."

"But?" She scowls.

I stare at her, lost for words. My heart is hammering hard in my chest.

If I take her virginity, she'll become needy and attached, and I'll only fuck this shit up. Girls fall in love with their first sexual partner, and I don't do love.

I so want to, though. I get a vision of myself teaching her the ropes, and my cock begins to weep. It would be so fucking good.

"Spencer, what's wrong?"

I swallow the lump in my throat, and I kiss her softly as I try to control my hunger.

She deserves her first time to be soft and gentle...neither of which are my strong points. Plus, I'm big. I'll hurt her.

Not if you warm her up first.

I get a vision of kissing her inner thigh, and my cock hardens to a painful level.

"You should go," she whispers sharply.

I stare at her in confusion. "I knew you were different the moment I laid eyes on you," I admit quietly. She's fucking perfect inside and out.

God, I want her. Everything in me *wants her.*

She stands abruptly and opens the front door in a rush.

"Goodbye, Spencer."

What? What the hell? "Wait, I-I don't want to go," I stammer.

Fuck, why did I hesitate? Now she thinks I don't want her.

"I want you to leave. Immediately."

"I'm not going anywhere," I say, standing my ground.

"You heard the lady," Wyatt growls from the front porch.

We both turn in surprise.

"Not now, fucker," I snap.

"Get out before I beat you to a living pulp."

"What the hell?" I frown, and my eyes flicker to the beautiful girl in front of me. "Charlotte?"

48

"Please leave, Spencer," she says as her eyes fill with tears.

My face falls, knowing that I've hurt her feelings.

She turns and runs up the stairs, leaving me no choice. Wyatt pushes me towards the front door, and I rip my arm from his grip.

"Don't fucking touch me!" I shout as I storm out onto the porch.

"Don't come back."

I turn to him. "I'll be back whenever it fucking suits me, you prick. Stay the fuck out of my way." I storm to my car, start it up, and rev the shit out of the engine.

I stare at her house for a moment, glaring at the fucking idiot guard dog standing on the front porch.

I don't even have her fucking phone number.

I tear out of the driveway and out through the large stone gates.

"Well done, Spencer, you stupid prick." I grip the steering wheel with white-knuckle force.

That was one gigantic fuck-up.

I sit at my kitchen table and type the words 'Charlotte Prescott' into Google.

It's now Sunday night, and I've been in a world of pain since Thursday when I last saw her.

I have never regretted not doing something so much in my entire life.

I sip my scotch as I wait for the results to come up. I smile as a gallery of images of the beautiful woman flash across my screen. I click through the images one by one, taking in her perfect angelic face.

There are photos dating back to her when she was a child in a private school uniform, and then at Polo events, a few charity events, but surprisingly there are very few images of her recently.

That's because she's never out.

Charlotte Prescott is the only daughter of Harold Prescott, and

*younger sister of fellow billionaires Edward Prescott and
William Prescott.*

*She became a multi-billionaire after her father split their family
estate five years ago to invest in legalised gambling. Prescott
holdings now has the largest casino portfolio in the world with
an estimated worth of twenty-nine billion dollars.*

*Famously known for her low profile, Charlotte was the driving
force behind the extension and establishment of the new £160
million National Philanthropic Fund in 2016.*

*The fund, which she chairs, was established by her late mother
over fifteen years ago.*

*She is also an arts patron who sits on the boards of the Art
Gallery of London and the United Kingdom Theatre Company.
Charlotte Prescott's estimated wealth currently sits at four
billion pounds.*

I raise my eyebrows, winded by what I've just read. *Fuck me.*
No wonder she's so guarded.

I sip my scotch with a shaky hand, and I read the next article.

*For almost twenty-five years, Harold Prescott's only daughter
Charlotte has been one of the great mystery women of the
United Kingdom. From birth, the third born child of Harold and
his wife Angelique was an enigma. Hidden away in private
schools from an early age, Charlotte grew up shy and socially
awkward until, as an adult, she became as fiercely private as her
father—inaccessible. Charlotte is rarely seen in public and is
stringently guarded, as she is considered to be her family's most
valuable treasure.*

*Some say that for the past five years, since her mother's death,
Charlotte has actively chosen to live a reclusive life.*

*Rarely seen in public, only usually attending charity events,
Charlotte resides in her family's private country estate*

Fuck. I slam my computer shut in disgust with myself. I keep seeing her disappointed face when I hesitated accepting what she so bravely offered. She thinks I didn't want her because she was a virgin. If only she knew how far from the truth that is.

I walk into the restaurant at 7:00 a.m. Masters and Sebastian are at our usual table and have already ordered for me. We do this every Monday. It's hard to find time to see each other, so we grab it while we can.

"Hey," I say as I slide into my seat.

They both frown as they look over at me. "What's wrong with you?" Seb asks.

"Nothing." I take a paper from the table and flick it open. "How was your weekend?" I ask.

"Better than yours, obviously." Masters tuts. "What happened in Nottingham last week?"

"Nothing." I sigh.

They both smile. "She wouldn't see you?"

I blow into my cheeks. "She saw me." I flick the pages of the paper angrily.

"Well, what happened? We want details."

"No details." I look up at my two friends. "You were right, though. She is well and truly out of my league."

"How so?"

"She's a virgin."

They both stare at me, and I swear, it's so quiet that you could hear a pin drop.

I throw my hands up in the air. "I know, right? What the actual fuck is that about?"

"Oh, hell," Masters whispers, running his fingers over his stubble.

"So, what happened? She told you she was saving herself for marriage, and then kicked you out?" Seb asks.

"Nope. She told me she was a virgin and I freaked out like a fucking baby, and *then* she kicked me out."

Masters stares at me. "You did what?"

I shake my head. "I can't deal with that kind of pressure, man. I can't even be monogamous to one woman for more than a week." I pinch the bridge of my nose.

Seb nods. "That's the truth."

Masters frowns at me, not saying a word.

"We had dinner and then went back to her house. Before we got inside, I had words with her fucking security guard."

"She has a security guard?" Masters asks.

"Yeah, and I reckon he is sweet on her. He was way too invested." I pause as I remember the look on Wyatt's face. "Once I got rid of him, we got busy and I told her we should fuck. That's when she told me she was a virgin."

Our breakfasts arrive to a table filled with silence.

I pick up my knife and fork.

"Fuck me," Seb eventually whispers. "Why does this shit never fucking happen to me?" He slaps his forehead. "I would give my left fucking nut to have a virgin."

Masters chuckles. "Right?" He cuts into his toast. "Imagine how hot the sex would be."

They both smile darkly.

"Stop it." I groan. "Don't even think about sex with her." I point my knife at Sebastian. "You go near her and I'll fucking kill you."

The two of them chuckle in unison.

"Jesus Christ, calm down." Seb laughs.

I run both my hands through my hair. "This woman has got me going fucking crazy."

"So, do something about it."

"I can't fuck her!" I snap. "You don't just fuck a girl like Charlotte."

"No, you don't." Seb shakes his head. "You fuck her, you marry her. Hands down, one hundred percent."

I begin to perspire. "See?" I point my knife at them. "I can't get married."

"Why not?" Masters frowns.

"Because I've seen the hell you two have been through and I'm not wired to be with just one woman."

"I didn't think I was either," Masters says.

"What made you change?" I ask.

He shrugs. "I didn't want anyone else touching me but her."

I stare at him.

"And I didn't want to touch anybody else. It stopped being just about the sex and more about when I got to spend time alone with her."

I shake my head in disgust and look at Seb. "See, this is what I'm talking about. Nothing good can come of this." I bite my food off my fork with force. "You're pathetic, by the way, Masters."

He nods. "I get it, Spence. Run. Run the fuck away now."

"I did."

"Then why is it pissing you off?" Masters ask.

"Because she's so fucking perfect, I can't even deal with it. I've jerked off so many times that my dick is chaffed, and I can't get any satisfaction from that. I didn't go out all weekend because I didn't want to sleep with anybody else."

Masters shakes his head. "Yeah, that sounds about right. Hate to tell you, but you're pretty much fucked already, man."

I close my eyes and pinch the bridge of my nose. "Sheridan is in town this week. She'll snap me out of it."

"God, you've been on and off with her for a long time."

"About ten years, I think."

"Why don't you just make a go of it with her?" Masters frowns.

I screw up my face in disgust. "It's not like that between us."

"So let me get this straight: you've been fucking this chick from New York for ten years and you don't even think about her once when you're not with her?"

"God, no, never," I answer with certainty. "I'm not being a stepfather to her three bratty kids, and I definitely don't want to move to the States. Nor do I want her moving here. We just have fun." I scowl and look up at the ceiling. "I think she's even got a boyfriend now."

"But she'll call you the minute she gets into town and you'll go to her hotel."

"Oh, yeah, I'll fuck her 'til she can't walk." I bite the food from my fork. "When she's in London, she's mine."

"How often does she come here?"

"Four times a year."

"How long does she stay each visit?"

I shrug. "Ten days or so."

"Like I said," Seb mutters. "Why doesn't this fucking shit ever happen to me?"

We continue to eat our breakfast, and the boys talk and chatter cheerfully, but my mind is in Nottingham...with Charlotte.

I hate that she thinks that this is about her. This isn't about her, it's about me and what I can't be.

If I go there, eventually I'll fuck it up. I know I will, and I can't stand the thought of that.

It's best to just leave it as it stands. *I can't see her again.*

I exhale heavily at the depressing thought, and I stare out of the window, feeling like shit.

"Fuck's sake, snap out of it." Masters groans.

"Whatever." I sigh, tucking into my breakfast again.

It's going to be a long day.

Charlotte

Lara falls into the seat opposite me. "Good Lord, I need a strong drink. Can you buy it by the bottle here?" She sighs.

I smile and sip my wine. "What happened?"

She throws her hands up in the air. "Ugh, where do I start?" She holds her finger up. "Oh, I know, let's start with the fact that there was a pubic hair on my desk this morning when I got to work."

"What?" I gasp.

"That stupid wench from accounts is fucking somebody, and she's doing it on my desk."

54

I put my hand over my mouth and stifle a laugh. "Are you sure?"

"Yes." She frowns, horrified. "I called the other girls into my office and we all agreed that the hair was definitely pubic. We had a two-hour discussion over it."

My eyes widen. "What did you do?"

"Disinfected the hell out of everything, and then put a complaint into management."

"I have no words."

She shakes her head in disgust. "I do. Get a fucking room." She pours herself a glass of wine, but she's so distracted that it sloshes over the side. "It's disgusting. Now, everywhere I look in the office, I imagine her huge, hairy vagina has been on it, getting pummelled." She sticks her fingers down her throat to fake vomit. "Oh, and don't even get me started on the kitchen. I'm never eating my lunch on that table again."

I tip my head back and laugh. God, Lara is really riled up about this.

"Anyway." She shakes her head. "How was your weekend?"

"Good." I shrug, and I feel a little sadness creep back in. I've been bummed all weekend over Spencer not wanting me. I'm embarrassed, and I wish the whole nightmare hadn't happened.

She sips her wine and watches me. "What is that look?"

"I saw Spencer last week."

She frowns. "What? Where?"

"He came to my work."

"Spencer Jones? *The* Spencer from the other night? The one you kissed at the wedding?"

I nod with a sad smile.

Her mouth falls open and she leans against the table. "What did he want?"

"We went out for dinner."

"What? Like, on a date?"

I nod and try to hide my smile. "He had the day off, and he waited outside work for me to finish."

She sits back in her seat. "Holy shit."

I shrug. "So, yeah, that happened."

She frowns. "What exactly happened?"

"Nothing."

Her eyes widen. "Charlotte... I am all for you finally going on a date and all, but with him? We both Googled him last week when you kissed him, remember?"

I twist my lips.

"He's a total womaniser." She tuts.

"I know that. I won't see him again, don't worry. It was just nice to do something out of the ordinary, you know?" I am not telling Lara the rest of the story. She just wouldn't understand.

"You're just bored." She sighs. "And I want you to break free, I really do."

I smirk.

"To be honest, it's time you broke out of Edward's reign," she continues.

Lara hates the way that Edward tries to control me, to the point they have had many an argument. I think they secretly like each other but would never admit it.

"Edward is..." I shake my head as I try to articulate my thoughts. "He's at the height of his controlling phase."

"Ha, what's new?"

"William came home this week and Edward called Penelope a whore. They had a huge fight, and William took off back to Switzerland."

"Penelope is a whore." She screws up her face. "I wish she'd gone back to Denmark with that German she was fucking," she adds. "If she just left William back then, he would be over her by now. Maybe he'd finally be with someone deserving."

"I know, she makes me sick." I sigh.

A comfortable silence falls over us, until Lara smiles at me, something clearly on her mind.

"What?"

"Why don't you move to London?"

"Lars." I sigh. "When are you going to give up on this?" She's been trying to talk me into moving for about eighteen months now.

"Never." She takes my hands across the table. "It's not like you can't afford it. Your trust fund is bigger than the Reserve Bank of England. Look, just move there for six months, date gorgeous men, have fun, meet new people. Elizabeth is in London, and you can go out and meet new people."

I stare at her.

"You are going to go crazy in that stuffy castle of a prison, Charlotte. You are wasting the best years of your life."

"It's not a prison," I retort. "I live there because of my father, and it's my home."

"Bullshit. Edward will control you while you continue to live there, and you know it."

I stare at her.

"He knows who you date, when you get home, what you are eating for dinner."

I sip my wine. "It's true, he does."

"All I'm saying is that it's great that you're ready to start dating, but do it in London, away from your brother."

"I love my brother, Lars. I know he's just trying to protect us all after Mum died."

"I know he is, too, and he's a good man. Just misunderstood." She smiles as she watches me. "He goes away tomorrow for six weeks, doesn't he?"

"Yeah." I frown. "How do you know that?"

Her face falters. "You mentioned it the other week."

I stare at her for a moment. I didn't even find this out until last week, and I haven't spoken to Lara in that time.

"What are you doing in town, Lars?" I ask casually.

Is she fucking my brother?

No. Don't be stupid.

"Oh, it's Mum's birthday tomorrow. I got the day off work, so I came home to see her. Do I need an excuse to see my best friend too?"

"No." I smile.

"Will you think about London?" she pleads.

"I have my job and I love it. I can't imagine doing anything else." I shrug. "If I'm meant to move to London, the universe will give me a sign."

"I know it will." She smiles knowingly. "Now, we need to talk about Spencer." She widens her eyes. "Tell me *everything*. Let's stalk him from afar."

I giggle.

"What does he do for work?" She frowns.

"Steel or something."

She takes her phone out and begins to search him.

"Don't tell me anything about the women you find on that thing," I snap. God, it's bad enough that he didn't want me, I don't need the women he *did* want rubbed in my face.

"Oh." She frowns as she reads. "So he's an architect who designs skyscrapers and he owns a steel company that supplies to most countries for said skyscrapers." She purses her lips. "His company has four hundred staff. Wow, he's no slouch."

"I never said he was. You did."

"Just don't tell Edward that he came to your work. He will go nuclear. Or your father, for that matter."

"I'm not that stupid."

Lara's eyes hold mine. "Promise me."

"Promise you what?"

"Promise me you won't fall for this guy's cheap pickup lines. He's a player—the player of all players."

"I know. I'm not stupid. Give me some credit, please." I sigh.

"Good." She smiles broadly.

I sip my wine and stare across the restaurant. If only she knew that I offered myself to him on a silver platter and he turned me down.

I close my eyes in disgust. *What the hell was I thinking?*

.   .   .

58

It's 10:00 p.m. and all is quiet on the estate. I pull the curtains back and stare out into the darkness. My mind keeps going over the fact that Lara knew Edward was going away tomorrow.

How did she know that? Had I told her and forgotten?

No. I hadn't even known it myself.

I see the two security guards walking down the road, performing their last sweep of the grounds for the night, and I walk out onto my front porch. "Hello," I call out as they approach my property.

"Hello, Charlotte." They both smile.

"Lovely night," I say, aiming for casual.

"Yes, and warm for this time of year."

"Does my brother have company tonight?" I ask.

They glance at each other. "I believe so," Ryan says with caution.

"Do you know who with?"

They exchange looks again. "A...female friend," Ryan answers.

I fold my arms over my chest. "And her name is?"

They once again look at each other. "We're not sure, Charlotte."

I tilt my chin and think for a moment. "Is this the first time she has been to the estate?"

"No, I don't believe it is," Ryan says. The two of them keep walking past in the hope that their interrogation will soon be over. "Good night, Charlotte," Ryan calls out, effectively ending the conversation.

"Good night." I huff, and I turn back into my house.

I head straight for the kitchen and flick the kettle on.

Edward and Lara? Surely not.

She sees other people. It was only last week that she went on a date with someone.

I think back over all the times over the years when they have had aggressive arguments with one another...mostly over me. Although, I must admit, they have always seemed to know a lot about each other.

59

Why would they hide it if something was going on?

Are they fucking?

No. They're not. I know they're not. I'm just imagining things that aren't there.

God, I really do need to get out more. Lara is right: I'm going crazy cooped up in this castle.

I make my tea and sit on the couch, my mind in overdrive.

I tap my tooth with my fingernail as I think. I wonder if Lara's car is at his house.

I go into my office and pull the drapes back. I can see the lights from his house in the distance.

He has his own road in and out of his place, just like I do, but because his house is at the end of the estate, I wouldn't have any clue who he has down there. Until tonight, I've never wanted to know.

Well, damn this.

I go out to my front porch, sit on the steps, and put my trainers on. I'm going to see exactly who Edward is bedding tonight.

And if it is Lara, there is going to be blood. Whether that's his or hers, I don't know yet, but I won't be impressed if they are sneaking around behind my back.

His, I decide. It will be his blood.

The thought of him sleeping with my best friend boils my blood.

She's way too soft and sweet for him.

I know for sure if I had someone here for the night, Edward would be here in an instant, ordering them home. I look down at my white sweater. Hmm, this won't do. I run upstairs and change into a black jumper and a black beanie. If I'm going to go spying, I may as well look the part.

I turn the torch on my phone on, and I look left and right to make sure the coast is clear. Then I slowly start to walk down the road towards Edward's house. It's a fair distance from my house, but I know the security staff have done their last check for the night and are tucked back in their office at my father's. Wyatt finished work at 6:00 p.m. because he thought I wasn't going anywhere.

I walk, and walk, and walk.

God, this seems a lot farther in the dark.

I finally arrive at Edward's house and duck behind a tree before I peer around it. Like my house, his house is made of sandstone and covered in ivy. Our houses are near identical, both two-stories with four bedrooms. The only differences being that he has had his house updated to his tastes and added another large living area at the back. Unlike me, he won't be leaving his house, so he has made it his forever home.

I tiptoe across the large circular driveway. There are no cars here, damn it. She must be parked in his garage, whoever *she* is.

The lights downstairs are off. I walk around to the side of his house and look up to the higher floor. Edward's bedroom light is on and the curtains are open.

Ugh, damn it, I wish I could just see who he has up there.

I blow out a breath and sit down on the ground for a moment.

I look around and wonder what to do.

About three metres out from his window sits a large tree. What if I climbed it? Just got a look at who is in there and then climbed down?

No harm done.

My heart rate quickens as I walk over and look up at the tree, smirking to myself.

What the hell are you doing, Charlotte?

I put my arms around the trunk and take the first step up, then another, and then another. Before long, I'm way up high. I just need to get to that taller branch and I will be able to see in. I step up and hug the trunk. It's pitch-black outside, but I can see into the lit bedroom clearly.

I watch in silence. Nothing's happening.

I peer down at the ground. Oh hell, I'm up really high. I cling to the tree as if my life depends on it, because at this point, it actually does.

I didn't think this through at all.

Then I hear movement. I squat down in a panic.

Edward comes into view, forcing me to hold my breath. He's facing away from me but...oh no.

He has no clothes on. My brother is naked.

The blood drains from my face.

He turns towards the window, his huge erection standing proud. He's holding handcuffs and spinning them around his finger as he talks to someone who is obviously still in his bed.

My eyes are as wide as saucers. Oh, dear God.

Not this. Anything but *this*.

I step back to try and get away. I slip, and I try desperately to grab the trunk. Unfortunately for me, I miscalculate and go hurtling down towards the ground, somehow managing to grab a branch along the way. It kind of breaks my fall for just a moment before I hit the ground hard with a thud.

"Ouch," I whimper as I lie in a crumpled heap.

What the fuck did I just see?

I stare up at the stars, hurting all over. I get a visual reminder of my naked brother and it makes me scrub my eyes with my fingertips to try and remove it from my brain.

I remain on my back, looking up at the dark sky for ten minutes in the dark, crumpled on the ground.

That really hurt.

Eventually, I crawl onto my hands and knees and push myself off the ground.

That is the last time I'm ever going to spy on anyone ever again.

What is he doing up there right now?

I scrunch my eyes together to try and block out the image of him with those handcuffs.

I feel nauseous.

I stand in the afternoon sun on the front landing of my father's house. My father and Edward are in their customary expensive suits. Their security staff are buzzing around, and the last of their luggage has been packed into the car. Five men are going with them, while the other five stay here to look after the house and me.

I wish it wasn't like this. I wish we didn't even have to have security. My father was, and still is, terrified that something is going to happen to me like it did to Mum. He knows that now that casinos and gambling are mixed in with the family empire, all bets are off. Security is at an all-time high.

My father's eyes rise to meet mine. "Will you please reconsider coming with us, Charlotte? Six weeks away would be wonderful for you."

"Dad." I sigh. "You two are going to be working the entire time."

"I'll have the plane pick you up. Maybe you could come out there for a shorter amount of time," he offers hopefully.

"No." I smile as I kiss his cheek and wrap my arms around him. "Have a great time, and I will see you soon. I will call you every day."

I turn and smile at Edward, who is unusually quiet today.

Don't think about it, don't think about it, don't picture it.

Last night's spying activities have traumatised me. "Have fun, Edward." I say.

He frowns, and I know he's worried about leaving me. "I can be back here in twelve hours if you need me to be."

"I'm fine." I step back from him. For all of Edward's faults and his overbearing ways, I know he really does mean well and is acting out of love for William and me. "It's six weeks, for God's sake."

"Please be careful, Charlotte. I couldn't bear it if anything happened to you. Don't go anywhere without Wyatt and Anthony."

Anthony is Edward's normal guard, and he is leaving him here to guard me. "I won't, I promise. I'm not stupid." My eyes glance over at Wyatt, who drops his eyes to the ground. Okay, fine, maybe I'm a little stupid, but I never will be again. I learnt my lesson, and thankfully Wyatt has kept his promise about keeping Spencer a secret.

Edward and my father get into the Bentley. Eventually, it slowly pulls out of the driveway, with security following in another car behind them.

I give them a wave and a smile as nerves flutter in my stomach.

I've never been alone for this long before.

I angle my face up to the sun and smile broadly, feeling the vitamin D sink in.

"Elizabeth is coming over for the night."

Anthony's face lights up. "What time will she be here?"

"Around six."

"Very well."

Anthony has had a crush on my beloved friend for years, and to be honest, I think she has a bit of a thing for him too.

I'm going to set them up on a date one day.

I turn and walk towards my house.

Six weeks all alone. I don't know whether to be thrilled or petrified.

Spencer

I hear the handle turn on my office door, and I glance up to see Sheridan standing before me.

"Hello." She smiles.

I grin brightly and stand to kiss her cheek. "Hello, darling." My eyes drop down her beautiful figure, which she's dressed in her usual power suit—a navy skirt and matching jacket with a white silk blouse unbuttoned to tease me just enough. Her long dark hair is up, and she is wearing tortoiseshell-framed glasses.

Sheridan is the CEO of a multinational conglomerate company. At the age of thirty-five, that's a huge accomplishment. My company supplies steel to her company, so we effectively work side by side but for different companies. Listed in the *New York*

Times as one of the most powerful women in the United States, Sheridan works hard and plays harder.

She gets me like nobody else ever has. We have a sexual relationship based on trust and friendship, but we both know this for what it is. No lies, no pretence that we're going to fall in love, and best of all, no bullshit.

"How are you?" I ask her.

"Why is Electra still here?"

I roll my eyes and drop into my chair. Electra is one of my PAs who gives us all nothing but trouble. She gets under Sheridan's nose, and the last time she was here, Sheridan demanded that I fire her.

"She's here because I can't fucking fire her. I gave her a written warning and she brought the damn union in to threaten legal action."

Sheridan points to the door with her thumb. "She's sitting out there messing around on Facebook."

I swing my chair from side to side, holding my pen between my fingers. "Wouldn't surprise me. Where are the other girls?"

"God knows. I mean it, Spencer, you need to fire her. It's not fair that your other two PAs have to do her share of the work."

"It's just not that easy."

"Oh, fuck off. It's dead easy. I'll do it now for you, if you like."

I smile as I look up at her. "Not everyone is an ice queen like you, Shez."

Sheridan makes grown men cry in her company. She's the hardest woman I know.

She strolls over to the window and looks out across the city, casually flicking through her phone before she hits call.

"Hello, this is Sheridan Myer from Universal Steel." She listens for a moment. "I need some security cameras installed throughout the offices, please." She listens.

"Immediately." Sheridan glances over at me, and I roll my eyes. "I need you here today, please. There are three offices that need to be fitted with invisible cameras after hours. Okay, great. You do know where we are? Yes, the fifteenth floor, and ask for Spencer Jones." She hangs up without saying a goodbye.

I sit back in my chair. "I don't need security cameras."

"Bullshit. That little troll is going to try and sabotage you. Mark my words, she's a nasty piece of work."

I smirk. "Because you're Mother Teresa, right?"

"I won't have you taken advantage of, Spence, and if she tries to wipe your computers or anything shady, at least we'll have proof."

She lets her hair down, kicks off her shoes, and walks back over to the window, leaving me to watch her. She stares out over the city for a moment, and then her eyes drift back to me. "You're different."

"How so?" I frown.

"You normally have me pinned to the wall within five seconds flat."

I sit forward in my seat and rest my chin on my hand.

"Have you met someone?" she asks.

I hesitate before answering, unsure if I want to discuss this with her. "Yes and no."

She walks back across the room and sits on my desk. She crosses her legs, and my eyes drop to her muscular thighs revealed by the split in her skirt. "What do you mean, yes and no?"

"Yes, I've met someone, and no, I can't have her."

"She's married?"

"Just the opposite." I pause for a moment. "Young and innocent."

She doesn't hide her amusement. "How young and how innocent are we talking?"

My eyes hold hers. "Very young, and as innocent as you can get."

She chuckles. "Oh God, Spence, she won't be able to hold you sexually. I can't, and I know how to fuck."

I run my hand up Sheridan's thigh and inhale sharply. "That you do."

She takes a hotel key card out of he pocket and slides it

across the desk. "I have a business dinner tonight, but I'll be back in the room by ten. My usual room, the penthouse at the Corinthian."

I pick the card up and stare at her for a moment.

She leans down and takes my face in her hands, and then she kisses me slowly.

My cock hardens instantly.

"See you then?" she asks as she tenderly brushes my hair back from my forehead.

I smile and run my hand up her thigh. "Of course."

She ties her hair back into her bun and slips her high heels back on. "I've got to go. My two PAs are in a café downstairs." She walks towards the door. "Can I fire the troll on my way out?" she asks hopefully.

"No, you may not. Goodbye, Sheridan."

"Until tonight, darling." The door closes behind her and I hear her say, "You're not getting paid to be on Facebook, young lady. Get to work."

I chuckle for a moment. She's a hard-ass bitch.

I walk over to the window in my office and stare out at the view. The city is bustling down below.

I wonder what Charlotte's doing now.

I get a vision of the look in her eyes when she thought I didn't want her, and my heart sinks, forcing me to exhale heavily.

It's not fair to start something when I already know its fate.

I'm doing the right thing.

It's best if I don't go near her again.

When the clock strikes 11:00 p.m., I walk down the corridor towards the penthouse of the Corinthian.

I know this hall; I've walked it many times, and always with anticipation.

Something's off tonight, though. I see the door up ahead and I stop and stare at it for a moment, sucking in a quivering breath.

67

I wish I was going to see Charlotte instead. She's the one I really want to see.

I exhale heavily, swipe the key card on the hotel door, and listen as it clicks on its release. The light in the apartment is muted when I step into it, with only the lamps lighting up the space, but I know where to find her.

I walk into the bedroom to see Sheridan naked on her hands and knees on top of the bed. Her long dark hair cascades down her back, and a white satin ribbon is tied around her neck, like she's a present.

My present.

On the side table sits an array of dildos and lubricant.

My cock instantly hardens.

"Hello, darling," she purrs before she slides a butt plug into her mouth and sucks it. "I was just about to start without you."

I smile as I take my jacket off and hang it in the walk-in robe. "You know, you really *should* play hard to get, Sheridan."

She moans, and I step back into the room to see her on her knees, bending over as she slides the butt plug deep into her ass. Her eyes close with pleasure, and I unzip my pants with a brand-new urgency.

"On your back, legs open," I growl.

Its 6:00 a.m. on Friday, and I'm lying in my bed, watching the morning news. Although I'm not paying much attention. I can hear it, but it's nothing more than background noise.

It's as if everything around me is on mute. This whole week has been on mute.

I feel like shit.

I fucked Sheridan, and the only way I could make myself come was by imagining she was Charlotte.

I've done it for three nights in a row.

The sex is hot—super fucking hot—but only because, in my mind, I'm fucking my angel. My Charlotte.

Not Sheridan.

And now the sick taste of betrayal rests constantly in my mouth.

I feel like I cheated on Charlotte, even though we are nothing to each other.

I hate that we're nothing.

I hate that I used Sheridan's body to ejaculate when I was thinking about another woman.

I've never done that before to any woman. I'm always completely focused on whomever I'm with. Thankfully, Sheridan has gone out of town now.

Regret runs deep in my blood.

What kind of man am I? Imagine if she knew.

I pick up my phone and check it.

No missed calls.

4

Charlotte

BETH CURLS HER NOSE. "What do you mean?"

I exhale and sink deeper in my seat. We're sitting on the living room floor after eating our weight in Indian takeout. "Just what I said. He turned up at my work and was being ridiculously gorgeous, so we went out for dinner." I shrug. "Things went well, and then we came back here. One thing led to another, we started making out, things got hot and... Oh, it was so good. Then the very next minute I ruined it by blurting out that I was a virgin."

Beth is deeply fascinated. "And?"

"And...he left."

"What?" Beth gasps, her disbelief evident.

"I know."

"But guys love virgins, don't they?" She frowns. "I don't get it?"

"But *do* they?" I scoff. "I'm twenty-four and I can't get a man to come near me at all, Beth."

She rolls her eyes. "Please, don't insult my intelligence. You get plenty of men who pursue you."

"Be serious for a moment and face the facts. I'm an ice princess who scares the majority of men away." I sigh sadly.

"Don't take offence to that. It's not you, it's Edward and every-thing that goes along with being a Prescott."

I drain my wineglass because, God, this is depressing.

"And you really liked this guy?" she asks quietly.

I shrug sadly. "Not specifically him, more what he represents, you know? He was fun, naughty, and gorgeous. He's older, too, and I would never be allowed to go out with him because he's a well-known player." I frown as I try to articulate my thoughts. "But... I just wanted to have fun for once. I'm not looking for a husband or anything, obviously. The only thing my family ever sees when they think of a man being with me is him only ever being with me for my money. I want men to be with me because of the woman I am. I want fun, carefree sex, like you get to have. Like every woman should be allowed to have in their youth."

She nods, her face full of understanding. "Who knew being wealthy was so boring?" She tuts and stares into space.

I refill her wineglass. "Totally." I pass her the glass. "And Wyatt was being all overprotective and annoying."

"That's his job. Don't blame him for that."

"Yeah, I get that, but Spencer was different. He wasn't trying to woo me. He was honest and told me he only ever has friends with benefits. He was nothing but himself, and you know what? It was damn attractive."

"So you want friends with benefits now?"

"No. I don't know what I want, but I know it isn't this."

"Hmm."

I exhale heavily and lie back on the floor. "I just want a fucking holiday away from myself for a while."

"Dropping F bombs now. You must be serious."

I chuckle. "Yeah, I am."

"What do you mean, you want a holiday away from yourself?"

"I mean I wish I was someone else for a while, with a normal shitty job, no money, and every man in the world trying to shag her." I smile as I imagine a different life where I don't have to constantly toe the line. "I want to feel desired and carefree, instead of having guards, Bentleys, Edward, and all the boring bullshit that goes along with being a Prescott." I exhale heavily.

Beth watches me for a moment, and I can feel her brain ticking. "If that's what you want, why don't you get it?" she asks.

"What?"

"Why don't you change your name and be normal for a while?"

"What do you mean?" I frown.

Her eyes widen with excitement. "And this is the perfect time, too."

I roll my eyes. Here we go.

"You said your father and Edward are away for six weeks, right?"

"Yeah, so?"

"*So*, why don't you take some time off from work while they're away? Why not move to London and go undercover? You could get a shitty job and pretend your name is something completely different."

"Like what?"

She bites her bottom lip and thinks for a moment. "Lottie Preston. Your friends call you Lottie, anyway."

"Have you lost your mind?" I gasp, sitting up at once.

She beams at me. "Just the opposite, this is fucking genius. Get a job in a café or a nightclub, pouring drinks or something. Nobody will know who you are, and you'll be treated just like the rest of us. You can run amuck."

I stare at her, wide-eyed as her idea rolls around in my head. "But what would I tell my father?"

"Hmm." She thinks for a moment. "That's tough, because he won't let you go anywhere without security."

I flop back against the couch, dejected that my plan is already screwed. "It won't work." I sigh. "Why doesn't Lara have the issues that I do?"

Beth rolls her eyes. "You and Lara are completely different."

"Why?"

"Both her mother and father come from money. She's had nannies and lived the high life her entire childhood. She has this entitled part of her personality that only rich people have. Your mother was different, Lottie. She didn't have money. She fell in love with a rich man. You never had nannies, and your main influence was your mother. She didn't rely on money or see it as anything special. That's why you're different. Money doesn't define who you are, and your family know that. That's why they feel you have to be protected so fiercely. They know that when you fall in love with someone, it could be with anyone. Social rankings mean nothing to you."

I become overwhelmed with emotion. "I never thought of it like that."

"Do you really think that your mother would want you to be a prisoner of your father's bank balance?"

My eyes tear up from knowing that's exactly what I am. I shake my head. "I don't think she would."

"Then let's do this."

"How do I get around the guards? Maybe I could just run away?"

"No. If you did that, your father and Edward would come home acting crazy only to drag you back here."

"That's true."

We both think for a moment.

"What about if you did run away, but more subtly so that you weren't detected," she says.

I frown. "How?"

"Well...you tell your job here that you are having eight weeks off to travel. But then you tell your father that you're going to be working the same job as usual, just from the London office for a few weeks."

This plan already sounds ridiculous. It will never work.

"But then you secretly get another job somewhere else."

I roll my eyes. "As if."

"The guards won't follow you into work; they never do. They

will hover around outside, but who cares, because you'll be inside, being someone else."

"But then where would I live?"

"Hmm." She thinks for a moment. "The guards don't guard you twenty-four hours a day, do they?"

I shake my head. "No, only when I'm out and about. Once I'm home safe, everyone relaxes."

"Okay. What about if you stay in a hotel?"

I twist my lips as I listen.

"Yes, I've got it." She holds her hands up in the air. "You stay in a swanky hotel where your suite is the only room on the floor. The guards come out with us or whatever throughout the day or night, but you specifically instruct that they stay at a distance so that nobody even knows they are there. Then, once the guards escort you home for the night, there is no security risk because nobody else can get to your floor without a key. They will stay in their rooms on the level below."

I stare at her.

"And then if you meet someone, I can take them up to your room after the guards have left, because I will have the only other key that gets me to your floor."

Excitement simmers in my stomach. "Are you serious?"

"Why not?" Her eyes are alight with mischief.

"Could this really work?" I whisper.

She shrugs, and we both smile goofily at each other.

"But what job will I get?"

"Well, it has to be in a fancy building that could compliment what you are supposed to be doing there. The guards and your family need to think you are doing the same job that you do here."

I nod as I think. "In reality it has to be a shitty job that has no responsibility. I don't want to let anyone down when I leave."

"Yes, of course. I'll look for one for you when I get back to London. Are you going to tell work on Monday?"

"Are you really serious about this?"

"Deadly. Fuck it, let's go crazy."

"I'll have to speak to my guards."

"Okay, ask them. But you know they will have to do whatever you want, anyway." She looks over at me and smiles mischievously. "Are you ready to have some fun, Lottie Preston?"

The nerves dance in my stomach at the sound of my new fake name. "It may not happen yet," I warn her. "There are a lot of what-ifs in this plan."

"But if it all pans out, will you do it?"

I imagine Spencer walking away and leaving me the other night without so much as looking back, and I know it's always going to be like this. Nobody will ever touch the precious Charlotte Prescott unless they want to marry her. Dealing with my family just isn't worth it. Who wants that kind of pressure on a first date?

"If the guards can go, and you can find me a job, you've got yourself a deal," I say flatly, convinced there's no way in hell that this will all come together.

She holds her glass up in the air and I clink it with mine. "I'm going to make this shit happen if it's the last thing I do." Her eyes already sparkle with victory.

I smirk. "Deal."

"Hello, this is Charlotte Prescott speaking," I say into the phone. It's Monday afternoon, and I'm at my dreary job.

"Okay, you got it. You start next week!" Beth squeals excitedly through the phone.

"What?" I frown.

"I got you a job, and you start on Monday."

My eyes widen. I glance around guiltily at all the normal, sensible people sitting at their desks. "Back in a minute," I mouth to Alison before I scurry towards the door.

"Sure, take your time," Alison says without looking up.

I push through the large glass doors and step into the outside garden area. "What do you mean, *you got me a job*?" I whisper.

"Look, it's nothing flash. You're going to be in the admin and mailroom. But it will be easy to do, and the shit jobs are where the fun is normally at, anyway. It's in the Belconnen Building, so your guards will have no idea you're not important. That building already has security, so it's a perfect scenario."

"You're serious?" I gasp.

"Completely. I'm coming to get you on Saturday to move you down to London."

My mouth falls open. "Elizabeth," I whisper angrily. "I thought you were joking."

"And I thought you were sick of getting no action," she hisses right back. "It's six fucking weeks, Charlotte. Loosen the hell up."

I close my eyes and pinch the bridge of my nose. "What if I get caught?"

"Then you turn around and come back straight home—no big deal. Your family are not going to disown you for having a working holiday in London."

"No, I... I mean the new job," I stammer. "What if I mess it up?"

"Oh, please, you're probably more qualified than most people in that shitty building. You could be the fucking CEO if you wanted."

Poor deluded Elizabeth has such a distorted view of me. She thinks I could rule the damn world. "Beth." I sigh.

"Don't *Beth* me. I'm coming to get you on Saturday, and we're going out clubbing on that same night. I'm buying you a huge box of condoms, too, because you're going to fucking need them."

I put my hand over my eyes. "Oh God." Nerves swirl deep inside my stomach.

"You want to have fun, Charlotte, and daring to do something different is the first step. You need to call your father and Edward tonight and tell them that you're working in London for a few days. They need to organise security, and then we'll just keep extending it so that it doesn't seem sus."

"This whole damn thing is sus," I whisper.

"Oh, and I called the Four Seasons to confirm they have a penthouse that takes up the entire top floor. I booked it out for six weeks. You'll have to pay on arrival, though."

I suck air into my cheeks, then blow it back out. "I can't believe you actually think this is going to work."

"Do you want to have a holiday from being Charlotte Prescott or not?" she snaps.

I stay silent for a moment before answering. "You know I do."

"Then stop being such a baby. See you on Saturday." She hangs up the phone and the line is dead.

I drop into a chair and stare at a tree in the garden for a moment. What the hell did I just agree to?

Edward is going to flip his lid.

The line rings, and my heart is thumping hard. It doesn't feel right to be lying to my father.

"Hello, my dear Charlotte," he answers.

I smile at the sound of his voice. I hadn't realised until now just how much I miss him. "Hi, Dad."

"How are you? What's been going on at home? You're up late, dear. It's after eleven here."

"Ah, yes." I hesitate. Lying to him is going to be harder than I thought. "I just wanted to speak to you and tell you something. I have to go work in London for a few weeks."

"Why?"

I wince. "There are some things that need to be taken care of in London, and I thought..." I twist the edge of my shirt between my fingers. "I thought now was a good time to go, while you're away, so I can spend some time with Elizabeth. It's just for a week or two."

"Can't it wait until we get home? I worry about you being in London on your own."

"I know, Dad." I bounce my leg as guilt fills me.

"I could come and stay in London with you when I get home, if that's what you want? I don't mind."

"Ah." Why does he have to be so damn nice all the time? "No. If

77

I go alone, then I'll be home when you get home and we can spend some time together where I don't have to work."

He remains silent, and I know I haven't convinced him yet.

"I'll take the guards, of course."

"Have you spoken to them?" he asks cautiously. "It may not suit them to go to London."

"I have, and they're both fine to come along. I'll book them into the room next to mine."

"I'll speak to Edward," he says sharply.

"Dad." I sigh. "You know Edward won't want me to go."

"Only for your own safety, Charlotte. You are my most prized possession, and if anything happened to you..." His voice trails off. "You are a target now, love."

"I won't take stupid risks, Dad, and I'll take the boys with me everywhere I go. I'm just going to be working through the day and going out to dinner with the girls at night. Nothing extreme."

He inhales sharply.

"Please, I need some time with my girlfriends." An unexpected wave of sadness rolls over me, because it really is true. "I'm lonely, Dad. I'll go crazy locked up here at the house alone for six weeks."

"I'll speak to Edward." He sighs.

"Thank you. I love you."

"I love you too." I hear the rustling of papers, and I imagine him sitting at his large mahogany desk, ruling the world from New York. "When do you want to go?"

"I have to be there for Monday, so I will go on Saturday, if that's okay."

"And where will you be staying?"

"I booked the Four Seasons penthouse so that I'm the only room on the entire floor. Nobody will be able to get in without a key." I smile to myself. "See, I really do listen to you."

"Okay." He inhales again, and I can imagine him leaning back in his chair. "Are you really all right, Charlotte?"

My eyes fill with tears because I honestly don't know if I am. "Missing Mum," I confess in a whisper.

"Me, too, darling. Me too."

We stay silent on the line, both lost in our own grief.

I smile sadly. "Thanks, Dad. I love you. I'll call you tomorrow."

"I love you, dear. Sleep well."

After hanging up, I make my way to the kitchen and put the kettle on. That wasn't a hard phone call, after all. However, the next one definitely will be, and if I know anything for certain, it's that Edward will call me in approximately fifteen minutes and begin freaking out.

My phone begins to vibrate on the kitchen bench, the name Edward lighting up the screen. Five minutes—a new record time.

"Hello, Edward."

"Charlotte, what do you think you're doing?"

"I'm going to London."

"Why?"

"I have to work."

"Send someone else instead."

"I can't, I need to do this."

"I'll come home and go with you. I'll only be a week."

"Edward." I sigh, exasperated. "I'm fine. I'll be with Elizabeth."

"That doesn't make me feel any better. Beth is out of control."

I get a flashback of him from the other night, and I want to blurt out the question, *Are you sleeping with Lara? Why is it a secret from me?* but I hold my tongue.

"Where will you be staying?" he asks abruptly.

"The Four Seasons penthouse. The only room on the floor."

"You've spoken to Anthony?"

"Yes. Anthony can come, and so can Wyatt."

"Hmm."

"It's just for work, Edward, and I'll have the guards with me the entire time."

"I don't like this."

"I know you don't, but you can't stop me from going. Dad said it was okay. I'm going to London for work, not Ibiza to party. Lighten up."

"Hmm." He groans.

I smile because I know I've got him. "I love you."

"Fine, but I'll organise their rooms at the Four Seasons myself. And I'm calling Alexander to keep an eye on you."

I smile. Alexander York is his best friend from school, and he just so happens to live in London. "Fine," I reply.

"And if I hear of you running amuck in London, I'm coming straight home and dragging you back to Nottingham."

I chuckle. "You're so dramatic."

He exhales heavily. "See ya, Lottie."

I grin with victory. I can't believe this plan is actually working out.

"Goodbye, Edward, I love you."

"Yeah... I love you too." Then he hangs up. I stare at my reflection in the kitchen window and smile. How the hell did I just pull that off?

The convoy of cars pulls into the Four Seasons at approximately 4:00 p.m. on Saturday.

I'm in Beth's car. The black Mercedes with the two security guards inside it is trailing silently behind us both.

I look over to Beth as she bounces in her seat. "My fucking God, can you believe you are doing this?"

"No." I hold my stomach. "I feel sick. What if I get caught?"

She shrugs as she pulls the car to a stop. "Who cares? What's the worst that could happen? Edward flips his lid, like he doesn't do that once a fucking week anyway."

I smile. It's so refreshing having a friend who doesn't give a damn.

Beth hands the keys to the parking attendant once we're parked, and we get my bags out of the boot of the car. I've warned the boys that they're to keep their distance. I don't want anyone to know that they are with me or are my security team. I want to appear normal. I *am* normal...it's just my life that isn't.

80

I walk up to the reception in the foyer with Beth by my side.

"Hello, I'd like to check in, please," I say timidly.

"Into the penthouse." Beth smiles proudly.

The girl types on her keyboard, and then frowns and types something else in instead.

Oh God, don't tell me they messed up the booking. This plan could all turn to hell before it has even started.

"Is your reservation for six weeks?" she asks with surprise.

"It is." I slide my credit card across the reception counter.

She scowls at the screen. "Just a moment, please?" She calls someone and turns her back to me, thinking that I can't hear her. "I have someone here for the penthouse for a six-week booking. Do you know anything about it?"

She glances over at me and her eyes widen. "Oh. Oh, yes, I see. Sorry, sir. Thank you."

She turns back to me and smiles an exaggerated fake smile. "Good afternoon, Miss Prescott. Welcome to the Four Seasons. It's our honour to have you stay with us for your time in London."

My shoulders sag as I stare at her. How does she know who I am?

"Your brother Edward has been on the phone with management all morning, making sure your arrangements are all in order."

He would have been going through their security with a fine-tooth comb.

Beth frowns, already unimpressed with my family's interference.

"The account has been settled in full. Welcome to the Four Seasons. I'll personally show you up to your room now."

I take my credit card back, feeling dejected. Edward would have paid my account without even looking at the amount.

Great.

"Can you issue me with three keys, please?" I ask. I want one for Lara and Beth so they can get up to my suite at any time.

"Certainly." She organises everything on her desk and then hands them over.

I glance at Wyatt and Anthony, who are walking through the front doors.

"Are those gentlemen with you?" the receptionist asks, already knowing the answer. She would be aware that we have two other rooms booked as well.

"Yes," I reply, embarrassed. There's no mistaking the two huge men dressed in black suits, staring at me.

"They are staying on the floor below, is that correct?"

"Yes. Thank you." I give the boys a small dejected wave. I guess they may as well come up and inspect the room now instead of later. She already knows who they are to me. So much for flying under the radar.

Damn it.

I turn to them. "Do you want to come up now and look at the room?" I ask.

"That would be great," Anthony replies without hesitation.

The receptionist, my two bodyguards, and Beth and I make our way into the lift.

I am silent and annoyed, sick of this fuss wherever I go.

As we ride up through the floors of the hotel, I stare at the floor, a sense of heaviness weighing over me. *Don't let this ruin it for you*, I try and remind myself.

It's okay, it's okay. I repeat the mantra over and over in my head. I hate to admit it, but when I'm with my family and the guards are with us, it doesn't seem to bother me at all. It's as if it's completely normal because they have it too. But when I'm alone with my friends, I want to be alone with my friends, and it becomes glaringly obvious that they have all this freedom while I don't.

The kind receptionist opens the door to the suite, and all of us tentatively walk in. "Holy shit!" Beth cries, her eyes flying around the room.

I smile at her reaction. There is nothing better than being with her when she experiences something for the first time. She can't hide her excitement at all.

The receptionist smiles as she walks through to the living area. "It's quite lovely, isn't it?"

"Yes, thank you."

I've stayed in some beautiful places before, and this is up there with the best of them. We walk into a large living area, and I glance up to the ceiling to see a mezzanine level with a cascading, ornate staircase.

"The apartment is two levels." She points upstairs.

The furnishings are complementing shades of coffee and creams. The space is filled with huge, luxurious, aqua-colored velvet sofas, as well as expensive curtains, with the room lit by beautiful free-standing lamps. We walk through to a large white kitchen. It has a large black marble island in the centre with stools lined up in front of it. The cupboards and cabinetry are black to match the island.

Wow, this is nice.

We continue on our tour, venturing into a large dining room, a bathroom, and a laundry room on the same level. We head upstairs to find three smaller bedrooms and another bathroom, and then to the end of the hall where the huge master suite happens to be.

I smile when I see it.

It's exotic and sexy, decorated and furnished with different shades of grey velvet. The bed has an oversized padded head-board, as well as a couch with a chaise lounge at the foot of it. The en suite bathroom is tiled in black and white marble. The feel of it is sheer luxury.

I turn to the receptionist, suddenly embarrassed that I can afford this place for six weeks. "Thank you, it's lovely."

She nods, realising she is being dismissed. "If you need anything, please call down to reception at any time."

"Of course." My eyes flicker to my guards. "Please look after the boys. I'll be fine."

She glances over to them. "Are you coming down to check in now?"

"Yes," Anthony answers. "We'll just perform our checks of the suite, and then we'll be down in a minute."

With one last smile, she disappears down the stairs and back to her job.

Beth starts to run up and down on the spot, and then she jumps up on the bed and begins to bounce. "Holy fucking shit, Lottie." She squeals in excitement. "This place is off the Richter."

The guards chuckle at my over-animated friend. She doesn't hide who she is from them. The guys check the wardrobes and the bathroom. They pull the curtains back to inspect the windows, and then disappear to check the rest of the suite.

I flop onto the bed, dejected from my overprivileged check-in.

"Who was I kidding, Beth? I can't escape who I am. Just look at this stupid apartment." I sigh sadly.

She falls down to lie beside me, and we both look up at the ceiling. "It's going to be so much fun sneaking guys in here," she says casually.

"What?" I look over at her.

"That cherry of yours...it's going down. In a big popping fashion."

5

Charlotte

I sit at the kitchen island with my glass of wine. I'm staring at the Google images before me. Beth will be here any moment to take me out to dinner. We decided that it's best if we play it safe this weekend and behave. The guards are on full alert, and we will get busted if we try to pull anything sneaky too soon. Even the thought of just going out to dinner with Beth is enough for me—something I don't normally get to do.

I click to the second page of images of Spencer Jones, studying photo after photo of him laughing and joking...*kissing beautiful women too*. I think back to my place that night, when I straddled his lap and we were making out.

His perfect kiss.

His hard body up against mine. His hands all over me.

It felt so natural. With his classic good looks and his sense of humour, I've thought of him often over the last ten days, and always with regret.

I wish I was experienced enough to please him. Lord knows I wanted to.

Beth is right: I need to change my life, and I need to start living.

My plan is to ease my father and the guards into this different life-style, and then when they get back into the country, I'm not going home.

I don't care about the consequences anymore. It is what it is. I'm not doing anything wrong by wanting some independence.

I'm staying in London to find myself, whoever she may be. I've done my time being a good girl and toeing the Prescott line. My pining for Spencer has shown me exactly what I'm missing out on:

Fun.

I would look for an apartment to rent permanently, but I know it will only instil a panic, and Edward will be here in an instant to drag me back to Nottingham.

I'm going to ease myself into it to—see if I even like living in London.

I hear the door open, and Beth comes into view. "Are you ready to hit the town?"

I snap my computer shut. "Sure am."

She holds her hands up in the air.

"What?"

"Anthony just checked me out on my way in."

"He did?" I smirk.

"He told me I looked gorgeous."

"Well, it's true, you do."

She narrows her eyes. "Do you think he has a girlfriend?"

"No idea. Edward would know."

"Next time you speak to Edward, ask him for me."

"Okay. You ready to go?" I ask.

"Sure am." She rubs her hands together in delight. "I'm going to prick-tease Anthony tonight 'til his balls fall off."

I grab my keys and bag. "That will be traumatising for me to watch, but whatever."

"This time tomorrow, he's going to be jerking off to the thought of me," she brags as she reapplies her lipstick.

I burst out laughing. "Beth."

"No, it's, *Oh, fuck yeah, Beth*," she says, feigning a man's voice as she pretends to wank herself off.

"Where did I pick you up?" I cringe.

She bats her eyelashes playfully and links her arm with mine. "From the Fun Friend Lottery. Now, let's go."

"So you won't let anyone see you, will you?" I ask Wyatt for the tenth time. It's Monday morning, and I am freaking out about my new job. The two of us are walking down the bustling street towards my new office building.

He raises his brows with exasperation. "I told you ten times... no, but I don't understand why anyone can't see us. They all know you have guards."

"It's just weird, you know. I don't want to seem odd to my new colleagues."

He rolls his eyes.

"And there are guards in the foyer of the building, so you don't need to hang around, Wyatt."

"Well, we sure aren't leaving you here."

"That's ridiculous," I scoff. "Go and do your thing for the day and I'll text you half an hour before my lunch break. Then you can come back and take me to lunch."

We arrive outside the tall building. We peer through the glass to see a metal detector and three armed guards.

"See." I smile. "This place is like Fort Knox."

One of the floors upstairs is the home of the American Embassy. I couldn't have planned it any better myself.

Wyatt looks around and exhales heavily. "Fine. Call me half an hour before your lunch break and I'll meet you back here."

I bounce on the spot as I grab his big arm and squeeze it tight.

"Thank you."

I take off through the large glass doors and hop into the lift, my nerves really beginning to rise.

The elevator is full, and people are all staring straight ahead. I clutch my handbag tightly, flinching when my phone beeps with a message. I scramble to read it.

It's from Beth.

Good luck today, Lottie Preston
xoxo

I bite back my smile and reply.

I'm so nervous, I'm about to throw up.
See you tonight.
xoxo

The doors open on the twenty-fifth floor, and I tentatively walk out and look around. There are people and desks everywhere. This place is a hive of activity. Where do I go?

I see a girl sitting at a desk, and I walk over. "H-hello. I'm starting today, would you know where I should go?"

She looks up at me and fakes a smile. "Hey, sure. Back office on the farthest wall." She gestures to the other end of the space. "Ask for Veronica."

I grip my handbag tightly. "Okay, thank you." I make my way to the office and stand by the door.

"Listen, if you continue to be lazy and not get through your work each day, I don't have a position here for you. Do you understand me?" I hear a woman chastise.

"Yes, Veronica," a man answers.

I swallow the lump in my throat and stand still. Shit, she sounds mean.

"Why weren't these reports done on time?"

"I've been doing three people's jobs, and I haven't had time."

"Then you make time," she snaps. "Get back to work right now, and don't make me call you in here again. I don't have the time or the energy to follow you around doing your work for you, Marcus."

"Yes, Veronica. It won't happen again." He turns and scurries past me, too rattled to even say hello.

The blood drains from my face.

"Yes?" she barks at me.

"Oh." I pause and step into her office. "My name is Lottie Preston. I'm meant to be starting here today," I whisper nervously.

She frowns. "Just a minute." She dials a number on her office phone, looking me up and down as it rings.

I shrivel under her glare.

"Yes. I have a Lottie Preston here, says she's starting today." She listens for a moment. "Okay."

I glance over at the door, wondering if it's too late to run.

She takes something out of her top drawer. "You're in the mailroom, follow me."

She stands and storms past me, and I swallow the lump in my throat. God, this woman is a rude pig. Not even an introduction? She's short and stocky with a strawberry blonde bob. I follow her as she powers through the office.

Who was I kidding? This was a stupid idea.

"You're on the tenth floor in the mailroom." She passes me a security card. "This is your key to get around the building."

I take it from her. "Thank you."

We get into the elevator and she hits the button hard. "I'm your manager. My name is Veronica, obviously, and as you probably just heard, I don't tolerate laziness."

My eyes widen.

"You'll be on time, you will work hard, and you won't gossip with colleagues and waste my valuable time. Do I make myself clear?"

"Yes," I murmur with wide eyes. "Of course."

The doors open on the tenth floor and she storms out again. This floor is different. There are huge conference tables everywhere, and over in the back corner I can see five small desks. Only one woman and a man are sitting at them, working on their computers.

89

"What are you doing, Paul?" Veronica snaps.

He spins on his chair, obviously not having heard us coming. "Hello, Veronica." He smiles cheerily.

"This is Laurel," she says to Paul, introducing me incorrectly.

"Lottie," I whisper.

She frowns and looks me up and down again. "Lottie." She rolls her eyes like I'm an inconvenience. "Lottie is starting in the mailroom today. Sarah, you can train her, please?"

The pretty girl smiles, and it's the first genuine smile I have seen aimed my way since arriving here. "Hello."

She has long dark hair and looks like a sexy Penthouse Pet with her huge boobs, silicone lips, and fake eyelashes. I feel so dreary in my sensible clothes.

"Hi," I croak.

"Back to work," Veronica says. "Laurel, if you need anything, come and see me in my office."

I frown. "It's Lottie." But she doesn't hear me—she's already power walking back to the lifts.

"Fucking slut," Paul groans once Veronica has disappeared.

My eyes widen.

"I swear to God, one of these days I'm going to stab that bitch in the eye with this letter opener." He pretends to stab something repeatedly.

Sarah smiles warmly and stands from her seat. "This is your desk, Lottie." She pulls out my chair. "Don't worry about Veronica. She's just a massive cunt."

My eyes pop. "Oh."

"Yeah, Cunty McCunt Face." She sighs. "I keep telling Paul to fuck her so she'll be in a better mood, but he won't."

"You fuck her," Paul cries out. "That vagina would be fucking green, I tell you. Nobody in their right mind would fuck her. I'm Paul, by the way." He smiles as he stands and shakes my hand. Paul is around thirty, at a guess, and he's quite good-looking with dark hair and height that towers over me.

I bite my bottom lip to stifle my huge smile. Nobody ever talks like this around me. It feels weird...and good.

"Hello, Paul." I hunch my shoulders together. "I have no idea what I'm doing, by the way."

"Neither do we," Sarah says casually. "We all hate this job. It completely sucks. You should run while you can."

I smile, unable to help it. "Then why do you work here?" I ask.

"Can't be fucked to look for a new job." Sarah sighs as she turns back to her computer. "That takes effort."

"I'm travelling. I'm only working here to save up for my next trip," Paul admits.

I smile and look around the office. "Makes sense."

"What are you doing here?" Paul frowns. "Why would you want to work in the mailroom of this shithole?"

I giggle at his language. "I was working in a nursery and wanted to come to London. This was the first job that I found."

They both nod, completely buying the story.

"So it's just the three of us here, then?" I ask.

"No, there are another two boys, but they are upstairs delivering photocopies at the moment. Or hiding in a storeroom somewhere," Paul mutters under his breath.

"Come on, I'll give you the tour," Sarah says.

"Okay." I follow her over to the large conference tables.

"So here is where we sort the mail every morning. We bag it into floor levels and then into departments. You and I deliver that every afternoon."

"Right."

She turns. "Don't ever let the boys deliver it, that's our job."

"Okay." I frown. "Why can't they deliver it?"

"Because it's the best fucking perving session ever. My God. There are some hot men upstairs. If we ever let the boys deliver it, they will never give the job back to us."

I smirk. I like this girl. "Makes sense."

"Do you have a boyfriend?" she asks over her shoulder.

"No."

Her eyes light up. "Well, you've come to the right place to work. This place is Hot dick city."

I laugh out loud. Hot dickcity? Who knew there was such a place?

"This room here is hell on Earth." I look in and see seven large photocopiers all lined up in a row.

"Why?" I frown.

"Because we have to print out and bind the training manuals for level nine."

"Is that bad?"

"It's the worst. We do that on Wednesdays. We usually all end up fighting, and then we have to go to the pub after work to recover."

I smile. Even that sounds fun to me.

"So, we do mail every day, making manuals on Wednesdays. Photocopying happens every day, and we have to answer delivery emails too."

"Delivery emails?"

She rolls her eyes. "If the twats upstairs are waiting for a package, they email us to ask where it is."

I really do like this girl. She reminds me of Elizabeth.

"All right. What else do we do?" I ask.

"We put up with a lot of crap from everyone. Especially Veronica."

"Where do we start?" I ask.

"We have coffee and toast while we wait for the mail to arrive."

"Sounds great." *Sounds normal.*

Four o'clock, and I'm pushing the trolley between the desks.

"Hey." A tall, dark, and handsome man smiles and leans back in his chair. "The mail cart is especially beautiful today."

I give him a weak smile. "Thanks."

"This is Lottie," Sarah introduces as she hands over the mail. "She's new, and doing a fab job, I might add."

If I could be excited, I would be, but I'm too exhausted from pushing this two-hundred-pound mail cart around the building for the last three hours.

I have been flirted with, teased, whistled at, befriended, and asked on four drink dates tonight.

This is the best day of my life...and the hardest.

I have never been so physically exhausted before. Who knew that all this mail has to be delivered to the whole building by hand? It seems so primitive and labour-intensive. And where the hell does it all come from? Hasn't anyone ever heard of emails, for Christ's sake?

I have paper cuts on my hands and blisters on my feet. My hair is a mess, and I'm quite sure I stink like a pig.

Sarah hands the last of the mail out. "Let's head back downstairs, Lottie."

Thank God. I smile and turn towards the lift.

"We only have an hour until home time. You did great today." She smiles.

"Thanks." I sigh.

"Monday is our easy day."

"This is the easy day?" I frown. "You can't be serious."

She giggles. "Yeah, I remember when I first started, I felt like I'd never done a day's hard labour in my entire life."

"I can relate," I mutter as we get into the lift and I push the button.

As we go down, I stare at the doors, thinking about the day I've had.

More people talked to me today than ever before. I was normal, one of the crew. People swore in front of me, hassled me, teased me, and asked me out. Veronica told me off three times, but apparently that's good for her.

I look down at my hands in front of me. They're dirty and grim. I drop my head and smile. I'm tired, exhausted, and utterly ecstatic with Lottie Preston's first day of work.

I did the right thing.

. . .

"Hi, Dad," I answer the phone.

"Hello, darling. How is my sweet daughter tonight?"

I smile broadly. "Good now that she's talking to you. What's happening?"

"Oh, not much, just meetings and whatnot. We're still in New York. We had a dinner on tonight and I came home early. Edward was talking to a woman, so I snuck out. What's new with you?"

My heart drops. I wish I could tell him about my exciting first day at work...but I know that I can't. "Just working at this end too," I lie. "William called me today. He's coming to meet me for lunch tomorrow."

"That's nice. What's he doing in London?"

"I'm not sure. He said he was here overnight for an appointment."

"Hmm." Dad thinks for a moment. "Let's hope it's with a good divorce lawyer, shall we?" He chuckles.

"We can dream. One day." I think for a moment. "Who was Edward talking to?"

"I don't know. I can't keep up with him. He dates a different woman every day. She was beautiful, I can tell you that much."

"Dad, have you ever heard Edward speak of Lara?"

"Why do you ask?" I can tell by his reaction that he must have.

"I just have a hunch that those two may be more than friends."

"I don't think so, darling. Edward wouldn't be interested in her."

"Hmm." I sigh, unconvinced.

"Anyway, I'll let you get to bed. Have fun with William, and I'll call you tomorrow night."

"Okay, I love you."

"I love you, too, dear. Good night."

. . .

I have to stop myself from running to him when I see William in the restaurant.

Oh, I missed my brother.

I laugh as I hug him. "This is such a pleasant surprise."

We hug a little bit harder, and I know he has something on his mind. I can feel it.

I fall into my seat. "What are you doing in London?" I smile.

"I could ask you the same thing." He smirks. "What the hell are you doing here? As soon as they leave the country, you have urgent business? It sounds suspicious to me."

I laugh. "I don't have urgent business at all. I'm just busting to do something different."

"Good." He smirks and glances outside. "Oh." His eyes widen. "How come Anthony is here?"

"Edward left him to watch me. He hasn't been too bad, to be honest. I think I had the wrong impression of him."

The waitress arrives with our drinks. I asked William to order before I got here, seeing how I only have an hour's break.

"So, what's new? What have you been doing?" He smirks.

"Working, spying on good-looking men, stuff like that." I roll my eyes.

He laughs. "I miss you."

I grab his hand over the table. "When are you coming home?"

He sips his drink. "I'm not." And then he shrugs. "Not to Nottingham, anyway."

"God, Edward is driving me completely mad, Will. He's completely out of control."

"My point exactly. Sorry about the other night—leaving without saying goodbye. He just makes me so furious that I can't even be around him."

"He's only worried about you. How are things going with Penelope?" I ask carefully.

"Up and down." He sighs. "I don't know, we have good weeks and bad weeks. The thing is, what I choose to do with my marriage

95

is my business. Imagine if you met someone and Edward stuck his nose in where it wasn't wanted."

"I can't think of anything worse, to be honest."

"Exactly. And Penelope's not perfect, God knows that. But I have a child with her, and I want him to grow up in the same house as me. What choice do I have?"

"It will be okay, and you know, you really are being amazing by staying with her and trying to repair your marriage for Harrison's sake. Not many men would do that."

"I don't feel so amazing some days." He smiles. "Anyway, tell me about you."

I sit back in my seat. "I met a gorgeous man."

"You did?" he asks in surprise.

"Yeah." I sip my drink. "It was a disaster."

"Why?"

"When he found out I was"—I hesitate—"inexperienced, he didn't want anything to do with me."

He scowls, confused. "Would he rather you be a stripper?"

I giggle. "Probably. Anyway, it was the push I needed to get out of Nottingham. Don't tell Dad or Edward, but I plan on moving here permanently eventually."

A big smile crosses his face. "You do?"

"Uh-huh." I smile proudly.

He takes my hand across the table. "Good for you, babe. Good for you."

"This stupid fucking prick of a machine!" Paul cries.

Sarah's hands are in her hair and her eyes are wide. "What the fuck do we do?"

I put my hand over my mouth to stop myself from laughing because this is hilarious.

The photocopier has gone crazy, and hundreds of papers are being spit out at record speed. It won't shut off and it won't quit printing. It's Wednesday, and we are supposed to be making training manuals for Veronica, but things aren't exactly going to plan. It seems to happen a lot in this dodgy mailroom. I have never laughed so much.

"Pull the plug out," I push out through my laughter.

"Yes," Paul says, scrambling for the power cords. He pulls them out, and the copiers all fall silent, leaving us to stare at each other for a moment.

There is paper everywhere. We have no idea what order the papers are in.

"That machine dropped some serious acid last night," Paul grumbles.

"Seems so." I look at the mess around us. "What do we do with all this?" I ask.

Sarah looks around too. "Shred it. We'll have to start again. It will take too long to sort this shit."

Sarah's phone rings. "Hello. Hey, Marcie..." Her face falls as she listens. "Oh no. Oh, damn it, Marcie. I've been waiting for this date for three fucking years."

Paul and I exchange questioning looks. Who is she talking to?

"Yeah, I know." Sarah sighs sadly. "That's okay. Who the hell am I going to get to come with me?" She exhales heavily. "Fine. No, it's okay, I'm just disappointed. I've been looking forward to it for months. He'll probably cancel on me now."

I begin to pick up the papers from the floor while Sarah finishes her conversation and hangs up the call.

"Fucking great!"

"What's wrong?" I frown.

"I have a double date on Saturday night, and the girl who was supposed to be coming with me has strep throat."

"So go alone." Paul picks up the papers with me.

"He won't come unless it's a double date."

Paul and I frown at each other. "Why not?"

"Because he doesn't even want to come at all. My uncle does business with him, and I've had a crush on this guy for years." She puts her hands on her hips in dismay. "My plan was to look gorgeous so that he can't help falling at my feet."

I smile. "Well, that's an excellent plan. Of course he will fall at your feet. Look at you."

"I know, right?" She smirks and gives a wiggle of her arse.

"Just get someone else to go with you," Paul suggests.

"I don't have anyone." She sighs. "This whole day is a fucking disaster." She kicks the photocopier in disgust.

"Take Lottie."

Sarah's eyes flicker to me. "Would you come?"

My face falls. "Oh." I shake my head. "I don't... I don't know the guy."

"I don't either. It'll be a blind date for both of us."

I stare at her in horror.

"*Please.*" She bounces on the spot and grabs my arm. "I really like this guy, and I can't go without someone else with me."

"You said you didn't know him!"

"I don't, but I really like the look of him."

I roll my eyes.

"Honestly, I've had the hots for this guy forever. Oh, please, Lottie. Please will you come?"

I stare at her. I mean, I could go. I have nothing else on... But a *blind date*? I really don't think that's such a good idea.

"What the hell?" Veronica cries out.

Our eyes widen, and we spin to see Veronica assessing the room from the doorway. Her hands are on her hips and her face is furious.

"This damn machine is on acid!" Sarah cries. "We had to shut the power off and everything." She throws her hands up in defeat. "We couldn't stop it."

Veronica looks at the papers all over the floor. She breathes deeply and closes her eyes. "I'm going to count to ten, and then I'm going to turn and walk out of here before I fire you all." She inhales in a dramatic fashion. "Clean this mess up and get those booklets finished before I lose my living shit."

We all drop to the floor and begin scrambling to pick up the papers. Veronica storms to the elevator and disappears, the doors closing behind her.

"Fuck off, you old mole," Sarah cries as she flips the bird to the closed elevator doors. "I hope the Grim Reaper comes around and fucks you up the ass with a baseball bat."

"Why can't you just say that to her face, Sarah?" Paul mutters, disgusted. "Then she wouldn't give us this shit." He throws a pile of papers into the bin. "And by the way, the Grim Reaper is too good for her. He has standards, you know?"

The situation overwhelms me, and I sit back on my knees, laughing. Loud, belly-cramping giggles take over, and I can't stop.

Sarah kicks the photocopier again, and then Pauls begins to laugh, too, until eventually Sarah joins in and the three of us are lying on the floor in uncontrollable fits of giggles.

"This job sucks hairy fucking balls, man," Sarah shouts up to the ceiling.

"Right?" Paul agrees.

I continue to laugh. If only they knew...

I think this is the best job in the world.

I glance over my shoulder at Wyatt and Anthony as they follow me across the street, making sure to keep their distance. I've warned them with murder if they blow my cover tonight. I told them I didn't want my new work colleague to know I have security, which is true, but I also don't want Sarah to find out who I really am.

I know her opinion of me will change if she finds out, and to be honest, I really like her company. She's refreshingly honest, and she likes Lottie Preston—the real me.

And I have to admit I like being Lottie Preston too.

It's Saturday night, and I have no idea how, but Sarah has somehow talked me into going on this blind date with her. We are meeting the guys at this restaurant-bar place.

I should be nervous. Charlotte would be terrified of going on a blind date with someone. But somehow, Sarah makes Lottie feel brave.

If we can handle Veronica and acid-dropping photocopiers together, we've got this in the bag.

I glance down at myself. I'm wearing a fitted black dress that has little capped sleeves and a gathered waist. I have my best black heels on, and my blonde hair is up in a bouncy ponytail so everyone can see my sassy red lipstick.

Wyatt looked me up and down when I walked out of the lift at the Four Seasons, and I didn't know whether he wanted to spank me and send me back into the room to change, or whether he wanted to kiss me.

Either way, he looked at me like I was different in this outfit. I'm not sure if I liked it.

Sarah links arms with me as we stride down the street towards our destination. Being this fake version of me gives me a confidence I didn't know I had.

"Where are we going?" I ask her cheerfully.

"Burbank. It's just up here, and it's the hottie capital of London."

"Remember, if it's not going well, we're out of here and we're going out just the two of us. You promised," I remind her. "I don't want to be stuck with a moron all night."

She nods. "I know, but trust me, my date isn't a moron. Just the opposite, actually. I hope his friend is cute for you. I'm sure he will be."

I roll my eyes, and she pulls me up the six sandstone stairs into the swanky-looking restaurant.

Seductive music is being piped through the speakers, and the decor is modern and eclectic. Large leather chairs are placed everywhere, with huge low-hanging lanterns over every table. The crowd seems trendy, and the atmosphere is fun.

I glance back out through the glass windows to see Wyatt and Anthony crossing the street towards the club.

I told them to get dinner and have drinks so that they don't look suspicious. Sarah grabs my hand and pulls me through the crowd.

"Where are we going?" I shout over the noise.

"To the back... I can see them."

"I thought you said you didn't know what they look like?"

"I know what my date looks like. I've stalked him for years." She cranes her neck to look over the crowd. "Oh, your date looks hot too."

I smile as relief hits me, and then we come into a clearing next to a table.

"Hi, I'm Sarah," she says nervously before she turns to me. "And this is Lottie. Lottie, this is my date, Spencer Jones, and your date here is Richard Marlin." She's beaming with pride, waiting for me to react.

The blood drains from my face.

Her date.

Spencer? *My* Spencer is *her* fucking date.

Big blue eyes come to rest on mine, and Spencer raises an eyebrow in surprise, a mischievous smirk crossing his face. "Hello, Lottie."

Oh. My. God.

6

Charlotte

"H-HI," I croak.

Sarah shakes Richard's hand, and then Spencer's. "It's so lovely to finally meet you."

They both stand, moving around the table to shake my hand, with Richard reaching for me first.

"Hello, Lottie." He smiles. He's handsome with dark brown hair and big brown eyes.

Then Spencer turns to me and takes my hand in his. It's hot and tingly, and I instantly remember the way it felt against my behind.

"Hello, Charlotte," Spencer purrs in his oh-so-sexy voice.

I push out a forced smile and tear my hand from his grip. "Hi." I fall into my seat.

"Her name is Lottie." Sarah smiles. "Lottie Preston. She just started working with me in the mailroom this week."

Spencer frowns, his eyes drifting back to mine with silent questions. Dear God, he's going to blow my cover.

This was the stupidest idea I ever had.

"You work in the mailroom?" Spencer asks Sarah, casting her a quick glance.

"For now...while I look for something else." Sarah says.

Spencer's attention turns back to me. "And...*you*...work in the mailroom, too?"

"Uh-huh." I fake a laugh, feeling my underarms beginning to perspire. "I need to go to the bathroom."

"Yeah, me too," Spencer says fiercely.

I practically run to the front of the restaurant and around the corner, but of course he follows me.

"What the fuck is going on?" he whispers angrily.

"Oh, Spencer," I whimper in a fluster. "Don't blow my cover. I'm pretending to be someone else."

He scowls hard. "Why?"

"Because I don't like being Charlotte Prescott."

"What's wrong with being Charlotte Prescott? I happen to like her." He quickly looks around the corner to see if we have been caught talking. "And what the fuck are you wearing?" he hisses when he looks back down at me.

"Sure." I huff. "You like Charlotte so much that you practically broke a leg when running away from her."

"Actually, it was your fucking bodyguard who threw me out...at *your* insistence."

"Because of the look of disgust on your face," I whisper angrily. How dare he throw this back on me? I've felt like crap for two weeks over this.

His eyes pop, anger radiating from him. "Disgusted?"

"Yeah, with my virginity!" I snap. "I'm so sorry to have disappointed you," I spit.

I don't know why, but we are both fuming mad with each other.

He throws his head back in disgust. "You have *got* to be kidding me?"

Something snaps inside of me, and I don't want to be sweet Charlotte Prescott for one moment longer.

"Well, you don't need to worry about me anymore, Mr. Spencer." I sneer, furious. "That situation has well and truly been taken care of."

He stares at me for a moment, connecting the dots.

"You slept with someone?" he finally asks, like he's been winded.

"Yep, and it was great." I glance back to the table. Screw him having the upper hand all the time. I'm not giving him the satisfaction.

"Do we have a problem here?" Wyatt growls as he approaches us, making us both jump.

Spencer throws up his hand in the air. "You. Fuck. Right off... right now. I am not in the mood for your shit tonight."

"Not a chance," Wyatt replies calmly, getting up in Spencer's face.

Good grief.

I roll my eyes. "Wyatt, can give us some privacy, please?"

Wyatt hesitates.

"Now!" I snap. "Don't blow my cover."

He glares at Spencer, and then he reluctantly walks off through the crowd, back to his table.

"Was it him?" Spencer growls.

"Huh? Was what him?"

"Did you sleep with fucking Wyatt? Because if you did, so help me God, Charlotte."

My mouth falls open...because that is literally the most ridiculous thing I've ever heard.

His eyes widen as he waits for me to answer. He comes closer to my face. "Are you fucking kidding me? It *was* him, wasn't it?"

I put my hands on my hips and narrow my eyes. "I'm going back over there to my date, and I'm going to continue to be Lottie Preston for the rest of the night. And you"—I poke him hard in the chest—"are going to shut your big mouth and not blow my cover."

He narrows his eyes and glares at me.

I turn to the back of the restaurant, inhale, and drop my shoulders before I walk back to the table with my heart hammering hard in my chest.

I find Sarah laughing out loud at something Richard has said, and I casually drop into my seat.

"So, Lottie..." Richard smiles. "Sarah was just telling me that you are new to London. What made you move down here?"

"Yes." Spencer sneers as he slides into his seat. "Please share. I'm fascinated to hear all about it." He steeples his fingers under his chin and smiles sarcastically.

I swallow the lump in my throat.

Oh God.

I fake a smile. "Well." I glance over to my two bodyguards, who are sitting at the front of the restaurant.

Thump, thump, thump goes my heart.

"Lottie worked at a nursery." Sarah smiles proudly and pours me a glass of wine. "Didn't you?"

The blood drains from my face. "Yeah." I pick up the glass of wine and nearly drain it in one go.

"I do love maternal women." Richard smiles and places his hand over mine on the table.

Spencer frowns and looks down at our hands, and then he narrows his eyes at me, his fury palpable.

I wither and drain my glass dry.

Spencer turns to Sarah. "Sarah, your uncle has been wanting me to come on this date with you for years. I hit his parked car in the car park last week, and I felt so bad about it that I finally conceded." He smiles, and everyone chuckles. "However, had I known you were this beautiful, I would have come on this date a long time ago."

She giggles into her wineglass nervously, and I find myself glaring at him.

Not funny, Spencer.

But it's like that, is it?

Game on.

"Richard." I smile. "Tell me all about you." I squeeze his hand in mine.

Richard's eyes light up. "Well, I work in the stock market, I'm thirty-two—"

"Thirty-two," I gush, interrupting him. "That's the perfect age, isn't it? Not too old."

Spencer looks at me, silently seething.

"How old are you, Spencer?" I smile sweetly. "I'm guessing around forty-five?"

He drains his wineglass, unimpressed, and I bite my bottom lip to stifle my smile.

"Spencer is the perfect age," Sarah coos. "I can see it in your eyes, Spencer, that you are just waiting for the right woman to come along."

He clenches his jaw. "Or just wanting to strangle one."

Sarah and Richard laugh on cue, and Spencer and I glare at each other across the table.

He composes himself and falls back into his role. "So you two are new friends?" he asks.

"Just this week." Sarah smiles. "Lottie came to work with me. I'm training her up."

"What is it exactly that you two do?" he asks as he acts fascinated.

"We're in the mailroom," Sarah replies.

Spencer's eyes hold mine, and Richard picks up my hand to kiss it. My eyes flicker over to Richard in shock.

What the hell? That's...unexpected.

I fake a smile and pull my hand out of his grip.

God, this night is a complete disaster.

Spencer's jaw tics and he continues to glare at me.

What is he so angry about?

I guess it could be my fake cherry popping, the fact that I'm pretending to be someone else and working in the mailroom, my tight black dress, Wyatt kicking him out of my house two weeks ago, or Richard kissing my hand. There are plenty of options, really.

I pour myself another glass of wine. Alcohol is the only remedy here, so I tip my head back and take a big gulp.

"Sarah." Spencer smiles seductively at her from across the table. "Do you like to dance?"

Her eyes light up. "I love to dance, Spencer."

"Me too. I can't wait for the real music to start."

Okay, now it's my turn to get angry. If he dirty dances with her, I swear to God.

"Do you like to dance, Lottie?" Richard asks.

I smile sweetly. "I do." I sip my wine. "You can tell so much about a person by the way they dance."

Richard grins like he's winning me over. The poor fella thinks he's getting in here. I kind of feel bad that he's tied up in this mess. "I'm going to the bar to get another bottle of wine for us." I stand before they can object, and I walk to the bar and wait in line.

What do I do? What do I do? Should I leave?

I don't want to be here if Spencer is into Sarah. Watching him with her would be my worst nightmare.

"What do you think you're doing?" Spencer whispers behind me.

"Washing my hair, what does it look like?"

"I don't know what kind of bitch pills you're on tonight, but fucking cut it out."

I turn to him and thumb my chest. "Me?" I shake my head and turn my back on him. "How about you cut it out?"

"Let's get out of here," he says suddenly.

I frown and look over my shoulder. "What?"

"I don't want to be on a date with her. I only ever intended on staying for an hour." He pulls out his phone. "Sebastian is calling me in exactly twenty minutes with my get-out-of-here plan. Let's go somewhere, just the two of us." He puts his hand on my hip bone, the contact unnoticeable to anyone else because we are covered by the crowd around us.

"Are you kidding me?" I whisper. "Sarah really likes you."

"Yeah, well, I don't like her." He squeezes my behind. "I like you."

I swat his hand away angrily. "You're a pig, Spencer Jones, and you're too late. You had a chance with me, and you blew it."

"You fucking blew it, not me!"

I turn to him, and I swear, I have never been so infuriated in my life. "I-I blew it?" I stammer. "You have got to be joking."

"You kicked me out and didn't call me."

I shake my head in disgust. "You are the most unromantic jerk I have ever met."

"Tell me something I don't know." He smirks and squeezes my hip bone. "Now, let's leave. If Wyatt gets in my way, I'm punching his lights out. Prepare yourself for my attack."

"Ha." I huff. "I would like to see that. He would wipe the floor with your wimpy behind."

"Yeah, we'll see."

I swat his hand away from my waist. "Stop touching me," I whisper as I shuffle forward in the line.

He immediately pulls me back against him to show me who's the boss here.

"I'm leaving in twenty minutes. Are you coming with me or not?"

"Not. She really likes you."

"And this is why I'm leaving. She's not my type. I have zero attraction to her."

I glare at him, unresponsive. Spencer links our pinky fingers together and his eyes drop to my lips. "You're my type," he breathes.

"Next!" the barmaid calls. I break out of his grip and step forward.

"I'll have a... erm..." My brain is completely fried from having him so close. "Can I have a..." Good grief, I can't even string two sentences together. What is it with this man?

Spencer steps forward to rescue me. "She'll have a bottle of

Louis Roederer." He smiles casually and leans down to whisper in my ear. "Give me your number."

His hot breath tickles my neck, and I feel goose bumps scatter up my spine.

"What?" I frown and find myself staring at his big, luscious lips.

"I don't have your fucking phone number. Give it to me."

My tingles instantly fade. "I don't want you to call me. And stop swearing all the time."

He rolls his eyes. "You can lie all you want about who you are to them, but don't lie to me. Give me your number."

The barmaid hands over the bottle, and I pay her without thought. Without another word to Mr Spencer, I walk back to the table.

He's such an asshole.

Moments later, he comes back to the table with another bottle of wine. He sits down and smiles calmly, placing his phone on the table.

My poor heart is hammering in my chest. This is devious behaviour at its very worst.

Sarah's date wants me to leave with him...and even worse than that is the fact that I want to.

Spencer's phone dances across the table, the name Sebastian lighting up the screen.

I roll my eyes. He has *got* to be kidding me.

"Hi, Seb," he answers cheerfully. "Oh no." His face falls as he pretends to listen. "Oh...really?"

I roll my eyes. Good grief. What next?

"Sure, yeah, I'll come and get you now." He listens and frowns at Sarah, shaking his head with fake annoyance.

I stare at him, deadpan. What a douche.

He ends the call. "Sarah, I am so sorry, but I have to go. My friend Sebastian has driven into a ditch about half an hour out of the city, and his pregnant sister is in the car. I have to go and help them."

Sarah's face falls. "Oh no."

"I'm so annoyed." He sighs. "This was turning out to be such a great night, too."

"What ditch?" I ask, raising my eyebrow.

"Dead Guard Ditch," he replies without hesitation.

I sip my wine and stare at him. "Sounds creepy."

He narrows his eyes. "It is."

He turns his attention to Sarah. "I'm sorry, but Richard will have to take over the reins tonight."

"That's okay, Spence, I can handle it." Richard smiles.

I roll my eyes yet again. It's obvious that Richard knew all along that Spencer was leaving early.

"Will you call me?" Sarah asks Spencer.

My heart drops for her. Damn him.

"Of course. What's your number?" he asks.

She smiles and reads it out to him, and he 'apparently' puts it into his phone.

"What about if I want to contact you at work?" he asks her. "Do you have a work email?"

"Yes." She smiles excitedly. "It's sarah@conradmailroom.com."

"Okay." He stands and shakes Sarah's hand. "Lovely to meet you. My apologies about tonight."

"That's okay." She giggles. "Call me."

Spencer shakes Richard's hand, and then he moves closer to me.

"Goodbye, Mr Spencer. Have a nice life." I tilt my chin to the ceiling.

He narrows his eyes at me again. "Have fun in that mailroom, Lottie."

I smile sweetly. "I intend to."

Our eyes are locked, and he raises his eyebrow in a *This is your last chance to come with me* way.

I wave. "Goodbye, Spencer." I sip my wine.

After a beat, he gives a subtle shake of his head and leaves the restaurant without looking back.

"Looks like I have two dancing partners tonight." Richard smiles, jiggling in his seat.

Sarah and I laugh at his goofy moves. "You sure do."

Spencer

I walk into another restaurant on a mission, riled up and severely pissed off.

She didn't want to come with me. She wanted to stay with him.

Her fucking bodyguard.

I should have knocked that fucker out on her porch like I wanted to.

My skin prickles. I bet he made his move on her that night after I left, the fucking snake.

Masters gives me a quick wave from the table they are sitting at along the back wall. I double-booked myself tonight. My first stop was with the date from hell, followed by my second stop of dinner with my three best friends.

I storm over and see Bree, Masters, and Sebastian glancing at their menus.

"Hi," I grunt, and fall into my seat.

"How did the date go?" Seb asks without looking up.

"Fucking disaster." I pick up his beer and drain it.

"Ease up." He snatches it back from me. "Get your own."

I raise my hand immediately to try and get the waitress's attention.

Spencer and Seb smile, exchanging a knowing look. "What was such a disaster?" Masters asks.

I throw my hands up in the air. "Where do I start?"

The waitress comes over. "Yes, sir?"

"Can I have a Corona, please?"

"Of course."

"And keep them coming."

The three of them sit tentatively, waiting for the story. "So, this

III

fucking idiot who I do business with has been hammering me for twelve months to take his niece out on a date."

Masters grins. "You're an idiot."

"You haven't heard half the story yet," I hit back.

"We don't need to." Seb chuckles, and they all exchange looks again.

"Anyway, I ran into his car in the car park last week, and he used it as leverage to make me feel bad, and he talked me into taking her out." I shake my head. They're right—I am an idiot. "I agreed on the condition that it was a double date, so then I could get out of there as soon as possible. I organised one of the guys from work to come with me, and he knew I was leaving early and was going to be left with two women. He's hoping for a threesome or some shit." My beer arrives. "Thank you." I take a long hard gulp of it. "Ah, that's the stuff."

"You were saying?" Bree frowns.

"My date, Sarah, arrives, and I will admit it, she's pretty hot."

"What's the problem, then?" Masters frowns.

"Guess who her friend was?" I snap. "The one set up with my friend."

"Who?" they all ask at once.

"Charlotte Prescott."

Their eyes widen.

I nod. "That's right. My dream girl who isn't into me is sitting across the table with my fucking friend holding her hand."

"What?" Seb whispers.

Bree puts her hand over her mouth and starts to giggle. "Oh, this is karma, Spence."

"Only she isn't Charlotte Prescott tonight. She introduces herself as Lottie Preston. A totally different person," I continue. "And she works in a fucking mailroom with Sarah now—Sarah, my *date!*"

"Wait, I'm confused." Bree frowns.

"That makes two of us," I snap.

"Why was she pretending be someone else?" Seb asks.

"I have no idea." I shrug and drain my beer. "But it wasn't long before I lost complete control of myself and followed her to the bar to start giving her shit about her kicking me out of her house two weeks ago."

Sebastian throws his head back and laughs out loud. "Why are you still going on about that?"

"Because it fucking pissed me off. No woman has ever thrown me out before."

Masters shakes his head and pinches the bridge of his nose.

"Well, what did she say?" Bree asks.

"She asked me not to blow her cover and said she wanted to be someone else for a while."

They exchange confused looks.

"I know." I shrug. "And she was dressed all sexy, and then I told her that I like Charlotte Prescott, and she starts going on about how I couldn't get away from her fast enough because she was a virgin—"

"That is true, though," Masters cuts in. "She did freak you out."

"Completely," I mutter as I sip my beer. "But she didn't know that."

"Well, she obviously did." Sebastian shrugs.

I exhale heavily. "And then the worst news of my life comes."

Bree giggles. "You're so dramatic, you really should go into theatre."

The boys both chuckle in agreement.

I raise my beer to them in a silent toast. "It turns out she isn't a virgin anymore."

Their mouths fall open, and I take an angry swig of my beer.

"So, there I was, being all gallant and leaving her fucking hot hymen in place for her future husband, and some other asshole has flown in and stolen it right out from beneath me."

The three of them all burst out laughing, thinking this is the funniest thing they have ever heard.

"This isn't funny!" I shout at them.

"This is fucking hilarious." Masters laughs.

I tip my head back and drain my beer bottle. "If I knew she was just going to give it away to any old prick, I would've fucking taken it...wouldn't I?" I roll my eyes. "I can't fucking believe this shit."

"Any old *prick* being the operative word," says Seb, and the three of them burst out laughing again.

I shake my head in disgust. "That's it, laugh at my expense, you arseholes. I'm getting new friends."

They eventually finish their fits of laughter. "Spencer, why are you here?" Bree frowns. "Why didn't you stay with her?"

I fake a smile because this story is so fucked up that I can't believe it myself. "Because she wasn't my date. My date was going gooey-eyed over the table at me...and she happens to be Charlotte's friend." I put my hand up for another drink. "If I'd stayed on that date, I would have had to stay with her friend, which means there is absolutely no chance Charlotte would ever go out with me because the friends rule overtakes all rules. And once you go out with the friend, there is no going back. You will always be the friend's ex."

They all nod, finally understanding my predicament.

"I did what I had to do."

"What?" Seb asks.

"I accused her of sleeping with her bodyguard and told her I was going to knock him out."

"You can't fight for shit." Masters chuckles.

"I know that! But I asked her to leave with me anyway." I shake my head and sip my beer, completely dejected. "She declined and told me to have a nice life."

The three of them burst out laughing again, and this time I can't help it...I find myself laughing too.

I drop my head into my hands.

"What are you going to do?" Seb asks.

"Get rolling drunk in hymen commiseration."

They all burst out laughing again.

"This isn't fucking funny!"

114

Charlotte

It's Monday afternoon and I'm sitting at my computer next to my work colleagues, each of us going through our emails and paperwork for the day.

Sarah checks her phone for the fiftieth time today. "Damn it, why hasn't he called?"

"He's an idiot." I sigh. "Forget about Spencer Jones, you can do a lot better."

At least he could have called her to tell her he isn't interested.

I hate that I like that he isn't interested.

"What was the other guy like?" Paul asks.

"Oh, he was really nice," I say. "And I think he liked Sarah."

"He did not." She sighs.

The three of us ended up having a really good time, and we danced the night away.

My email pings, the name Spencer Jones appearing in front of me.

My heart skips a beat.

I glance to the other two, who are only a metre or so away from my desk.

Shit, shit, shit.

Hello, Lottie,
I would have called you,
but I don't have your number.
Would you like to have dinner tonight?
Spence.

Oh my God. I quickly close the email, get up, and move away from my desk.

I don't want to be suspicious, so I scurry to the kitchen.

"Anyone want a coffee?" I ask them.

"Please," they both answer.

I can't believe Spencer is emailing me when I am sitting next to someone who is waiting for his call.

Good grief.

I make the coffees with my mind in overdrive, and then I take my time returning to my desk.

Just say no. *Yes.*

Okay, I'm just going to email him and say no. That's easy.

I open the email and hit reply.

Mr Spencer
I cannot think of one good reason why I should
want to go out with you. My answer is no.
Lottie.

I look left then right and hit send. A reply hits my inbox in an instant.

Dearest Lottie,
You are mistaken
I can think of at least thirty reasons why you should go out
with me.
Spencer.

Poor conceited fool.

Mr Spencer,
Name them

I hit send and smirk against my coffee cup.

I answer a few emails, and then another reply comes back.

Lottie,
Although I have many obvious attributes, I will
happily oblige your request.
1 – I have white teeth.

2 – I love my grandma
3 – I bake delicious cakes.
4 – I have blonde hair like you; we could dress as twins on fancy dress.

I giggle before I catch myself.

5 – I don't tell lies
6 – I like naughty kittens.

I put my hand over my mouth and close the email before I laugh out loud.

This man is an idiot. Can't he at least pretend to be cool. I head to the bathroom to try and calm myself before I go back to my desk and open the email again.

7 – I am a size 13 shoe. You work out what that means.

I bite back my grin.

8 – I'm not scared of your brother.

My heart drops. If only he knew how important that point is to me.

9 – I'm taller than you.
10 – I can't stop thinking about you.

Charlotte

I QUICKLY CLOSE the email and sit back in my chair.

He can't stop thinking about me.

Well, the feeling is completely mutual. I've thought of nothing but him since Saturday night. I stare at the computer screen for a while, wondering what to do.

He really hurt my pride the other week at my house, but worse than that, he hurt my feelings. I don't like the power he has over me. Nobody has ever had the ability to hurt me before.

But I know he could do a really good job of it... *will do a good job of it.*

I blow out a dejected breath. Spencer Jones may be the most fun man I've met in a long time, but we are better off just being friends. I already know what the future holds for us. I don't want to be one of his harem. He made it very clear that he isn't interested in virgins.

And even though I told him that my virginity ship has sailed, I also know deep down in my heart that telling him I was no longer a virgin was an appalling lie, and he isn't actually attracted to women like me.

He likes the challenge.

I would too if I were him.

God, I can't believe that he actually thinks I may have slept with Wyatt. That's laughable.

"Do you want to come up to level fourteen, Lottie?" Sarah asks.

"What for?" I frown.

"It's Callam's birthday. They're having cake." She wiggles her eyebrows, and I smile.

"How old is Mr Hot Dick turning?" I ask.

"Who cares? All I know is that he's old enough to do terrible things to my body."

I giggle as she pulls me towards the lifts and we get inside.

"I just wish he would get with the program and do it already." She sighs.

"You should ask Callam out."

"Yeah." She thinks for a moment. "Maybe I will." She shrugs. "If I used my brain and had some foresight, I would have popped out of his birthday cake."

I burst out laughing, getting a vision of her covered in whipped cream and popping out of a huge cake. "I don't think level fourteen is prepared for your level of hotness, Sarah."

"I know, right?"

The ceiling of my room is plastered with fancy, swirling circular shapes, and my apartment is dead quiet as I stare up at it. It's the early hours of the morning, but I can't sleep. I'm preoccupied with this weird feeling—one of realisation. It's as if my eyes have finally been opened to what I'm missing out on by being a Prescott.

Working, laughing, and being asked out every hour at work by gorgeous men have all made me happy—the happiest I've been in a long time.

And this isn't even my life.

It's one big fat lie.

I roll over and punch my pillow in disgust. Who am I kidding?

Most people on the planet would give their right arm to have what I've been born into and the privileged life that I live.

I'm being ungrateful, I know I am. I mean, I do appreciate everything that I have.

I stare into the darkness as a tear rolls down my face and onto my pillow.

I feel so lost.

Maybe there's something wrong with me? Maybe I need to go back to my grief counsellor?

Yes...that's probably it. I'll call and make an appointment tomorrow. I haven't been for over a year now.

I get out of bed and walk to the bathroom to stare at my reflection in the mirror.

Big blue eyes and pale skin stare back at me. My blonde hair is in a high messy bun, and I'm wearing odd pyjamas. There's nothing special about me. I'm just a normal girl who happens to have four billion dollars in the bank.

I storm back to bed and pull the covers over me to stare up at the ceiling again.

I'm lonely as hell.

My email pings. Spencer Jones again.

I smirk and look around guilty. It's 4:00 p.m. on Tuesday afternoon, and I hate to admit it, but I've checked my emails every half hour today.

I don't want him to email me, but then I kind of do.

Dear Lottie
I am so sorry to hear that you've had a terrible accident and broken all of your fingers and are unable to email me back.

I smirk.

*I shall, however, as usual, pick up your slack and continue with
my reasons as to why you should have dinner with me.
11– I am a specialist in broken-finger first aid.*

I put my hand over my mouth to stop myself from laughing out loud. He's an idiot.

12 – I don't have a YouPorn profile.

I frown. What does that mean?

*13 – I have nice feet
14 – I can fold a fitted sheet.
15 – I have huge muscles.*

I roll my lips to hide my goofy smile. Why does he have to be all cute and adorable?

16 – I read ten books a week.

Pfft, I highly doubt that.

*17 – I'm nocturnal
18 – I manscape.*

He *manscapes...* My shoulders begin to bounce as I try to hide my giggles.

19 - I am on the navigation team for Santa Claus's sleigh.

I burst out laughing, unable to catch myself.
Sarah looks over. "What's funny?"
I close the email quickly. "Nothing, I was just..." I pause as I try to think of something. "I was just remembering something I watched last night."

"What was it?" She keeps typing.

"Oh, just this weird guy was playing tricks on people." I widen my eyes. Good grief. "It was hilarious," I add.

She raises her eyebrow, unimpressed. "Hmm, sounds like it." She stands. "I'm going to the bathroom. Does anyone want a coffee while I'm up?"

"Please," we both say.

I drop my head to desperately try to stop myself from laughing out loud. Spencer's on the navigation team for Santa Claus. Now I really have heard it all. I click the email open again and read the last reason.

20 – Because I know you like me too.

I click it shut immediately. How does he know that? I've not given him any reason to believe I'm interested in him.

Shit. I stare at my computer for a long time.

What do I write back? I think for a moment.

Dear Mr Spencer,
Thank you for taking the time to outline your personal attributes, which I must say, are very impressive indeed. However, unfortunately, at this time, your application for a dinner date has been unsuccessful.
I wish you luck with your future endeavours.
Santa Claus's navigation team? You really are an inspiration.
I must go, as I'm typing this with my nose due to my severely broken fingers and I am in terrible pain.
Lottie
xoxo

I hit send with a hint of sadness. Damn it. I hate that my pride won't let me go out with him. He has no idea how much he kicked my confidence to the kerb.

And besides, I've only just started to have fun. If I begin to run around with him now, it will just bring attention to me, my plan, my job, and my time in London will come to an abrupt end.

It's a hopeless situation, anyway... It is what it is.

Now is not the time to start something with Mr Spencer.

My email pings.

Dear Miss Charlotte,
I reject your rejection.
Give me your phone number immediately or
I'm calling you at work on your work number and asking for
Charlotte Prescott on 07826653350

My mouth falls open. He wouldn't, would he?

"W-what's our work phone number?" I ask, trying to act casual.

Paul looks up. "07826653350."

My eyes widen. Shit, he knows the number. I immediately type back.

Don't you dare call me at work!
Sarah is sitting beside me, and she is waiting for you to call her.
But of course, you are too much of a coward to do that.

I hit send in a fury. God, this man drives me mad. I close my email in disgust.

Sarah's phone immediately rings, and my heart drops. Damn it, what have I done?

My phone rings at the same time, shit.

I quickly answer it. "Hello."

"Hello, Charlotte. It's Alexander," the deep voice purrs down the phone.

Alexander is Edward's best friend. Edward said he would be checking on me. I glance over to Sarah to see who she is talking to.

"Hello," she answers, and her face breaks out into a smile. "Hi, Spencer."

It's him.

"How are you?" Alex asks me on my call.

"I'm great, busy with work," I add. "And you?" I glance back at Sarah.

"Oh, that's okay, I know you're busy," Sarah says. She listens for a moment. "Oh." She sighs.

Damn him.

"We need to catch up while you're in London," Alexander says.

What I really need to do is hang up so I can listen to Sarah's conversation properly. "Yes, we do," I agree in a rush.

"What are you doing Saturday night? I have my mother's charity ball on. You must come," Alexander suggests.

Sarah drops into her chair. "Oh, I see." She smiles sadly. "She's a lucky girl," she says.

What the hell is he saying to her?

"Of course, Alex." I exhale. "I'm really busy, though, I'm at work."

"Okay, I'll let you go. I will message you with the details."

I watch Sarah, and she frowns as she listens. "He said that?"

I need to end this call. "Yes, Alex. Sounds great, see you Saturday." I hang up in a rush.

Sarah is smirking as she stares down at her desk.

"Oh, I don't know." She smiles. "I'll have to think about it." She listens for a moment. "Thanks for letting me know. Yeah, it's okay. I completely understand."

She hangs up and turns to me. "Well, that's that." She throws her hands up in the air. "Spencer Jones just dumped me."

"What did he say?"

"He said that he wasn't over his old girlfriend and it wasn't fair to start something with me."

I stare at her. That was the last excuse I ever thought he would give. "Oh."

"He said that Richard had asked him if he could call me because he felt that he and I had hit it off."

"Really?" I smile in surprise. That was nice of him to say that to boost her confidence.

She shrugs and tries hard not to smile, but I can tell she's flattered. "I don't think I'll go out with him, though. He isn't really my type."

"I thought Richard was hot." I smile.

"Really?" She frowns.

"Yes, really."

My email pings again.

Lottie,
I need to talk to you. You are worrying me. I don't understand
what's going on???
Please give me your number.
Spence

I blow out a dejected breath. He doesn't know what's going on because I hardly know myself. I loiter around work for half an hour and finally come to a conclusion: there's no harm in talking to him, I suppose.

Mr Spencer
My number is 07712345678

A reply comes back immediately.

I have a business dinner on tonight. I'll call you when I get home
around 9 p.m.
Spence
xoxo

I stare at the hugs and kisses, and I feel my heart flutter. He's calling me tonight. I want to spin around on my chair in excitement.

I won't, of course. I'll pretend, even to myself, that this is an inconvenience.

I click the email closed and turn my attention to Sarah and Paul. "You guys want to go to the pub for drinks after work?" I ask.

Paul shrugs. "Yeah, why not? May as well. I've got nothing but mouldy cheese in my fridge at home, anyway."

Sarah smiles and types away on her keyboard. "Yes, but can we go to the Grange?" "Sure, but why?"

"That place is Hot Dick City."

Paul rolls his eyes. "I take it you've gotten over that other chump in the last half hour, then?"

"God, yes." She fixes her hair. "His loss. I'm way too hot for him, anyway. Spencer bloody who?"

I glance at my watch: it's 9:30 p.m. Maybe he isn't going to call after all.

I make myself a cup of tea and sit at the kitchen island. I love this apartment. It already feels like home.

My phone dances across the bench and an unknown number pops up.

It's him.

My heart begins to race, and I blow out a deep breath to try and calm myself down.

"Hello."

"Hello," his mischievous deep voice says down the phone. I find myself smiling just from the sound of his voice.

"Hello, Mr Spencer."

He chuckles. "Always so formal."

I press my lips together, too nervous to speak in case I say something stupid.

"What's going on?" he asks.

"Nothing serious. I just wanted to see what it was like working in another environment where people didn't know my father. You won't say anything, will you?"

"To who? I don't know any of your family's aristocrat peers."

"I know," I murmur, suddenly feeling stupid.

"Does your father know where you are?"

"He knows I'm in London, but he thinks I'm working at my regular job. Edward and Dad are overseas for six weeks. I thought it was a good opportunity to have some fun."

He inhales sharply. "By fun, you mean sex?"

I smirk. Why does he always have to be so up front? "No, I mean spend time with Beth, my friend. Work a different job. Meet new people, things like that."

"Haven't your guards snitched on you?"

"No. They don't know what I'm doing either. They stay on the ground floor of my office building and meet me on my breaks or when I finish."

He hesitates. "Let me get this straight—you've moved to London for six weeks and are pretending to be someone else and nobody at all knows?"

I run my finger along the edge of the kitchen counter. "Beth knows, and now...you."

"And what about him?"

I frown. "Who?"

"The man you slept with?" He's clearly annoyed.

"Oh." I scrunch my eyes shut. God, this is the biggest lie I've ever told. "No, he doesn't know."

"So he's still communicating with you as Charlotte."

"Yes."

He stays silent for a moment. "I take it you are in a relationship with him, then?"

My eyes widen. "N-no," I stammer. "No, it was just a one-time thing."

"Why would you give your virginity to someone for a one-time thing?" he snaps, and I can hear tension in his voice.

Shit. I close my eyes. "It just happened, Spencer. It's over now, and I would rather not talk about it, please."

"Is that why you moved to London and are carrying on with this façade? You were hurt? Or were you just running away from him?"

"No. It really was a one-time thing, and now it's over. Did you call me to talk about my past? Because I'm quite sure there is a lot of *your* history that we can discuss instead."

He falls silent, eventually speaking softly. "Can I see you?"

God, I would like that.

"Perhaps we could go out to dinner when my father gets home?" I offer.

"Why not now?"

"Because if I'm seen with you, my guards will tell my family, and then I'll be watched extra carefully. I've come this far with this fake identity, and I want to carry on with it for the full six weeks. I'm really enjoying my job and the friends I am making."

"You don't think I'm worth the risk?"

I roll my eyes. "You *are* being very high maintenance tonight, Mr Spencer. Did you call me to nag me to death?"

He laughs out loud. It's deep and intoxicating, and I feel myself smiling goofily down the phone.

"Well, I've never been called that before." He chuckles.

"There's a first time for everything." I smile as I sip my tea.

"What are you doing now?" His voice has dropped to a sexy, playful tone.

"I'm sitting at my kitchen bench in my pyjamas with a face mask on, drinking tea."

"Good grief, woman. Lie to me."

I giggle. "Okay." I pause and try to think of a good lie. "I'm on a yacht."

"Yes," he whispers.

I try and stop myself from laughing. "I'm sailing through Croatia. The sun is setting, and I can hear the water lapping at the side of the boat."

"Yes," he purrs.

"With my husband." I smile.

He makes a buzzer sound. "Wrong lie. Try again."

"What lie are you hoping for?" I chuckle.

"Something along the lines of you being naked and thinking about me."

My eyes widen. "Oh, that one." God, he's fun. "Well, you have to ask me again."

"What are you doing now, my beautiful Charlotte?"

The sound of him calling me beautiful makes me smile. "I'm taking a bubble bath."

"And?" I can tell he's smiling.

"Drinking champagne."

"Are you lying back against the edge?"

I get a vision of myself naked in the bath, drinking champagne. "Yes," I breathe.

"Is your hair up?"

"Yes."

"Is the room full of steam?"

I feel arousal start to tear through my bloodstream. "Yes."

"What are your legs doing?" he whispers.

I swallow the lump in my throat. God, this man makes me think naughty things.

"They're open, my knees touching the sides of the bath," I whisper.

He inhales sharply.

We stay silent as we both picture the setting. My sex begins to pump.

"Have you ever touched yourself while you thought of me?" His voice is husky, aroused.

I cringe. "Yes," I breathe. He could make me orgasm just by talking to me like this.

"I'm going to call you tomorrow night at 9:30, angel, and I want you in the bath, naked with your legs wide open so we can continue this conversation."

My eyes widen.

What?

"Do you understand me?"

"Yes."

Silence hangs between us.

Eventually, he replies, "Good night, angel."

I press my hand on my chest as I try to control my breathing. I don't want him to know how much he turns me on with his voice alone, and I most definitely don't want to get off the phone. I want to play more games tonight.

"Good night, Spence."

We both wait. I just want to ask him over to my place, and I know that's what he's waiting for.

Not yet.

"Goodbye," I whisper, and I force myself to hang up.

Beth's eyes nearly bulge from their sockets while she sucks her straw. "What do you mean, lie to him?"

I shrug and laugh. "Just what I said. I told him I had pyjamas and a face mask on, and he said 'lie to me'."

"Oh, this guy is fun, I like him."

The two of us are at dinner and I'm filling her in on the latest Spencer gossip. I hate to admit it, but I have been wearing a goofy grin all day...the man makes me giddy.

"So, tonight, you have to be in the bath when he calls you?" she asks.

I shrug. "Apparently."

She smiles broadly. "Get in the bath and ask him to come over to wash your back." She chews her food. "With his dick."

We both laugh out loud. "Can you imagine?"

"Do you reckon it's big?"

I giggle and snort my wine up my nose. "Beth?"

"Seriously. He's so overconfident, he would have to be packing heat."

I laugh myself into a coughing fit. "Packing heat?" I cough. "Who the hell says 'packing heat'?"

She puts her finger up. "I do."

I laugh and shake my head, and then she falls serious.

"Go home, get naked, and get into a big hot bath, then wait for Mr Size Thirteen to call."

I raise my wineglass in the air, and she clinks hers against it. "Mission accepted."

The room is filled with steam as I lie back in the deep bath. I'm so aroused, I might orgasm when the phone rings...and right on cue, it does.

"Hello," I answer.

"Are you in the bath?" he asks seductively.

"Yes," I breathe.

"Are your legs open?"

Just get straight to the point, why don't you? My eyes close. I've never had anyone talk to me like this before. It's insane.

"Yes," I whisper.

"Run your fingertips down over your stomach." I can tell he's already aroused too.

"Did you call to talk dirty to me, Mr Spencer?" I tease.

"Shut up and fucking do it."

"Is that filthy mouth of yours always so bossy?"

"Angel, you have no idea."

I smile and dust my fingers down over my stomach.

"Tell me what you feel?" he asks.

Oh God...

"My skin."

"Is it soft?"

"Yes."

"Lower." He exhales.

I drop my fingers between my open legs.

"Circle your four fingertips over your clitoris."

I shudder because just hearing him say that heats my blood. No man has ever spoken to me like this. I do as he asks, and I close my eyes to let the pleasure take over.

"Imagine it's me who's doing it. My open lips are on your neck."

My head falls back.

"Talk to me," he whispers through ragged breaths. "I want to hear your voice when you're aroused."

My fingers get to work, and I moan softly, my legs parting wider, seeking his invisible touch.

"Hmm, fuck yeah." He hisses.

I smile at the arousal in his voice.

"Are you going to come for me, angel? Because I've been coming for you for two weeks."

"Hmm." I smile, my eyes still closed.

"I've had to imagine I was with you during sex or I couldn't come."

What?

My eyes snap open. "You imagined you were having sex with me when you were inside another woman?" I snap.

"Oh... Shit... I mean..."

"You've had sex with someone else since we met?"

"Ah..." He hesitates as he tries to get himself out of this. "So-so did you, Charlotte," he stammers. "Did you imagine it was me?"

My blood begins to boil. "No, Spencer. I did not."

"You should have. I'm way better in bed than him."

I get out of the bath in an instant. The water sloshes all over the floor. "No, what you are is an *idiot!*" I snap.

"I know. Wait. What are you doing?"

"Ending this call."

"Don't hang up on me," he pleads.

"Go and do what you've been doing with the others."

"What do you mean?"

"Imagining having sex with me is as close as you're ever going to get. You big, stupid jerk."

I hang up, wrap myself in a towel, and then storm out of the bathroom.

The man is a first-class idiot.

. . .

I watch my phone dance across my side table while I lie in bed.

It's late on Thursday night now, and Spencer has been calling me nonstop since our disastrous call on Tuesday.

I don't want to answer. I mean, what is there to say?

While I've been pining over here for him, he's been out screwing around, imagining my face when he was with someone else.

I'm shocked and appalled, but if I'm being totally honest, a little relieved that he had to imagine me to climax. That's God punishing him for being such an asshole.

And why does he have to be so damn honest all the time?

It's infuriating.

Beth thinks I should speak to him, and that in his eyes, I have double standards because he thinks I slept with someone else too. She thinks I'm making a big deal out of nothing. Maybe I am.

But maybe I'm just not cut out for casual dating, and this was just the gentle reminder I needed. He had me naked in the bath, touching myself, for Christ's sake. Talk about being putty in his hands.

The phone stops vibrating, and I stare at the ceiling, a sad, dejected feeling sweeping through me. I feel like I'm back to square one with him—below square one, because now I know he's having sex with other women.

Maybe I should have answered his call and had it out with him. Perhaps it would make me feel better?

I exhale heavily and pick up my phone to start scrolling through Instagram when the phone starts to vibrate in my hand again.

I stare at it for a moment.

Screw it. "Hi," I answer.

"Are you fucking serious?" he snaps.

I stay silent, unsure what to say.

"Okay, firstly...don't you dare hang up on me."

I roll my eyes.

"Secondly, yes, I am well aware that telling you I imagined you during sex was probably the stupidest thing to ever come out of my mouth."

"Who was she?"

He hesitates.

"I want to know who she was."

"Her name is Sheridan, and she's an old friend. She lives in America."

I get a vision of a beautiful woman with my Spencer, and jealousy twists in my stomach.

"You know her well?" I ask.

"Yes."

I don't know if I want to know the answer to this question, but I ask anyway. "How long have you been sleeping with her?"

"Do we have to talk about this?" he asks.

"Depends."

"On what?"

"On whether you want me to listen to what you have to say."

"Ten years."

My eyes widen and my stomach drops.

"It's never happened before," he says softly.

"What hasn't?" I frown.

"I've never thought of someone else when I was with her."

I stay silent, waiting for him to go on.

"I wasn't prepared for it."

"Do you think of other women often when you're having sex?" I ask, confused.

"God, no. I've never done it, I just told you. I can't stop thinking about you. It's constant, and it's driving me fucking insane, to be honest."

I twist the quilt between my fingers. "So Sheridan is your girlfriend who lives in another country?"

"No, she's just a friend."

"Who you have sex with?" I'm trying to understand the dynamics of their relationship.

"In the past, yes."

"What about your future?"

"Charlotte, the only person on my mind at the moment is you. If I were with you and it bothered you, I wouldn't be with anyone else."

If it bothered me? What the hell?

"It would bother me, Spence, of course it would bother me. I don't like to share."

"Then you won't."

I get a lump in my throat, and I want to believe him.

Silence hangs between us.

"What are you doing?" I ask.

"I'm on a yacht, sailing around Ibiza."

I smirk at the make-believe games he plays. "Yes."

"And I'm working out a plan to come and kidnap this girl in London who I'm obsessed with." His voice has dropped to his playful tone.

"What are you going to do with her once you have her?"

"What wouldn't I do with her, if I had her." He breathes out heavily.

I smile softly.

"I'm sorry I thought of you while I had sex with someone else," he tells me. "It wasn't fair."

I frown, and for some stupid reason, my eyes fill with tears. *No, it wasn't.*

"I won't do it again, angel, I promise."

I listen.

"Can I see you?" he asks.

"Erm." I run through my schedule in my mind. "I have something on tomorrow and Saturday night," I tell him.

"Sunday night?"

"We'll see." I sigh.

"Lottie."

"Yes?"

"Have you ever felt like you know someone better than you actually do?"

I bite my bottom lip to stifle my smile. That's exactly how I feel with him, and I don't know where this attachment to him is coming from, because it shouldn't be there. I really don't know him at all. After a pause, I reply, "Perhaps."

"I'll see you Sunday, then?"

"Yes." I find myself smiling like a fool.

"What am I going to do with myself 'til then?"

"Why don't you have a bath and spread your legs?" I smirk.

"Already done that. My dick is chaffed from jerking off to thoughts of you."

My mouth falls open. "Spencer Jones, you are the crassest man I have ever met."

"I'll take that as a compliment. And I'm not crass, I'm just honest." I can tell he's smiling.

"Goodbye, Spencer."

"Are you sure you don't want to come over here and make up in person?"

"I'll see you Sunday." I smirk.

"That you will. I'm excited to see you."

I don't really want to say goodbye to him. Making up with him in person does seem like way more fun than this. We both stay silent and eventually I have to end the call.

"Goodbye, Spencer," I eventually force out.

"Good night, angel. Dream of me."

The line goes dead, and I smile goofily into the darkness.

I have no resistance to this man. None.

I walk into the ballroom with Alexander. It's Saturday night, and we're at a charity auction. I would rather be out with Beth, but I did promise Alexander I would come. Besides, it will keep my father and Edward appeased.

Alexander stops to talk to someone, and I look around, freezing on the spot.

Oh no.

136

Spencer is by the bar.

What the hell is he doing here?

His wavy hair is messed up to perfection, and his square jaw and piercing blue eyes meet mine. Wearing a black dinner suit, he looks so handsome, and I feel myself melt a little.

He raises an eyebrow at me, and then just as suddenly as we connect, he snaps his eyes away from mine.

Spencer

"You never know what the future will bring." Leoni smiles.

"I guess." I sigh as I look around.

Charlotte—*my Charlotte* has just walked into the ballroom on someone else's arm.

What?

Alexander York?

My skin prickles. You have got to be kidding me.

Him—my archnemesis. We've known each other for years and hated each other for just as long. We met at a party years ago. Alex did some trading for me on the stock market and they turned bad. Then I dated someone he wanted, and it's gone downhill ever since. We've had harsh words on more occasions than I care to remember, and right now, I want to kill him with my bare hands.

"Yes, the universities are wonderful over there," Leoni says.

I inhale sharply as I try to focus on what she is saying, although I'm quite sure she can see steam shooting out of my ears.

Was it him?

Did she sleep with Alexander fucking York?

My nostrils flare in fury and I tip my head back to drink my beer. This woman will be the death of me. The two of them walk through the crowd, and Charlotte finds my gaze and falters, as if shocked.

She's wearing a gold crystal-beaded dress, and her thick honey hair is set into large curls. She looks curvy, glamorous, and beautiful.

Perfect.

My cock instantly hardens with appreciation...and she's fucking here with someone else.

I put my hand into the pocket of my black dinner suit and stare at her, my eyebrow rising involuntarily.

I'm livid and force myself to look away.

Leonie keeps banging on about the most boring thing I've ever heard and Charlotte stands still, her hands both clutching her gold purse nervously as Alexander stops to talk to someone. She can't even look at me, while I can't look away.

I've caught her out. This is why she won't see me. She's fucking *him*.

Agreeing to the date on Sunday night was probably just to shut me up.

I want to storm over there and drag her out of here.

I inhale deeply, trying to get a hold of myself. It's been a long time since a woman has gotten to me like Charlotte Prescott has. If ever.

I don't like it, I don't trust it, and I don't fucking want it...much to Masters's and Seb's amusement. They've told me that I am, without a doubt, the stupidest man on Earth to say that to a woman. I agree with them.

Lesson learned.

I tip my head back and drain my beer.

Alexander keeps talking, then Charlotte says something to him and walks over to a table. When she gets there, she turns and walks back to the bar where I am standing, approaching me slowly.

"Excuse me." I smile at Leonie as she talks.

"Oh, sure." She frowns.

"Hello, Spence." Charlotte smiles up at me.

"Hi," I push out.

"I didn't know you were coming," she says nervously.

I stare at her, physically biting my tongue from, once again, losing control and showing my feelings.

"You're here on a date?" I ask flatly.

Charlotte's eyes widen. "No. God, no. Alexander is a family friend, that's all."

I stare at her as she dusts my arm with her hand. "Honestly, I swear."

Relief fills me, and I smirk, feeling stupid.

"Were you jealous?" she asks.

"Green-eyed-monster jealous."

She's all big lips and dimples, and I feel my lust for her all the way to my balls.

"I wish I was alone with you," I say. Damn it, why does this woman make me blurt shit out?

Her eyes hold mine. I feel like she wants to say something, but she remains silent.

"How was your day?" I ask to make conversation.

"Good." She smiles. "I was waiting for a phone call. Weren't you calling me today?"

I smile, my anger dissipating. "I was waiting until I got home tonight and was naked in my bed."

Her breath catches.

"I wanted to touch myself to the sound of your voice," I confess.

She smirks and the air between us crackles, our eyes locked.

"You are a scoundrel, Mr Spencer," she whispers.

I dip my head, pick up her hand, and kiss the back of it. "At your service, my lady."

Her hand stays in mine for an extended time, and eventually, good manners prevail. "Would you like a glass of champagne?"

She smiles. "That would be lovely. Thank you."

"Back in a moment." I walk to the bar and wait in line to order our drinks.

"What the fuck do you think you're doing?" someone growls from behind me.

I turn to see Alexander York. "I'm getting a drink, you idiot, what does it look like?"

"I mean what the hell do you think you're doing talking to Charlotte Prescott?"

I turn to him as my anger begins to pump. "Charlotte is none of your concern."

"The hell she isn't. We've been family friends all of our lives, and she's way out of your fucking league."

Unable to help myself, I smile smugly. "What's the matter, York? You jealous?"

"Fuck you."

I really want to say, *that's what she's going to do later,* but I hold my tongue.

"I saw you kiss her hand. What do you think you're doing with her?"

I turn to him, raise our two champagne glasses, and throw him a wink. "Whatever the fuck I want to."

8

Charlotte

SPENCER APPEARS through the crowd and comes to stand beside me. He passes me my drink and we clink glasses. "Thank you." I smile.

His glowing eyes linger on my face.

"You're staring, Mr Spencer." I get butterflies in my stomach when he looks at me like that.

"I know," he whispers. "I can't help it."

"Hello, sorry we're late," a girl's voice interrupts us from behind. I turn to see a pretty woman and a man standing beside us. She's heavily pregnant. Actually, I think she is the one from the wedding the first time I met Spencer.

Spencer turns immediately. "Charlotte, this is Julian Masters and his wife Brielle—Bree for short."

"Hello." I smile nervously and shake both of their hands.

They both smile back at me, and the woman hunches her shoulders in excitement before she rubs Spencer's.

I can tell they are very fond of each other.

"Where's Sebastian?" Spencer asks. "Typical. He signs us up for this shit and then turns up late."

Julian smiles. "What would you expect?" He turns to Bree. "Would you like a drink, sweetheart?"

"Uh-huh." She exhales heavily. "I would like ten glasses of champagne, actually."

Julian raises his brow. "Lemonade, then?"

"Ugh, fine." She sighs and moves closer to me.

Julian falls into natural conversation with Spencer. I look around at all the people dressed in their black-tie outfits, and I notice that there really are some beautiful gowns here.

"When are you due?" I ask Bree, simply to make conversation.

"Seven weeks."

"Exciting." I smile. "Is that an accent I detect?"

"Yes." She laughs. "I'm Australian." She takes my hand in hers. "I'm so glad to finally meet you." Her eyes drop down my dress. "You are absolutely gorgeous, just as Spence said you were."

I frown. "You've heard of me?"

She glances at Spencer to check he can't hear us. "Of course I've heard of you. Spencer has been going on and on about you since the two of you first met," she whispers.

I try to hide my smile but fail miserably. "So you know him well?" I ask. I don't know why, but I already feel at ease with this woman. I'm guessing she's around my age too.

"He's Julian's best friend, along with Seb, of course." She looks over at a man with dark hair who is approaching us through the crowd. "Speak of the devil."

"Hello, troublemaker," Seb teases Bree as he bends to kiss her cheek.

"Sebastian, this is Charlotte," she introduces with a broad smile.

Sebastian is tall, dark, and handsome, and he has a natural wave to his hair. Good grief, these men are seriously good-looking.

Seb's eyes light up, and he picks up my hand to kiss the back of it. "Lovely to meet you, Charlotte, but you really should run away with me instead of Spencer." He winks mischievously.

"Hey, cut that out," Spencer cries from behind us. "Lips off her immediately."

Julian and Sebastian chuckle.

"Hello, Sebastian." I smile.

"Where is your date?" Bree asks Sebastian.

He rolls his eyes. "Long story, but you're my surrogate date tonight."

Bree and I chuckle.

He stands and falls into conversation with Julian and Spencer.

"He seems nice," I say.

"He's dreamy," Bree agrees. "But he attracts the worst women."

"Why?"

"I have no idea. They all end up being crazy bunny boilers."

I giggle.

Bree looks over at her husband. "Jules, how is my lemonade going? I'm dehydrating over here while making your baby."

"Sorry, babe." He takes off to the bar immediately.

"Are you kidding me, Jones? What the hell are you doing here?" a male voice barks from behind us.

We turn, and Spencer laughs out loud. "What the fuck, Stanton? What are you doing here?" Spencer shakes the hand of the man in the black dinner suit.

"My wife Natasha runs this charity with our friend Nicholas. We fly everywhere for them." He points to an attractive brunette woman talking to a large European-looking man. Jeez, good looks run in the family.

"Charlotte, this is my friend Joshua Stanton. Joshua's brother Cameron studied medicine with my brother in the States. We've been to many a weekend away together over the years." Spencer smiles.

"Hello." He smiles over at me.

"Hi." I smile back. I look at Bree, who is staring at the god in front of us.

"This is Julian Masters and his wife Bree, and this is Sebastian Garcia."

143

They all shake hands, and the men fall into easy conversation.

"I'm on my way to the bar," Joshua says.

Spencer's eyes find mine. "I'll get us another drink."

I smile and nod, and he disappears with his friend.

"Holy heck," Bree whispers. "Who was that guy?"

"God's gift to women, I imagine."

She giggles and clinks her lemonade with my champagne. "I like you, Charlotte Prescott." She beams.

I smile. "Please...just call me Lottie. I'm trying to lose my surname for a while."

She frowns. "You don't like the name Prescott?"

I smile bashfully. "Yes, of course, just not everything that comes with it."

"What do you mean?"

"My family have rigid rules." I shrug. "That's why I've moved to London. I just want to be Lottie for a while."

She smiles. "That's why I moved to London too."

"How did you and Julian meet?" I ask.

She smirks as her eyes seek him out. "I was his nanny."

My eyes widen. "What?"

She nods. "Yep. Cliché, isn't it?"

I bite my bottom lip, and I take a look Julian's way. "So he was your boss?"

"Uh-huh. I thought I was coming over here to work for a woman, and when he picked me up from the airport, I nearly died."

I make eye contact with Spencer at the bar, and he gives me a sexy wink. My stomach flips, and I have to drag my eyes back to Bree.

"It was all forbidden attraction and fireworks. Anyway, that's enough of me, let's talk about you and Spencer."

My face falls.

"Oh." She frowns. "What's that look?"

"Nothing." I sigh.

"You can talk to me. I won't say anything, I promise."

144

I stare at her for a moment.

She crosses her finger over her chest. "I promise."

I shrug. "I don't know. His playboy ways are..." My voice trails off.

She offers an understanding nod. "I can imagine."

"It does kind of make you wonder, you know?" I shrug.

She glances over at the four men over at the bar. "The thing is, Charlotte, when you date a thirty-eight-year-old man who has never been married before, he's going to have some baggage with him."

I look for Spencer and, once again, catch him watching me. My heart skips a beat, and I turn back to Bree. "What was Julian's baggage?"

"God, what wasn't Julian's baggage? It wouldn't fit into this ballroom." She smirks with an eye roll.

She, too, looks at Spencer, and she smiles watching him watching me. "The way Spencer looks at you—" She hesitates.

I wait for her to finish the sentence, but she doesn't. "What?" I whisper.

"I haven't seen him look at a woman the way he looks at you, ever."

Hope blooms in my chest, and Spencer comes back to stand with us again.

"How handsome that Joshua Stanton is," Bree says without missing a beat.

"He's okay, I guess." Spencer's mischievous eyes find mine. "Not as handsome as me, though, is he, angel?" He links our pinky fingers together.

My heart skips a beat at him calling me angel in front of everyone.

"No, Spence." I smile sarcastically and release my finger from his grip. "No man could ever be as handsome as you."

Our eyes linger on each other, the air between us crackling.

Bree fans her face with her hand. "Good lord, the sexual tension between you two is ridiculous."

I drop my head and chuckle, embarrassed that we just forgot she was here with us.

This man makes me giddy.

"A word, Charlotte," Alexander demands, appearing from nowhere.

I turn, suddenly remembering that I'm here with him. Damn it, how could I forget that?

I fake a smile. "Of course." I suddenly feel awkward. "Alex, please meet my friends, Spencer and Brielle," I say.

"We know each other," Spencer says flatly.

Alex nods, and they glare at each other.

I frown at the obvious animosity between them.

This is awkward.

"I'll see you later, Bree. It was lovely meeting you." I'm in a fluster.

"You, too, Lottie. Come back and see us later." Bree smiles warmly.

"I will!" I call over my shoulder as Alexander leads me through the ballroom, over to the wall at the back of the room.

"What are you doing talking with Spencer Jones?" he asks angrily.

I frown. "What does it matter to you?"

"Do you know who he is?"

I twist my lip in annoyance. "No, why don't you tell me who you think he is?"

"He's the biggest womaniser in all of London."

"And how do you know that?"

"Everybody knows that, Charlotte. Take a look at the tabloids. Is Edward aware that you know him?" he whispers.

"He's Brielle's friend." I roll my eyes. "I don't even know him."

He stares at me for a moment, trying to work out if I'm telling the truth.

"I'm not stupid, you know?" I add.

"I know you're not." He rubs my arm. "Just...whatever you do, don't mess with him."

"Why not?"

"Because you will be the next bit of town gossip." He holds two fingers in the air. "Spencer Jones dates two women in the same day. Two."

My heart drops, but I smile on cue—that fake smile that has been ingrained in me through my years of schooling. The same fake smile that I wear when Edward is scolding me in public for someone I have talked to who he didn't approve of.

"Alexander, I have no interest in Spencer Jones. Now, if you'll excuse me, I'm going to the bathroom."

"Of course. I'll go sit down and wait for you over there." He gestures over to the table we are sitting at.

"I'll see you in a moment."

I walk out through the foyer and into the bathroom. I push into a cubicle and sit on top of the closed toilet seat.

Regret, annoyance, and disappointment course through me, all rolled into one stupid lead ball that sits in the base of my stomach.

Part of me wants to go home right now. My night is ruined, all because of one snide comment from Alex, even though I know he *was* only trying to be a good friend and look out for me.

I hate that Spencer has this reputation. I hate that everyone knows it, and I hate that I enjoy his company as much as I do.

His friends were so nice.

I exhale heavily as I try to come to grips with the reality of who Spencer is. No matter how honest he is, everyone has already made their judgements on his reputation. I don't feel that the two sides of Spencer correlate at all, at least not in my mind.

I finish up in the bathroom, wash my hands, and stare at my reflection in the mirror, giving myself a silent pep talk.

Go out there and finish the night. Just put the information to one side and process it tomorrow once you're at home.

I reapply my gold lipstick.

I wish I was here with Spencer...and that nobody else knew who the hell he was.

147

Spencer

I stare at her from across the room. She's sitting with him, laughing, talking, completely in her comfort zone with the table full of London's aristocratic society. She's one of them, and I can't seem to connect the sweet, innocent girl I'm attracted to to *the* Charlotte Prescott she is.

I wish she wasn't one of them, and just a normal girl from Nottingham instead.

"You can't take your fucking eyes off her for a moment, can you?" Seb sighs.

I sip my beer. "Nope."

"How is this going to go?" Masters frowns. "She isn't allowed to be seen even talking to you. What exactly do you think is going to happen here, Spence?"

I roll my eyes and exhale heavily, choosing not to answer that particular question.

The music grows louder, and people flock to the dance floor now that the formalities are officially over.

I haven't spoken one word to Charlotte since Alexander dragged her away from me.

My phone vibrates in my pocket, and I take it out to read the message. It's from her.

Hi

I smile and text back.

Hi.

She replies.

Meet me at the bar?

"She's texting me as we speak." I smirk to my friends, and then, without thinking, I stand and make my way to the bar as she requested.

She appears beside me a moment later, and my heart flutters in my chest.

"Hello." She smiles up at me, her face full of hope.

"I don't like you here with him," I tell her honestly.

"We're just friends, I promise." She glances over at Alexander, who is talking to a group of people while we are shielded from the crowd. "You and Alex don't get along?" She makes it sound like a statement and a question.

"Not at all. It started with work a few years back. Since then, we've had a few run-ins with each other over the years. He doesn't get on with Masters or Seb either."

"Masters?"

"Julian. His last name is Masters. He had a run-in with Alex at work too."

"What does Julian do?"

"He's a judge."

"Oh." She frowns.

"He will warn you away from me, no doubt," I mutter into my drink. "Apparently, I'm the Devil." I raise my eyebrow in a silent dare.

Defend him to me. See what happens.

She stares at me for a moment, and I have no idea what she's thinking.

Have I misjudged this whole thing with us?

"We haven't spoken about you at all," she tells me.

My eyes hold hers and I know that she's lying. He did warn her away from me, and God, I would like to rearrange his face for his efforts. Unfortunately, I'm a lover, not a fighter.

What I should do is let my friend Joshua Stanton take care of him instead. Joshua cage fights...for fun. That bastard is mean as shit.

"I'd like to see you alone."

Her eyes hold mine. "I'd like that too."

"I can come to you. Tonight?" I offer.

She frowns again, her mind going into overdrive.

"Give me a key to your room, Charlotte. I'll wait for your guards to leave and sneak in. They won't even know I've been. We can have coffee and dessert." I shrug. "We can just talk..."

Her chest rises and falls heavily.

I can almost hear her brain ticking.

She glances over to the side of the ballroom, and I follow her gaze, only to see Wyatt standing silently, his back against the wall. I hadn't even noticed him; I was too preoccupied with York.

"They will see me give you the key," she whispers. "And how will I get into my room when I get home?"

"Leave the key somewhere here for me to pick up without being seen, and then just ask them for another key at reception when you get there. Tell them you left it in the room."

"Where?"

I think for a moment. "Go out the foyer. There's a storeroom. Just text me to tell me where you leave it."

Her eyes hold mine as she swallows a lump in her throat.

I link our pinky fingers again. "I need to see you alone," I whisper. "And this is the only way we will get any privacy." Charlotte licks her lips. "Okay?"

She nods softly, not saying another word before she heads off in the direction of the foyer.

I turn and order my drink, elation filling me.

Finally.

I clutch the key in my pocket and casually stroll through the grand foyer of the Four Seasons. Charlotte left the function an hour ago, but she's only just texted me to give me the all clear.

Don't get caught, don't get caught, I remind myself.

I don't really care if I get caught, but not getting to see her if I do has me worried.

I'm having trouble walking to her... I want to run.

Fast.

I get into the elevator and scan the key. The penthouse floor lights up, and I exhale heavily, my heart racing. Being nervous around a woman is new for me.

Don't fuck it up. Don't fuck it up.

The doors eventually open. I drop my shoulders, exhale heavily, and walk out into the foyer. A large set of black double doors stand before me, and I tentatively turn the door handle.

It's open, and I walk in.

Charlotte is in front of me, still in her ballgown and just as beautiful as I remember. My heart skips a beat at the sight of her.

Her eyes search mine.

I smile softly and then step forward to take her into my arms. "Alone at last."

Charlotte

He's here, and I'm finally in his arms. Arms that are big and warm and hold on to me tight. The smell of his aftershave is all around me. He's tall—so much taller than me without my shoes on—and his hair is messed up to perfection.

Leaning down, he kisses me slowly and with just the right amount of pressure. He smiles as he tucks a piece of hair behind my ear.

"I've been through torture tonight watching you with him."

"He's just a friend."

"Does he know that?" He takes my hand and leads me farther into the apartment.

This is my house. I should take the lead—be brave for once.

"Would you like a drink?" I ask with fake confidence.

He kisses my fingertips, his eyes locked on mine. "Please."

Oh, he's just so...

I guide him to the kitchen, where he stops me and spins me towards him again. I stare up at him and feel the air leaving my lungs. Spencer has this intensity about him that I've never seen on him before tonight. I don't know if it's because we are completely alone for the first time, because we're sneaking around, or because we're in my apartment and we both know that anything could happen. But everything feels magnified tonight. Every glance, every smile, every touch.

Perhaps it's my nerves that are making everything seem so...extreme.

He takes my face in his hands. "I have to kiss you. It's been too long since I've felt your lips." His mouth dusts mine, and his tongue slowly slides out and runs across my lips. I feel the thrill of it all the way to my toes. He goes deeper and his tongue connects with mine softly, as if coaxing me to come out and play.

I smile against him and put my arms around his broad neck.

He walks me backwards into the kitchen, and then we stop for a moment, and he holds me in his arms, looking down at me.

The air swirls between us and we stare at each other as we drink in our close proximity.

His eyes are smouldering, and I can feel the power his body is emanating. He licks his lips, and I can see he's debating whether or not he should take this slow.

Please...

"Where are your wineglasses?" he asks smoothly.

"R-right," I stammer. "Good idea." I point to a cupboard in a fluster. I need a drink...or ten. I take two champagne flutes, grab a bottle of Grange, and pass them over to him.

He smirks when he sees the label. "The good stuff." Little does he know I just ordered this in a panic from room service only twenty minutes ago. The cork pops, and he pours the bubbly liquid into our glasses.

He passes me a flute and then holds his glass up in the air.

"What are we toasting?" I smile shyly.

"Our first date."

"This isn't our first date."

"That other one didn't count. That was just a practice run. I completely screwed that up. Erase it from your memory. I want a do-over."

I smile, relieved that he acknowledged our last disastrous date, and clink my glass with his. "To do-overs," I whisper.

He touches my glass and takes a slow, controlled sip. His eyes hold mine and he slowly licks his lips.

What *is* that look? "What's going on in that mind of yours, Mr Spencer?" I whisper.

"I'm wondering what the hell is going on here."

I frown.

"You see, I..." His voice trails off, and he places his drink down, stepping towards me to take me in his arms. His lips drop to my neck, and then his tongue comes out and he slowly licks me.

My insides melt, and I close my eyes. "You see what?" I ask. "What were you going to say?"

"I'm wondering what's so different with you. Why does my heart race when you look at me?" He breathes against my skin.

I smile and look up at the ceiling as his mouth slowly caresses my neck.

"I'm wondering why the fuck you make me so nervous, like nobody ever has before."

He nips me with his teeth, and I flinch.

"I'm wondering how just the sound of your voice over the phone can make my cock so hard that it weeps."

I whimper as his lips begin to assault my neck with more force. His hands have now dropped to my arse.

"So many mysteries," I whisper, trying to control my breathing.

"You're the eighth wonder of the world." He chuckles, moving his kisses to my shoulder before he trails his tongue across the skin there.

"Why do you lick me like that?" I ask, breathless.

He lifts his eyes to mine and cups my cheeks. "Because I need to taste you."

My stomach clenches. "When you say things like that...it does things to me."

"What things?"

"Strange things that make me feel my pulse where I've never felt it before."

With his dark eyes locked on mine, he trails his fingers down my face, down over my breasts, and then lower.

"Here?" he whispers as he gently rubs his fingers over my sex through my dress. "Do you feel your pulse here?"

I nod, my erratic breathing ragged, desperate to suck in precious air.

He leans closer, his mouth at my ear, his breaths dusting my skin. "I want you to feel my pulse here." He grabs my sex aggressively, and he hisses sharply. My legs nearly buckle.

I pull out of his arms and step back, panting wildly. Fear takes over.

What the hell? This is too much. Too...full-on.

I don't think I can do this.

A frown creases his brows. "I'm sorry, I didn't mean to frighten you, angel."

My eyes search his. I shrug weakly, ashamed that he can sense it.

With a shaky hand, I sip my champagne.

He shifts around, uncomfortable, turning his attention to the apartment. "This...this is a nice place."

"I-it is..."

He takes a seat at the kitchen counter and refills his glass. "Top up?" he asks casually.

I nod and pass him my glass.

We stare at each other as we drink again, and it feels like he's choosing his next words carefully because I simply don't know what to say.

"We can just take it slow." He shakes his head. "I don't mean to rush you. I'm just so damn attracted to you that I can't help myself."

"It's okay, Spence." I pause, taking a moment to compose

myself. "I'm attracted to you too. It's just...this is new for me. I'm sorry," I whisper shamefully.

He leans over and kisses me again, as if he's unable to help it, and then he runs his hand up my thigh.

"Ouch." He winces. The crystals on my dress are sharp. "This dress is like a beautiful, yet very lethal crustacean."

My mouth falls open. "A crustacean?"

He chuckles. "Yeah, you know...a soft little thing in a very hard shell. All lethal like a sea anen—" He pauses and tries again. "A sea amen-emey."

I laugh. "A sea *anemone*."

He laughs too. "Fuck, that's a hard word to say."

"You sound like something from *Finding Nemo*."

"What a great movie that was."

"A classic." I smile at him, trying to lighten the subject. I love that he's trying to ease my fears.

He takes a sip of his drink. "Dory was my favourite—by far the best actor of all time."

I giggle. This is the last thing I thought he would talk about. "Mine too."

"I've watched this movie many times over the years at Masters's house with Willow and Samuel. I think Sebastian knows every word of it by heart." He drinks again and then scowls softly. "What was the kid's name, again?"

My eyes widen. "You did not just say that."

His grin is full of mischief.

"Nemo. The kid's name is Nemo, Spencer."

"Oh." He laughs out loud and raises his eyebrows in embarrassment. "Right."

We both smile as we sip our champagne, our eyes lingering on each other's. He takes his black dinner jacket off and hangs it over the back of one of the stools, loosening his bow tie in the process. Watching him do that feels strangely sexual. Spencer steps forward again, and the two of us embrace to kiss softly. It's not a passionate kiss like before. It's an affectionate kiss, one that feels natural, comfortable, just right.

"Can you answer a question for me, Charlotte?" he asks as he tucks a piece of my hair behind my ear.

"Yes."

"Why do I feel like I know you?"

"I could ask you the same thing. I feel a familiarity with you that shouldn't be there."

He runs his hand up my leg again. "Ouch." He shakes his hand. "This dress is fucking lethal. It has its own built-in security system. Did Edward buy it for you?"

I laugh. I've worn this dress a few times before but never realised the crystals were so sharp to the touch. Nobody has ever touched me like this while I've been wearing it before.

"Is this where you tell me to slip into something more comfortable?" I smirk, feeling brave.

His eyes darken. "As cliché as it sounds, and at the great risk of being kicked out, yeah. This is exactly where I ask you to slip into something more comfortable."

"I'll let you in on a little secret," I say.

"Go on..."

"I couldn't get the zip undone to take it off, and I didn't want to call for help because I knew you were coming here."

His eyes widen. "And who do you normally call for help, may I ask?"

"Wyatt." I giggle.

He shakes his head in disgust. "This is one of those moments where you need to lie to me, Charlotte."

I laugh. *Oh, he's fun.*

"I'll ask you one more time: who do you normally call for help?"

"Beverly, my assistant." I smile.

"Much better."

I smile goofily as I take another drink of my champagne. The air between us is electric. Our lips touch, and I feel so naughty and carefree. We get carried away and he leans forward, accidentally knocking my glass of champagne over. It spills over the bench and onto my dress.

"Oh, fuck!" he barks, and without missing a beat, he begins to unbutton his white shirt. All I can do is watch with my heart in my throat. *What is he doing?*

He takes his shirt off and wipes the bench down with it.

His chest is broad and tanned, and his stomach is ripped with muscles. He has a scattering of dark hair across his chest, and then a trail from his navel that disappears into his pants. I've never seen a more beautiful man. I've never seen *any* man, but jeez, he's one hell of a first.

"We have tea towels for wiping up spillages," I say casually.

He kisses me. "I needed an excuse to take some clothing off." He lays me back over the bench. "You thought that was an innocent spill, didn't you? It was completely strategic."

Playful Spencer I can handle. He doesn't scare me. I laugh out loud, and he slides his hand up my stomach.

"Shit!" He pulls his hand away. "That's it. This fucking dress is coming off. It has teeth."

I lie on the bench, looking up at him. My hands are above my head, and my blonde hair is splayed out. He smiles and points at me. "Ah, I see what's going on here. Well played, Charlotte. Well played."

"What?"

"The old sea anemone dress trick." He smirks. "That's an oldie, but a goody, Prescott."

I giggle.

"You wore that dress knowing full well that I would have to take you into the bedroom and take if off you, didn't you?"

I smile up at him.

He runs his index finger down my neck, between my breasts, and down to my pubic bone.

Our eyes are locked, and the air leaves my lungs in a rush.

"Didn't you?" he whispers.

This is it, the moment I've waited so long for. I know he thinks I've done this before, but hopefully I can fudge my way through it. So far, so good.

"Well?" he asks with a raised brow.

This just all seems to be moving so fast. I have no idea at what pace it should be going. Is this normal?

I nod softly. "Yes."

He pulls me up by the hand. "Luckily for you." He grabs my hips and pulls me down from the bench. "I am an excellent personal assistant and will happily oblige."

We fall serious, and he kisses me, his tongue sweeping deeper into my mouth as he holds my face. My sex begins to throb. "Where is your bedroom?" he asks against my lips.

"Up-upstairs," I whisper. Oh, this feels like it's going way too fast. He just got here. "Can we just...?"

His eyes meet mine and his face softens. "Slow it down?" he whispers as he kisses my lips softly.

I nod. "I'm sorry. I just..."

"Once again, I'm getting ahead of myself. Spencer Jones needs a leash."

I laugh out loud at him talking in third person. He takes my jaw in his hands and stares into my eyes. "Will you dance with me, Charlotte?"

"Here?"

"Right here." He takes out his phone and opens Spotify. "What's your favourite song?"

I smile and think for a moment. "Umm." I shrug. "I have a playlist on my phone."

His eyes widen and he feigns surprise. "You *do*?"

I giggle. "I do." I pick up my phone and he takes it from me. "What's the code?"

I smirk and snatch it from him, typing the code in myself. "I'm not giving you the code to my phone." I scoff.

"But how am I supposed to spy on you if I can't get into your phone?"

"You're an idiot." I giggle. "*All Hands on Deck*" by Tenashe begins to play.

He snakes his arms around my waist, the sexy beat playing out around us, and he pulls my body closer to his. "That's better." He smiles down at me.

I'm dancing in my kitchen with a gorgeous man who has no shirt on.

Who am I?

My hands roam over his bare shoulders. I can feel his warm skin on my face as I lean on him. "Is this one of your strategic moves?"

He chuckles and twirls me around. "Yeah, but I didn't think it through too well."

"Why?"

"Your dress is biting me." He winces at the crystals pushing up against his chest. "This is painful."

I laugh out loud and he spins me around.

"But do you see how brave I am?" he asks.

"It really is very impressive." I smirk.

"Anything for you, Lady Charlotte." He leans down and kisses me softly. "What are the words to this song?" He frowns as he listens. "All hands on deck, all in the front all in the back," he repeats.

He has the ability to switch between intense and playful within seconds. I've never met anyone like him before.

He raises a sexy brow. "All part of your strategic planning, no doubt, Prescott."

"What is?" I laugh.

"All in the front, all in the back."

"They're words to a song." I shake my head.

"Ah, but are they." He puts his hands on my arse. "Or are you giving me directions to where you want me to touch you?" His tongue takes mine with purpose. "A roadmap, as such. Is this a secret code I needed to crack?"

"A roadmap to where?" I whisper.

"To wherever you want me to take you." His tongue dances with mine.

This is it.

This is what I want. I don't want him to go home, I want him to stay here with me and take away the ache.

What are you waiting for? Just do it.

His lips linger over mine, and my arousal is beginning to ache between my legs.

"Spence." I run my fingers through his hair.

"Yes, angel." He smiles at me, already knowing what I'm going to say.

"I want you to take me upstairs and I want you to take this dress off me."

He smiles and holds me close. We stay in each other's arms for just a moment, and then, without another word, he takes my hand in his and leads me out of the kitchen. My heart begins to race as he pulls me through the apartment and over to the stairs.

"I would carry you up, but I don't want you to think I'm showing off."

I laugh. "That's a relief. I do hate a poser."

With every step closer to my bedroom, the less air there seems to be in my lungs.

You can do this, you can do this, I chant over and over again in my head.

Spencer falls quieter, as if sensing my nerves. "And what are we changing you into?"

If I could answer him, I would, but I'm too busy having a complete internal freak-out.

He's so experienced. What if I'm a dud in bed? I probably am—I have absolutely no idea what I'm doing.

"Where is your bedroom?" he asks.

"Up at the end of the hall," I whisper.

Hearing my voice, he turns and frowns, concern on his face. "What's wrong, angel?" He takes my hands in his.

I shrug, embarrassed, "I'm..."

"You're what?"

"I'm not. I mean... I don't." I shake my head. God, this all seems so fast. "I mean, I do..."

He smiles softly. "You're nervous?"

I nod, horrified at my own inexperience.

"Do you want to do this?"

I nod. "Yes."

"This is only your second time?"

My eyes search his. I want to say first, but I don't want to scare him away, so I nod again.

Spencer smiles and leans down to kiss me. It's tender, lingering, and gentle, and in that moment, I know he's going to look after me.

"You do know that I'm going to find who was your first and kill that fucker, right?"

I smile goofily.

"You have no idea how badly I've been beating myself up about this," he says as he turns and pulls me into the room. "It keeps me awake at night."

"It does?"

"God, yes." He tuts and turns me towards him, his face softening when our eyes meet. "Let's just pretend this is your first time, yeah?" he whispers. "For my sake."

I frown. "Why would you want to pretend that this is my first time?"

"To make me feel better about what I missed out on. Biggest fucking regret of my life."

My heart swells, and some of my confidence returns. "Spencer—"

"Spence," he corrects me with a soft kiss.

"Are you going to take this anemone off me, or am I going to die in it?"

He chuckles. "God, yes, this dress is going in the bin."

"This is a Dolce & Gabbana. I don't think it's garbage-worthy."

He grabs me and kisses me roughly, walking me backwards. "Dolce can Gabbana off."

He turns me away from him, and I close my eyes as the zipper in the back of my dress slowly begins to slide down. It's laced up with gold ribbon towards my lower back, and I can feel Spencer begin to unlace it. He slowly slides one shoulder off, and then the other, eventually peeling it down over my hips. He stays focused on his task, and all I can do is watch his face through the mirror in front of me.

What's he thinking?

I'm so nervous, I think I might throw up.

"Lie to me," I blurt out.

His eyes come up to mine in surprise. "What?"

"Tell me something about yourself to take my mind off this."

Tenderness crosses his face. "Angel...how beautiful you are."

I frown as I desperately try to control the oncoming heart attack.

He falls into his requested role-play with ease. "Did you know I was in the Guinness Book of Records?"

"You were?" I frown, unsure if he is lying or serious.

"Yes, for having the smallest dick in the world."

I burst out laughing and look over my shoulder at him.

"True story. This dick has never hurt a soul." He winks.

He's trying to calm my nerves. I'm not scared of him hurting me, I'm scared of letting him down.

I turn back to him. "That's useful information." I smile. "Although, I'm unsure you should spread that one around."

"I do try to keep it on the down low. I don't want every virgin in the city knocking on my door."

"Are you always such an idiot, Mr Spencer?"

"It's a talent." He slides my dress down over my hips, letting it pool on the floor. He holds my hand and helps me step out of it.

His eyes slowly drop to my toes as he drinks me in. I stand before him in a satin gold strapless bra and thong.

162

"Holy mother of fuck, Charlotte," he whispers in awe. "You are so beautiful."

He leans in and kisses me, his lips lingering over mine, seeking permission. I wrap my arms around his neck and deepen our kiss.

"I'm just going to take the lead here. You tell me if something doesn't feel right, okay?" he breathes against my lips.

I nod slowly.

He kisses me, walking me back until we hit the bed, and then he lays me down and lies beside me, leaning up on his elbow. My body is snug up against his, and I can feel his erection against my hip.

He kisses me, and with every slip of my tongue, his body moves to cover more of mine. His hands run over my bra and down over my underwear, and I can't help but writhe beneath him.

For a long time we kiss and drink each other in. It's perfect. With every flick of his tongue, every bite of my neck, I feel myself floating higher and higher. It's like he has a manual to my body and knows exactly what to do to drive me crazy. I can't get close enough.

Our kisses turn frantic until he's lying on top of me, his erection pressed against my sex. He's hard, and his breathing is ragged. I feel out of control with this beautiful man on top of me.

He feels so good.

He leans and rests on one elbow, and with his eyes locked on mine, Spencer slides his hand into my underwear, sweeping his fingers through my wet, swollen flesh.

"Fuck me, you're so wet, baby," he whispers. "You're soaking."

I grip his forearm, eyes searching his. I should stop him...but I don't want to.

His fingers begin to circle my clitoris, and *I* begin to see stars.

"Spence," I moan, my back arching off the bed.

This is something else. It's not at all awkward or horrible like I'd imagined it could be.

Spencer sits me up and reaches around to unclip my bra. His

smile breaks free when his eyes drop to my full beasts. He leans down and kisses each of them in reverence. "So... beautiful."

He slowly slides my underwear down my legs, removing and discarding them to the side.

"Fucking hell." He groans, his hips driving forward without thought.

I close my eyes to try and block him out. All of this adoration from him is frying my brain.

I watch as his lips drop to my nipple, and he sucks carefully, his eyes closing.

"Hell, Charlotte, *you are* fucking delicious."

I rock against him, our eyes locked. His fingers circle and tease me, the sound of my arousal hanging in the air.

Is being this wet normal?

This is the weirdest thing. My body already knows what to do.

"That's it, angel," he whispers. "Ride my fingers."

I pant and my legs clamp shut at once, but Spencer continues to circle...and circle, and...oh my fucking God.

He pulls his fingers out, and I blink rapidly.

"What are you doing?" I whisper, lifting my head from the pillow.

"I'm going to slip into something more comfortable." He smiles and throws me a sexy wink.

I pant wildly, and my head flops back to the bed with a thud.

That wink is the Devil at work, I swear. It could talk me into anything.

"Keep your eyes on my face," he instructs as he hops out of his pants.

When he pulls down his briefs, my eyes widen in horror.

"You're an appalling liar, Spencer Jones. *That* is not the smallest dick in the world." I gasp. "That's the biggest."

His dick is large and hangs heavily between his legs. It's dark pink and engorged with thick veins running down the length of it.

Good God.

Heaven help me. It looks scary...and hungry.

"I told you not to look there." He smirks. He digs in the pocket of his trousers and takes out three condoms, placing them on the side table.

Oh my God, oh my God...

He pushes me back down on the mattress and then he kisses my breasts, my stomach, travelling lower and lower until I find myself cringing.

"No, Spence," I whisper, placing my hands on the back of his head.

"What?" He looks up.

I shake my head. "Not that. Not tonight." God, that's just too intimate. I can't stand the thought of it.

His face falls and I can see his disappointment. I internally kick myself. Damn it, why did I say that?

"Okay, baby," he whispers softly.

"I... I'm sorry." I put my hand over my face.

"Don't be sorry." He crawls back up to lie beside me, smiling as he leans on his elbow and looks down on me.

I run my fingers through his stubble and stare up at him.

"You're staring," I whisper.

"I know." He leans down and kisses me. "You make *me* nervous, Charlotte." He takes my hand and puts it over his heart where a hard, heavy thumping beats beneath my palm.

My eyes search his. "Why would you be nervous?"

"They were right. You are completely out of my league."

I smile softly. "Let's just pretend it's your first time too."

He chuckles and rolls over me, never breaking our kiss.

"How did you lose your virginity?" I ask him.

He spreads my legs and pushes a finger inside of me. "You don't want to know."

My mouth falls open...

Oh God.

Satisfaction flashes across his face as he watches me, and he adds another finger, grinding himself against my hip to relieve some of his own tension. Another finger is slipped inside of me, and my head falls back. Slowly in and slowly out, his circular movements stretch me. I can hear the sound of my arousal as he works my body.

"Open your legs wider, angel," he whispers.

My body rocks from the pressure of his fingers, and I shudder. He slowly pulls his hand away.

"You're ready," he whispers.

I swallow the lump in my throat and nod. Am I?

Will I ever be ready for this?

He grabs a condom and rolls it on, and then with a succession of perfect kisses, Spencer rises above me.

"I'm just going to go quick, angel, okay? There is no easy way. It will sting for only a moment, I promise you."

I stare up at him and my heart swells. Even as aroused as he is, he's thinking of me, conscious of not hurting me.

"I trust you." My breaths quiver as I stare up at him. He positions himself at my entrance and smiles down at me.

I giggle at the pure mischief on his face. "That is the look of the Devil if ever I saw it."

He smirks coyly, and then he pushes forward and pins me to the mattress as hard as he can.

I cling to him, my face twisting in pain.

"*Ooh...*" I whimper.

His eyes find mine and I see confusion staring back at me. That's when I know...*he knows.*

Suddenly, I'm panicked, and this is too much...too intense.

"Spence," I whisper.

"It's okay, angel." He slowly pulls out. "Kiss me," he breathes before he pushes himself back in.

We kiss, tenderly and loving at first, as he slowly eases himself in and out. His breaths are ragged, and he jerks and shudders. His face is twisted up like he's the one in pain.

"W-what's wrong?" I stammer, holding his face.

"Fuck." He groans. "Angel, you feel too good. I can hardly hold it."

What?

He closes his eyes, and I feel like he is trying to block me out while he gets into a rhythm: in, out... in... out.

It burns like fire.

He goes deeper and circles his arse, trying again to stretch me open. I get my first taste of pleasure and I can't help but smile up at him.

His eyes open and see me. "You like that?"

I nod.

He does it again, and my smile grows.

"God, I do like that," I rasp.

"What about when I do this?" He moves forward with force, almost winding me.

I frown, but not because I'm in pain, and Spencer circles again, forcing me to smile.

He grabs my ankle and wraps my leg around his hip, and then he begins some kind of heavenly circular rhythm, while I feel like I'm going out of my damn mind.

His lips descend on mine, his hands finding their way underneath my behind as he lifts my body onto his so his dick is deep inside me...stretching me in ways that feel impossible.

Something deep inside begins to build, and I grip his shoulders to get closer to him. "Spence?"

"I know, angel. So fucking good."

Our bodies begin to slap together, and I suddenly lurch forward, overcome with a feeling. I shudder and moan deeply, feeling a release from deep within me.

"Oh...fuck." He groans, and he begins to hit me hard.

Slap, slap, slap goes our skin.

His eyes roll back and then he holds himself still, deep within me, unable to stop the sound of ecstasy leaving his lips.

I smile and cling to him. *Did he just...?*

He drops his head to my shoulder, and the two of us lie there panting. I can feel his heart beating hard against mine.

"You didn't tell me you were in the Guinness Book of Records too." He pants.

"What for?" I frown.

"The most perfect sex of all time."

He kisses me and holds me close, making me feel overcome with emotion.

He holds me tight as we pant and our hearts beat hard.

This feels special and intimate, and I smile broadly as a silly thought crosses my mind.

"And just like that, Dolce fucked Gabbana."

Spencer bursts out laughing and rolls off me, falling beside me as his deep belly laugh breaks the tension.

I smirk and lean on my elbow, resting my cheek in the palm of my hand. "What?"

"I think it's Gabbana who fucked Dolce."

I giggle. His joy is infectious. "Yeah, well, shut up or I'll do it again."

I wake to the feeling of his warmth behind me, and I smile sleepily, relieved to know he's still here.

Spencer...

He didn't want to leave me last night. He wanted to sleep beside me.

I roll over to face him, and he rolls onto his back, still fast asleep.

My eyes roam over his muscular arms and broad chest, slipping lower to his chiselled stomach, and then a 'V' of muscles that run from his stomach to his groin.

He has short, well-kept pubic hair, and his dick is semi-hard resting up against his stomach. His legs are spread wide, and even his quad muscles are large and powerful.

He's so beautiful.

His plump lips part and his eyes flutter open.

"Hmm." He inhales deeply and reaches for me, pulling me across his chest.

"Good morning, my angel." He kisses my temple and holds me close.

"Good morning." I smile goofily, dropping a chaste kiss to his chest.

Now, that's a good way to wake up.

He runs his fingers through my hair. "How did my girl sleep?" He kisses my forehead again.

"Great, thanks."

I can feel his erection growing harder by the second.

"Is that thing hard in your sleep?"

"Men's testosterone is replenished while they sleep, that's why they wake up with an erection. Testosterone is at its highest in the morning."

"Good to know."

"I need the bathroom," he says. When he gets up, the blanket falls off me. Feeling self-conscious, I quickly pull it back to cover myself. He frowns when he notices, but he doesn't say anything. He simply disappears into the bathroom and returns with my robe.

"Here you go, baby." He passes it to me with a soft kiss to the lips.

"Thank you." I smile, my heart swelling. *Thoughtful.*

Spencer disappears back into the bathroom.

I quickly jump up and throw the robe on. "Would you like some water?" I ask.

"Please!" he calls out.

I walk out and down the stairs to go into the bathroom down there. I don't want him to hear me on the toilet. This is all so foreign to me. I have so much to get used to.

I wash my hands and smile goofily at my reflection in the mirror.

"Oh my God," I mouth to the messy just-fucked blonde in the reflection.

"I know," she mouths back.

I run my hands through my hair and wash my face before I head back upstairs.

When I get there, I find Spencer in the shower, and my heart sinks.

Is he leaving?

"Charlotte, come here, angel," he calls to me.

I twist my fingers together nervously and walk in to find him soaping up his groin. "Are you getting in with me?" he asks.

"Oh...erm." Shit.

He smiles warmly. "I've already seen you naked. Just get in with me so I can wash you." He turns his back so I'm less self-conscious.

I smile, feeling stupid, and slowly untie my robe and take it off. Then I step in behind him.

He turns and his eyes hold mine. He wraps himself around me, pulling me under the hot water. He takes the soap and begins to wash my back, my stomach, my shoulders...my sex, eventually turning me back to him for a kiss.

"What are you doing today?" he asks.

"Nothing."

"I'm not ready to leave you."

"You're not?"

"Can I stay?" he asks, brushing his lips against mine.

"For as long as you want."

"I'll stay today and leave tonight after your guards have gone." He exhales slowly.

"Okay."

We kiss and he holds me tight.

"Are you sore?" he asks.

"I'm okay." I am sore, but I want him.

Our kiss turns frantic. Eventually, he turns the shower off and pulls me out.

"I need you in bed. Now."

He wraps me in a towel and dries me off. Before I know it, he is leading me out into the bedroom. Ah, this could be painful. I didn't think this through at all.

"Can we try something different?" he asks.

I stare at him. Like what?

"Can you get on your knees for me?"

Still, I stare at him.

"I won't hurt you, I promise."

I nod, unable to string two words together. He positions me on the bed on my knees, and then pulls me over to the side of the bed. He points to the mirror in front of us. "Watch, Charlotte." He leans down and kisses my behind. "Watch me fuck you."

My breath catches, and I look up into the mirror. I watch him slowly roll the condom on, putting saliva onto his fingertips before he rubs it into the lips of my sex. He hisses when he feels me. I'm already wet.

He smiles darkly at our reflections and positions himself at my entrance before he slowly pushes himself inside.

My mouth falls open at the feel of him.

He pulls out and then pushes back in, and he gives me a sexy wink through the mirror.

Unable to help it, I giggle. "You and that wink," I tease.

He pulls out and then slams in hard, forcing my mouth to fall open.

"No talking while I fuck you." He smirks.

"Yes." I smile.

"Yes, sir."

He circles his cock deep inside of me, and that is one hell of a delicious movement. Before I know it, he has my hip bones in his hands, and he is riding me hard.

His mouth hangs slack as he watches us in the mirror, and I can do nothing but hold on. He hits me hard, his eyes flickering with arousal.

Last night was for me. This is for him.

The sheer pleasure on his face is a wonder. My breasts bounce as he hits me, and I'm totally entranced by the sight of this beautiful man in all his glory.

"Fuck, fuck, fuck." He shudders as if he's about to lose control.

He reaches around and circles his thumb over my clitoris, making my body contract.

"Let me have it," he growls as his cock hits me harder and harder.

"Oh God," I sigh. "Oh...oh!" I cry out, and I grab the sheets beneath me as an orgasm rips through my body at once. Spencer pushes me down, forcing my arse in the air, and then he takes what he needs.

Deep, hard thrusts hit me until I'm seeing stars. He goes on and on, and then he holds himself deep inside, and I feel him jerk and lose control.

I fall to the bed in a heap. Spencer tenderly kisses my shoulder from behind. "You're a fucking deviant," he pants.

I smile against the sheets.

"I think I'm addicted."

The hot water runs over us and I smile against the warmth of Spencer's large chest. It's Sunday afternoon, and we are in the shower and in some heavenly alternate universe. Spencer soaps up his hands and begins to wash me again. This is our third shower together. And I have to say, I'm addicted to having someone worship my body under hot water this way.

He rubs his two soapy hands over my breasts.

"Hmm." He wraps his large arms around me and holds me tight. "I have to go to the pharmacy."

"What for?"

"Condoms."

My face falls. "Oh." I think for a moment. "If you leave now, you can't come back. The guards will see you."

He frowns. "Fuck's sake." He exhales heavily, turns me, and continues washing my back.

"I don't like this at all. How long are you going to hide me?" he huffs.

"I could go to the pharmacy?" I offer. "You could stay here and rest. I'll go with the boys. Just tell me what you need."

He turns me by the shoulders and smirks down at me. The water is running down over his face. He looks simply gorgeous.

"Don't you think they're going to be suspicious of you buying twenty-nine boxes of monster-cock condoms?"

I burst out laughing. "Well, probably, but how about one box of snake-cock condoms instead." I run my fingers through his stubble. "They'll stay outside while I go in. I do have *some* privacy."

He falls serious as he stares down at me. There's this feeling of closeness between us that I can't explain.

"We're good together," he whispers.

I smile up at him. "I know."

He kisses me and holds me tight, and the emotion in his kiss nearly tears my heart wide open.

"What are you going to cook me for dinner?" I ask, just to take the seriousness out of the situation.

He grabs my behind and pins me to the wall. "Cock stew."

Half an hour later, we are sitting downstairs in the living room. I'm wearing a white robe and Spencer is wrapped in a white towel. He's been naked practically ever since he got here.

He pulls me onto his lap and I straddle him. We kiss and he flicks the towel to the side, grinding me over his hard penis.

He lifts my gown so that we are skin on skin. "This beautiful pussy of yours is going to get me in trouble."

I smile down at him. Who knew I could be so naughty?

"Spencer."

He bites my neck.

"We have no condoms left," I remind him.

His mouth begins to ravage my neck, and he growls playfully. I have to get up and run to the kitchen to escape him.

He sprints after me, each of us on either side of the kitchen island.

"When I get you"—he smirks—"you're going to pay for running away from me."

I raise a brow. "And what are you going to do to me?"

His eyes blaze with arousal, and he chuckles. "I'm going to teach you how to suck my cock." He wiggles his sexy eyebrows. "No condoms required for that."

My mouth drops open and I laugh out loud. *This man kills me.*

The front door suddenly opens.

We both stop still, eyes wide.

"Who's that?" he mouths.

"Lottie? It's me, Beth. I found Alexander in the foyer of the hotel. I brought him up with me," she calls loudly. It sounds like the two of them are walking through the apartment.

"Hi, Lottie," Alexander calls.

"Just a minute!" I call. "I'm not decent."

My eyes widen, and I begin to slap a very naked Spencer in total panic.

"Oh my God," I whisper.

Spencer's eyes light up with excitement. He thinks this is hilarious.

Oh.

My.

God.

9

Charlotte

I JUMP AROUND in a panic while Spencer laughs.

Well, he hasn't seen Edward angry. This is no joking matter.

I look over to the sliding door of the balcony and see it is still open from our time when we were lying out in the sun this morning. I push Spencer backwards, shoving him to the balcony and out of the door. I slam it shut and flick the lock.

"What the fuck?" he mouths through the glass.

I draw the heavy drapes shut and try to act calm.

"Hello?" I call out to them as I walk out into the living room, fixing my robe in place.

Alexander's face falls when he sees me in a state of undress.

"Oh, I'm terribly sorry, Charlotte, forgive me for intruding." He frowns.

"It's okay." I fake a smile. "I'm just not well today." I wrap my robe tighter around me and glance over at the window.

"What is it?" Alexander asks.

I put my fingertips to my temples. "Just a headache. It's nothing to worry about."

I can't believe I have locked Spencer on the balcony naked.

I can only imagine what he must be doing out there, and I bite my bottom lip to stop myself from smiling.

"I'm going to take a lie down, though," I say, widening my eyes at Beth. For God's sake, take the hint.

I glance over to the window, and I can see Spencer pushed flat up against the wall. It must be nearly zero degrees out there. I bite the inside of my cheek to stop myself from laughing out loud.

"I shall leave you in peace." Alexander smiles.

"Thank you." I kiss his cheek. "And thank you for checking in on me, I appreciate your concern."

He smiles warmly. "Can we have lunch one day this week?"

"Of course." I begin to guide him towards the door, practically pushing him out of it.

Just leave already.

"Where are you working now?" Beth asks Alexander.

I widen my eyes at her for starting a conversation, and she frowns in confusion.

"I'm still in merchant banking."

"That's great! See you later," I snap, holding my hand out. "I really must get to bed."

A frown crosses Alex's face at my sharp dismissal. "Goodbye, ladies." He walks out and I close the door behind him, immediately putting the chain on. As soon as I can, I turn and run to the sliding door, opening it in a rush.

"What the actual fuck?" Spencer shivers when he walks inside.

He looks up, and Beth's eyes widen to the size of saucers. Her mouth falls open in shock.

He covers his dick with both his hands. "Charlotte!" Spencer cries.

I put my hands over my mouth, and I burst out laughing.

"Oh my God, I'm so sorry." I run to get his towel, and I hold it up to shield him from Beth's bulging eyes.

He wraps it around his waist and glares at me.

I'm still laughing. "You..." I point to the balcony. "And you didn't..." I can't stop the hysterical laughter. "Elizabeth, please meet Spencer."

She gasps. "You're Spencer?"

He hunches his shoulders together and throws her a cheeky grin, holding his two hands in the air. "In all my glory."

She shakes her head. "I have no words."

I put my hand over my mouth. She's seen everything.

"In my defence, it was *very* cold out there," he tells her.

Beth and I burst out laughing, and Spencer shakes his head. "I can't fucking believe you locked me out there...naked. My dick could have frozen off."

We throw our heads back and hoot with laughter. This is the funniest thing I have ever seen.

"I'm glad you two think this is so funny. I'm going to have a hot shower. I'm frostbitten."

I smile over at him and my heart sings. *I really like him.*

He narrows his eyes at me, and then, as if silently reading my mind, he kisses my temple when he walks past me.

"Lovely to meet you, Elizabeth!" he calls out.

Elizabeth's mouth drops open and she slaps me on the arm. "Oh my fucking God," she whispers. "Tell me everything."

I put my finger to my lip in a hush signal and wait for Spencer to disappear up the stairs.

"I'm confused. I thought you weren't seeing him until tonight."

"He was at the ball last night and we organised for him to sneak in here afterwards."

Her mouth falls open. "He *stayed* here?"

I nod with a huge smile.

Her eyes widen. "Did you...?"

I nod again.

She puts her hands over her mouth. "I can't believe this. And he's gorgeous."

"I know," I whisper. "I have to go to the pharmacy. Do you want to come with me, and we can maybe have a quick coffee?"

"But he's still upstairs."

"I know, but if he leaves, he can't get back in past the guards. He wants to stay tonight too."

She jumps up and down on the spot, grabbing my arms. "Holy fucking shit."

I put my hands over my mouth and laugh at her reaction.

This conversation seems surreal.

"Just wait here," I whisper. "I'll go up and tell him we're going out for half an hour."

"Wait, why do you have to go to the pharmacy?"

"We're out of condoms."

She bursts out laughing, and I slap my hand over her mouth again. "Shut up." I look around guiltily.

"How many times did you do it?"

"Three."

Her eyes bulge again.

I giggle at her reaction. "I know. Look at me all sex kitten–like." I flap my hands around in excitement. "Back in a minute."

I head upstairs and find Spencer in the shower. I try really hard to calm my schoolgirl excitement before I see him.

"Hi." I smile casually as I walk into the bathroom.

He turns towards me and smirks. "You locked me out on the balcony in the nude."

I smile and lean in to kiss him. "I'm sorry." I cup his face. "I didn't know what to do."

Spencer soaps up his groin. How in the hell is he so comfortable naked? Where does one get this confidence?

"I'll tell you the first thing you can do," he says.

"What's that?"

"Tell Alexander fucking York to never come here again." He puts his head under the water in annoyance and rinses his hair.

"He was just checking in on me."

"I don't want him coming around here."

I smirk. "Are you jealous, Spence?"

"Yes." He falls serious. "I am, actually, and I don't like it."

This is the first time I've seen him angry this way.

"Okay." I smile softly and lean in to kiss him again. "No more home visits from Alexander. I'm going to go out to the pharmacy now. I won't be long."

He frowns. "How long is this going to go on for?" he asks.

"What?" I frown.

"This sneaking around?" Hmm, he really is getting a little shirty here. I haven't seen this side of him before.

"Not long." I run my hand down his chest and to his groin. I take him in my hand like he showed me to. "Let's just have today, okay?" I give him a slow stroke to sweeten the deal. "I want you to myself for a little while longer, that's all."

His eyes flicker with arousal. "I'll be on my back in your bed, waiting for you." He grabs my behind with both hands and grinds me against his dick. His tongue dances through my open lips.

Oh, hell, the man can kiss.

"Okay." I smile. "I'll be quick." I make my way out of the bathroom, turning back to him at the last moment. "What do I buy again?'

He smirks. "A bottle of lubricant and a few boxes of condoms." He turns the shower off. "Take my card."

"I think I'm good for it."

He smiles and wraps a towel around his waist.

I hesitate for a moment, knowing this is probably a stupid question. "Are all condoms the same?"

His face softens, and he steps forward, wrapping me in his arms. "Do you have any idea how beautiful you are to me?"

I smile up at him. "Me not knowing anything about condoms is beautiful to you?"

"It is." He kisses me. "And I need the large ones."

I widen my eyes. "I knew it."

He turns me around and slaps me on the behind. "Be quick."

. . .

"So?" Beth smiles against her coffee cup. "Tell me everything."

I exhale heavily and sip my coffee. "Oh, Beth." I frown. "He's beautiful."

"I can see that. Was it good? The sex, I mean."

I wince a little. "Well, the first time…" I pause as I try to articulate my thoughts. "Honestly, it was kind of awkward."

Her face falls.

"Not awkward—that's the wrong word. He helped me through it. More like limped me through it, actually."

"He didn't come?" She gasps, horrified.

I glance around to the other people in the coffee shop and to the front door, where Wyatt and Anthony are standing out on the street. "He came, but I know he was being super careful about what he said, and he did because he knew I was so nervous."

"You told him it was your first time?" She frowns.

"No. God, no. He thinks I did it once before, but my inexperience was obvious. I hope I fooled him anyway.

"He was being sweet, gentle, making jokes and trying so hard to make me feel at ease."

She smiles and takes my hand over the table. "Lottie, I'm so glad you waited for someone who actually took the time to read your body language."

"Me too." I smile. "But I know what he's like, and… I'm just trying not to let myself get inside my own head, you know."

"What do you mean?"

"When we were in bed, I didn't think about losing my virginity or him or…anything, really. I was just trying to get through it. It fucking hurt." I widen my eyes. "A lot."

"It must have. He isn't packing heat, he's packing the whole fucking oven."

I giggle. "And you saw the shrivelled-up version."

She laughs.

"The aroused version is very angry, let me tell you."

"Imagine walking around with a thing of that size in your pants. It must get in your way."

"I know, right?"

"Okay...so the first time was just okay."

I smile. "It was good for me, but I know he wasn't being himself. I still think he liked it."

"Ah." She nods. "What about the other two occasions?"

"This morning." I smile, remembering it all. "But afterwards, there was this feeling of... I can't explain it. The way he was holding me close. It was really nice. And then the last time was different again."

"How so?"

"He was intense, and the way he kissed me." I fake a shiver. "God, it's just good, that's all I know. It gets better each time we do it. I'm trying to play it cool, though. I'm not asking for any more dates, I'm just going to see where it goes," I tell her.

"Good."

"It's one thing to be a virgin, but to be a clingy virgin is the worst."

"I agree. But you've done it now, and whether this turns out to last or not is irrelevant, really. He was sweet and gentle. He put your needs before his."

I smile. "He really did. You should have heard the goofy jokes he was making to try and take my anxiety away from me."

"Like what?"

"He spilled my champagne and then took his shirt off to wipe it up. He eventually confessed that it was a strategic move on his part."

She smiles as she listens.

"Then we were joking around about the sharp crystals on my dress and he was talking about *Finding Nemo* to be all cute. Then he told me he was in the Guinness Book of Records for having the smallest dick."

She laughs. "We both know that's a lie."

"We do."

Her face falls. "Just be careful, Lottie. You know that it may not work out, right?"

"I know that."

"And it's okay if it doesn't," she reminds me with a smile.

I nod. "At this point, Spencer is just a friend who helped me through a very awkward situation in a really sweet way."

"That's true."

"And if we keep being friends for a while, that's great. If not, that's okay, too."

She grins, looking proud. "Look at you being all grown up and sensible. I'm so happy you are seeing this for what it is. I was so worried you were going to fall madly in love with the first guy you slept with." She sips her coffee.

"Don't be stupid." I fake a smile, and from somewhere deep inside I hear a little voice whispering, *Too late.*

There's a crime show of some sort on the television. Someone has just been murdered but the body hasn't been found, although they are searching high and low for it.

"It was obviously the guy from the apartment block," Spencer says.

I smirk. "It wasn't him; he had an alibi."

"I'm telling you, it was him." He looks up at me. "I have a sixth sense about these things. I should have been a cop."

I kiss his forehead. "You poor, deluded man. You would have made a terrible cop, because it wasn't the guy from the apartment block."

"Just wait and see, Prescott. Just wait and see."

It's late at night and neither of us wants to go to sleep. That will mean that our date is over. Spencer is well and truly focused on solving this crime, but my focus is on the man next to me who has his head on my chest.

I'm in my nightdress and, of course, Spencer is naked. We have fucked ourselves into some kind of sated bliss.

We are lying here just enjoying the show and each other. Every now and then he kisses my breast and my fingers run aimlessly through his hair.

This physical touch thing is so real.

I've never had it, and now that I do, I don't want to let it go.

"You know on our first date, you told me you had an idea about what you wanted to do with your law degree..."

"Yes." I play with his hair, wondering where this is going.

He pulls back to look at me. "What was your idea?"

I sigh. "I had this crazy idea of opening a law firm that represented charities for free."

"What do you mean?"

"Charities need contracts drawn up and legalities looked over, but the fees come out of the money they raise. It can run into the thousands. I had this idea that I could open a practice and represent charities without charging them a penny."

"Charlotte, that's a great idea."

"And a pipe dream."

He frowns and waits for me to explain.

"I have no idea how to run a company. I wouldn't even know where to start."

"Well, you just decide you're going to do it."

I smile. "If only it were that easy."

"It is that easy, Charlotte. You just decide you're going to do something and you find a way to make it happen."

I stare at him for a moment. "Is that what you did? Decide you were going to make it happen and it just miraculously happened?"

"No. I worked hard and educated myself on what I had to do to make it happen. Then I worked fucking harder and harder. You just need to take a chance and back yourself. If you don't believe in you, nobody will."

I run my fingers through his hair. "Are you going to turn into my life coach now, Spencer Jones?"

"No." He bites my nipple through my nightdress. "I'm your sex coach. I can't be everything to you."

My eyes hold his. "Who said you can't be everything to me?" I whisper.

The air tightens around us.

That sounded soppy and needy. Why did I have to say that?

"And besides, you would be a terrible coach of anything besides sex, because the guy in the apartment didn't do it," I add to lighten the mood.

He rolls his eyes. "Good grief, you really have no idea what you're on about. You're a terrible fake cop. Perhaps I should take over your whole life." He goes back to watching the show.

I smirk as I watch the television. Life coach, sex coach...love coach. What else could I possibly need?

Spencer Jones could be my everything. I know he could.

Large arms circle me from behind, and Spencer's big, dreamy lips kiss the side of my face.

"Good morning, angel," he whispers sleepily.

I smile and turn my face to kiss him softly. "Morning, Spence."

Our naked bodies are a tangled mess.

It's just after 5:00 a.m., and Spencer's alarm has woken us up. He has to go before my guards get up.

"Maybe we could just run away together instead." He sighs with his eyes still closed.

I giggle. "That would be something, wouldn't it?"

He rolls me over so that half of my body is over his. I snuggle into his chest and he kisses my forehead. "Are you sore?"

"Yes." I smirk. "Who knew that would be a question you would have to ask me so often?"

"Hmm." He sighs. "I'm not going to get my wakeup sex today, then, am I?"

Should I just do it anyway? I want him to leave satisfied.

Stop it!

This isn't all about him. I need to pull myself out of this clingy mood. I get up and go to the bathroom to break the tension. When

I come back, Spencer is still on his back in bed. His honey-blond hair is messed up, and his broad, naked chest is on display with the white blanket pooled over his waist.

"You probably should get going," I say quietly.

He nods.

Our eyes are locked, and it's as if he is waiting for me to say something.

I go to the wardrobe and take out his shirt. "I washed this for you yesterday."

"Thanks."

After being in his arms all weekend, the thought of him going home feels horrible.

I'm not sure what to do. What do you say in this situation?

As if sensing my turmoil, he holds his arms out for me. "Come here, baby."

I sit on the bed beside him and he pulls me close into an embrace. I scrunch my eyes closed against his strong neck.

I don't want him to go. I'm just getting the hang of all this.

I can be better. I know I could have been better in bed.

Stop it!

I pull out of his grip and stand. "I have to shower." I bend to kiss him, and then I walk into the bathroom and turn the shower on. My heart is beating hard in my chest. I know this may be the last time I see him, but I'm not asking the question.

I just want him to go so I don't have to wait for him to ask about seeing me again. This is like slow torture.

I want it over with.

I take a long shower. When I eventually walk back into the bedroom, I find him standing next to the freshly made bed, wearing his black dinner suit. My heart free-falls at the sight of him.

"My word, you do look handsome in that suit, Mr Spencer." I smile softly.

He takes me into his arms and kisses me. "Can I see you again?" he whispers.

I nod and smile against his lips.

And just like that, the day is saved.

"I'll call you tonight, okay?"

"Okay."

He studies my face and runs his finger down my cheek and over my bottom lip.

"You are one beautiful woman, Charlotte Prescott."

I smile, feeling emotional.

"I'll talk to you later?"

I nod, unable to talk because of the lump in my throat.

With one last lingering kiss, he finally pulls away and walks down the stairs. I hear the front door click shut when he leaves.

I flop onto the bed and smile goofily at the ceiling, running my fingertips over my lips to get closer to his touch.

Spencer

I walk into the restaurant and see my two best friends sitting at our usual table.

Breakfast time—our Monday ritual.

"Hey, Spence," Masters greets me.

"Hey," Seb mutters, studying his phone.

I take a seat and smile smugly.

They both look up and watch me for a moment. They frown together, and then exchange looks.

"What's wrong with you?" Seb asks cautiously. "You're being creepy."

"Ask me where I've been all weekend."

Masters rolls his eyes. "Where have you been all weekend, Spencer?"

"With Charlotte."

They both sit up, suddenly interested. "What?" Seb frowns.

"I went back there on Saturday night and snuck in."

Masters frowns. "Why, you old dog."

"And?" Seb prompts me.

"And she is the most beautiful fucking woman I've ever been with."

"Did you have sex?" Masters asks.

I nod, trying my best to act casual. "Uh-huh."

"And?"

I lay my napkin over my lap. "And that's it." I put my hand up for coffee.

They exchange another look before glaring back at me. "What do you mean, that's it?" Seb asks.

"I mean, I'm not giving you the details."

Masters grunts. "We always get blow-by-blow accounts of your sex life."

"Yes." Seb bites into his toast. "Don't you know we're living vicariously through you."

"Not with this one." I smile as the waitress fills my coffee cup. "Thank you."

"So, was the sex...?" Seb's voice trails off.

"The sex was..." I inhale dreamily. I get a vision of how nervous she was when we were walking to the bedroom for first time. She was literally shaking. The memory makes me smile softly.

"What is that look?" Masters pins me with a stare.

"What look?"

"That Mary Poppins I'm-pathetic look."

I chuckle and get an image of her clinging to me the first time we did it. It hurt her, I know it did, but she soldiered through it... for me.

"I don't know what you're talking about." I smirk.

"Are you seeing her again?" Masters asks.

"You can bet your fucking life I am," I say as I bite into my toast.

"And you're not going to tell us one single detail about her?"

"Nope. Only that she is..." I narrow my eyes. "She is the most perfect woman on this planet."

"Oh yeah?" Seb frowns, clearly fascinated. "What's so good about her?"

"I don't know." I chew my food. "But she makes me fucking nervous."

"You?" Masters smirks. "When have you ever been nervous with a woman?"

"Never," I reply. "I was getting all fluttery when she looked at me, and it wasn't even about the sex."

"Jesus Christ," he mutters against his coffee cup. "Here we go."

"She's different. So, so different from anyone I've ever met."

"Good God." Seb rolls his eyes. "What next?"

I get a vision of my angel lying next to me in bed this morning.

I think I lay awake and watched her for half the night; she was too perfect to miss a second of.

Her thick blonde hair splayed across her pillow, her perfect skin with dimples, and the way her chest rose and fell as she breathed. Damn.

I want to turn around and drive back there right now. I turn my attention to my two best friends instead. "What have you two boring fucks been doing all weekend, anyway?"

Seb looks at me dryly. "Fighting with The Wicked Witch of the West."

"Ugh. I hate that fucking woman." I tut. Seb's ex-wife Helena is the most conniving little slut on the planet. She slept with their gardener and is now bleeding the money out of him, day by day. "Masters, you know some criminals. Get her knocked off for us, will you?" I mutter.

Julian shakes his head. "Don't think I haven't thought about it."

We eat in silence for a few moments.

"What were you fighting about?" I eventually ask.

"She wants Bentley."

I drop my fork and it hits the plate with a clang. "She's not taking fucking Bentley!" I snap in an outrage. Bentley is the brown Labrador that Masters and I bought Seb for his birthday one year. He's adored, and he stays with me when Seb is away. I love that dog like he's my own.

I point my knife at Seb. "If she takes that fucking dog, I'm not even joking, I will have her knocked off, no questions asked. I might even do it myself."

Masters and Seb laugh.

"And this is why we thank God that you don't have an ex-wife, Spence." Masters laughs. "You're a nasty bastard when you're crossed."

"You don't fuck the gardener, take the house, fight for maintenance and spousal support, take the fucking dog, and then live to tell the tale." My blood boils just thinking about it. "God, I fucking hate her."

Honestly, the woman infuriates me like nobody else on Earth. Why the hell would anyone ever cheat on Sebastian Garcia? He is the sweetest, most loyal man I have ever met. I didn't like her before any of this, though. I knew what she was like by the way she used to look at me. She wanted me, and if I'd have let her, she would have fucked me in an instant.

She never loved my best friend, not even in the beginning.

Luckily, I do.

Of course, Seb doesn't know any of this. Masters does. He could pick up who she really was too. She wasn't exactly subtle.

It boils my fucking blood. How many men did she fuck behind his back before she got caught? The next woman he falls for better be fucking good, or else there will be hell to pay. To be honest, I don't think any woman will ever be good enough for him. Not in my eyes, anyway. My anger pulses through me as I eat the remainder of my breakfast.

"What's happening on the agenda today?" Masters asks me.

"I'm finally going to sack my stupid PA. All she ever does is piss about on Facebook and bitch about everyone else. The other girls have had enough of covering her work."

"Ha!" Seb laughs. "I'll believe that when I see it. You've been sacking her every Monday for two months."

I exhale heavily. "I know, I hate firing people even if they are assholes." I sip my coffee. "And she is a queen fucking asshole."

"Get Sheridan to do it," Masters suggests. "She lives for firing people."

A sense of unease fills me.

Sheridan.

What am I going to do about that one?

She's due here in the next couple of weeks.

But I'm not thinking about her right now. I want to think about Charlotte.

I smirk to myself, remembering one story I can share with the guys.

"Charlotte locked me out on the balcony of her hotel room yesterday...while I was naked. My pecker almost froze off. I wouldn't be surprised if some old lady had a heart attack on the street below."

"What the hell? Why?" They both laugh.

"I was chasing her around her suite and...get this." I narrow my eyes. "Fucking Alexander York turns up unannounced, tagging along with Charlotte's friend, not knowing I was there. The friend let him in."

They both fall serious. "Is York after your girl?" Masters asks me.

"Maybe."

"Fuck him." Seb winces.

"I'm planning on digging a double grave. One for Helena and one for Alexander. I'll call it the snake pit."

I'm reading through an email for the second time when I hear my office door open.

"Hello, darling," the familiar voice purrs.

I look up, startled. "Sheridan?"

She smiles as she turns the lock to ensure our privacy. She walks over and kisses me, her lips lingering over mine for too long before I pull out of the kiss.

"What are you doing?" I ask.

A scowl creases her forehead. "What do you mean, what am I doing?"

"You can't just kiss me like that."

She smiles darkly. "I can do whatever I want to you." She kicks her shoes off, lets her hair down, and sprawls on the couch in my office. Why is she so damn comfortable around here?

She taps the couch beside her. "Come lie with me."

"Sheridan." I sigh.

"What? I've missed you. You were weird the last time I saw you."

I roll my lips as I watch her, knowing it was because I was thinking about Charlotte the whole time I was with her.

How do I say this?

"Is that why you're back so quick?" I ask her.

"I needed to see what was going on with my man."

I remain at my desk, despite the way she keeps tapping the couch for me to go to her.

Her phone rings. "Excuse me." She answers it. "Hello." She listens for a moment. "No, I won't be there for another twenty minutes. Stall them." She hangs up without saying goodbye. Her attention turns back to me. "Let's go out to dinner tonight. We can paint the town red."

"I can't."

"Why not?"

"I'm seeing someone."

She smirks. "Since when does that matter to us?"

I stare at her, not saying a word.

She gets up, saunters across the office, and places herself in my lap. She tries to kiss me again, but I turn my head away.

"We belong to each other first and foremost, Spencer."

"This one's different, Shez."

She frowns. "Meaning what?"

"Meaning I'm not going to sleep with you while I'm with her."

"She'll never even know."

"*I'll* know."

"Don't be so ridiculous." She leans down and kisses my neck, and I instantly push her off me.

"Stop it!" I snap.

"Spence." Her face falls. "What's going on?"

"I really like this girl. I'm not going to risk fucking it up by sleeping with you."

She raises her chin in defiance. "Is this the young one?"

"Yes."

"Are you in love with her?"

I shrug. "I don't know, it's only new."

She smiles, sarcasm dripping from her face. "You can't do monogamy, Spencer, you're just not wired that way."

"I've never tried it."

She laughs. "Exactly. So why are you trying it now?"

I glare at her.

She puts her shoes on, her temper evident. "You've decided you want to be in a relationship and play happy families, is that it?" She fixes her hair. "You want a house in the country with two point four children, is that it?"

"What, like you have?" I roll my eyes. "Sheridan, stop with the dramatics. I don't know what I want. All I know is I only want to sleep with her right now."

"Is the sex *that* good?" She sneers.

"It's not about the sex," I fire back without hesitation.

Her face falls and she stares at me for an extended period of time. "That hurt more than it should have," she murmurs softly.

I drop my head. "I'm sorry."

"Where does that leave us?"

"There is no us at the moment."

"But we're always going to be together. We made a pact seven years ago that we would always come first with one another."

I pinch the bridge of my nose.

"Remember?" she asks quietly.

I nod and put my hands on my hips as I stare at her. We did

promise each other that years ago, and until now, it has never even been a problem.

She walks over and slides her key into my pocket, pressing a soft kiss to my lips. "Women will come and go with you, Spencer, but I'm here forever and, unlike them, my love for you is unconditional."

I stare at her.

"I'm here for ten days," she whispers.

"I'm not coming."

"We'll see." She turns and walks out of my office, closing the door quietly behind her.

Her perfume lingers in the air, along with my regret, and I drop into my seat and stare into space.

Sheridan has been the only stable in my life for so long.

This is a really weird feeling.

Charlotte

I sort through the mail with a goofy smile on my face. I'm thinking of Spencer naked and laughing in the shower. He makes me melt. The way I lay in his arms after having sex, and the way we talked and laughed like old best friends...

The way he looks at me.

The way he makes me feel.

The day has flown and I'm in my fangirl element.

Spencer Jones.

I'm seeing him tonight, and oh, it's all going so well.

I think back to the emails he sent me, and I go through the list of his qualities in my mind.

I don't have a YouPorn profile. What does that even mean?

"What does YouPorn mean?" I ask Sarah and Paul. They look up from their task.

"What do you mean?" Sarah asks.

"I heard someone say the other day that they don't have a YouPorn profile. What does that mean?"

"Oh." They exchange looks and both laugh.

"You know... YouPorn?" Paul says.

"Nope." I shrug. "Should I know what that is?"

"They should teach this shit at school. This is vital information," Sarah says. "YouPorn is a platform like YouTube, but people upload sex videos to it."

"Honesty, I wouldn't even know how to fuck if it hadn't been for this when I was a teenager." Paul laughs.

"Me too." Sarah nods enthusiastically. "I remember I used to practice the blow job tutorials."

Paul laughs. "I remember I used to watch the guys fingering the girls to see what I was supposed to be doing down there. I had no fucking idea."

"Did you practice?" Sarah smiles.

"Yep, on a watermelon."

We all burst out laughing.

"You need to get on it and watch it, Lottie." Sarah smiles. "See what we're all missing out on. There are some seriously hot dudes on there who make the rest of the male population look very lame indeed."

"Oh, yeah, because all you women let us blow on your faces." Paul tuts. "Men are more depressed by that site than women are, let me tell you."

"Yes." Sarah gasps. "What the fuck is with that? Nobody is blowing on my freshly straightened hair while I kneel with my mouth open." She shakes her head in disgust. "Honestly, as if women do that in real life."

I giggle, pretending to know what they are on about. Shit, I really need to study this YouPorn thing tonight.

"Delivery for Lottie Preston," a voice calls out.

I turn to see one of the security team from the foyer walking through with the biggest bunch of red roses I have ever seen.

"Holy shit!" Sarah cries.

My eyes widen, and the man walks over to me. "You Lottie?" he asks.

I nod.

He passes me the huge bouquet, and I turn bright red.

"Oh my God!" Sarah cries. "Look at the size of the heads on those roses."

I inhale their scent—a deep and beautiful perfume—and I open the card.

> Lottie,
> Thanks for an amazing weekend
> I can't wipe the smile from my face.
> Dolce.

10

Charlotte

I HOLD the card to my chest as happiness literally beams out of me. It *was* an amazing weekend, and I can't wipe the smile off my face either.

Oh, and he signed it Dolce...so sweet that he remembered our stupid game.

"Who the hell are they from?" Sarah gasps as she touches the petals. "Look at the crystal vase they are in. Those will have cost a pretty penny. The fucking vase alone."

I swing on my chair in glee.

"I got back with my ex-boyfriend," I lie. I'll just go along with Spencer's story. It seemed to work okay.

Sarah nods in approval. "He knows his shit, that's for sure."

I place them on my desk and read the card again.

"I'm just going to call him quickly, is that okay?" I ask.

"Yeah, sure thing, go for it," Sarah says, and the two of them turn back to their work.

I dial his number, smiling as it rings.

"Hello."

I walk out of earshot from my colleagues.

"Hi," I breathe. I can hardly contain my excitement. "I just got a delivery of the most beautiful red roses I have ever seen in my life."

"You did, huh?"

"Thank you. They're beautiful."

"I should be thanking you. I had an amazing weekend."

"Me too." I'm practically beaming.

We both wait for the other to say something.

"What time are you coming over tonight?" I finally ask.

"I'll come over and cook you dinner."

"Really?"

"Yeah, I'm a great cook."

"You're great at a lot of things."

He chuckles, and I imagine him swinging on his chair in his office.

"How will you get in?" I ask, aware that the guards are going to be an issue, as always.

"I'll park in the basement and catch the lift straight up."

I bite my lip as I think. "Okay. About seven thirty. That way, they know I'm in bed for the night."

He grunts, unimpressed. "Okay."

"Do I need to get anything? Any ingredients?" I ask.

"Just be waiting for me in something sexy."

"Okay, I can do that." I blush.

"Goodbye, angel. Have a nice day."

My heart bursts when he calls me angel.

"You too. Bye." I hang up and go back to work, and I have to concentrate really hard to not jump on the desk and punch the air.

This is a good day.

The best.

"Just down here," I say to Wyatt and Anthony. I power walk across the street as the lights change.

"Where are we going?" Wyatt asks. I'm on my lunch break and I'm on a mission.

"Victoria's Secret," I say casually, as if I say that to them every day.

Wyatt frowns at Anthony but quickly recovers.

I march down the street and they try to keep up with me. I know this looks suspicious. I'm going to buy lingerie on my lunch break, making it seem like I have a date.

Well, too bad, because I do.

I walk inside the store and the two men come in and look around to check the surroundings.

"You can wait outside for me if you like." I smile awkwardly. I don't want them to see what I buy.

"Okay, sure thing." They head off outside and wait near the front doors for me.

I exhale heavily as I look around. Right, what do I want?

Something sexy.

There are rows upon rows of skimpy satin and silk bras, as well as panties. I take a black bra and thong set and keep walking. I keep going until I get to the corsets. I grab an ice-pink lace-up corset and matching thong. I keep walking until I get to the night-dresses, and I smile. This is more me.

I spot a cream baby doll nightdress that is completely see-through with a fuchsia-coloured satin ribbon weaved through the lace under the bodice. A delicate flower pattern is entwined into the lace. It's beautiful. The lace bottoms are the same fuchsia colour with pretty cream bows.

This is it. I grab my size and head to the counter. I look at my watch and realise I've been here for all of twelve minutes.

Don't mess with me when I'm trying to be sexy. I'm a woman on a mission.

I walk through the foyer of the Four Seasons with Wyatt carrying the biggest bunch of flowers in history—vase and all.

"Where did you get these?" Anthony asks.

I fake a smile. "A secret admirer from work. Someone on level four, apparently."

Wyatt frowns from behind the flowers. "Who?"

"I'm not sure, but I'm hoping it's the guy from accounts."

Anthony smirks, and I smile cheekily. I'm going to throw them off the Spencer scent.

We get into the lift, and I have to concentrate on keeping a straight face. Every day it's the same routine. We come back here, they check my apartment and check the fire stair doors are still locked from the outside, and then, after they are satisfied that it is safe, I'm left alone.

We arrive at my floor and Anthony walks inside first as Wyatt and I stay outside. Then Wyatt goes in while I wait for them to give me the all clear.

I listen to them walking through the apartment. It's never really occurred to me before now how bizarre this actually is.

"You can come in!" Wyatt calls. I walk in to find my roses have been carefully placed in the centre of the dining table.

"Thank you." I walk in and throw my handbag on the foyer table. I kick off my shoes, turn the television on, and walk through to the kitchen to boil the kettle.

I listen as Anthony walks around upstairs and Wyatt does his balcony checks. Eventually, they both come down to the kitchen to find me.

"Are you going out again tonight?" Anthony asks.

"No. I'm having room service and going to bed early," I lie. "I won't be needing you again this evening."

"We'll be here in the hotel the whole night," Anthony assures me.

I smile. "Thank you for taking such good care of me. I appreciate you both."

They head to the front door, and Wyatt turns to look at me as if he knows something is off.

I smile calmly and hold eye contact with him.

Flowers and lingerie, you idiot.

He knows.

"Good night, boys." I smile. "I'll head down to the gym at 6:00 a.m. You don't have to come if you don't want to."

"We'll see you there," Wyatt says flatly, and then they both walk out into the corridor.

"See you then." I close the door, turn the lock, and run through the apartment and up to my room.

Next stop: YouPorn.

I open my laptop and type the words 'YouPorn' into the search bar as I sit on my bed. The site opens up in front of me and my eyes instantly widen.

Oh shit.

The page is full of little squares of images of things—things that I have never seen before. My mouth falls open, but I find myself leaning closer. There are women bent over, men ejaculating, dicks—lots of dicks.

I swallow the lump in my throat as I scroll through the images.

I click on the next page and read some of the headings.

Slut Fucks Teacher. Anal to Mouth. Anal to what? That's a thing? Hubs Watches Wife Fuck His Friend. Dual POV? What does that mean? Cream Pie! What the hell is a cream pie?

I scroll through the pages, completely overwhelmed. It's very intimidating seeing images of naked people having sex. Dicks, lots of hard dicks, in every shape and colour...they're everywhere.

I click out of the site in disgust, slamming my laptop shut.

It feels cheap to even be looking at it.

I shiver in disgust and get up to go take a shower.

Ten minutes later, as I stand under the hot water, I think about what I've just seen. I want to know how to please Spencer. I want to know what to do.

There is only one way to learn. It's not like I'm going to be able to see this stuff anywhere else.

I'm going to have to go out there and make myself watch a few things.

I turn off the shower with renewed determination, and I storm back out to my bedroom to reopen my laptop. I scroll through the categories.

Romantic? Yes, I want romantic. I keep searching until I find one that looks okay, and I hit play, leaning back against my headboard.

It involves a couple, both about my age, and both dark-haired. They're naked in bed and kissing.

His hand slides down to between her legs, and I watch, transfixed.

They begin to kiss, his hand moving lower. I sit forward as he slides two fingers into her.

My mouth falls open. Oh, I feel my arousal rolling in as I watch him turn her on. I can see the muscles on his shoulder contract as he works her. Her legs are opening wider and wider. This is hot.

My eyebrows rise, and I swallow the lump in my throat. I look around guiltily. This feels so naughty. I exhale as she moans and thrashes, her back arching off the bed. I can almost feel it myself. I rub my legs together to ease some tension.

The man lies back, and she kisses down his chest and over his stomach. Then she begins to suck on his penis.

His hands are on the back of her head.

I hold my breath.

Fascinated, I watch her bring him to his undoing. He groans beneath her, unable to control himself. His legs are wide, and his face...

Oh, I want to do this to Spencer.

Like a cat ready to pounce on her prey, I sit at the kitchen island in my sexy little nightdress.

It's 7:30 p.m., and I hate to admit it, but I watched people having sex for over an hour this afternoon. Soft sex, hard sex, messy and wet sex—all of it was hot. Damn, Sarah was right. I have been missing out.

I sip my wine and smirk to myself. Who the hell am I?

Working in a mailroom, sneaking men into my suite, watching porn, getting flowers and sitting here in sexy nightwear, waiting for the most gorgeous man of all time to come and cook me dinner.

I feel so alive, like my whole life is just getting started.

I hear the door open and my heart flips.

"Charlotte?" Spencer calls, securing the chain in place on the door.

I bound out of the kitchen. The second he sees me, he drops the shopping bags that were in his hands, and he smiles broadly. I laugh and jump up at him, loving the way he wraps his big arms around me when he catches me and lifts my feet from the floor.

"Hello, Mr Spencer." I smile.

We kiss and his tongue slowly slides between my waiting lips.

"I'll send you flowers every fucking day if this is the hello I get."

I giggle. "Thank you."

We kiss again and again, and Lord, I need him. He walks me backwards to the lounge and falls onto the sofa so I can straddle him.

He looks up at me. "You're different," he whispers.

"I feel different."

His hands slide under my nighty and over my bare hips. "I like this...*different*."

"Hmm," I murmur as I rub myself over his hard cock.

All my arousal from the last hour of porn has me ready to explode. I kiss him with an urgency like never before. His eyes flash with arousal, and his tongue dances with mine. The kiss is deep, slow, and long, and my body begins to grind over his hard cock, taking on a rhythm of its own.

I can't hold it. I want to do this, and I want to do it now.

I drop to the floor, positioning myself between his legs, and he inhales sharply, completely shocked.

Our eyes lock.

I want to suck him. I want to bring him undone. I slide the zipper of his jeans down and he frowns, confused by my sudden show of bravery. I hardly touched him last time we were together.

He lifts his hand to cup my face, and I tug at his pants a little harder. I want this. Eventually, he stands and takes them off, and I lift his T-shirt over his head.

"Jesus," he mutters.

I rub his shaft through his briefs and his eyes flutter.

"Fucking hell, those roses are miracle workers. I'll buy the fucking company tomorrow."

I giggle and lick my lips, sliding down his boxers before I push him back to his position on the sofa.

I drop back down to the floor and kiss up his thigh.

His scent intoxicates me, and this is the hottest thing I've ever done.

His places his hands to the back of my head carefully. "Fuck," he whispers.

I look at his dick. It's hard, engorged, and so thick. I don't know what I'm doing here, but I'm going to go with what I watched today.

I lick the top and his hands slide to my face. With our eyes locked, I slowly take him in my mouth, enjoying the way he hisses in approval.

"Tell me if I do it right," I whisper around him.

"Angel, you're doing it fucking perfect." He brushes my hair back from my face.

I take him deeper and deeper, and my eyes close when I get a taste of his pre-ejaculate. It's salty and different to anything I've ever tasted before.

I get into a rhythm and begin to work him with my hand. His body relaxes and he lies back against the couch.

"Fucking hell," he moans.

I work harder and harder. His hips are rising to meet my rhythm. I place my fingers around his balls and he shudders.

"Stop that or I'll come."

I smile around him and do it again. Spencer shudders and his eyes roll back in his head.

"Get up here," he growls.

I ignore him and keep sucking him until he pulls me off, guiding me so that I'm kneeling over him. He swipes his fingers though my flesh.

"Holy fuck, you're dripping wet," he whispers.

I moan against his lips, circling my hips to work myself onto his fingertips.

"Condoms," he groans, sounding pained. "Oh shit, stop right there," he demands at once. He pushes me off him and runs up the stairs two at a time. Moments later, he returns with a box of condoms. I watch as he carefully rolls one on and then he falls back into place on the sofa.

"Where were we?" He smiles.

His excitement is infectious, and I kneel over him again with my hands on his shoulders. His fingers find that spot between my legs, and his eyes close as he enjoys the way I feel for him.

"You are so fucking hot," he growls.

I wiggle my hips so he knows that I want it. Our kiss turns frantic and he bites my nipple hard through my nightdress, making me yelp.

This untamed aggression in him is new.

I like it.

He holds the base of his cock up and positions me over him. I frown and come down on him a little.

Fuck, he's so big.

"Wiggle from side to side," he tells me.

I shimmy and he puts his thumb over my clitoris, circling it with just the right amount of pressure. I moan deeply, unable to keep my eyes from closing.

"That's it, angel, ride my cock."

Hearing him say that does something to my insides, and I shudder as I am flooded with wetness.

"Fuck, yeah," he growls. "You like me talking dirty to you, baby. Do you?"

I continue to wiggle down to get him in.

"You open up that creamy cunt, angel, and let me in. I'm going to give you what you need." He bites my bottom lip and I jump. He grabs my hips and pulls me down on him with force. "I'm going to blow your fucking mind with this cock of mine."

Goose bumps scatter my skin, and he grabs a handful of my hair, guiding my head back so his mouth can ravage mine. The kiss is out of control.

This is so different than the other times—so much better.

We keep struggling, trying to find a way for my body to accept all of him.

"Open!" he commands, pulling my hips down hard. As if my body understands who's in control, it opens, and he slides all the way in.

Our mouths drop open together, and we stay silent, just staring at each other.

Thump, thump, thump goes my heart.

He's so deep inside of me, so big and so perfect.

"Did you miss me today, angel?" he whispers.

I nod, overwhelmed by the feeling of him. "Yes."

"Does my girl need to be fucked hard when she's missed me?"

I nod. I can't even talk. This feeling is incredible. "Yes," I whisper. "So hard."

He lifts my hips and slams me back down at once, forcing me to cry out.

Oh shit...

Why did I say that for?

Spencer starts pumping me hard. His hands are gripping and moving me with such force that the air is knocked out of my lungs.

But he wouldn't be able to tell, because he's totally lost all control.

His mouth is hanging open and his lips are roaming from my jaw to my nipples to my lips.

"Legs up." He bites my nipple, paralysing me further.

I lift my legs, and he slams me back down again.

"Fuck, fuck, fuck," he growls as he works.

I shudder, the feeling of him taking over me.

"Spencer," I pant. I grip his arms for balance, the muscles there bulging as he lifts me.

Fuck, this is too hard...but too good.

I lurch forward and scream out as he slams me harder. The sound of our skin slapping echoes around my apartment, and Spencer tips his head back and groans as he comes deep inside of me. I feel his dick jerk as it empties out.

My heart is hammering in my chest and I'm struggling to catch my breath.

Honestly, this euphoric feeling he gives me with an orgasm is the best thing I've ever experienced.

He lifts me off him carefully, positioning me so I'm sitting upright, and he pushes my legs open.

Huh? What's he doing?

He drops between my legs, and I hold my breath, watching him as his tongue swipes through my swollen, hot flesh.

"I want your orgasm on my tongue," he whispers darkly.

Holy *fuck.*

I put my hand on the back of his head and I watch him lick me up and down. His eyes are closed and it's like he's worshipping me. For ten minutes, he sucks and licks at me like I'm his last supper.

This can't be happening. This is too good.

He shuffles forward, and I can see that he's still hard.

"I need you again, angel."

I nod, my arousal tearing through my veins.

He picks me up and rolls me over so that I'm on my knees on the couch. I hear him opening another condom packet. His hand runs up and down my back and behind, and then he grabs a handful of my hair and pulls me back, easing himself in.

"Jesus Christ, Charlotte. You're blowing my fucking mind here, baby."

I smile, half in relief, half with fear.

And when he starts, I can only hold on as he takes what he needs from my body.

Which is everything.

This time, he lets go, and he's loud, moaning and groaning as much as he wants. It's the hottest thing I've ever heard. His body is wet with perspiration.

"So. Fucking. Tight." He grunts again and again.

I close my eyes and try to deal with him. This is hard. God, so hard.

His grip on my hair becomes painful, and I cry out.

"Come now!" he yells.

"Ah!" I cry. He's an animal.

"Clench for me, angel. Clench and you'll come. Trust me."

I do as I'm told, and sure enough, it spirals, and I begin to convulse. He holds himself still, so deep inside of me, and he cries out. I feel his cock shudder before he falls forward.

We both pant in time with each other. We're wet with perspiration, and I find myself smiling into the cushion on the sofa.

"Holy shit," I whisper.

He chuckles as his lips kiss the side of my face tenderly. "You will wear that nightdress every night from now on."

I giggle, breathless as the two of us rest cheek to cheek. "Yes, sir."

It's later that night, and Spencer and I are facing each other in bed. My hand is in his, and he has this satisfied, dreamy look on his face. We showered and he washed me in that way I'm getting used to. He cooked me dinner and we watched a movie.

Now this.

This is something else. There's a bond I can't explain. It's like I already know him, like I've always known him. The room is lit only by the lamp, neither of us wanting to go to sleep.

"You know, when you smile, your dimples go from here"—he reaches over and touches my face—"to here."

I smile on cue and turn my head to kiss his fingertips.

"I don't think I've ever smiled so much in one day," I admit in a whisper.

He leans in and kisses me softly, his hands snaking around my waist to pull me to him.

"Me either." He stares at me for a moment, as if he's contemplating saying something else.

"What is it?"

He frowns. "This is new for me."

"What is?"

He rolls onto his back and brings me with him. I lie with my head on his chest, rubbing my cheek back and forth on his skin.

"I feel like I..."

"What?"

"I can't stand the thought of..." His voice trails off.

"Spencer?"

"It doesn't matter." He kisses my forehead. "It's nothing."

"No, tell me," I urge. "What were you going to say?"

"Who did you sleep with, Charlotte?"

What the hell is he thinking about this for?

"Why does that matter?" I ask.

"I don't know." He shakes his head. "It just does."

Should I tell him? No, don't wreck this.

"He doesn't matter to me," I tell him.

"Are you sure?"

I frown as I look up and watch him. What's going through that mind of his? "Spence, why are you thinking about me with another man?"

He exhales heavily. "Because I don't like it."

"Like what?"

"Feeling jealous."

I lean in and kiss his big, soft lips. His tongue slowly slides through my open mouth, and that addictive feeling is there again.

208

Closeness.

"There's nothing wrong with a little jealousy. I would be worried if you didn't care." I run my fingers through his messy blond hair.

He frowns at the ceiling, as if processing my words.

"Does it normally bother you if a woman you are seeing has been with another?" I ask.

"No."

"Would it bother you if I were with someone else now?"

"Yes," he replies without hesitation.

I smile softly and stay silent.

It's like he's going through some kind of inner turmoil and doesn't know how to handle it.

"I won't be, Spence." I kiss his chest. "I won't be with anyone else. But you already know that, don't you?"

He stares straight ahead.

"Is that what's bothering you?" I ask. "The fact that I don't fuck around—that this is special to me?"

His jaw clenches, and I know I've hit a nerve.

"Does it bother you that this is special to you too?" I whisper.

His eyes search mine. "It shouldn't."

"That's not what I asked."

He pulls me close, so close that he nearly crushes me, and I smile against his shoulder as I wrap my arms around him.

He doesn't have to answer me. He just told me the answer to my question without using his words.

Whether he likes it or not, this means something to him too.

This is special.

Click...

I wake with a start. It's dark, and I've just heard the front door open. Spencer is sound asleep next to me.

I sit up in a rush.

Who's that?

I throw my robe on and glance at the clock. It's 6:20 a.m.

I pick up my phone and see ten missed calls from Wyatt.

Damn it, my phone was on silent.

I walk out into the hall and quickly close the bedroom door behind me before I head downstairs. Wyatt is already halfway up them.

"Is everything all right?" He frowns.

"Yes, sorry. I slept in." I continue walking down the stairs to guide him away from my bedroom.

"You didn't come down to the gym. When I couldn't reach you on the phone, we were worried."

"I'm sorry," I apologise.

"Perhaps you should take my number too," Spencer offers sharply.

I look up to see Spencer with a towel wrapped around his waist, and he's walking down the stairs towards us.

The blood drains from my face.

"What are *you* doing here?" Wyatt growls.

Spencer glares at him. "Visiting my girlfriend. What does it look like?"

11

Charlotte

WYATT NARROWS his eyes and steps forward when Spencer gets to the bottom step.

"Spencer!" I stammer, glancing between the two men in total panic.

Shit.

"How did you get in here?" Wyatt asks roughly.

"I walked through the front door and used my key." Spencer folds his arms over his chest.

"I don't think so." Wyatt sneers.

Spencer smirks. "Really? So, do you think I scaled the building instead? Perhaps a helicopter dropped me on the roof?"

Anthony walks through the front door and stops sharply when he sees Spencer wearing nothing more than a towel.

Wyatt turns and looks at Anthony, a silent message passing between the two of them.

"Spencer is a guest of mine," I say quickly.

"I don't think Edward's going to like this," Wyatt tells me, stating the obvious.

"Edward's not going to know about this," Spencer warns. "Not until Charlotte tells him herself."

Wyatt narrows his eyes, his disapproval clear.

"What exactly is your role here, Wyatt?" Spencer asks calmly.

I hold my stomach as my heart has a fit.

"Is your role to guard Charlotte and keep her safe, or are you here to spy on her for her overbearing brother?"

"Spencer," I whisper. "Please—"

Spencer holds up his hand, cutting me off.

Oh no...

"My role with Lady Charlotte is none of your concern," Wyatt fires back.

"The hell it isn't!" Spencer snaps. "Whether you like it or not, I'm with Charlotte now, and you will report to me from this moment forward with regards to her safety."

Oh God, my knees feel weak.

"I report to Edward Prescott only."

Spencer smiles sarcastically. "Okay, then you can tell him that Charlotte has had a visitor every night for a week while you and Anthony got plastered in the hotel bar. I'm sure he will be thrilled about your professionalism."

The men exchange looks.

"Here's how this is going to go: Charlotte is perfectly capable of making her own decisions. She deserves your respect, and you're going to allow her to have some fucking privacy for once. You will tell her family about me *when she* is good and ready."

"But—"

"No fucking buts. Take out your phone," Spencer demands. He rattles off his phone number to Wyatt. "Now, if you have any concerns for Charlotte's safety, you call me."

The two men glare at him.

"If you don't give Charlotte the privacy she deserves, you can find another job immediately."

Oh my God. "Spencer..." I whisper.

"One day soon, you will work for me. Guarding Charlotte for

me. I don't give a fuck about the Prescott money. My concern is for Charlotte's safety only, and so far, you two are the worst fucking guards I've ever seen."

The men stare at him, shocked.

"If you go against Charlotte's wishes, you'll hand your resignation in on the same day. Because I won't fucking have it," he growls. "She is your boss. She is the only one who gets to make the decisions around here. Not me, not you, and most certainly not fucking Edward."

The three men glare at each other while I hold my breath and wait.

"Do I make myself clear?" Spencer asks.

They stay silent.

"Do. I. Make. Myself. Clear?" he yells.

"Yes," Wyatt mutters angrily. Anthony nods.

Emotion overwhelms me, and I stare at Spencer through tears as I smile softly. He's the first man to ever stand up for me—for my privacy.

If I didn't love him before, I do now.

Spencer turns his attention to me. "I'm going to get ready for work, angel."

I nod, embarrassed. "Okay."

He turns back to the boys. "We'll be going out for dinner tonight. I assume you'll be accompanying us."

They nod and step back, clearly defeated.

"We'll be leaving at seven. Don't come into this apartment unannounced ever again without calling me first."

"Yes, sir," they both reply.

Spencer walks up the steps and I drop my head, ashamed that I liked what he just did.

"I'll be ready for work at eight," I say quietly.

Wyatt's eyes hold mine. "Are you all right with this? Him being in charge?"

"Yes," I whisper, enjoying the way my heart fills with hope. "I really am."

. . .

Wyatt and Anthony leave, and I linger in the foyer for a moment, trying to process what just happened.

One day soon, you will work for me. Guarding Charlotte for me. I don't give a fuck about the Prescott money.

I'm not imaging this; he *does* think this is going somewhere. He wouldn't be saying these things if he didn't think we had a future together.

One day they will be working for him... What the hell?

I take the stairs two at a time to find him stepping out of the shower and drying himself in the bathroom. My eyes find his across the room.

He smirks and holds his arms out. I move to him, wrap my arms around his body, and hold on tight.

"I apologise for overruling you down there." He kisses my temple, and I look up at him. "I can't let this go on, angel. I won't have it." He shakes his head. "Nobody gets to control you anymore."

"Except you?" I whisper.

He smiles softly. "Not even me." His hands slide down over my behind. "I like strong women, Charlotte, and just because you haven't been allowed to be one, it doesn't mean you aren't one."

Tears fill my eyes.

"Hey." He cups my face. "What's wrong?"

I shake my head, feeling stupid, and he kisses me softly. I stare at him for a moment as I try to articulate my thoughts. "Not many men are comfortable being with strong women, Spence."

"Lucky for you that I'm not like other men, then, isn't it?"

"Do you think I'm weak?"

He gives me a slow, sexy smile. "From the first moment I saw you, I knew you weren't weak. The way you carried yourself, the sway of your hips, the self-respect you have for your body. I wouldn't be with you if I thought you were weak, and I most definitely wouldn't be planning a future with you in it." He wipes my

214

eyes with his thumbs. "I think your life is just about to begin, and you will become the woman you were born to be." He tucks a piece of my hair behind my ear. "Don't be afraid of being strong, angel."

My eyes search his. It's like he's reading my soul.

"You are a powerful woman. You're beautiful, intelligent, and wealthy." He kisses me softly. "It's about time you let the rest of the world know it." He hesitates for a moment. "More importantly, I want you to believe it for yourself."

I hold him close, pressing my face against his chest. Who knew that the biggest player in all of England would become my hero?

My email pings with a new message and I open it up. A broad smile crosses my face when I see the name Spencer Jones.

> **Good morning, Miss Preston**
> **What is my favourite mail girl up to?**

I smile and hit reply.

> **Dear Mr Spencer,**
> **Your favourite mail girl is working her fingers to the bone.**

He replies quickly.

> **Wrong answer**
> **Lie to me.**

I smile and close my screen down while I think of what to say. This is so awkward to be sitting next to Sarah while Spencer messages me. I have to tell her about the two of us. I can't lie like this. It's eating me alive.

I exhale heavily.

Dear Mr Spencer,
I'm just going through my warm-up exercises
I go on stage in twenty minutes.

I smirk as I wait for his reply.

Fascinating. Do tell...

What will I write now? I think for a moment.

My stage name is Angel Leroo, and I'm a prima ballerina.
Perhaps you've heard of my recent show? The
Nutcracker?
Ironic, really. Breaking penises happens to be my hobby.

I hit send and giggle. How on earth do I come up with this
stuff?

Dear Angel Leroo,
That is one break I will personally look forward to.
I'm happy to oblige all of your broken-penis fantasies.
And I look forward to you kissing it better.
Where do you want to go for dinner tonight?

Does he have any idea how gorgeous he is?

Surprise me
I'm unable to concentrate at the moment.
I'm busy doing splits.

I smirk as I look around.

Your legs won't be the only thing splitting tonight.
Thank you for warming up for me: So thoughtful.
We'll be having Italian food.

Pick you up at 7:00 p.m.

Spence

xo

I feel myself blush and I close the email. He's just so naughty.

Two hours later, I'm sitting at my desk, staring out the window. Spencer's pep talk the other night about deciding to do something, and then going forward and doing it, is playing on my mind.

Perhaps he's right.

What *is* holding me back from turning my business dream into a reality?

I mean, I have the money, I have the qualifications, and I definitely know more about the charity sector than most people do. It could be a really great service that could help so many charities.

I just don't know where to start. How would I even go about it?

Would I get an office here in London and just work by myself for a while until I got established? Or would I go for it straight away and employ a few people so we could hit the ground running? I tap my pen on my chin as I think.

I don't want to fail.

"I'm so horny." Sarah sighs beside me. "I think my vagina's closing up."

I smile and click open my emails as I listen to her. "I don't think it has the ability to close up...does it?"

"Did you know that you can lift weights with your Kegel?"

"Huh?" I frown. "Isn't a Kegel what the actual exercise is called...not your...?"

She rolls her eyes. "Fine, with your vagina or whatever. But, yeah, it's true. Nutjobs tie stuff to a weight that they put in their snatch, and they lift then squat and stuff. I saw a chick on Facebook who was carrying a surfboard down the beach once."

"What?" I gasp.

She giggles. "Imagine that, you ask some guy to meet you down the beach and you rock up with a surfboard hanging out of your pussy." She widens her eyes as if making a great epiphany. "I should put this on my Tinder profile." She holds her hands up. "I can carry your surfboard with no hands."

I laugh out loud. "Honestly, Sarah, what next?"

She laughs and then falls serious. "I think I'm going to look for another job."

"You are?" I frown. "What do you want to do?"

"I don't know. Maybe be a receptionist or something. Anything other than spending my days in this shit mailroom."

"That sounds fantastic." I smile. "You'd be great at that."

"Do you think so?"

"I know so."

"But what would you do if I left? I can't leave you in this shit-hole by yourself with Paul. He does nothing."

I sigh. I have to tell her one day, so I may as well tell her now. "Can I tell you a secret?"

"What?"

"But promise you won't get mad with me."

She rolls her eyes. "As if I'll get mad. Did you give someone upstairs a blowie?"

I laugh. "Why does it always come back to blowies with you? And no, most definitely not. I didn't really use to work in a nursery."

"You didn't?" She frowns.

"No." I watch her for a moment, pondering how much I should elaborate. Damn it, I should just tell her everything—lay it all out on the table.

"I just wanted a stress-free job for a while."

"Oh...okay."

I exhale as I brace myself for her reaction. "You know how I told you that I recently broke up with my boyfriend before I moved to London?"

"Yes."

"Well…" *Oh, how do I say this?* "I recently ran into him again, and we realised that there was still something there between us."

"Obviously, if you got back with him."

"And now it's really awkward because, well, I don't want to upset you."

"Why would you upset me?"

"Because I ran into my ex-boyfriend when I was with you."

She frowns in confusion. "When?"

"He was your date on our double date. His name is Spencer Jones."

Her mouth falls open. "Fuck…off," she whispers.

I cringe. "I'm so sorry. I didn't know how to tell you, and that's why Spencer left early that night. He was horrified."

"What?"

"I didn't know how to tell you at first. It was all so weird, and then I spent the weekend with him, and he sent me those flowers yesterday. The thing is, I really like you, and I can't lie to you anymore," I blurt out in a rush.

She shakes her head and exhales heavily. "And what is your real job?"

"I'm a lawyer," I whisper in embarrassment.

"Of course you fucking are." She leans back in her chair and hangs her head over the back. "So let me get this straight. You're smart *and* you're going out with my dream guy?"

I shrug. What else can I do?

"Hmm." She turns back to her computer.

"What does hmm mean?" I ask as I watch her.

"You can't carry a surfboard with your snatch like me, though, can you?" She raises her eyebrow sarcastically. "I bet you Spencer doesn't know that."

I giggle. "What? You can't do that."

"I could if I wanted to. If it's on my Tinder profile, it must be true."

We both burst out laughing.

"I'm sorry for lying to you. I just didn't want to upset you." I reach over and take her hand. "Are you angry with me? You have to imagine my horror when I realised who your date was."

"Nah." She shrugs. "I get it. He's totally hot, but please put me out of my misery and tell me he's a complete dud in bed."

"Completely shit," I lie.

"Good." She smirks. "I knew it."

I trail my lipstick over my lips and smile at myself in the mirror. I can't wipe the stupid smile from my face.

A date with swoony Spencer Jones, the dreamboat.

I've floated through today ever since I told Sarah the truth. I feel like a weight has been lifted from my shoulders. She was fine and says she doesn't hate me.

I mean, there is still that small issue of me telling my family about the two of us, but I'll cross that bridge when I get to it. Who knows, we may not even be seeing each other by the time my family get back.

Of course we will.

I'm trying not to let myself get attached to him, but it's hard not to. He's funny, smart, sexy, and he makes me feel so special.

I laugh the whole time I'm with him. What's between us feels so grown-up and real. I turn and take a look at my behind in the mirror. I'm wearing a tight grey dress that has long sleeves and a plunging neckline. My hair is swept up, and I'm wearing long silver earrings to match my high stilettos. I smile as I look over myself.

I look different.

I feel different.

It's as if Spencer has awakened something inside of me that has been dying to get out for years. Suddenly, I want to dress sexily because he makes me *feel* sexy. I've had this dress for ages, but I've never worn it, not once. I've put it on before but taken it off before I went out because I thought it was too much.

But I want to be too much for him. I want to be everything.

I hear the front door open, and I smile with excitement.

"Angel?" he calls from downstairs.

"Coming!"

I take one last look at myself and make my way to the stairs. Spencer stares up at me and gives me a slow, sexy smile as I walk towards him.

His hands are tucked inside his suit pockets, and the way he is looking at me might just set me on fire.

"Hi." I smile bashfully when I reach him.

"Hi," he whispers, his eyes dropping to my lips.

There it is.

The air crackles between us. "You look fucking beautiful." He takes my hand and kisses the back of it. He turns my hand over and his tongue darts out to slowly lick my wrist.

Oh, he's *just so…*

"Thank you," I murmur, distracted by the feel of his tongue on my skin.

"Maybe we should stay home and eat English instead," he whispers darkly.

My insides melt. He means he wants me to eat him instead.

I lean forward and take his face in my hands. I kiss him, softly at first, then deeper. I kiss him with everything I have because, damn, he makes me feel everything.

Spencer inhales sharply, his hands coming around to my behind. "Don't kiss me like that, angel, not unless you want to be flat on your back with your legs over my shoulders within the next thirty seconds."

I giggle against his lips. "So romantic, Mr Spencer."

He chuckles as he holds me close. "Four nights," he murmurs into my hair.

"What?" I frown.

"This is the fourth night in a row that we've seen each other."

"You say that like it's a rarity for you." I smirk.

"It is. I've never seen a woman four nights in a row before."

I smile up at him and straighten his tie. "I guess I'd better make this a perfect date for you, then, hadn't I?"

His eyes twinkle with something I haven't seen before. "You just have to turn up for my night to be perfect."

We stare at each other and something runs between us. I don't know what it is exactly. Affection? Closeness? Electricity? *Love?*

I lean up and kiss his big, soft lips. "You make me happy, Spencer Jones," I whisper.

He grins brightly, almost looking bashful. It makes my heart melt.

"Do you want to go eat some Italian now?"

"What about eating my English?" I smirk.

"Oh." He chuckles. "It's *your* English now, is it?" He grabs my behind and pulls me against his erection.

"Yes, you're my English. And no to *that*. We're going out." I take him by the hand and lead him to the door. He tries to grab my behind and I swat him away. "We *are* going out, Spence," I repeat.

He laughs. "Yeah, yeah, fine. Italian it is."

Four hours later and I am being twirled around the dance floor while smiling dreamily up at my gorgeous date.

We've talked, laughed, and eaten. It's really surprising how well we actually get along. Even without the crazy attraction and mind-blowing sex, we have something special going on between us.

"I told Sarah about us today," I admit.

He smirks down at me and raises his eyebrow. "And what did you tell her, exactly?"

One of my hands is resting in his while his other hand is resting on my hip. As usual, we're the only ones on the dance floor. I love how he doesn't care if anyone else is dancing. I think he likes it because he gets to hold me in his arms.

"I told her I was seeing you...casually."

"Oh?" His eyes hold mine as he waits for me to elaborate.

"Although there was that thing you said yesterday."

He spins me. "What thing?"

I hesitate. "When you told Wyatt and Anthony that I was your girlfriend."

He frowns. "I did, didn't I?"

I smile goofily up at him. "Uh-huh."

"What possessed me to say that?"

"At a guess, I would think that if you told my bodyguards you were my boyfriend, it was probably because you didn't want me to see anybody else."

"Really?" He smirks.

I nod. "Uh-huh."

"Do you want to see other men?" he asks.

"No." I frown. "Do *you* want to see others?"

"What would happen if I did?"

I stop dancing. "Then I would leave you to it!" I snap, annoyed. "I don't share, Spencer."

He laughs as he pulls me closer. "Are you getting possessive of me, Prescott?" I pull out of his arms, but he brings me right back to him. "I'm joking with you." He leans down and whispers in my ear, "I don't want to see anybody but you."

"That wasn't funny," I whisper back.

I feel him smile above me as he holds me close.

"What is this?" I ask.

"What's what?"

"This," I murmur. "Between us. What is it?"

He smiles down at me and then kisses me softly. "I don't know, but it's fucking good."

I smirk, mollified for the moment, and we continue to sway to the music.

"Maybe we should try this boyfriend girlfriend thing," he finally says.

I press my lips together to hide my smile. "Are you sure? I'll be a high-maintenance girlfriend. I'm not entirely sure if you're up to the job."

He spins me as he chuckles. "No?"

"I'll need lots of massages with oil, and..." I exhale heavily. "There's the whole teaching-me-about-sex thing. That's a full-time job in itself."

He smiles mischievously.

"And my family are a nightmare," I add.

"I don't want to date your family."

"And I'm setting up my own business soon, so I'll be working a lot."

He stops dancing. "You're going to do it?" he asks, suddenly falling serious.

"Do you think I can?"

"I know you can."

My eyes search his. "You know, you're the only person who believes I'm strong enough to do this."

He starts swaying us to the music again. "Isn't that what boyfriends are meant to do? Believe in their girlfriends."

I smile against his lips. "I'm glad we met, Spencer Jones."

"Me, too, angel. Me, too."

We're in bed, facing each other. It's late, but we don't want to sleep.

We're holding hands and staring at each other in the semi lit room.

It's my sixth day with Spencer, and it's been six days of utter bliss.

Six days of having this wonderful new person in my life who pleases me beyond anything I've ever dreamt of.

Tonight, over drinks in a bar, we wrote a business plan together. He helped me with costings, and we worked out steps in order of what I needed to do.

I think I'm really going to do this.

I feel like I've met the other half of myself.

I smile softly at him, and he reaches up to brush his thumb over my bottom lip. "What are you thinking about, Angel Leroo?"

I giggle at him remembering my lie from the other day. "I'm thinking that being a ballerina is really hard work."

His eyes dance with delight. "What other job would you consider doing?"

"Maybe I could be your private call girl?"

His eyes flicker with arousal. "We would have to do a lot of training to get you up to call girl standards."

I crawl over him and rub my sex along his length. His eyes hold mine as the electricity buzzes between us. "Can we start now?"

"As a matter of fact, we can."

"Just a few more stores," Spencer says. He's leading me through the shopping centre on Thursday night.

"I'm tired," I moan as he pulls me along. God, the man is on a shopping spree from hell. We've looked in at least a hundred shops in the last two hours... At least, that's how it feels.

"Stop whining, woman. You've got hours to go before bedtime." He gestures to Wyatt and Anthony, telling them that we are going across the street. He's grown accustomed to having them with us a lot more easily than I thought he would.

"We're not having sex tonight," I warn him.

"So you say." He smirks. "You'll do as you're told." He cranes his neck. "I just want to look in this toy shop up here. I think they might have what I'm looking for."

I smile as I walk behind him. Who knew that Spencer Jones, the player, would be so worried about getting just the right gift for his five-year-old niece?

He can act tough all he wants. I know better. The man is a pussycat.

"Spencer?" a man says from somewhere behind us.

We turn on the street, and Spencer's face falls immediately. He steps back as if he's just received a physical blow.

The man is in his mid-to-late fifties. He's good-looking and well-dressed.

"You got a hug for your old man?" the man asks.

Spencer stares at him but doesn't reply.

The man turns to me and smiles, holding his hand out to shake mine. "Hello, I'm Arthur."

My eyes widen. He is the mirror image of Spencer...or vice versa. *His father.*

Spencer grabs my hand and pulls me behind his back, as if I need protecting from his dad.

"Don't speak to her. Don't you dare fucking speak to her," Spencer growls.

The man's face falls. "Son..."

"Don't call me that!" Spencer snaps.

I look between the two men as they stare at each other, and my heart drops. Spence is so hurt. What on earth did his father do?

"When are you going to forgive me?" Arthur asks.

Spencer glares at him. "When hell freezes over." He turns and storms off, dragging me along behind him. I have to practically run to keep up.

He's physically shaken.

I stay silent as we walk, and once out of sight, Spencer turns to Wyatt and Anthony. "That man is not to come near Charlotte under any circumstances, do you understand me?"

Wyatt and Anthony look back at Arthur to get a better visual. "Okay."

Spencer clenches his jaw as he turns and powers through the people.

"Where are we going?" I call.

"Home," he says sharply. "I want to go home."

I lie in the deep hot bath between Spencer's legs. It's late.

Spencer has said about five words since we saw his father four hours ago.

He stares straight ahead, and his jaw is continuously clenching.

His hands run over my breasts and back down to my stomach again and again while he remains lost in thought.

I turn and kiss his bicep softly.

"When was the last time you saw your father?" I ask.

"Ten years ago."

I frown. That's a long time.

Spencer takes the soap and lathers his hands before he begins to wash my back without saying another word.

"You don't get on?" I ask.

"I despise him."

"Why?" I whisper.

He stares straight ahead for a long time, eventually kissing my temple. "When my mother was pregnant with her last child..." He pauses and frowns, as if it pains him to say the next words out loud. "He got her baby sister pregnant."

My eyes widen. "He was sleeping with your mother's younger sister?"

"Yes."

"How old were you?"

"Two."

I frown as I process the information. "What happened?"

"My aunt was seventeen..." His voice trails off. "She killed herself before the baby was born."

My mouth falls open. Dear God.

"How old was your mother?"

"Twenty-two with three children under three."

I roll over to face him. He stares at me, his eyes cold.

"And you have always hated him?"

"Just the opposite. I loved him once," he says sadly.

My heart drops.

"Every sports game, every school concert, I would look for him."

I lie down on his chest as I listen. I hate this story.

"For years I would lie in bed every night crying, and I'd pray to

God that I could be smarter so that Dad would come back and love me."

My eyes fill with tears as I imagine him being so small and crying himself to sleep. "Spence," I whisper.

"When I was twelve, my mother met my stepfather, and for the first time in my life I had a man around who was actually interested in me. Then, as I got older and I understood the dynamics of what Dad had actually done, I got angry and started to hate him for being who he was. What kind of man sleeps with his pregnant wife's sister? My aunty was only seventeen when he started sleeping with her." He shakes his head in disgust. "What kind of man walks away from his own children?"

He drops his head back to the edge of the bath, lost with a faraway look in his eyes as if he's regressed to that time. "Masters, Seb, and I found out where Dad lived when we were fourteen. We went to his house and broke in when he wasn't home, and we smashed up everything he owned."

"Did that make you feel any better?"

"No." He clenches his jaw tight. "I hate that I'm like him."

I frown instantly. "What? You're not like him, Spencer."

His sad eyes find mine. "Yeah, I am. All my life, all I've ever heard is how much I'm like my father."

"Only in the way you look," I huff. "Spence, if you were like your dad, you would have taken my virginity without a single thought for my well-being."

He runs his fingers through my hair as he looks at me.

"Spencer, is this why you've never let yourself get close to anyone?"

He blinks in surprise.

"You're so scared that you're like your father, the thought of hurting someone horrifies you and you'd rather be alone."

He clenches his jaw, and I know that's exactly how he feels.

I crawl up over him. "Baby," I whisper. "You're nothing like your father."

His eyes search mine. "How do you know?"

I smile. "I just know. If you were like him, you'd be on your fourth wife by now and have six kids to six different women."

He stares at me.

"You haven't even had a girlfriend before, you big dope."

A trace of a smile crosses his face.

"When I look at you, I see an honourable man with good morals—a man I am proud to be with."

We stare at each other for a moment before he crushes his arms around me and holds me close. I smile into his neck.

I think I just found Spencer Jones's baggage.

Big, warm hands slide around my waist from behind, and the smell of his heavenly soap lingers around me.

"Good morning, Mr Spencer." I smile as he turns me to him.

He's wearing a navy suit, his hair messed up to perfection yet again. Wearing his expensive shoes and watch, he looks every bit the multimillionaire businessman that he is.

One thing I've learnt about my man over the last week is that he has two distinct personalities. There's the carefree, funny Spence I first met who makes me laugh, and then there's the serious businessman of Spencer Jones. He's strong, deliberate, and he doesn't take shit from anybody.

Both men are beautiful, and both men are mine.

He grabs my waist and sits me up on the counter, spreading my legs around his body. He holds my jaw, angling me the way he wants me, and kisses me deeply as he slides his hands beneath my robe.

"Let's go away for the weekend."

"Really?" I smile up at him. "Where to?"

"I don't know, I'll surprise you."

"You're just full of surprises, aren't you?" I smile playfully.

He pulls my hips forward so I can feel his erection through his trousers. "How about I surprise you here on the kitchen counter with a bit of hard dicking?"

I giggle. "I am completely dicked-out."

"There's no such thing." He bites into my neck. Goose bumps scatter up my arms.

It's early on Monday morning, and after spending the most wonderful weekend in the history of all weekends, it's time for us to separate and go back to work.

"I have to go, angel," he whispers.

I smile and nod as our eyes search each other's. I feel so close to him, and I know he feels the same. There's this tenderness between us. I can feel it in his touch. When he thinks I'm asleep, his hands roam over my body in reverence, and he kisses me softly...continually...and he doesn't even know I'm awake.

He worships me.

He's so beautiful.

Spencer runs his finger down my face. I feel like I want to blurt it all out and tell him that, yeah, maybe I think I love him.

But I won't because it's too soon.

We've been together for all of ten days. Maybe I'm misjudging our closeness for love. I don't even know what the protocol for this is. When is it okay to acknowledge how you feel? When is it okay to say it out loud?

His big blue eyes hold mine. He lingers, waiting, and I have to wonder...does he feel it too?

Whatever *it* is.

"Spence..." I whisper.

"Yeah." He kisses me softly.

My stomach twists as I try to hold in the words. "I'm going to miss you today," I breathe out.

He gives me a slow, sexy smile. "Good." He kisses me deeply. "You can show me how much when I see you tonight."

His tongue slides through my lips, and he gently tugs at my bottom lip with his teeth. We kiss again, only this time he's using the same force he uses when we fuck.

There's no mistaking it, Spencer's fucking-kiss is a hell of a lot different to his relaxed-kiss. It has an edge that's as sharp as a knife. Not that I'm complaining, of course.

He lies me back over the counter, pulls my robe to the side, and slides two thick fingers into my sex. His eyes drop as he watches my body take him in.

My mouth falls open.

He gives a subtle shake of his head. "You'll be the fucking death of me, woman. I can't get enough of this sexy body of yours."

I giggle quietly.

He removes his fingers and puts them in his mouth. When he sucks them, his eyes darken and he hums in appreciation.

"I'm going to be late, Prescott."

I nod. "Go..."

With one last kiss, he turns and picks up his briefcase. "See you tonight." He flashes me a sexy wink. "Behave yourself today."

I smile from my position on the kitchen counter. "Bye."

The front door clicks closed.

I lie for a moment in a state of awe. How he can get me from zero to gagging for it in five seconds flat is beyond me.

Finally, I drag myself upstairs and make my way to the wardrobe.

I look around and smile. It's filled with Spencer's suits and clothes. Four shirts on hangers and three suits hang there like they own the space. There are also two pairs of dress shoes, a watch, his deodorant, aftershave, a laptop, and his earphones. He's taking over this damn wardrobe.

He's taking over me.

All of his things are mixed in with mine, so I begin to hang his on the other side, organising him his own space. I pick up a coat hanger with a pair of suit pants on it, and the pants slide off the hanger. I catch them midair and feel something in the pocket.

I reach inside and pull out a hotel key. I stare at it in my hand.

The Corinthia.

Why would he have a hotel key to The Corinthia? That's weird.

I move around a few things and put them in their place, but my mind is already in overdrive.

Who does he know that stays in London from out of town?

Sheridan.

Don't be stupid.

I put the key back into his suit pants, and I hang them back up in disgust.

Think about it, Charlotte, I tell myself.

He has everything dry-cleaned. He's almost OCD when it comes to his suits, so that's not an old key.

Why would he have a key to her room?

I begin to pace in the bedroom, back and forth, back and forth.

He's been seeing her for ten years. She comes to London for business often. Has she been here this week? If the suit pants are here, it means he's worn them this week while we've been together.

Has he met with her?

I pace for another twenty minutes with my mind in overdrive. This is going to send me insane.

It's an old key. It has to be an old key.

There's only one way to find out.

Stop it!

More pacing.

"Why does he have that key?" I ask the universe, hoping to get a reasonable response.

Damn this, I need to know.

I get dressed in record time and take the key from his pants again. I grab my handbag and I run to the foyer, hitting the elevator button as quickly as I can. If I go now, I can be back before the boys come to get me for work.

Fifteen minutes later, the taxi I'm in pulls up outside The Corinthia, and I tentatively step out.

What are you doing here, you fool?
Trust him!

I walk in casually, and I make my way to the elevator. I get in and scan the key, watching as it lights up.

My heart drops at once. The key is still active.

He's seen her recently, he has to have to have to have gotten this key.

I begin to hear my heartbeat ringing in my ears, and I stumble out of the elevator and lean up against the wall, unable to go upstairs. Knowing the key is active is enough.

The second elevator opens beside mine, and a beautiful woman with long dark hair steps out of it. She's wearing a navy skirt suit, and I can tell her figure is amazing. The power she emanates is overwhelming. The hairs on the back of my neck stand to attention as I watch her, and somehow I just know.

I know it's her.

"Here you are, Sheridan," a woman calls as she steps towards her and hands her a cup of coffee.

"Thank you, darling." She smiles. "Do we have the spread-sheets ready?" she asks in an American accent.

My heart drops again. That's her. She's here.

Spencer has a key to her room.

My eyes fill with tears. All I can do is stand still as I watch her and her two assistants climb into the back of a black cab and drive away.

I don't remember getting back to the Four Seasons. My mind is a clusterfuck of emotions. My heart is hammering hard in my chest.

One side of me is unable to believe that my Spencer is capable of cheating on me.

The other side is unable to believe that ten days with me could ever compete with ten years with her.

She's beautiful.

Lara's words come back to me from the first time we saw him.

"He dates power women. CEOs, fashion designers, models, women like that."

I stumble up the stairs and place the key back inside the pocket of his suit pants. I sit on the bed in a state of shock.

I have no idea what to do.

It's just gone 6:00 p.m., and I'm sitting at the kitchen counter with a glass of wine in my hand. I've had a horrible day.

Imagining him with her, all their years together, the history they share...it's driven me insane.

Does she satisfy him better than I do?

Of course she would.

My phone rings and the name Spencer lights up the screen.

"Hello," I answer.

"Hi, angel." His happy voice is practically singing down the phone.

"Hey." My nerves begin to swirl deep inside my stomach.

"Listen, baby, I forgot that I have a work dinner on tonight."

I close my eyes and get a lump in my throat. "Sure." I force the words past my lips.

"I don't know what time it's going to finish, so I'll just see you tomorrow night, okay?"

My eyes fill with tears. He hasn't slept away from me since we got together. "Okay," I whisper.

"You okay?"

I shake my head as I screw up my face in tears. "Sure," I lie. "I'll see you tomorrow. Have a nice night." I hang up, unable to hide my emotions from him for one moment longer.

I drop the phone and walk up the stairs, my body working on autopilot. I open the wardrobe door and go to the suit pants to feel inside the pocket. I check the other pocket and I check again.

The key is gone.

It was there this morning.

Spencer came back here today while I was at work to get the key.

I drop to the floor of the walk-in wardrobe, and my face creases with the agony of it all.

He's with her now.

12

Charlotte

I LIE IN THE DARK, sprawled on the sheets that still smell of him.

But he's not here.

I'm trying my hardest not to think the worst, but he came back here to get the key today when I wasn't home. It's the only explanation. Nobody else would have taken it. Nobody else even has a key to this apartment.

I have an ache in my throat from holding back all my tears. If I allow myself to cry, I will lose all control and howl to the moon all night long.

Well, Charlotte, you wanted an adult relationship, and you got one.

Warts and all.

Part of me wants to forget that I even know about the damn key, to listen to my gut and trust him.

The other part of me, my brain, wants to get dressed and go and wait at the bottom of the elevator so I can catch the bastard red-handed when he slips out of there in the morning.

If he wanted her, why isn't he just with her?

Why would he pursue me if he wanted her? Why would he stay here every night? I don't understand.

The sex. It has to be about that. The sex they have must be incomparable to what he has with me. I get a sharp twist of pain in my heart as I imagine him with her, naked and hard. Does he kiss her the way he kisses me?

I angrily swipe the tears from my eyes with the back of my hands. He told me that the last time he was with her, he imagined he was with me.

Does he imagine her when he's with me?

I close my eyes, tasting bile. The thought is sickening. My mind goes back to the conversation I had with Lara on that first night when she told me who Spencer was.

"Mr Spencer. Don't bother even looking at him," Lara said.

"Why not?"

"He's the most eligible bachelor in London, and an appalling rake." She raised an eyebrow for effect. *"He's loaded...and I don't just mean his wallet."*

I close my eyes in disgust. I was warned. Many times, I was warned, but like a moth to a flame, I had to have him anyway.

Do they make gentle love, or does he fuck her hard? I get a vision of him naked again. And her...she's beautiful. I bet she's even more beautiful naked.

I clench my jaw so hard, my teeth ache.

My fury begins to pump, and I angrily swipe the tears away again. How dare he do this to me? How dare he throw me to the side as soon as she comes to town?

He made me feel so special, and then to lie to my face... Oh, this is a different type of betrayal than I've ever felt before. This one hurts.

I roll over and punch the pillow hard, and that's when I hear the door downstairs. Huh?

I sit up to listen.

I hear keys hit the side table, and I glance at the clock. It's 10:10 p.m.

He's here.

I quickly wipe my eyes and lie back down, pretending to be asleep. My heart is beating so hard, I lie in the silence and I screw up into my pillows.

Stop it, stop it, stop it. Don't let him see you weak.

I lie with my back to the door on my side. When he walks in, I can feel his presence.

He stands still and watches me for a moment.

Does he feel guilty? I hope so. More tears fill my eyes.

"I'm home, angel," he whispers as he sits beside me on the bed. He leans down and kisses my cheek.

Unable to help it, I turn to him and his face falls. My eyes are red and swollen. I've been in tears since I found the key was gone.

"You've been crying." He frowns. "What's wrong?"

I stay silent because I don't know what to say. I mean, what is there *to* say? What can I possibly say that will make this better?

"Charlotte?" he whispers as he flicks the lamp on to see my face. "What's wrong, baby?"

"You tell me."

He frowns. "What does that mean?"

My eyes hold his. "Do you have something to tell me, Spencer?"

"Like what?"

My traitorous tears fill my eyes again. Damn these weeping bitches.

"Charlotte, why are you crying?" he demands.

I shake my head and roll away from him. I can't even look him in the eye.

"What the fuck is wrong with you?" he snaps.

I clench my jaw. "Get out."

"What?"

"You heard me. Go back to Sheridan."

"What the hell?" He stands, daring to look completely outraged. "What the fuck is that supposed to mean?"

Angry blood rages through my body like a rapid river. Does he

238

think I'm fucking stupid? I roll back onto my back as contempt fills me.

"Did you come back to the apartment today, Spencer?" I ask him calmly.

His eyes narrow, and he swallows a lump in his throat. "Yeah, I did, actually."

I smirk. "Did you imagine my face again when you were fucking her tonight?"

His eyes widen and he shakes his head, connecting the dots. "I didn't... I don't...it's not what you think."

"Get out," I say coldly.

"It's not like that."

"Get the fuck out!" I cry as I lose all control. The stupid tears break free again, stealing my bravery act. I wipe them away with my forearm.

"She...she came to me last week," he stammers. "She wanted to see me. I said no."

I stare at him.

"Someone came into my office just after she left, and I shoved the key in my pocket to hide it from them. After that, I forgot all about it."

I feel my back molars nearly crack from me clenching my jaw so hard.

"I remembered it this morning on my way to work." He runs his hands through his hair. "I panicked, Charlotte. I didn't want you to find it and think the wrong thing."

I roll my eyes in disgust. Likely story.

"I came back here today, got it, and I threw it in the bin."

I fly out of bed like a madwoman. "Of course you did." I storm to the door. "Right after you fucked her."

"Charlotte, I promise you, I haven't been with Sheridan."

I stare at him through my tears.

"I was at a work dinner. I have clients who have flown in from China."

"Why didn't you tell me she came to you?" I cry.

"Because she doesn't fucking matter to me!" he yells back.

My face screws up in tears. "Do you love her?" I sob.

"No, I fucking love *you*." He shakes his head. "And I have no idea how that's even possible. I've known you for five fucking minutes."

I stare at him, lost for words.

"People who love each other don't tell lies, Spencer."

I turn away and storm downstairs. I can't be near him right now. I have no idea what to believe.

"What about you?" he calls from the top step. "You haven't told me one fucking lie since we've been together?"

I turn to him sharply. "Never! I have not lied to you once. Not once."

"Bull-fucking-shit." He charges down the stairs and grabs my arm, dragging me out of the front door and into the corridor near the elevator. "Look in the bin."

"What?"

"Look in the fucking bin. I threw the key in there this morning on my way out of the apartment." He picks up the bin in the corridor and tips it upside down like a crazy person. The lid flies off, and a lone hotel key card falls out onto the carpet. "Check the security footage from Mr Wong's in Chinatown, you fucking know-it-all. I was there until twenty minutes ago."

With that, he turns and storms back into the apartment, leaving me to stand still as my heart beats hard in my chest.

I close my eyes, instantly full of regret.

Shit.

I walk back inside the apartment to find him marching up the stairs.

I follow him carefully and quietly.

He's furious, raging like a bull. He storms into the wardrobe and begins throwing his stuff on the bed like a madman.

I fold my arms over my chest. "What did you expect me to think?" I snap. "I find a key in the morning then I come home and

240

find it's gone. Then you've conveniently had something on all of a sudden and won't be coming over."

"While we're talking about lies... I want to know yours." He sneers.

I wither. "I don't know what you're talking about."

"You are pissing me off, Charlotte Prescott," he growls. "Get out of my fucking face before I lose my shit." He storms up the hall, and I find myself running after him.

"What lie?" I cry. "What are you talking about, Spencer?"

"Don't tell me that you don't have feelings for the man who took your virginity, because I know you do. It's fucking eating me alive."

Huh...?

"Do you really fucking expect me to believe that you wait twenty-five years to lose your virginity, only to give it to someone you don't care about?"

I roll my eyes.

"I'm not fucking stupid," he barks, making me jump. "Who is he?"

We stare at each other as we pant, both of us furious. I'm not telling him like this, he's too angry. He'll go berserk about me lying to him in the first place.

I go to touch him, but he flicks my hand off his arm. "Don't fucking touch me, you piss me off." He storms out. I hear him walk down the hall, and then the spare bedroom door slams shut.

I drag my hands through my hair.

I walk up to the spare bedroom and stand outside the door.

I hear him kick off his shoes, and then I hear something hit the wall. I hear the blankets get thrown back. "Fuck off!" he mutters angrily to himself before something else hits the wall.

I slide down the wall and sit on the floor in the hallway. At least he hasn't left me.

But what now?

Edward

I run through the profit and loss sheets for Macao, checking the losses myself with a calculator. They're two percent higher than expected, and I want to find where we are slipping. My father is in his office next to me, going through some refurbishment details with our interior designers.

My phone rings, and the name Alexander York lights up the screen.

I smile and answer with, "Yorkie, how are you?"

"Good, good." He laughs.

Alexander is one of my closest friends. The two of us went to boarding school together and have only gotten closer over the years.

"Why are you calling me at..." I glance at my watch. "5:00 a.m. your time? Did you wet the bed?"

"Ha, very funny. I've been contemplating calling you all week. It's finally gotten the better of me."

I frown, suddenly interested. "What's up?"

"You know how I took Charlotte to the charity ball last Saturday night?"

"Yeah."

"There was this guy sniffing around her."

"Who?"

"Spencer Jones."

I immediately type the name into Google on my laptop.

"Define sniffing," I urge while I wait.

"Well, that's the thing: I don't know anything for certain, but it's left me feeling uneasy all week, so I thought I'd better let you know."

A collection of images appears, and I scroll through each of them, reading the first headline.

Bad Romeo Caught with Three Women in the Same Day.

I clench my jaw. "What happened?"

"That's the thing, they seemed to know each other. They were familiar when talking, and then he was kissing her hand."

"Kissing her?" I snap and sit forward in my chair. "You're fucking kidding me, right?"

"Afraid not. I approached Spencer at the bar when he was out of her earshot and asked him what he was doing with Charlotte Prescott."

I continue to scroll through the images of him with different women.

"What did he say?"

"He said, and I quote, *Whatever the fuck I like*."

I narrow my eyes. "Do you know this guy?"

"Yes, and I fucking hate him. He's a womanising cad who sleeps with every supermodel in town."

"Who is he?" I Google his bio.

"He owns a successful steel manufacturing company...does all right for himself."

"Why do you hate him?"

"The guy stole a girl off me years ago and it escalated from there. I've had run-ins with his friends too. He hangs out with Julian Masters and Sebastian Garcia."

I narrow my eyes even farther. I know Julian Masters. Our fathers have done business together in the past. I saw him once at Madison's when he was coming out of a suite. He didn't see me, though. If he goes to Madison's, Spencer would too.

"What happened at the ball?"

"Nothing while I was there. He talked to Charlotte, he and I had words, and then later in the night, my mother fell ill, so I had to take her home an hour before it finished."

"You left Charlotte there alone?" I frown.

"She was with my sister Mariella, and she knew everyone at our table. Her guards were there, too, of course. But here's the thing, as soon as I left, she was back at the bar, talking to Spencer Jones again."

My fury begins to rise. "Did they leave together?"

"No, separately." He pauses, as if he has something else to say.

"What?"

"Look, I don't know if I'm imagining it, but I called around to see her the next day unannounced and she was...half-dressed, and she most definitely did not want me in her apartment."

I sit forward in my seat, glaring at the images of this Spencer Jones with what seems like every beautiful woman on the planet. "You think he was there with her?" I ask.

"No, but it was obvious she didn't want me there." He pauses. "I don't know, it just felt off, man. I can't put my finger on it."

"Hmm."

"Anyway, it's been eating at me ever since, so I thought I should let you know. Spencer is the last fucking person that Charlotte should be associated with."

I glare at the computer screen with a sarcastic smile plastered on his face.

"I can see that." I inhale sharply. "Don't mention this to Father or anyone else."

"I won't."

"I'll check it out, thank you. You're a good friend." I hang up and sit back in my chair, studying the playboy in front of me.

"Over my dead body will you get your hands on her," I whisper. "Over my dead body."

Charlotte

I wake with a start, and I can tell by the light of the room that it's now early morning. I get out of bed, go to the bathroom, and tiptoe down the hall.

My man didn't come and get into bed with me when he'd cooled down like I thought he would. I've been thinking about it all night, and Spencer is right... I should have asked him before I jumped to conclusions. But he should have told me she came to him, and he was being deceitful when he hid the key from me. We're both in the wrong here, and I won't take all the blame.

I open the bedroom door and my shoulders slump. The crumpled-up bed is empty.

He must have just left, although he normally leaves at 5:30 a.m. Great.

I head downstairs and make myself a cup of tea, then I sit at the kitchen counter as I drink in silence.

What the hell do I do now?

Damn this, I'm not spending the day worrying.

I take out my phone and dial his number.

"Hello," he answers in a clipped tone.

"Hi." I smile nervously. "Why didn't you wake me up before you left?"

"What's the point?"

"Spence," I sigh. "What did you expect me to think?"

"Exactly what you did." He pauses. "I am my father's son, after all."

My heart drops. "Stop it and come back home. We'll work it out."

"I can't, I have to work."

I close my eyes. Damn it, why did I fly off the handle before talking to him?

"Will I see you tonight?"

"I'm busy."

I frown.

"See you later." He hangs up.

Five hours to stew on something is a long time. I sort through the mail on the table like a zombie, my mind with Spencer and how he doesn't think he'll see me tonight.

He said that he loved me.

"Are you okay?" Sarah frowns. "You've looked like shit all day."

"Not really, I feel sick," I lie.

"Go home." Paul tuts. "We don't want it."

"Yeah, go home," Sarah says. "We're entitled to sick days. Just go, and we'll tell them after you leave that you were throwing up."

"Really?" I could go and see Spencer at work. "Is that okay?" I ask.

"Sure! Off you go."

I can't stand the thought of him thinking that I think he's like his father.

I need to fix this situation right now.

I'm worried sick about this.

Half an hour later, I'm walking into Spencer's building with Wyatt and Anthony close behind me. I read the lists of businesses in the directory in the foyer.

Universal Steel — Fourteenth floor

We take the elevator up, and my heart beats furiously in my chest. Up until last night, I wouldn't have thought Spencer had a temper, but now I know that he does, and it's a little scary. The doors open up to reveal a huge office space. It's modern and decorated black and white with huge, brightly coloured abstract paintings along the walls.

The entire back wall is made of windows that overlook London.

Wow, this is something else.

Wyatt and Anthony stand by the door. I turn and give them a nervous smile. "I won't be long."

I walk through to the large reception area with my stomach in my throat. What if he doesn't want to see me?

"Can I help you?" the receptionist asks.

"Yes." I smile awkwardly. "I'm here to see Spencer Jones."

"Do you have an appointment?"

"No."

She looks me up and down, and I raise my eyebrow. *Who is this?* The way she looks at me sparks something in my brain, and I

246

hear the words leave my mouth before my filter kicks in. "Tell him that his girlfriend Charlotte is here."

A frown crosses her forehead before she quickly recovers. "Just a moment."

She taps a number on the phone and speaks through the headset.

"Yeah," I hear Spencer's bored voice say.

"I have a Charlotte here." Her eyes come back to mine. "She says she's your girlfriend."

He exhales heavily. "Send her in."

My stomach drops. It's not exactly the enthusiastic response I was hoping for.

Maybe this *is* it?

She fakes a smile. "This way, please."

I follow her through the office and people stop what they are doing to look over at me. I keep my eyes on the floor. I'm so nervous, I can hardly lift my head.

She opens the last door and fakes a smile.

"Thank you." I look nervously into the office, and there he sits behind a large black desk made of wood and glass. He's wearing a grey suit, white shirt, and a pink tie, looking as edible as I've ever seen him. His eyes rise to meet mine and his jaw clenches.

The door shuts behind me.

"Hi," I say nervously, twisting my fingers in front of me.

His eyes hold mine, and he rolls a pen across the desk with four fingers. "Hi."

I walk around and sit on the desk in front of him, watching as he leans back in his chair.

"I shouldn't have jumped to conclusions."

He stares at me, devoid of emotion.

"I'm sorry."

He nods once.

"But I'm not the only one in the wrong here," I add.

He nods again.

"This is where you say sorry, too, Spence."

"I was only trying to protect you."

"From her?"

He shrugs.

"Do I need protecting from her?"

He shrugs again and remains silent. I don't think he knows what to say.

"I saw the key was missing, and then you called to say you weren't coming home."

"I know how this looks." He sighs.

"Then why are you angry with me?"

"I'm not angry, I'm disappointed."

"That I thought you were with somebody else?" I frown.

"Yes. Why would you think that? Have I given you any reason to doubt me?"

"No, baby," I whisper as I crawl into his lap.

"This is about your ten years with Sheridan," I say softly. "I don't know how to compete with that kind of history, Spence, and it scares the hell out of me."

He slides his hand up my thigh. "I told you I'm not in love with her."

I smile softly. "You said you loved me."

His eyes fall to the desk, and I place my finger under his chin to bring his face back to mine. "Is that still true?"

His jaw clenches as his eyes hold mine.

"Spencer..."

He stares at me.

I wrap my arms around him and hold him tight.

"Okay, well, I have something to tell you." I run my fingers through his stubble. "You were right, I could never sleep with someone I didn't have feelings for."

Spencer

My heart sinks from her admission. "Who is he?"

She smiles softly. "He has white teeth and he wears a size-thir-

248

teen shoe."

I frown.

"He's on the navigation team for Santa Claus."

My face falls. "What?"

"He likes naughty kittens because he's a big naughty kitten himself."

"I don't understand."

She gives a subtle shake of her head. "There was no other man, Spence."

My eyes search hers.

"Only you," she says softly.

I frown in confusion.

"You're the only man I've ever slept with—the only person I have feelings for."

My heart free-falls. "Are you serious?" I whisper.

She smiles and nods gently. "I wanted it to be you—"

"Why would you lie to me about that?" I breathe out, cutting her off.

I should have made it better for her. I try and remember how I took her the very first time. Was I rough? Did I hurt her?

"I knew that you were too scared to go through with it because you thought I was going to fall in love with you," she admits.

My eyes hold hers.

She bends and kisses me softly. Her tongue gently slides through my lips, and I feel my arousal roll in.

"And it turns out you had a good reason to be scared of that... because I have," she whispers.

I drop my head as emotion takes over, our foreheads coming together.

This feels so...real.

She puts her finger under my chin and brings my face up to meet hers. "I know this is crazy and we don't even know each other properly yet, but I was devastated last night when I thought you were with Sheridan."

I shake my head and look up at her. "How does this happen in ten days, angel? I don't understand what's going on here."

She smiles. "You always hear people say that when you know, you know, right?"

Oh God...this beautiful woman.

"I know," I whisper against her lips.

"I know too. I've known all along." Her lips take mine and our kiss is deep and passionate. It's everything I've never had. Suddenly, I'm desperate to be alone with her—to show her what she means to me.

"Let's go home," I murmur into her hair.

"To your house?"

I stare at the perfect angel in front of me, and a thought of pure horror runs through my mind.

She can't stay in my bed.

I need a new mattress before we stay at my house. I don't want her sleeping where I've been with another woman.

I want a new start...*with her.*

"Let's go to your house. It's easier for the boys," I lie. "We'll stay at mine tomorrow night when we've made arrangements for them."

"Okay."

I stand and take her in my arms, holding her tight.

There's no other man.

Only me!

This feeling, this overwhelming feeling I get from her, is like nothing I've ever felt before. I can't get close enough.

It's comforting, and yet it terrifies the hell out of me. She's not just anyone, and I know for certain that her family are not going to accept me. I grip her tighter as the reality that I may lose her sets in.

"Let's go home, baby," she whispers against my shoulder.

I kiss her big, soft lips. "Let's go."

I pack up my desk and we walk out through the reception area hand in hand.

"I'm leaving for the day," I tell Rosalie, my PA.

"Okay, Mr Jones." She smiles as she looks us both up and down.

"Goodbye." Charlotte smiles to her. "Lovely to meet you."

"You too!" Rosalie calls back.

We walk through to the foyer to find Anthony and Wyatt waiting patiently.

"Hi, guys," I say to them both.

"Hey," they both reply.

The four of us get into the elevator and I push the button.

I want to know why Charlotte is guarded. There has to be something more sinister going on than she is led to believe, and I intend to find out exactly what that something is.

"My car is out on the street today. Where are you parked?" I ask them. I don't want Charlotte to be without them with her for a moment.

"Around the block," Anthony answers.

"We'll just go down and wait in my car until you come around, and then we'll pull out in front of you, okay?" I ask.

"Okay, good," Wyatt replies.

We walk out of the building hand in hand, across the quadrangle area.

"Charlotte?" a man calls out. "Charlotte Prescott..."

We both turn and see a photographer smiling as soon as he realises it's her. Before we can do anything, he begins to take photos. The camera clicks away picture after picture.

Charlotte's step falters.

"Keep walking!" Wyatt snaps.

Charlotte puts her head down, and I drag her by the hand as Wyatt approaches the photographer.

"Get the fuck off!" the photographer cries out when Wyatt tries to take the camera from him. They get into a struggle, leaving Charlotte and me to head to the car as quickly as we possibly can.

"Meet us at home!" Anthony yells, turning and running back to help Wyatt confiscate the camera.

I open the car door and Charlotte slides in. I run around to my side and, once secured in, we take off quickly.

I look out through the rearview mirror to see the two guards in a full-on scuffle with two photographers now.

"Oh my God," Charlotte whispers, dropping her head into her hands.

I grip the steering wheel with white-knuckle force, trying to concentrate on the road ahead.

Looks like the war is about to begin.

13

Spencer

WE DRIVE IN SILENCE, but my eyes keep drifting back to the road behind us to make sure we aren't being followed. Charlotte sits in the passenger seat, staring through the windscreen.

I pick up her hand and kiss her fingertips. "We have four or five days before those pictures go live, and that's if we're lucky."

She glances over to me. "How do you know that?"

I clench my jaw. "I just know. If they want top dollar, then they'll have to approach several tabloids to sell the images."

She pulls her hand from my grip and gives a subtle shake of her head, somewhat annoyed that I've been through this before.

I hate that I have too.

I exhale heavily as my eyes drift to the road behind us once again. They can't find out where she's staying, or her job is gone.

Great. It's just my luck that a photographer who recognised her was outside my place of work. What are the chances? Nobody even knows who she is in London.

"You'll need to tell your father that you went out with me," I say. "Warn him of the images that could be coming out."

She runs her hands through her hair. "It's not that easy, Spencer."

My eyes flicker over to her. "It is, actually. You are allowed to see people."

"You don't understand." She rolls her eyes.

"Then why don't you help me to."

"Don't get snappy with me. You think I like this drama?"

"All I'm saying is that you are an adult, and you're doing nothing wrong. If they can't be happy with our relationship, then it's too bad for them."

She folds her arms over her chest.

"Am I right?" I snap as my eyes flick between the road and her.

She stays silent.

"You tell me right fucking now, Charlotte. What are you going to do when they find out?"

She shrugs.

"I'm waiting."

"I don't know how to handle them." She gets teary and shakes her head. "It's overbearing, Spence, and I hate that they're going to judge you without even knowing you."

I screw up my face in disgust. "I don't give a fuck whether they judge me or not. But they will not judge you. I won't have it."

She stares at me blankly. "What's that supposed to mean?"

"It means that you're an adult, and if they try to stop me from seeing you—"

"Which they will," she interrupts.

"What are you going to do about it?"

She shrugs, her face sad.

It's obvious that this is too much for her to take on by herself.

"I'll take care of it," I tell her.

"Meaning what?" She frowns.

"I'll take care of Edward and your father for you."

She huffs. "You haven't met them, Spencer. They don't get taken care of."

I glance over at her. "It's taken me thirty-eight years to find you, Charlotte. I won't be forced out of your life by your family."

"I don't want you to be." She softens and reaches over to raise and kiss my hand. "They'll push you away, though. I know they will. They'll make it so difficult for you that you'll eventually leave." Her voice cracks on the last word.

I pull the car over to the side of the road and turn to her. "Angel..." I smile softly and cup her face in my hand. "I'm not going anywhere."

Her eyes search mine. "Promise me that they won't come between us."

"*I'm* the one asking *you* to promise *me* that."

"What do you mean?" She frowns, confused.

"We'll go to Nottingham together and tell them you are moving to London. Then you'll leave with me, with or without their permission."

Her face falls and she shakes her head. "Spencer, they'll go insane if I do that. I can't do it that way. They'll come after me with guns blazing."

My eyes hold hers. "Charlotte..."

She stares at me through her unshed tears, already terrified of their reaction.

"It's time," I say calmly.

She drops her head and stares at her hands in her lap.

"You are not a child. You are not a possession to be owned. Stop allowing them this control over you. You're with me now. We're happy, and we're not hurting anyone."

"But..." She stops herself from saying something.

"But what?"

"What if I leave them and then..." Her voice trails off.

"And then we don't work out?" I frown.

Her eyes rise to meet mine, and I know that's it—that's what she's most afraid of.

"Then we make it work out," I tell her.

"How do you make something work out?"

I smile softly at the beautiful woman in front of me, and I lean over and kiss her, brushing her hair back from her face. "I don't know. I've never done it before. We'll work it out together."

She wraps her arms around me, and we hold each other close.

"Just give me the permission I need to handle this for you... please," I say into her hair. "You're driving this ship, angel, not me."

"What are you going to do?" she whispers.

"Nothing sinister, but I'm not taking their shit, and I can't stand by and let them have you living in fear like you do."

"They're my family, Spence. I love them."

I cup her jaw. "I know, angel, and they love you back. Once they see you're happy and taken care of, they'll ease up. They *will* accept us eventually."

She smiles softly.

"But you need to let me lead us into battle, okay? It's not just going to happen without a fight." I kiss her. "You already know that, and you need to prepare yourself for a few hard times."

She stares at me.

"They'll tell you I'm not the man for you, and to not rush into anything. They'll refuse to let you move to London if you let them, and what happens then? You live in Nottingham miserable, and I'll live in London, unable to visit you. Your security will be tightened, and we won't see each other again."

Her eyes hold mine and then she nods with renewed purpose. "You're right. That's exactly how it will go." She turns and stares out through the front windshield, deep in thought, and then she turns to me again. "You take the reins."

I lean over and kiss her softly, placing my hand on her thigh. Once she's calm, I pull back out into the traffic.

That's exactly what I'm going to do.

I sip my scotch as I sit at the bar of the hotel. I'm waiting for Wyatt and Anthony. When we got back here, I took Charlotte up to the room and called the two of them, asking them to meet me here instead of at the apartment. I need to talk to them without Charlotte hearing.

I dial Seb's number while I wait for them to arrive.

"Hey." I sip my scotch. "Man, I need a huge favour."

"What is it?" Seb asks.

"Can you go to the shops for me in the morning and buy me a king-size orthopaedic mattress and get it delivered to my place by tomorrow?"

"Erm, why?"

"Because Charlotte is coming over tomorrow night and I have meetings all day tomorrow. I'm snowed under with crap over here."

"What the fuck do you need a new mattress for?"

"I can't have Charlotte sleeping on that mattress."

"Why not?"

"Do you know how many women I've had in that bed?" I whisper angrily as I try to keep my voice down.

"Oh, for fuck's sake," he snaps. "You're being ridiculous. She won't know."

"I'll know. I need a new fucking mattress. I won't have her sleeping in it."

"What the fuck is happening to you?"

"I don't know!" I snap. "Just do it."

"Why don't you get one of your PAs to do this shit for you?"

"Oh, yeah, like I can say, *Can you get me a new mattress so my new girlfriend won't have to sleep on my sex-stained old one?* You just don't say that shit to your personal assistant, Sebastian."

He chuckles. "Spence, you're the most fucking ridiculous man I know."

I smirk at the sound of his laugh. "Right?"

"This is like the *Princess and the Pea* fairy tale."

I roll my eyes and sip my scotch. "Yeah, and the fucking villain is about to come home. Paps photographed us together today."

"You reckon the old man's coming home to cut your balls off?"

"Without a doubt."

"Ha. The fun's about to begin. I'll get popcorn."

"Can you help me tomorrow or not?" I sigh.

"Why do I get to do all your shitty jobs when you have staffing of four hundred?"

I smile broadly. "Perks of being my best friend."

"Stop sucking up, asshole."

I sip my scotch. "What have you been doing, anyway?"

"Angela called me today."

I close my eyes and pinch the bridge of my nose. "No. Get that shit out of your fucking head…right now."

He laughs. "I knew you'd love that one."

Angela is his ex-wife's sister. She's a widow with kids, and Seb has had a soft spot for her for years. "What did she want?" I ask.

"Just to check in on me."

I roll my eyes. "I bet she did." I huff. "I'm sure she has venom in her veins like her sister. It probably runs in the family, like a witch thing."

He laughs again. "Good Lord, if Prescott doesn't kill you first, I'm quite sure one of your cellmates will fuck you to death once you go inside for my ex-wife's murder."

I roll the scotch around in my mouth with a smirk. "It would be worth it to rid you of that wench."

He exhales heavily. "So, what am I buying?"

"King-size orthopaedic cushion-top mattress. Make it hypoallergenic."

"Okay, I'll call you from the store."

"I have these Chinese clients in town, so I'll be with them most of the day. I can be home from four for the delivery."

"I've never heard of a bed being delivered on the same day as the purchase."

"Can you just make it happen?" I sigh, holding my forehead. "Fuck the saleswoman in the back room if you have to."

He chuckles. "Where are you? It sounds noisy."

"In the hotel bar. I'm waiting for Charlotte's guards. I want to talk to them with her not around."

"Why, what's up?"

"I want to know why she's so guarded."

"Yeah, me and Masters were talking about this the other night. Something must have happened in the past, we reckon."

"I agree." I sigh.

The stool next to me shifts, and Anthony and Wyatt slide into the seats. "Got to go," I tell Seb. I hang up and turn to the boys. "Did you get the film?"

Anthony exhales heavily. "Nope. There were two of them with cameras. If we were caught manhandling them, it would have all been caught on camera."

"Shit." I sigh. "You guys want a drink?"

"No, I'm good," Wyatt says.

"We're off the clock now. You've finished for the day," I urge. I want them relaxed.

"Okay, just a beer. Make it two Coronas," Anthony replies.

"Can I have two Coronas and another scotch, please?" I ask the waitress.

"Sure." She smiles as she moves away to grab the drinks.

"Well." I sigh. "Those pictures will be live in a few days. They'll be selling them to the highest bidder as we speak. You're both going to have to call your boss and let him know that Charlotte and I have been on a date if you want to keep your jobs."

Anthony nods. "Looks like it."

"I'll take care of Edward," I tell them.

Wyatt smirks. "Edward Prescott is not someone you can take care of." The waitress puts the drinks down in front of us. "Thank you," they both mutter before taking a sip.

I rub my fingers through my two-day growth. "What makes you so sure that he won't approve of me seeing Charlotte?" I ask.

Anthony shrugs. "Nobody will ever be good enough for her in his eyes."

"I can see why," I mutter under my breath. "Most certainly not me."

Wyatt smirks and sips his beer.

"Tell me, for interest's sake, why is she so guarded?" I ask.

They exchange looks.

"I won't say anything to her or anyone else, of course. I don't want her frightened." I sip my scotch. "But I would like to know what we're dealing with here."

Their eyes meet again, and Wyatt shrugs.

"There was another car involved in Francesca Prescott's fatal car accident."

I frown. "Her mother?"

"Yes, but it's never been known who was driving the other car."

I think for a moment. "Does Charlotte know this? Are they sure the other car was there intentionally?"

"No, not at all. Charlotte's not to be told. The tyre marks suggest that she was run off the road by another vehicle. No trace on who, though, and no proof that it is actually sinister, but it's just enough for the fear of God to have been put into them about Charlotte's safety." Anthony drinks his beer. "She's adored."

"By all that know her," I agree.

They nod.

"And that's it?" I ask. "The car accident five years ago is what keeps you two in a job?" I shrug.

Anthony exhales, and his eyes hold mine. That's when I know there is more. "What else?" I ask sharply.

"I've been with the Prescotts for ten years," Anthony says. "I've witnessed a lot of meetings going on, and there is bad blood around the family...a lot of it."

"Such as?"

"When it comes to business, they're ruthless. Nobody stands in their way."

I frown. "Just Edward?"

"Both of them. If someone wanted to hurt them, Charlotte is the way to do it." He sips his beer. "The *only* way to do it."

"Do you feel she's in danger?" I ask, my eyes holding his. "I mean amongst the people you've seen them deal with, in your honest opinion, is Charlotte a target?"

260

"Massively," he answers flatly. "Why do you think she has two guards on her all the time? Why do you think they keep her hidden at the estate and away from paparazzi?"

I exhale heavily, and my mind begins to race. We remain silent as we fall into our own thoughts.

"Can you do me a favour?"

"What?" Anthony asks.

"Give us a few days before you tell them, if you can. I've organised to sublet an apartment in my building for you two. Charlotte will be staying there with me from now on."

The boys exchange looks, and Wyatt smirks. "You really think they're going to let her stay with you?"

My eyes hold his. "They won't have a fucking say in it."

Anthony raises his eyebrow and sips his beer.

"What does that look mean?" I ask.

"That means you should watch your fucking back, man. I wouldn't want to be on the bad side of Edward Prescott."

"I'm not scared of Edward. Charlotte is the only person who matters to me." I stand and take my wallet out, throwing some money onto the bar. "Catch you guys tomorrow."

I walk through the bar and out into the foyer. I take out my phone and scroll through my numbers.

Alan Shapiro

I dial his number and nod at a woman as she walks past me.

"Hello, Spencer," Alan answers cheerfully.

"Hi." I smile. "How is my favourite lawyer this afternoon?"

"Good, good. I haven't spoken to you in a long time. How can I help you?"

"I need a contract written up urgently."

"Sure thing. What kind?"

I frown, not knowing how to put this. "I have a new girlfriend, and we may be moving in together."

"Oh, okay. You need a cohabitation agreement. How much are you prepared to give her when you break up?"

"We won't break up, and it's not for my protection. It's for hers."

He pauses. "I don't understand. What do you want to give her?"

"I want a contract drawn up saying that I want none of her money if we separate."

"I doubt she'll have more money than you." He scoffs.

"Trust me, she does."

"Okay, so you want the contract stating that you both leave the relationship with no financial crossover. What you both came in with, you leave with."

"Yes."

"What's her name."

"Charlotte Prescott."

There's silence on the other end of the line.

"You there?" I ask.

"Not Harold Prescott's daughter?"

"That's her."

"Fuck." I hear him typing, and I know he's Googling her estimated wealth. "Spence, you need to cover yourself. Don't be stupid and walk away from that fortune. If you marry her, you're entitled to it."

"I don't want it." I roll my eyes as I feel my anger begin to bubble. "Just write me up the fucking contract, okay?"

He exhales heavily. "Think this through, will you?"

"No. Can you do me the contract, or will I need to get someone else to do it? I don't want a single penny of her fucking money."

"Four billion pounds, Spencer."

"I don't give a fuck. Get the contract to me as soon as possible."

"You're an idiot if you sign this."

"Stop pissing me off," I snarl.

"You pay me for advice. My advice to you is to not sign a cohabitation agreement. Not if she's not asking for one."

"Goodbye, Alan. Email me the contract tomorrow, please."

"Don't say I didn't warn you." He sighs.

I hang up and stuff my phone into my pocket angrily. For fuck's sake, why can't Charlotte be a broke orphan? My feelings for her would be the same, and I wouldn't have to deal with all this fucking bullshit that goes with her name. I inhale heavily to try and calm myself down, and I take the elevator up to her floor and apartment. I walk in and close the door behind me, and suddenly I feel calm.

It's a peaceful calm that I only get from being alone with Charlotte.

It's just me, her, and all the rest of the bullshit is on the other side of that door.

"Angel?" I call.

"Up here." I hear her sweet voice call from the bedroom upstairs.

"I hope you're naked."

She laughs, and I know she is. I smile and take the stairs two at a time.

I walk into the bedroom to find her lying in bed. Steam is flowing from the bathroom, and I know she's freshly showered.

"Hi," she whispers.

"Hi." I feel the blood start to rush to my cock.

"Everything all right?"

"It is now."

"Now?"

"Now that I'm here with you."

She smiles softly and holds her arms up for me to go to her. She's in her robe, lying on her back, which is propped up against the pillows. The smell of her soap floats through the air.

"Are you naked and in bed for any particular reason?" I ask.

She smiles and gets up on her knees, crawling over to the side of the bed. I bend and kiss her. Her lips are big and soft, and all coherent thought begins to leave me.

I can't think when she's naked near me. I lose my ability to think clearly.

"I'm naked for my man." She pulls me to her by the suit pants. I watch on as she slowly slides down my zipper and kisses my cock through my briefs.

I run my fingers through her hair as I watch her. She's blossoming before my eyes.

Every day, a little more of her sexuality comes out. She becomes a little more daring and I feel myself fall that little bit harder. She kisses me through my black boxers. I kick off my shoes and push my trousers down. She takes off her robe and then goes up on her knees, unbuttoning my shirt as I smile down at her. I'm conscious that I need to let her take the lead whenever she wants to.

Slowly but surely, she's getting there—getting to the place where soon I'll be able to take her as I want to. It took her a week just to be comfortable being naked in front of me.

It's been hard holding myself back, to consider her needs before mine, because I'm petrified of hurting her.

She slides my shirt over my shoulders, and then her hands drop to my boxers, and she slides them down my legs. Her hand goes around my cock, and a deep rumbling begins in my balls. I put my hand over hers to guide her, slowly stroking myself as she watches on in wonder. Pre-ejaculate beads at the head.

"Lick me, angel," I whisper, brushing her hair back from her forehead. "Taste me."

She smiles and in slow motion bends. I watch as her tongue slides out and over my end. I clench my stomach in appreciation.

Every time, every fucking time I'm with her, I have to concentrate not to blow too soon.

She's too perfect.

This, what's between us, is too perfect.

She takes me into her mouth, and with her eyes glued on mine, she takes me deep down her throat.

Fuck.

My mouth falls open as I watch on. Her eyes are closed.

No man has ever had her before. I had my suspicions. I thought I felt her hymen break, but I wondered if it was wishful thinking on my part. Thank God it wasn't.

She's mine. *All mine.*

As she sucks, I close my eyes and drop my head back. It's so good.

I need it harder...so much harder. I put my hand over hers as it follows her lips, and I stroke myself harder. "Like this," I whisper to show her.

She nods and follows my lead, making me hiss in appreciation.

I lift my foot to rest it on the bed next to her. Watching her naked and sucking my cock is too much to bear. I push her back to the mattress and hover over her.

"Open your legs."

She smiles and arches her back off the mattress. My eyes roam down her body, to large, firm breasts, hourglass hips, and a small patch of perfectly groomed, light pubic hair. Her legs are long, toned, and currently spread wide just for me. But it's the look of hunger in her eyes that turns me on. She wants me, she wants what I can give her...and only me. *Nobody has ever touched her.*

She's every man's fucking wet dream.

Unable to help it, I take my cock back in my hand and begin to fist it hard. My jaw is clenched as I work myself.

"Touch yourself," I instruct.

Her eyes widen as I jerk my cock harder. Fuck, I want to come. I want to come looking at her. I want to come on her...in her.

My shoulder flexes as I grip my cock with white-knuckle force, and her back arches off the mattress again.

"Spence," she pleads. "I need you."

I grab the lube from the wardrobe as quickly as I can and squeeze it out onto my fingers then through her soft, wet flesh. It's practically pulsing beneath my fingertips.

"You feel so fucking good, angel," I whisper as I bend and take her nipple into my mouth. I suck it hard and slow, just how she likes it.

"Hurry," she moans.

I smile. This sense of urgency from her is new.

I like it.

"I've got to warm you up, baby," I whisper as my fingers circle through her swollen lips and over her clitoris.

"No, now."

All I can see is her.

I roll a condom on, climb over her, and spread her legs wider so that they touch the mattress. Then I line myself up at her opening.

"For God's sake, hurry up, Spencer," she gasps, frustrated.

I chuckle and lift her right leg, placing her foot on my chest. Her eyes widen. "This one's going to be deep, baby," I whisper. "That okay?"

I see fear flash in her eyes before she disguises it and nods softly.

I pull the end of my cock back and forth through her lips, enjoying the way she hums in appreciation.

Don't hurt her, don't hurt her, don't hurt her.

The usual mantra runs through my mind. Every time we have sex, I repeat this in my head over and over again. I never want her to be scared of me. I push forward at once, and she cries out as searing pleasure sucks my cock in.

So...wet. So fucking tight. I can feel every muscle inside of her as it contracts and ripples around me.

Mine.

I pull out and her eyes dilate. My breath quivers in appreciation.

So.

Fucking.

Good.

I press my hands above her shoulders to pin her in position, and then, holding myself up with straightened arms, I pull out and push back in again. My knees are wide to give me better traction.

She moans and her hands go to my behind.

I do it again and again, and soon we have a rhythm, and she begins to thrash beneath me.

"Spence," she moans.

I clench my jaw to try and hold it, to stop myself from coming, but she's too beautiful.

I can't.

The bed begins to hit the wall with force. I bring her other leg up to my chest and we both stop suddenly as our eyes lock.

Her eyes search mine, and she brings her hand up to cup my cheek.

"I love you," she whispers.

My eyes roll back, and I drop to my elbows to take her lips with mine. Our kiss is soft, hungry, and prolonged. Her hands move to my shoulders as her legs wrap around my waist.

This is what happens with her every time.

She blows my mind with this intimacy thing she has going on. I can't get enough.

I'm addicted.

She begins to thrash. "Now, Spencer."

I smile, knowing this is the first time she has begged me for an orgasm. I lift myself and slam in deep. She cries out, so I do it again, and she contracts and clenches around me. My cock jerks and I blow so fucking hard, I roll my head back and moan loudly.

Damn this fucking condom.

And then we kiss, and it's just the two of us. Nothing else matters in my world but her.

I hold her tight and smile against her lips.

"What?" She smirks.

"You're getting very good at that."

"I have a good teacher." She giggles as she kisses me again.

"Baby, we haven't even started yet." I pull out and roll onto my back, bringing her body over mine. I kiss her temple as we lie close. I can feel her heart still beating hard in her chest.

"What are you making me for dinner, Jones?" She looks up at me.

I run my hand down and over her ass. "Whatever room service is delivering."

. . .

I sit at my desk and stare at the plans in front of me. It's late in the afternoon and I've been hectic all day, taking endless meetings with clients.

My phone rings and the name Seb lights up the screen.

"Hi." I smile and lean back in my chair.

"The mattress is in your room and waiting for the princess. Completely sex-stain-free...for now."

I chuckle. "Thanks, man, I owe you one."

"And I may have fucked the sales assistant to guarantee your delivery."

"What?"

He chuckles, and I know he's joking.

"Where's my old mattress?" I ask.

"They took it away. It caught fire as soon as it saw daylight."

I laugh. "I don't doubt it." I hear the door click, and I turn to see Sheridan walking in. She turns and locks the door behind her.

I frown. Oh shit.

"I've got to go," I tell Seb.

"Hey, so you know how Angela called me..." he continues, ignoring me.

Sheridan sits on the desk in front of me. She leans down and kisses me, and I pull away quickly, shaking my head in disgust.

"Stop," I mouth at her.

"Angela wants me to go over tonight," Seb continues.

I frown. "What for?"

Sheridan drops to the floor in front of my chair and I shake my head. "Stop," I mouth again.

"She wants to talk to me about something," Seb says.

Sheridan grabs my fly and begins to unzip my pants. "Will you cut it out!" I snap, quickly closing my legs.

"What?" Seb asks.

"Mate, I have to go, sorry," I snap. "Shit's going on here."

Sheridan grabs my cock through my pants and strokes me. I

268

swat her hand away.

"Call you later," I snap and hang up. "What the fuck, Sheridan?"

"Oh, darling. Don't act like you don't love it when I do this."

My phone buzzes and my receptionist's voice rings out. "Mr Jones?"

I push Sheridan away. "Fucking stop it, will you?" She drops her head to my lap and bites me through my pants. "Get up!" I snap. I push the intercom. "Yeah?" I say.

"I have an Edward Prescott here to see you."

My eyes widen.

Oh fuck.

14

Spencer

Oh hell. This is the worst timing ever. I exhale heavily. Shit, what does he want?

"Tell him I'll be a few minutes. I'm with a client," I splutter.

"Okay."

I hang up and stand in a rush. "Fucking hell, Sheridan." I drag her from the floor by the arm. "What the hell are you doing?"

She smirks. "Pleasing my man. What does it look like?"

"I'm not your man, and you need to stop coming in here unannounced and touching me."

She rolls her eyes. "Are you still going on with this nonsense?"

"Yes." I grab her biceps. "Fucking listen to what I'm saying. This has to stop." I gently push her away from my body. "Please," I urge.

Her eyes search mine, and realisation sets in that I actually mean this. Her eyes fill with tears. "Spence," she whispers.

My heart drops and I sigh. "Shez...don't."

"But you said it would always be us."

"I know I did."

"I love you," she whispers through tears.

"What?" I frown. What the fuck...*she did not just say that.*

"For years, I've loved you, Spence."

My eyebrows rise. "And you didn't think to say something to me before now?"

"Because I didn't want to lose you." She shrugs. "But if you're ready to settle down, I'll move here, and we can try to make it work. Maybe you can have the house in the countryside and the two-point-four children...but with me."

My shoulders slump, and I tuck a piece of hair behind her ear. "It's not that easy."

Tears fill her eyes even more, and damn, if it isn't the worst thing I've ever seen. Sheridan is the toughest chick I know.

"Please," she murmurs helplessly.

My heart constricts at the sight of her begging. "Shez." I take her in my arms and hold her tight as her tears roll down her face. "Don't be upset." I kiss her temple. "I can't stand seeing you like this."

"Then give me a chance. We can try. I'll move here. You know I can make you happy, Spence."

I glance at the door. Edward is still out there. I completely forgot about him for a moment.

"Sheridan, my next appointment is here," I whisper in a panic.

"Can I see you tonight?" she pleads.

"No."

Her face scrunches up. "Ten years together, and you can't even have dinner with me to talk about this?"

Fuck, I'm a selfish prick.

"Tomorrow night," I whisper. "We'll meet tomorrow night." Right now, I just need her out of here. I'll deal with her tomorrow.

She smiles, mollified for the moment. "Okay." She leans in and kisses me softly on the lips, rubbing her fingers through my stubble. "I'll call you tomorrow?"

Fuck, why is nothing fucking easy? "Sure. Now I have to see my next appointment. Clean yourself up, you look like a mess."

"Then stop upsetting me." She huffs as she walks into the bathroom.

I pinch the bridge of my nose in frustration. Jesus fucking Christ, how do I get myself into this shit? I exhale heavily as she washes her face and redoes her makeup.

"Will you hurry?" I snap.

"Stop it," she scolds me. "I'll be ready to leave when I'm ready to leave and not a minute before."

She reappears with her power suit firmly back in place, and I smile at the sight of her. "That's better."

She smiles bashfully. "What have you done to me, Spencer Jones?"

Sadness fills me. I do love Shez, just not in the way I love Charlotte. I don't know how to make this right for her.

Ten years is a long time.

"I'll see you tomorrow night?" She smiles hopefully.

I nod. "You will, speak tomorrow."

She kisses me softly on the lips, and I wrap my arms around her, holding her close. There is a familiarity in her touch that comforts me. My eyes close with sadness because I know that this is our last embrace. As if sensing it too, she squeezes me tight and we stay in each other's arms for an extended moment. I pull back and cup her face in my hand, rubbing my thumb over her bottom lip.

"I do care for you, you know that, right?" I whisper.

Her eyes fill with tears anew. "But not love?"

"Baby, don't..." I sigh.

She breaks from my arms and stares at the floor for a moment while she pulls herself together. I see her transform back to the power woman the world knows. She picks up her bag and heads for the door.

"Speak tomorrow," I say.

Without another word, she leaves, and the door clicks shut behind her. I know I don't have to worry about her saying anything to anyone or looking upset out there in reception. She would rather die than show any weakness. I hate that after ten years, she just opened up to me and I kicked her out.

Such an asshole.

I press my eyeballs with my fingers and pace back and forth for a moment, trying to calm myself down.

Fuck, Edward is here and Sheridan loves me.

This is one fucked-up day.

I go to the bathroom, wash my hands and face, and take a seat back at my desk as I prepare myself. Once ready, I press the intercom. "Send my next client in, please."

The door opens and a man in a navy suit comes into view. He's tall, dark, and good-looking. Not what I was expecting at all. I thought he would be fair like Charlotte. Anyway, whatever.

I stand and hold my hand out. "Hello, I'm Spencer Jones."

He shakes my hand. His grip is strong as he holds direct eye contact.

"Mr Jones," he says flatly with a forced smile. "I'm Edward Prescott."

I gesture to my desk. "Please, take a seat."

He sits and I fall into my chair at the same time. I'm not exactly sure why he's here. I asked the guards not to tell him yet. Have the images of our kiss been released already? No...because for him to get here so quickly, he would have had to leave Vegas or wherever he was yesterday. The flight is fourteen hours. I'm just going to keep quiet until I know what he's doing.

"How can I help you?" I ask calmly.

"Do you know who I am?"

My eyes hold his. "Should I?"

He raises an eyebrow, sits back in his chair, and crosses his legs. He has a distinct air about him, although I can't quite put my finger on exactly what that is.

Is he arrogant or entitled? Or perhaps just misunderstood.

"I understand you met my sister recently," he says.

"And your sister is...?" I ask as I play along.

"Charlotte Prescott."

I smile. "That I did."

Our eyes are locked.

"Where did you meet?" he asks sharply.

"I'm sorry, why are you asking me questions about Charlotte?" I interrupt.

He smirks. "Let's stop fucking around and get straight to the point, shall we? I have reason to believe that you are sniffing around my sister."

I chuckle. "I'm not sure what kind of dog you're used to, but I can assure you I don't sniff around."

"That's not what my friend Alexander York told me. You were kissing her hand and didn't take your eyes off her all night long at a recent charity ball."

Ah, he's here because Alex told him about us. What else does he know?

"I wouldn't be throwing the name Alexander York around and connecting him as a friend if I were you."

He glares at me.

"I think you and I both know what his character is like," I add. "A reference of any sort from him doesn't mean much."

He raises an eyebrow in a silent dare. "No, why don't you tell me?"

"The man's a snake and there is no love lost between us." I stand from my chair and walk over to the window, placing my hands into my trouser pockets before I turn back to him. "But you already know that, don't you?"

"Alexander is not my concern, Mr Jones."

"Please, call me Spencer."

"Spencer." He nods once.

"What exactly is your concern?" I ask. "Why are you here?"

"Charlotte."

I raise an eyebrow. "And why is she a concern to you?"

"She is not the kind of woman you are...*accustomed* to."

I smile. "Is that what York told you? Ah, he said that I'm a scandalous rake and that I can't be trusted anywhere near your sister, didn't he?"

We glare at each other for a moment.

"Have you contacted her since you met?" he asks me boldly.

I smile. The fucking nerve of this guy.

"Let me tell you this, Mr Prescott." I exhale heavily. "If I were to contact Charlotte at any point, it is none of your damn business, only mine and hers."

"The hell it isn't my business." He jumps up from his seat and moves to stand in front of me. "My job is to protect her from men like you."

"I thought your job as her brother would be to love her?"

He raises his chin in defiance, unimpressed with that hidden accusation I planted there. "I protect her from everything. Sleazy arseholes like you being one of the more specific threats."

"Is that what you think I am?"

He steps forward until our faces are close. "Stay away from my sister, Mr Jones."

I glare at him. "Or what?"

"Or you'll deal with me."

"Do you really think that you could keep me away from her, if she were truly who I wanted?"

"Is she?"

I smirk. "I will not discuss my intentions with you, but I will say that you underestimate her greatly. She is intelligent and old enough to make her own decisions."

"She is not accustomed to men like you."

"And what kind of man would you have her go out with?" I fire back. "Alexander York, perhaps?" I smirk. "I'm quite sure he would love to be part of the Prescott family."

His face falls before he quickly masks it. "Don't be ridiculous, he's a friend to her."

"Does he know that?" I ask with a raised eyebrow. "Have you seen him with her?"

The best form of defence is attack. I'm going to throw him off the scent.

"Maybe you should ask Charlotte about Charlotte and stop jumping to ridiculous assumptions. Have you really driven all the way from Manchester to London just to see me?"

Satisfaction flashes across his face, and that's when I know he's just fallen for my fake ignorance of his family. If I knew her well—which he doesn't need to know I do...not yet—I would know Manchester isn't where they live, or where he has just travelled thousands of miles from.

"I was in town doing business," he lies.

"Well, it was nice meeting you, Mr Prescott."

His eyes hold mine and we glare at each other.

"I don't want to have this conversation again. Stay away from Charlotte. Do I make myself clear?"

I smile broadly. I would just love to throw it in his face right now for being such a conceited prick, but I won't. I won't...for Charlotte's sake. Edward doesn't respect her, but I do.

"Perhaps next time we meet, you will be a touch more well-mannered, Mr Prescott." That's the only answer I give him. "Or at least have some idea what you are talking about. I don't have time for childish, half-thought-out assumptions. I'm a very busy man."

His eyes blaze with anger, and he steps forward so his face is only millimetres from mine. "I don't like you."

Our eyes are locked.

"You don't have to." I smirk. "Now get out."

We stand toe-to-toe as fury boils between us. Eventually, he turns and leaves without another word. The door clicks closed, and I inhale a deep breath as I drop into my chair.

Fucking hell, this really is going to be World War Three.

Charlotte

I push the heavy mail cart though the office. "Lottie!" Scott calls as he leans back on his chair.

"Yes?" Scott is the cheeky man from level six. He's good-looking and so, so much fun.

"Are we on for tonight?" he teases with a wiggle of his eyebrows.

I hand him the wad of mail for his department. "No, we're not on for tonight. I tell you that every day."

He winces and tips his head back to the heavens. "Oh, come on, you don't know what you are missing out on. I'm every woman's dream, you know?"

I chuckle and keep pushing my trolley.

"Call me!" he cries out in a girl's voice. I smile as I walk along and continue handing out the mail. Who knew that this shitty job could make me so happy? I look up ahead and see Sarah swinging on a chair as she talks to three girls. She glances over at me.

"This cart is heavy, you know..." I huff.

She ends her conversation and skips over. "Oh, I was just getting the gossip. Apparently, Tiffany broke up with Zane because she caught him having sex with Brittany from level two. They were doing it in her car in the basement car park."

I wince. "Oh shit."

"But apparently Tiffany gave Darren a blowie the other night in his car when he drove her home, and that's why he fucked Brittany. It was his payback."

My mouth falls open. "Who told you that?"

"Darren told Paul, Paul told me, and I just told them."

"God, it's so sleazy. Who gives other guys blowies when they have a boyfriend?"

"I know." She takes the cart for me. "I told you, this place is Hot Dick City, and every woman is here for herself. Women can't control themselves."

I giggle as I walk beside her. "Have you ever given anyone here a blowie?"

"Yeah." She nods. "Last year at the Christmas party I had a threesome in one of the offices on level eleven."

My mouth falls open. "Sarah," I gasp. "What the hell?"

"I know, right?" She shrugs. "Weirdest night of my life. It was like the twilight zone, and it was totally shit."

"Why?" I frown. I've been watching this stuff on YouPorn and it looks anything but shit.

"Frigging hell, there was just too much going on, you know? One minute I'm riding, then I had a dick getting shoved down my throat at the same time. Then the other one is flipping me around and doing me doggy, while the other one is pulling my hair so I can suck his dick *just how he wants it*. I couldn't concentrate on any one task enough to do a good job of it."

I burst out laughing, imagining her getting flipped around like a rag doll while trying hard to concentrate.

"Honestly, threesomes are like some kind of Olympic pentathlon except you have to do all the events at the same time. Good in theory." She puffs air into her cheeks and shakes her head. "Not so much in practice."

I put my hands over my face and laugh. I'm never going to think of Olympic pentathlons the same ever again. I love this girl, but a sadness fills me. I'm going to miss her when I leave.

Maybe she could come with me?

Enjoy every day while I can.

My phone rings in my pocket and I take it out. The name Spence lights up the screen.

"I'm just going to take this," I whisper.

"Sure thing." She continues pushing the cart.

I step into the stairwell. "Hello."

"Angel." His deep voice purrs, and a broad smile crosses my face. Even his voice makes me giddy.

"How are you?" I ask dreamily.

"Missing my girl."

"Well, you get to see her in"—I glance at my watch—"approximately five hours."

"I'm counting the minutes."

I swoon. He's so gorgeous.

"I'm calling to give you my address."

"Oh." I bunch my shoulders together in excitement. "That's right, we're having a sleepover at your house tonight."

"We are," he purrs. "What time will you be here?"

"I'll finish at five and go back to grab my stuff, and then I'll be over."

"Bring a few days of clothes."

I smile. "Is this an extended sleepover?"

"Mmmhmm, it is. Don't shower before you come."

"Why not?" I frown.

"Because that's fifteen more minutes that I don't get to see you. Besides, I like to wash you."

My heart sings in my chest. He does love to wash me. I've never felt so adored in all of my life.

"Okay," I whisper. I've told him I love him a few times, and he hasn't said it back yet, not since that first time he said it when we were arguing about Sheridan. I'm trying not to be needy.

"Goodbye, Spence," I say.

"Where's my I love you?" he asks.

Relief hits me. "I love you." I smile.

He inhales sharply. "And now my day is complete. See you tonight, angel." He hangs up and I frown. I stare at the phone in my hand for a moment. Why does he notice when I don't say it to him, but then he never says it back to me?

Men.

Well, that's it, I'm not saying it again until he does. I walk back into the office to find Sarah laughing out loud with a group of girls, and I find myself smiling broadly. Who's slept with who now?

I'm sitting in the back of the Mercedes wagon that Wyatt is driving. Anthony is sitting in the passenger seat beside him, texting Spencer to let him know we will be arriving in a few minutes. It turns out that Spencer has called them about the details of where they will be staying tonight too. The two of them have overnight bags with them as well. It seems surreal that he looks after the boys as if they're his own staff. If I'm being honest, he seems more caring about their welfare than Edward has ever been. I'm usually the only one who worries about them.

"Where is it exactly?" I ask, craning my neck to look up the street.

"Just up here around the corner."

"Do we have a key?"

"Spencer is meeting us in the foyer. He has to take us up."

"Okay." I look out the window at the bustling streets as we drive. It all feels so surreal, that I'm with him and he's with me when only a month ago I was completely alone and still a virgin. What a difference a month can make. Finally, we get to a tall, swanky-looking building.

"This is it," Anthony says as we pull in.

Wow, this looks nice.

Wyatt parks the car, and Spencer walks out through the large double front doors. His face lights up when he sees me. I have to stop myself from running and throwing myself into his arms.

"Hello, angel." He smiles.

"Hi," I beam. I hate that I can't touch him in public yet.

"Hey, guys," he says to the boys as he takes my bag from me.

"Hello, Spencer," they say as they walk behind us.

We walk through a marble reception with a concierge and two doormen, making our way over and into the elevator. The door closes and Spencer immediately takes my hand in his and smiles. His eyes stay fixed on the back of the closed door.

I love that he's so touchy with me.

The doors open on level two and he strides out with purpose.

"This way." We walk down a corridor until Spencer stops and opens a door, handing Wyatt the keys. "This is your apartment. It has three bedrooms and everything you should need while you're here. I sublet it. It's one of the other residents' staff members, but they're out of the country for a few months," Spencer tells them both.

Wyatt and Anthony walk in and look around.

"It's nice." I smile.

The boys smile, seemingly impressed with their new hangout.

"Everything is still the same. Once Charlotte and I are in for the night, you're off duty, but you should continue to be with her when she is out and about, please."

"Of course," Anthony replies.

"Would you like to come up and go through my apartment?" he asks them.

"Please," Wyatt says.

Spencer takes my hand again and strides back down the corridor to the elevator that's still waiting. We ride in silence to the fifteenth floor.

We arrive at two huge black double doors. Spencer swipes his key and they click open. When he reveals his room to me, my heart catches in my throat.

Holy cow!

I look up at a mezzanine level that hangs over the main living space and I smile to myself.

The room I'm in has polished concrete floors, with a beautiful pale timber ceiling. It looks like something out of a trendy home magazine. Perhaps a ski lodge in Aspen.

"This is your house?" I ask.

He winks at me.

Wyatt and Anthony look around, back at each other, and then back to Spencer as if shocked.

"What?" Spencer smirks. "Not what you were expecting?"

"You're rich too?" Wyatt frowns.

Spencer smiles. "I do all right for myself."

I bite my bottom lip to hide my stupid smile.

Spencer walks through the apartment. "I'll give you the tour." He holds his hand out as he walks past us. "This is the kitchen." He points to a stainless-steel kitchen with a huge timber island bench sitting in the middle. He then points to the glass wall. "City of London, obviously." We all peer out to see an expansive view of London before us.

Wyatt rolls his eyes, as if completely unimpressed.

Spencer chuckles. "I do love showing off my house, I have to admit."

"Couldn't tell," Wyatt mutters dryly while Anthony and I giggle.

"This is the dining room." There's a large, rustic, oval dining table that seats ten around it. There are differently upholstered chairs there, all of which kind of match but don't really. "Living room." That's a huge living area with slouchy chocolate-colored leather couches and a big gas fireplace sitting in the middle.

Wow.

"This is the guest bedroom." He points to it as we walk into the hallway, and I stop in my tracks.

"Oh my God," I gasp.

The whole length of the hallway is lined with black book-shelves filled with thousands of books. It's a lot wider than a normal hallway, and it gives off the feel of a library. It even has one of those rails with a ladder going up to the top shelves.

"You *do* read?" I ask in surprise.

He smirks over his shoulder, grabbing my hand to lead me along. "I told you I did. I don't lie, Lady Charlotte," he teases. "My office." He continues with the tour, and I peer inside to see an office with a large mahogany desk facing the door, a big high-back black leather office chair sitting behind it.

"Laundry, gymnasium," he says as he points to several rooms we walk by.

I peer in and see a large room with a treadmill, rowing machine, and weights. A television is mounted on the wall.

I can hardly wipe the goofy smile from my face. I thought my hotel room was nice.

It has nothing on this place.

"Upstairs." Spencer gestures as he continues to play tour guide. We all peer up to see a floating staircase that hangs out of the wall. The bannister is nothing more than a sheet of glass.

"This place is beautiful, Spence," I tell him.

He smiles proudly and looks around. "I do love it."

We all follow him up the stairs. "Spare rooms, bathrooms, and then at the end is my bedroom."

We get to his room and I smile so wide that my face nearly splits in two. It's a huge white bedroom with all different textured fabrics. There's a king bed covered in white linen, white wingback chairs, a black and white charcoal artwork piece on the wall. The floors are a herringbone timber too.

"Look around as much as you wish," he says to the boys.

They walk past him and open the walk-in wardrobe doors, and then they go into the bathroom, leaving me to wrap my arms around Spencer's waist and smile up at him.

"I like your house," I beam.

He kisses me softly. "I like you."

From the corner of my eye, I see Wyatt roll his eyes at Anthony, and I giggle. What must they think?

"Let yourself out, boys, we won't be needing you again tonight."

"Okay," Anthony says before they disappear out of the door. "See you in the morning."

"Thank you," Spencer calls.

I would love to be a fly on the wall to see what they say when they're in private.

"Alone at last." Spencer smiles down at me before kissing me softly. His lips linger over mine and his tongue sweeps through my open mouth with just the right amount of force.

Dominant, caring...the man is as hot as hell.

"Well, Mr Jones." I look around his room. "I did not expect this."

"Expect what?"

"A house that looks like a *Vogue* home living shoot. You are full of surprises."

"I'm an architect, what did you expect?"

I shrug. "I don't know."

"I designed this building."

My eyes widen. "You did?"

"Yes, and this apartment was always going to be mine." His hands run down over my behind. "Just like you were."

I frown up at him in question.

"You were always going to be mine, Charlotte."

I giggle against his lips and walk him backwards towards the bed until he stops me. "Not yet. I'm starving, woman."

"Party pooper. What are we eating?"

"I'm cheating. I had my housekeeper pick up some Indian food for us. It's in the fridge."

"Sounds perfect." He leads me back down the stairs and out into the kitchen, sitting me at one of the bench stools.

"Red or white?" he asks.

"White, please."

I watch as he pours our wine and then hands me mine. We clink our glasses together and smile stupidly at one other. "I like having you here," he says.

"I like being here." I reach up and drag him to me. We kiss and my eyes close to absorb every second of it. I really am pathetic when I'm around him.

He pulls out of our kiss. "Stop distracting me, I'm about to pass out from lack of sustenance. Do not kiss me again unless you have a defibrillator in your possession."

I giggle. "Always so dramatic."

He takes the Indian food out of the refrigerator and grabs a few saucepans.

"Why don't you just microwave it?" I frown.

"You must be kidding. Have you ever had reheated Indian food that way?" He frowns.

"Many times."

He rolls his eyes. "And here I was all this time thinking you were cultured."

I giggle against my wineglass and watch on as he pours the food into the three saucepans.

"Have you thought about where you are going to live when you move to London?" he asks.

I shrug. "Not really. I guess I'll have to start thinking soon, though." I watch him for a moment. "What are your thoughts?"

He continues stirring. "I have a few." He sips his wine. "The Spencer Jones in me wants you to get your own kickass apartment and decorate it however you want. To have your own things and come and go as you please."

I smile and wait for him to go on.

"He wants you to gain your independence and live life without the restraints from your family." He thinks for a moment. "I mean, you should. That's what you should do. That's the smart thing to do."

It's clear he has something else on his mind, though. "And what do you want?" I ask.

His eyes find mine.

"That's what Spencer Jones wants me to do," I say. "What do you want me to do?" I ask. "The selfish little boy inside of you... what does he want?"

"Well..." He pauses. His eyes hold mine as he decides whether to share. "The selfish little boy in me can't stand the thought of spending even one night without you, and he wants you to move in here."

15

Charlotte

WHAT?

"I mean…" He shrugs, as if embarrassed by my shocked reaction. "That's only if you wanted to, and I'd completely understand if you didn't." He's speaking way too fast, tripping over his words as he tries to recover.

I smile and remain silent as I watch him.

He continues to stir the pot, shaking his head as he thinks. "That was…" His voice trails off. "That was a bad idea, forget I said anything."

"Spence?"

He keeps stirring with his head down, unable to look at me.

I get off the stool and walk around in front of him, wrapping my arms around his neck. "Spence?"

His eyes meet mine.

"Why don't we just see how we go?"

A frown creases his forehead. "What does that mean?"

"It means that we've been together for five minutes, and I think that maybe we should stop moving so fast."

"You don't like the way things are going?"

I kiss him softly. "I love the way things are going, but this isn't a race."

He holds me tight. "It feels like it is."

I pull back to look at his face. "Why?"

He shrugs. "I'm waiting for the shoe to drop and everything to turn to shit."

"Spence," I breathe. "It's not going to."

"This is new for me, angel. All this." He shrugs. "Feeling..."

I giggle. "You think this is new for you? Try being me for a moment. I'm getting used to having sex, falling in love, as well as an ex-girlfriend of yours who is slipping keys into your pocket."

He smirks and pulls out of my arms. "Oh, I saw her today."

My face falls. "You saw her today?"

"Yeah." He goes back to stirring his pot of Indian food, choosing not to elaborate.

"And?" I frown.

"Long story."

"I've got time."

He dishes out our meals and places them on the counter in front of us. He refills our wineglasses, too, leaving me to just... watch him.

He sits down and begins to eat, as if he hasn't a care in the world.

"Spencer! Are you going to tell me what happened or not?"

He blows out a deep breath. "It was a day from hell."

"Why are you always so dramatic?"

He chuckles. "No, seriously, today was a day from hell." He shovels some food into his mouth. "Like...literally."

I take a mouthful of food for myself. "Why?"

"So, Sheridan turns up and tells me she loves me."

My mouth falls open in surprise.

Don't say anything, don't say anything.

"She wants to move here and make a go of it with me."

"I thought you said you were just having sex?"

He shrugs. "I thought we were too. I was bowled over."

"Well, what did you say to that?"

"I said no, that we were never like that." He chews his food casually, as if he has this conversation every day.

"And you've told her you're with me?" I ask. Damn this sneaky bitch.

"She knows I'm in love with you. I told her."

"You told her that you love me. In those words?"

"I think it was in those words." He shrugs. "Anyway, she knows."

"How come you tell her you love me, but you don't tell me you love me?" I ask.

He looks at me, deadpan. "Really? That's all you got out of that sentence?"

I raise my eyebrows. Hmm, his snarky attitude is pissing me off tonight.

"Anyway, so I'm dealing with her crying and shit."

"How were you dealing with her?" I frown. "Define *dealing with her*."

He rolls his eyes. "I was hugging her."

I get an image of them in a passionate embrace while he comforts her. "Did you kiss her?"

"No, I did not kiss her. Will you let me tell the fucking story?"

I shovel food into my mouth with force. Do I have to? *I hate this fucking story.*

"Anyway, so she's crying and begging for two kids and a house in the countryside."

My anger begins to rise. Is she kidding?

"She asked you for two kids?" I snap.

"Because she thinks that's what I want with you."

I stare at him. "Is it?"

"Is it what?"

"Is that what you want? Two kids and a house in the countryside?"

He shrugs. "I don't know, you've got me thinking all types of crazy shit that I haven't ever considered before. I did just ask you to move in with me and got shot down in flames for my trouble, didn't I?"

"I did not shoot you down in flames." I smile. "It was more like a gentle slingshot."

He rolls his eyes. "Whatever you call it, you didn't say yes. So, Sheridan is in my office crying and shit, and then my receptionist buzzes through to tell me that Edward Prescott is there to see me."

My eyes widen. "What?"

"Yep."

"What the hell?"

He holds up his hands in the air. "Fucking crying ex-girlfriend in my office. New girlfriend's crazy-ass brother in the waiting room, ready to kill me."

"I thought you said she wasn't your girlfriend."

"Again with the pointless shit from that sentence." He rolls his eyes. "The only part of the sentence you should have heard was *ready to kill me*."

I smirk. "You are an idiot."

He gives me a sexy wink as he bites the food from his fork.

"So then what happened?"

"I got rid of Sheridan, and then I saw Edward."

"And...?"

"Nothing, really. Stupid Alexander York told him I was sniffing around you."

"Sniffing around?" I frown. "That's uncouth."

"I really did want to tell him how good you tasted. You know... to infuriate him more."

"Spencer." I smirk. "Now you're being uncouth. Will you stop joking around and tell me what the hell happened?"

"Nothing other than he warned me to stay away from you. I told him that it was none of his business. He told me he didn't like me, and then I kicked him out of my office."

I stare at him as my brain misfires.

He winks that cheeky boy wink again.

"Tell me you're joking."

"Nope. That's exactly how it happened."

"You kicked him out?" I gasp.

"He told me he didn't like me."

"You-you could have *tried* to be nice to him at least," I stammer.

"I'm not putting up with his shit, Charlotte. Nobody comes to my office and makes demands without getting kicked out."

"Sheridan does," I retort.

He rolls his eyes. "Don't start that shit."

"Don't start?" I snap. "Oh, I haven't started yet. How did it end? What was the last thing you said to her?"

"I told her I would have dinner with her tomorrow night to talk about it."

"*What?*"

He shrugs casually. "It's the least I could do. I won't be long. A few hours tops."

"No."

His eyes come to mine. "What do you mean, no?"

"I mean no. You're not going."

He frowns.

I point my fork at him. "If you think for one minute that I am staying home while you go out with your ex–fuck buddy, you can think again."

His eyes hold mine.

"I am inexperienced, Spencer, not a fucking idiot."

"She's just a friend."

"Who wants two kids and a house in the country with you." I get up and scrape my plate of food into the bin with force. "She will get there and want a goodbye fuck, and then the two of you will fall back into this pattern of sleeping together behind my back."

"What?" He stands in an outrage. "I wouldn't do that to you."

"But she would, and I'm not giving her the fucking chance."

"Since when do you swear every second word?"

"Since fucking sluts piss me off!" I yell.

"Don't call her that."

"If the shoe fits." I storm upstairs.

"You don't even know her," he calls after me.

I turn and storm back down the stairs. "Oh, but you do. Very well indeed. Isn't that right, Spencer?"

He narrows his eyes and puts his hands on his hips. "What's that supposed to mean?"

"It means if you want any type of relationship with me, you will cut all ties with her immediately...or else."

"Or else what?" he fires back.

"Or else I'm out of here, and you can go back to sleeping with her whenever you want."

"I don't want to sleep with her. Stop being a fucking bitch about it."

"A fucking bitch?" I yell. "You haven't seen a fucking bitch yet."

"I think I just have!" he yells. "They can see your bitchiness from space. NASA is picking you up on bitch cam right now."

We glare at each other.

"I'm going to have a shower while you decide which one of us you want." I sneer sarcastically.

He throws his head back in disgust. "And you reckon I'm fucking dramatic." He tuts. "You're going for a fucking Oscar here."

"If it's not me, Spencer, then get out," I say. "Go stay elsewhere tonight."

He puts his hands on his hips. "This is my house. You can't kick me out of my own house."

"I just did, and guess what? I *am* moving in."

"Maybe I don't want you to move in now."

"Tough shit!" I yell as I storm up the stairs. "You have no say in it."

"And you think I'm fucking crazy," he calls after me. "Can you hear yourself, Charlotte? You don't want to move in with me until someone else does." He laughs sarcastically.

"You're not going out with her!" I yell down to him.

I walk into his bedroom and slam the door shut. I can feel the adrenaline pumping through my body.

Calm down, calm down, calm down.

I shake my hands to try and expel some of my negative energy. I am so angry right now. I walk into the bathroom and inhale deeply. I turn the shower on hot, and the water begins to stream down heavily.

I handled that badly, but honestly, what did he expect? I look around for a towel and can't see any. There are none on the towel rails, none folded anywhere. I go to the top of the stairs.

"Where are the towels?"

"In the linen cupboard. Where do you think?"

"You're an idiot. And the worst host ever."

"I thought you fucking lived here now. That makes you the host."

"You're lucky this is an apartment building, or I would bury you under it." I hear him laugh out loud in surprise, and I turn and stomp back up the hall.

I'm not even joking. I probably would.

Twenty minutes later, I'm standing under the hot water, feeling my anger running down the drain along with the water.

At least he told me about Sheridan coming to him today. He didn't try to hide it, I suppose.

Maybe I overreacted?

He walks into the bathroom a second later, flashing me a lopsided smile. I can't help but give him one back. He takes a seat on the side of the bath and watches me.

"Sorry for screaming at you." I sigh.

He exhales heavily. "I'm sorry for calling you a bitch."

I smirk and pick up the soap.

"What are you doing?" He frowns.

"Washing myself. What does it look like?"

"I told you that I wanted to wash you."

"Well, you're not doing a very good job of it." I widen my eyes. "Are you?"

He chuckles. "Jesus Christ, where is the shy, sweet Charlotte I first met?"

"To be honest, I don't know. What on earth have you done to me, Spencer Jones?"

He stands and begins to unbutton his shirt.

"Don't bother taking off your shirt until you decide what you're doing tomorrow night."

He frowns.

"I mean it, Spence. I don't want you seeing her."

"Angel." He sighs. "I gave her my word, and I'm a man of my word. If I make a promise to someone, I keep it."

"And you made a promise to me that we are exclusive and making a go of this. Meeting with your ex does not fit in with that, Spencer." My eyes search his. "Please try and see this from my point of view. If I had an ex, would you want him coming into my office and me comforting him about our breakup, then making plans to see him at night?"

He walks to the edge of the shower and watches me for a moment. He runs his hand down my cheek and then cups my breast, deep in thought. His thumb dusts over my nipple and it hardens beneath his touch. "No, I wouldn't."

I rise on my tippy toes and kiss him. My face is wet as it rests up against his, and his big hand drops to my naked behind.

"Keep your promise to me, Spence," I whisper. "No matter how many times you meet with her, it isn't going to get any easier. Just the opposite. It will get harder, and you will end up either in bed with her or having a huge fight. There is no in between with the two of you, you know that."

He drops his eyes to the floor. "I just feel bad, you know?"

I smile softly. "I know." I begin to unbutton his shirt. "That's because you're a good man."

"I didn't know that she felt like this." He sighs.

I push his shirt over his shoulders, and it falls back to the floor. "Of course she would feel like this. I imagine all women you meet fall madly in love with you."

"I can't comment." He gives me his best cheeky smile and shrugs. "I know you do hate a show-off."

I giggle. "Lucky I like idiots, though, hey?"

"If you don't want me to see her, I won't."

"I don't."

He exhales heavily. "Okay."

I pull him in under the shower, and he wraps his big arms around me. His lips take mine and his tongue slides slowly through my open mouth. He towers above me and his large frame takes over the space.

He smiles as he kisses me.

"What?"

"You do know I concocted that whole story just to get you to move in here with me, right?"

"You're a terrible liar."

"You're terrible at finding towels."

I laugh out loud. "Is that the best you've got?"

"For now, yeah." He grabs my behind and pulls my cheeks apart. His open mouth drops to my neck, and I feel his large erection up against my stomach.

His open mouth ravages my neck, and he bites me hard, forcing me to wince.

And there it is.

The perfect moment where Spencer Jones loses control and he returns to his primal, natural instincts. Where his body needs to orgasm, and he'll take it whether I want to give it to him or not. He switches from the sweet, lovable man I know to a hungry predator who needs to fuck.

There is always a bite, a subtle hint that he's reached his limit. Some days it comes faster than others, but it's always there. I'm addicted to this man of mine and the way that he makes me feel.

He gets out of the shower and disappears into the bedroom, reappearing moments later as he unwraps a condom. I watch on in awe as he slowly rolls it on. It doesn't matter how many times I watch him do this, it always fascinates me.

When his eyes rise to mine, I see the hunger in them, and my stomach dances with nerves.

Then he is on me. I'm pushed up against the wall as his open mouth takes mine. His hand holds my jaw just the way he wants me, and he grinds his hard cock up against my hip bone.

"We need to fuck, angel."

"Yes," I whimper against his lips. He lifts me and wraps my legs around his waist. I'm pinned between him and the wall by his hard body. He kisses me slow and deep as he slides his hard dick through my swollen wet lips.

"You want my cock?"

"Hmm." I hold onto his shoulders for balance. His tongue slides through my open lips again as he takes what he needs. Does he honestly think I can string two words together when he has me like this?

With two hands, he brings me down on him hard, and I feel the familiar stretch as his body dominates mine.

My eyes close and I release a whimper.

He smiles darkly and circles himself deep inside of me. "You like that?"

"God, yes."

He lifts me and slams me back down again, knocking the air from my lungs.

I throw my head back against the tiles and he builds a rhythm. The room is steamy and hot. Water is streaming down over his face, yet the way he is looking at me might just set me on fire. He goes faster and deeper, lost to his own concentration. He stares straight ahead as our skin begins to slap together.

"So. Fucking. Good," he pushes out.

My body convulses forward, and he sees that as his signal to really let me have it. With both hands over my shoulders, he slams into me again and again, and I screw up my face and cry out as a freight train of an orgasm steals my breath.

He lifts me like a feather on and off his large muscle.

"Oh, that's it. Clench that beautiful cunt for me, baby. I want to feel it."

Slam.

Slam.

Slam.

"Clench!" he growls.

So, deep...too deep.

"Charlotte, fucking give it to me."

My face creases up as I try and deal with him. He's like an animal when he gets to this point. The only thing he's thinking about is the orgasm his body craves.

My head begins to hit the tiles as he really loses control, and the sound of our skin slapping is deafening around us.

"Fuck, yeah," he cries as he holds himself deep. His whole body lurches forward, and I feel the telling jerk of his cock as he comes in a rush deep inside of me.

I can hear my pulse ringing in my ears.

And then he kisses me, and it's soft, tender, and a reminder that my gentle man has returned. He smiles against my lips, his body still having me pinned to the wall. I can feel his heart beating hard in his chest, and I bury my head into his neck as he holds me tight.

This is it. This is what I've been searching for all this time.

He stays deep inside of me. I smile against his neck with my legs still wrapped around his waist.

"I thought you were washing me," I pant.

"Hmm." He kisses me again. "I thought I should get you dirty first. This is the deluxe car wash."

I giggle and our lips linger over each other's. "Did you just call me a car?"

"Maybe?" He smiles and pulls out, gently lowering me to the floor. "You're not dirty enough, though." He pulls his condom off in disgust. "I hate these fucking things." He huffs as he puts it in the bin beside the shower. We stay in each other's arms under the hot water. The room is quiet with the sound of the shower the only sound to be heard. I can feel myself begin to relax.

"What are you going to do about tomorrow night?" I ask.

"I guess I'll call her when I get out."

My eyes hold his.

"You can listen, if you want?"

"No. I don't need to listen."

He smiles down at me and fixes my hair in a bun on top of my head. "You know, you're kind of hot when you're angry."

"Can I have that on tape, please?"

He chuckles and picks up the soap to lather my body. "Except for the death threats and all."

"It wasn't a death threat," I say. "Only a burial threat. There's a big difference."

His soapy hand goes down to between my legs. "Should I be sleeping with one eye open, Prescott?"

I laugh out loud. "Seeing as you kicked my brother out of your office today, I think you should."

It's late, and I'm in bed alone. I can hear Spencer downstairs on the phone...

To her.

He's been on the phone for forty minutes and he seems to be listening a lot. She obviously has a lot to say.

The green-eyed monster in me is fuming and wants to stomp down there and make him hang up, but the woman in me feels sorry for her. I can't imagine what it would be like if he told me he was in love with someone else. But then, I could never imagine sleeping with him for ten years casually. Did she get the same Spencer that I get?

Or was he different with her?

How did they meet in the beginning? Was it always about the sex? My mind begins to go off on a tangent as I imagine him going to her hotel whenever he met her.

Did they have a routine?

Would they go straight to bed and fuck? Or did they spend time with each other like we do? Having dinner, talking, and laughing.

I close my eyes in disgust with myself.

Stop it! He's ending it.

My mind keeps picking up speed, though. When they had sex, was it better than what we have? Did she do what I don't know...anal?

My stomach flips imagining him fucking her. I wonder, do they kiss while they do it like we do?

Did he look at her after it was finished the way he looks at me?

I get a vision of her from the hotel that early morning—her and her power suit, with a figure to die for. She was confident in every way, which is the exact opposite of me.

I close my eyes as the disgusting taste of bile fills my mouth.

I can't stand the thought of him with her...touching her.

I can hear his voice rise, and I sit up. What's he saying? I get out of bed and sneak out of the bedroom, down the hall, and sit on the top step. He's in the dining room and can't see me from where he is. He, thankfully, has no idea I can hear him.

"Because she's right!" he snaps. "We both know she's right. If we meet up, we'll either end up in a huge fight or in bed. That's how we are."

My heart drops.

"But I don't want to end up in bed, Sheridan. Fucking listen to me. I'm going blue in the face here."

He listens for a moment.

"No, I don't want that."

He listens again.

"No. Look, this is going nowhere. You're not fucking listening. I'm changing my phone number and I'm telling my receptionists that you are not to come into my office unannounced again."

He listens.

"Because of you dropping to your knees under my desk today!"

he snaps. "You can't fucking touch me. I've asked you multiple times to stop and you won't, so it's quite obvious to me that we can't be just friends."

What the hell? She dropped to her knees under his desk? Did she go down on him?

Oh my God, what the hell happened in his office today?

What if Edward hadn't interrupted them?

My heart begins to hammer.

"For fuck's sake, stop it!" he snaps. I can tell by the tone of his voice that he's beginning to get angry. "No, you listen to me: you do not go near Charlotte or there will be hell to pay."

She says something that makes him pause.

"She makes me happy, Sheridan. You always said you wanted me happy." He listens again. "There is a big difference between the two, and besides, have you forgotten that you have a fucking boyfriend?"

She has a boyfriend. What the hell?

"I don't care if you're in an open relationship. No. I don't want you to end it with him. For the first time in my life, I don't want an open relationship. I want Charlotte all to myself and I can't think of anything worse than having sex with someone else who isn't her. This is why I can't be with you. I don't physically want to be. I'm not into it like I was before I met her."

I smile to myself.

"Don't you fucking dare bring this back on me," he whispers angrily as he tries to keep his voice down. "I'm blocking you, and if you dare to go near Charlotte, you'll see what fucking happens."

I hear a bang, and it sounds like his phone has been thrown across the room.

Shit.

I get up and run back to bed, diving under the covers.

After a brief bout of silence, I hear ice being poured into a glass from his refrigerator.

I lie in the darkness as fury pumps through my bones... How fucking dare she?

299

She goes to his office, drops to her knees even when he's told her that he's in love with someone else, and now it sounds like she threatened him that she's going to come to me.

And say what?

Well, she's got another thing coming if she thinks I'm taking her shit.

I've waited a long time for Spencer to find me, and I'm not handing him over to a woman who fucks at the drop of a hat.

I'll be waiting, Sheridan.

Come at me.

I blow into my coffee cup while sitting at the kitchen counter. It's now 7:00 a.m. and I'm up and dressed for work early.

Spencer didn't come to bed until very late last night. I was fast asleep by the time he did, and the last time I checked the clock, it read 3:00 a.m.

What was he doing downstairs?

Did he call her back? Was he having second thoughts?

My mind is in overdrive, but I'm not falling into the insecure trap. Well, I'm trying my best not to, anyway.

I'm not sure about this love thing. It's like you hand your heart over to someone and hope to God that they don't break it.

Part of me feels sorry for Sheridan. I can only imagine how she must feel to have lost him. But part of me is terrified that one day I'll find out for myself. I exhale heavily and stare out of the window to look out over London.

Stop thinking like this! It's destructive to both of us.

Nobody needs an insecure girlfriend.

"Good morning, angel."

I turn to see him walking into the kitchen, his CEO attire firmly in place. Today he's wearing a navy suit, crisp white shirt, and a paisley tie. His golden hair is just washed, and he's freshly shaven too. Spencer exudes opulence...way more than I do.

The expensive watch, the shoes, the ridiculous good looks...

he's the whole delicious package. Lara's words of warning come back to haunt me. He's heartbreak in a hot suit.

His big blue eyes meet mine before he kisses me softly. "I missed waking up with you this morning." He smiles down at me.

"Good morning, Mr Spencer." I smile and wrap my arms around him. His tongue slowly slides through my open lips and he sucks on me with just the right amount of pressure.

The way he kisses me is just so...

His eyes drop to my toes and then back up to my face. "You look fucking edible today, angel."

I force a smile. "Thanks." I'm wearing a tight grey skirt that hangs just below my knees, and a white silk shirt with a matching grey suit jacket. It's a power suit...the kind I know he likes.

Stop it.

Damn it, I hate this insecurity nonsense. This isn't who I am at all.

His eyes drop to my feet again and then up over my hips. I feel the heat from his stare burn my skin, and he readjusts himself in his suit pants.

"What time did you come to bed?" I ask.

He licks his lips as his eyes drop to my breasts, and he cups one of them, fascinated. "Late."

My eyes hold his. "Did the phone call go well?"

His lips drop to my neck and he holds my jaw in his hand. He bites me and I feel goose bumps scatter up my spine.

"Yeah," he murmurs against my skin.

"What did she say?"

He bites me on the base of my neck and his hand drops to my behind as he grinds me onto his hard cock.

"Spencer..." God, the man's an animal. Is sex all he thinks about?

"Hmm, why are we talking about Sheridan?" He kisses me again. "I only want to talk about you in this fucking edible outfit."

"Because I want to know what she said."

He pulls away from me and my body instantly hates it. "She was pissed off and carrying on."

"What do you mean?"

"She wants to meet you."

My eyes hold his. "Why?"

"Because she wants to intimidate you and make you feel insecure." He grabs me by the waist again and drags me to him.

It's too late, she already has.

"You fought?" I frown. He begins to unfasten my buttons one by one.

"A bit."

"Did you call her back? Is that why you came to bed late?"

"No." He concentrates on my buttons. "I stayed up because I was angry, and I didn't want you to have to see me like that."

I pull his face to meet mine. "I don't want you to hide your emotions from me."

His eyes darken and he puts his hands under the hem of my skirt, lifting it up over my hips. "You want to know what emotion I'm feeling right now?" He sits me up on the counter and slips my high heels off.

I nod, although I have a pretty good idea already.

He kisses me, all suction, all domination, and he lays me back over the counter. With his eyes locked on mine, he pulls my panties to the side and slides two thick fingers deep inside my sex.

"Oh." My eyes close involuntarily.

He pumps me hard and then lifts my legs up so that my feet are resting up on his chest in front of me. He begins to work me, deep and aggressive, his eyes dark and holding mine.

"You want to know what I'm feeling right now?" he whispers as his hand begins to really work me. My body begins to move on the counter from the force of his hand.

"I'm feeling like I can't let you go to work looking like that without feeding that beautiful cunt of yours."

My stomach flips.

302

God, he's filthy. "She's a very hungry girl," I whisper. "Starving."

He curls his lip in arousal, and his fingers work me so hard that I wince from the sting.

He unzips his fly, drops his pants and briefs, pulls my panties to the side, and then he lifts my legs over his shoulders and slides in deep.

The sheer size of him takes possession of my body, and I lose all coherent thought. His eyes flicker with a dark arousal.

"Fuck, yeah," he hisses.

He pulls completely out, and then he uses his hand to bounce his hard cock onto my pubic bone a few times before he slides back in and repeats the delicious movement.

My body ripples around him. The man is a god.

He adds a deep circular movement that makes my eyes roll back in my head.

He pulls completely out again and bounces his cock back onto my pubic bone. When he slides it deep inside me again, my insides melt. What must we look like? Him dressed in a suit and ready for work, me laid out for his pleasure.

That's what this is: his pleasure, and I'm just the lucky woman who gets to give it to him.

Spencer Jones takes what he needs. He doesn't care about the rules. When he wants it, he takes it.

This is the best breakfast date ever.

Within moments, he has me arching my back as he fucks me with his thick, weeping cock. I lurch forward, coming *hard*. I'm going to have bruises from this kitchen counter tomorrow on my spine, but I don't care. Every second of pain is worth it.

He tips his head back, groans, and comes deep inside of me. He closes his eyes as he slowly empties himself, and then he stops and pants, looking down at me the whole time.

He smiles as he licks my ankle and then kisses it tenderly before he slowly pulls out. His eyes drop to my sex and he smirks.

303

He puts his fingers back into my sex and then takes them out, rubbing his fingers across my bottom lip.

He licks his lips and smiles darkly.

"What?" I smirk.

"You look really good all freshly fucked with your legs open like that." He pushes my hair back from my forehead. "Especially with my come on your lips."

"You are a filthy bastard, Spencer Jones."

He chuckles and zips up his pants in one quick movement. "I am, and now I'm a satisfied filthy bastard."

I wrap my arms around him and we kiss. It's unrushed and perfect.

"I booked us a weekend away while I stayed up last night," he says as he looks down at me.

"You did?"

"We're going to Greece for the weekend, so you'll have to take Monday off."

My face falls. "Greece?"

"Uh-huh." He leaves me and picks up his phone and briefcase.

"But I can't take Monday off." I frown, rising up to rest on my elbows.

"You need to." His eyes drop down my body like he's hungry for it again.

"What?" I smirk.

"Just taking a photographic picture to remember you by. I'm going to jerk off today to the thought of how hot you are like this."

"Spencer," I gasp. "You're going to jerk off at work?"

"I'll be in my office bathroom, of course." He gifts me with a very sexy wink. "You're the main star of many a lunchtime fantasy."

I laugh out loud and throw my forearm over my eyes. "You're an animal," I huff.

He kisses me softly. "Agreed." He walks towards the door. "See you tonight, angel."

I drop my head back and look up at the ceiling. A huge, goofy grin spreads into my cheeks. Holy hell... I'm in love with a sex maniac.

And he's taking me to Greece.

16

Spencer

I STRIDE into the restaurant with my racing heart, spotting Masters and Seb in our usual seats. I fall into my position around the table.

"Hey." I pick up a glass of water and drain it. I refill the glass and drink it all down again immediately.

Masters and Seb frown as they watch me and then exchange looks.

"Can I get you a coffee?" the waitress asks.

"I'll have a beer. Actually, no, make it a scotch." I circle my fingers over my temples. "On the rocks."

"Jesus Christ," Masters mutters under his breath. "What now?"

The waitress walks off to the bar, looking a little perplexed.

"Have you even been to bed yet?" Seb frowns.

"Yes, of course," I bark.

"You know it's seven in the morning, right?"

"Yes! I know what fucking time it is!" I snap. "I've fucked it. I fucked the whole thing."

"What thing?" Masters frowns.

"Charlotte's pregnant."

"What?" they both gasp, widening their eyes.

I drag my hand down my face. "Oh God, she was all sexy and shit, and I didn't see her last night because of fucking Sheridan. One minute I was saying hello, the next minute I was finger fucking her with her legs over my shoulders, and the minute after that, I'm giving it to her on the kitchen counter. I forgot all about a fucking condom," I blurt out.

They both stare at me, horrified. "When was this?" Seb asks.

"Twenty minutes ago." I sigh with a sad shake of my head.

"Oh God, you idiot. So she's not really pregnant?" Masters throws his head back and laughs out loud, placing his hand over his heart in relief. "You had me there for a minute."

"Well, she soon will be. This isn't fucking funny, Masters, you prick." I put my head in my hands. "She's young and never been on the pill before." I try to think of an analogy. "She's like a giant, golden uterus, just waiting to be fertilized."

They chuckle together.

I shake my head in disgust. "Seb, Google what age a woman is most fertile," I whisper in a panic.

He takes out his phone and consults Dr Google.

The waitress arrives with my drink and hands it over. "Thank you," I whisper and take it with a shaking hand.

Masters winces as he watches me. "Bring him another, please."

The waitress frowns and looks between us. "Is everything okay?"

"No!" I splutter. "I've fucked it, I fucked the whole thing. And everything was going so great, too."

She purses her lips, unsure what to say to that.

"Thank you," Seb says to the waitress, obviously trying to get rid of her.

I drain my glass of scotch while they watch on.

"Why would you have unprotected sex?"

I shrug. "I don't know. It was so good that I completely forgot I was a mere human with super potent bodily fluids."

"Fuck's sake," Seb mutters in disgust. "I need sex that good. I

307

have fucking repetitive strain in my wrist. I think I'm going to have to start going back to Madison's."

"Did Charlotte forget too?" Masters frowns, ignoring Seb.

I shrug. "I don't know."

"Did she remind you?"

"No."

"Did she freak out after?"

"No." I shake my head.

"Fucking hell." Masters rolls his eyes. "I thought you said she was all pure and wholesome. Surely she would have thought of this."

"Ah." I point to them. "She isn't pure at all, though. She's as fucking dirty as I am and she didn't even know it." I run both of my hands through my hair. "Give it a few months and she will be running rings around me, I'm telling you. She loves it."

"Or waddling like Bree with a huge pregnant baby bump." Masters smirks.

Seb interrupts us with his search results. "Okay. It says here that a woman is most fertile at the age of twenty-four."

My eyes widen in horror. "Charlotte is twenty-five," I gasp.

"Oh fuck, you're doomed."

Masters laughs again. "What's the problem, anyway? I thought you said she was perfect?"

"She is."

"So..." Seb frowns. "Masters is right, what is the problem?"

"I can't have a kid. I only just got my first girlfriend. I can't even have a dog yet."

"You're thirty-eight, Spence," Seb says, deadpan.

I put my head into my hands. "It's just a fucking number, okay! And you sound like my mother."

"When is her period due?" Masters asks.

"I don't know."

"When did she have her last one?"

"I don't know." I look between them. "Should I know this?"

"Uh, yes." They both look at me as if I'm stupid. "You should definitely know this."

I think on it. "She definitely hasn't had one since we've been having sex." I shrug. "I know that much for sure."

"How long has that been?"

"Umm." I frown and try to remember. "About three weeks or so. Maybe longer."

"Which means she's probably due around about now," Masters tells me.

"Has she been feisty over the last few days?" Seb asks.

My eyes widen. "Yes." I point to him. "Very fucking feisty, in fact. She threatened to bury me under my house and all."

They both laugh. "You're safe," Masters tells me just as our breakfast arrives.

We all thank the waitress when she puts our meals in front of us.

My nerves temper a little. "You reckon it's okay?"

"I know it is." He takes a bite. "Hormones turn women into the devil. Death threats definitely qualify."

"Right," Seb mutters.

"Good, good," I mutter under my breath, and I drag a hand down my face. "What a fucking morning," I huff. "Best sex ever followed by a complete freak-out in the elevator."

They both chuckle. "You didn't even realise what you'd done until after?"

"Nope." I shake my head. "I'm slipping, man."

Seb giggles. "It's a good thing you're off the market. You're getting sloppy, Spence."

"Or perhaps just happy." Masters smirks, cutting through his toast. "Children with the woman you love are a blessing."

I exhale heavily as the scotch begins to warm my blood. "How is my Breezer?" I ask.

"Huge." Masters smiles. "Fucking beautiful."

"How long have we got?"

"A few weeks or so."

"Tell her to keep her legs crossed until I get back from this weekend."

"Why, where are you going?"

"Greece."

"I take it this thing with Charlotte is going really well, then." Masters smiles.

I shrug as I chew. "I asked her to move in with me."

Seb's fork hits the plate with a clang, and they both stare up at me, shocked.

"Are you joking right now?" Masters frowns.

"No, why?" I ask, surprised by their reaction.

"You've known her for six weeks."

"I know, and in such a short time I've become completely pathetic. I can't stand a night away from her. Her idiot brother came to my office and warned me away from her. On top of that, Sheridan threatened to pull the account from me if I refuse to keep seeing her."

"What?"

"Yeah, get this. Sheridan comes to my work when I was on the phone…to you, actually, Seb." I take a sip of my scotch. "She drops to her knees on the carpet and tries to give me a head job while I'm on the phone."

Seb frowns as he chews. "When the hell was this?"

"The other day, when you called me about the mattress. So, she's on her knees, and she tells me she loves me. Then she starts crying and shit. All this is going down the exact same time the receptionist buzzes through to tell me Edward Prescott is there to see me."

Masters chuckles and pinches the bridge of his nose. "Only fucking you, Spence. You have the best stories."

I roll my eyes. "Then I get rid of Sheridan with the promise of having dinner to discuss our relationship. Edward waltzes in and proceeds to tell me that fucking Alexander York has been spinning tales to him about Charlotte and I being together—"

"Well, it is true," Seb interrupts. "So it's not really a tale."

"What did you do?" Masters frowns.

"He's so fucking arrogant." I shake my head. "We instantly despised one another. In the end, I kicked him out of my office."

"Jesus Christ," Masters mutters. "You don't do that shit to the future in-laws, Spence."

"Yeah, well, what am I supposed to do? I'm not putting up with his entitled shit. He doesn't give a fuck about Charlotte, and unfortunately for him, I do." I take an angry bite of my breakfast. "You know what pisses me off the most about the cockhead? He flew here yesterday from wherever the fuck he was, and he didn't even call Charlotte to see how she was doing."

They both frown.

"He doesn't give a fuck about her feelings or well-being. All he cares about is his fucking self." I chew my food as my anger begins to rise. "I mean, who the hell does he think he is? He doesn't fucking control her. How dare he even think that he does." I put my hand up for another drink.

Masters looks down at my two empty scotch glasses. "Are you working today?"

"Yeah."

"You're going to work drunk?" Seb asks carefully.

"Looks like it!"

"Why did Charlotte want to bury you for?"

"Oh." I throw my hands up in disgust. "That's a whole other story. Sheridan wanted me to have dinner with her to discuss our relationship. I said yes just to get her out of my office because Edward was in the waiting room. Last night, I told Charlotte, and she lost her ever-loving shit over it. Like, she went full crazy-bitch mode on me, saying it's her or Sheridan from now on."

They both smile at me.

"Not funny. Then I had to tell Sheridan that I wasn't able to see her. That's when she pulled the whole 'if you won't see me, how are we supposed to work together' bullshit. Maybe I need to find another steel company to do business with."

Their faces drop. "How much is her contract worth to you?"

I pinch the bridge of my nose. "Fucking millions. But I don't care, she's not blackmailing me into being with her."

"God." Seb sighs.

"Anyway, that's my week in a nutshell." I sigh.

"Sounds fucking hectic." Seb winces.

My eyes widen when I remember that there's more to the story. "Oh, and some pap took a photo of me and Charlotte together. I'm assuming that will be everywhere soon, too."

Masters bursts out laughing while Seb shakes his head in disbelief. "I thought that once you got a girlfriend, things might be quieter for you."

"So did I." I huff as my next scotch arrives. "So. Did. I."

Charlotte

Beth smiles at me. "Tell me everything." The two of us have met for lunch today. She's been on a work conference for a week, although it feels like she's been gone a month. I have so much to tell her.

"Oh, Beth, he is..." I shake my head. "Words just don't do him justice."

"Here we go. What happened to you playing it cool and not falling for him?"

"I couldn't help it."

She sips her drink, unimpressed.

"We had the talk."

"What talk?" She frowns.

"He wants to be exclusive and—"

"What?" she interrupts me.

"Honestly, I'm telling you, it really is something special between us. From his side, too."

"Ugh, okay, so he's fucked you into submission. I get it."

I giggle. "Ah, the sex. How have I been missing out on this for so long?"

She laughs. "I told you. And you do look stupidly happy."

I take her hand over the table. "I am, Beth. I'm so happy."

"Good for you, Lottie Prescott." She glances over and makes eye contact with Anthony, slowly turning her attention back to me. "Could you give Anthony my phone number?"

I glance around, and Anthony looks away guiltily. "Has something happened?"

"He just looks at me like he wants to eat me."

I roll my lips to hide my smile. "That could be kind of good... couldn't it?"

"Fuck, yes. Pass him my number and just say *'I'm setting you up with Beth, so here's her number. Give her a call and she'll fuck you real hard.'*"

I laugh. "I am *not* saying that."

"Fine, say whatever you want. Just make sure he calls me."

"Okay."

"Now tell me what's happening tonight." She smiles.

"I'm cooking Spencer dinner at his house," I announce proudly.

Beth smirks. "Look at you, being all domesticated."

"Do you want to come over?" I ask.

"Hopefully I will be occupied with Anthony's dick in my mouth. Give him my number straight away when you leave. Don't forget, will you?"

"He might not even call you."

"As if he won't."

Swoony Mr Spencer.

It's funny how quickly things become a habit.

And by things, I mean Spencer Jones.

Every night, we talk and eat dinner together, and then we lounge about and laugh all night before he takes me to bed and makes me feel like the most beautiful girl in the world. Well, it's not always sweet lovemaking. He mostly fucks me like he hates me, but man, I love it when he hates me hard.

I never dreamed that it could be this good or that I could feel this satisfied. For the first time in a long time, I'm living completely in the moment. I laugh all day at work and then my nights are full of Swoony Mr Spencer.

Things are good—really good.

I'm sprawled on the sofa, reading my book. My feet are in Spencer's lap and he, too, is reading. He wasn't joking in that email. He really is an avid reader.

"Can you turn the television off?" Spencer asks, never letting his eyes stray from the page.

"No, I have to have it on."

He looks up from his book. "What do you mean, you have to have it on?"

"I hate silent houses, haven't you noticed? I have the TV on all the time."

He frowns. "But you don't even watch it."

"I know." I turn the page of my book. "I need the noise." I can feel his eyes on me, so I glance up. "What?"

"Why do you need noise in the background?"

I shrug. "It keeps me company."

"Why would you need company from the television?"

"Well, I don't now that I have you."

"When did you need company from a television in the past?"

I roll my eyes. "Fine, if it's that big of a deal." I hold up the remote and switch it off. I go back to reading.

"Charlotte."

I glance up at the tone of his voice. One thing I've learned about Spencer is that he only calls me Charlotte when something is on his mind. The rest of the time I'm his angel. "What?" I ask.

"Will you answer my question, please?"

"What was the question?" I sigh.

"When did you need company from the television?"

"Ever since my mother died."

He stares at me, and I can practically hear his brain ticking over from here. I drop my attention back to reading some more.

"Have you heard from Edward this week?" he asks.

I shake my head. "No."

He glares down at his book.

"Why?" I ask.

He turns the page so hard, he nearly rips it. "No reason."

"Tell me."

"I'm just wondering why your brother flew across the world to accost me about spending time with you, and yet he didn't even fucking bother to see you for himself."

I shrug sadly. I've been thinking about this all day too. Disappointed is an understatement. "He's very busy." I sigh.

"So busy that he has all the time in the world to scare everyone away from you, but none to actually spend time with you himself." He turns the page angrily again. "Makes me fucking sick," he mutters under his breath.

"Spence." I sigh. "Just drop it. It's not like that with Edward and me. William is the one I'm close to. Edward loves me in his own way, he's just misunderstood."

"Or perhaps just a selfish prick." His eyes hold mine for a moment and then, as if feeling guilty, he asks, "When do I get to meet this beloved William whom you talk so fondly of?"

"Soon," I beam, and then I quickly go back to reading my book. But, once again, I can feel his eyes on me. I glance up. "What is it now?"

"When is your period due?"

I smirk. "Why?"

"Because we had unprotected sex and you don't seem to care."

I smile and go back to my book. "It will be here early next week."

"How do you know?"

"Because I'm on the pill."

"You're on the pill?" he gasps. "Why wouldn't you tell me that? This is need-to-know information. Why have we been using condoms?"

"Because I don't know where you've been."

"In condoms, Charlotte," he snaps. "In condoms."

"You can stop stressing."

"I wasn't stressing."

"You were, you've been stressing all week over it, I know you have."

"How do you know that?"

"Because I'm getting to know you, and I know when something is bothering you."

"Why didn't you say something to put me out of my misery?"

"Because I wanted you to ask me when my period was due and have this conversation."

He narrows his eyes and crawls over me, holding himself up on his elbows. "I have a good mind to punish you right now for freaking me out about impending fatherhood. That was evil. I've been fucking frantic."

I laugh out loud. "You idiot. Why didn't you just ask?"

He kisses me, and that's his only answer.

"We're going to Greece tomorrow, remember?"

He smiles broadly. "We are."

"What are we going to do in Greece?"

"Eat, drink, swim, and fuck."

I laugh out loud. "You are a born romantic, Spencer Jones."

My phone dances on the table, the name Dad lighting up the screen. "You need to be quiet." I jump up and get it.

Spencer rolls his eyes, unimpressed.

"Hello, Dad." I sit back down beside Spencer.

"Hello, darling." My father's kind voice drifts down the phone.

Spencer's eyes light up with something, and he drops to the floor between my legs. My eyes widen and I shake my head, mouthing the word "No."

He smiles mischievously and begins to tug my pyjama pants down. I push his head away. "What's been happening, Dad?" I ask, trying to sound casual.

"Just working, as usual. I went to a Broadway show this week. I have business dinners a few nights this week. What are you doing? What's new with you?"

Everything.

Spencer nips my sex with his teeth, and I slap the top of his head. "Just lounging around, getting ready for bed," I lie as I widen my eyes at Spencer. "Stop it," I mouth.

He tears my pyjama pants down my legs and pulls me forward to the edge of the couch, where he spreads my legs.

"Oh my God," I mouth. "What's the weather like, Dad?" If only he could see what I'm doing now.

"It's been very hot. Vegas is muggy."

Spencer's thick tongue slides through my flesh, and I tremble as I try to hold it together. "I can imagine," I breathe out.

Spencer slides two thick fingers into my sex, forcing me to close my eyes.

"How's work going, love?" Dad asks.

Spencer pumps me hard, and I clench around him. Our eyes are locked, and I can hardly hear what my father is even saying. "So good," I murmur.

"Great."

My father's voice snaps me out of my moment.

"Dad, I-I have to go to the bathroom. Can I call you back tomorrow?"

"Of course, dear, speak soon. I love you."

"I love you too."

I hang up, chuck the phone, and grab Spencer to drag him to me. The minute our lips touch, I kiss him deeply. A thought runs through my mind. Shit. I scramble up and run across the room to pick my phone back up to check it's definitely off. I don't want my father to hear me say the next sentence.

"Fuck me," I breathe.

"That's exactly what I'm about to do. Get those fucking legs up."

. . .

We walk into the airport, hand in hand. Spencer has a trolley with our bags while Anthony and Wyatt trail behind us with theirs. There are people everywhere, and when I see all the queues, my eyes instinctively go back to Wyatt for reassurance.

"It's okay," he says.

Spencer frowns down at me. "What's wrong, angel?"

"Nothing," I lie.

Spencer looks at Wyatt in question.

"She gets a bit overwhelmed with crowds," Wyatt tells him.

Spencer's face falls. "Oh. I didn't know. Are you all right?"

I force a smile. "Yeah, I'm fine, lead the way."

He leads me by the hand, and we make our way to stand in the back of the check-in line. I look around at all the people, feeling very out of my comfort zone indeed. Spencer stands behind me with his hands on my hips. He's talking to the boys. He's wearing a navy blazer and blue jeans with a white T-shirt. He'll look delicious in any country. I feel his lips come to my temple while I concentrate on staying calm amongst the crowd.

"Have you ever caught a commercial flight before?" he whispers.

I shake my head, embarrassed by my stupid lifestyle.

"As you will see, airports suck."

I smile and nod.

"Does your father have a plane?"

I nod. "Three."

He rolls his eyes. "Only three. The poor fucker."

I smile bashfully. We make our way through the check-in and eventually walk through all the security and out into the restaurant. The boys take a seat at the bar and we sit in a booth.

"What do you want to drink, angel?" Spencer asks as he looks through the drinks menu.

"I'm easy."

His eyes rise to my lips. "You're only easy for me," he whispers darkly.

The air crackles between us.

I lean forward, resting my elbows on the table between us. "I really can't wait to suck your big dick tonight, Mr Spencer," I whisper.

He winks. "I'll look forward to it."

I find myself smiling again. Who would have ever thought I would have it in me to be like this?

"What drink do you want?"

"Margarita."

"Good choice. I'll join you." He closes the menu and goes to the bar.

As I wait, I glance over and see a bookstore just across the way. I might get a new book for by the pool. I get up and walk over to the boys.

"I'm just ducking into this shop to get a book. I won't be a moment. You stay here."

Wyatt, ignoring me, immediately stands and follows me. He waits outside while I walk in and look around. I pick my book and stand in the line to pay, when I look down at the magazine stand and my heart drops.

A picture of Spencer and me with the heading:

Bad Romeo Strikes Again

What?

I pick up the magazine with the sound of my blood pumping hard in my ears.

How humiliating... *Bad Romeo.*

"When did this magazine get released?" I ask.

The bored shopkeeper looks up. "Oh, it's not due out until tomorrow. We got it early."

I force a smile. "Thanks." I pay her and storm back to the table to find Spencer sitting with our two margaritas in front of him. He smiles cheekily up at me. "Here you go, sustenance for your cock-sucking duties tonight."

I slap the magazine on the table, and he looks down at it

immediately. It takes him a few seconds to realise what he's looking at before he frowns.

"What the hell?"

I fall into the seat and flick through the pages until I get to the story.

Spencer begins to drink his margarita and watches on. Wishing he were anywhere but here.

There are about twenty images of him and me together. There are even some of Wyatt and Anthony struggling to get the camera off the photographer. I read the story out loud.

"Renowned Playboy Spencer Jones is at it again.
Caught with the enigmatic and fiercely private billionaire Charlotte Prescott.
The two were captured on a lunch date hand in hand on Tuesday. Once spotted, her bodyguards physically attacked photographers to try and retrieve the film.
Two days earlier, Spencer was snapped with model Tiffany Boland on a yacht in Ibiza. He has also been linked in recent weeks with reality TV star May Allywell.
Charlotte Prescott is most definitely new to our radar.
We sense fireworks are coming when Daddy Megabucks finds out.
Watch this space!"

17

Charlotte

"WHAT THE FUCK?" Spencer splutters, wide-eyed. "They're fucking liars. I wasn't in Ibiza. You know this shit is made up, I was with you the whole time. And I don't even know May Allywell."

I glare at him.

"This isn't my fault," he wails.

I sit forward in my seat. "Spencer, go to the bar and get me another drink, please. Why couldn't you just keep your fucking dick in your pants all these years?" I whisper angrily.

"Believe me, I wonder the same thing," he splutters in a fluster as he stands. "How many drinks do you want?"

I glare at him, feeling like red steam is shooting out of my ears.

"I'll just get the whole bottle," he mutters under his breath.

I continue my glaring and he scurries away to the bar to escape my rage.

I inhale deeply to try and calm myself down.

This is *not* going to plan.

. . .

Three hours later, and I'm reading my book on the plane. The engine is droning out all sound. On a normal trip, I would be fast asleep by now.

"Are you still angry with me?" Spencer whispers.

"I'm not angry with you," I say, deadpan, my eyes firmly on my book. I'm not even reading; I'm too mad to see the words. I have no idea how I'm going to explain this situation to my father and Edward once they see this story. What's worse is that this is exactly what they didn't want to happen. I feel like a fool, knowing everyone thinks he's playing up on me, even though I know that's not true.

"You seem like you're angry with me. You're not exactly being friendly. You haven't said a word in three hours."

I look at him deadpan. "I am allowed to be angry with a situation. The whole world doesn't revolve around you, you know."

He widens his eyes. "Jeez." He thinks for a moment. "Is this your PMT talking?"

I stare at him.

"I mean, what would you say to me if you didn't have those bitch hormones running through your blood right now?"

Steam shoots from my ears once more. This man can't be that stupid, surely.

"What I would say to you is *shut the hell up.*"

He chuckles and lifts my hand to kiss the back of it. "You're hot when you're angry, Prescott."

I exhale heavily and turn back to my book.

"You know it's not true, right?"

"Yes."

"So why are you still mad with me?"

"Because I look like a fool."

"No, you don't."

"I do."

"But we know the truth." He frowns.

"Nobody else does."

He exhales heavily. "Why are you so worried about what everyone else thinks? Care about what I think."

I stare at him for a moment. "Okay, what do you think?"

"I think these people who work for the media and the magazines are idiots, and like I told you before, half of the shit they put out there is completely fabricated."

"A picture tells a thousand words."

"But does it? I've even been photographed with Seb's girlfriends in the past and been in the stupid tabloids for it."

"Why do they target you? I don't understand why they target you specifically." I do, actually. He's gorgeous, wealthy, and has enough boyish charm to light up the world...but I'm not letting him know that.

He shrugs. "It started about five years ago when I dated a girl who also happened to be a model. It was her they were after, and they got a few images of us together. Then I met another girl who, unbeknown to me, was an actress. We were photographed leaving a club together and they just assumed I was seeing both women at the same time. That's when they began this whole love rat bullshit."

"Were you seeing both women at the same time?"

He smirks. "Possibly, but each of them knew we weren't exclusive, and they were seeing other people too."

I stare out the window and a wave of disappointment runs through me. Unable to stop it from happening, my eyes fill with tears.

"Angel," he whispers, wrapping his arm around me. "Don't be upset."

"This isn't how I wanted to announce my first relationship to my family, Spence," I whisper.

"I know, baby." I sit back and rest my head on his shoulder. "It's shitty." He kisses my temple. "But don't let this crap affect our relationship. I don't care what everyone else thinks, I don't care if they hate me, but if I lose you because of shitty lies from people who don't even know me..." His voice trails off.

He's right. This isn't his fault.

"Can we start the weekend again, please?" I ask hopefully.

He smiles down at me, his eyes filled with empathy. "We can do anything you want, angel."

The car pulls into the private garage and I hunch my shoulders in excitement.

We're in Santorini, Greece.

"Your villa is two doors down from ours. You have your own pool," Spence tells the boys. "The key is in the mailbox at the side."

"Thank you." They both smile, and I think that, secretly, they're just as excited as me.

I love how Spencer always books their things and looks after their welfare, making sure they are well looked after. They have taken to him well and look to him for guidance now. It means a lot to me, and it says a lot about the type of man Spencer is.

"We'll just check out your place first, if that's okay?" Anthony asks.

"Of course."

The boys grab our bags and then disappear inside, leaving me to bounce around in the car. I can't remember ever being this excited. Spencer opens my door and holds his hand out for me to take.

"You ready, angel?" His face is alive with mischief, and I already know the place he's booked is incredible.

"I am." I beam at him as I take his hand and get out of the car. "Thank you for organising this. It's amazing."

"You haven't even seen it yet." He chuckles. "This isn't our place. We're camping on the beach with no bathroom." He throws me one of those sexy winks he does so well. "I thought we could rough it. Really get to know each other."

I laugh. "That would be amazing too."

He takes me into his arms and kisses me. "You are very easily pleased, Charlotte Prescott."

"As long as I'm with you, I'm happy."

We kiss again as the air around us swirls; our tabloid disaster has thankfully been left behind on the plane. We've decided not to think about it until Monday when we return. There's no use worrying and ruining our time here over something that's already done.

We are on the side of the mountain in Santorini, just near a village called Fira. All the houses and villas are white and overlook the sea. It looks like it's straight out of a travel brochure.

"Let's go inside," I urge

"Wait for the boys to finish first."

Oh, he wants privacy. I love it when he wants privacy.

I giggle up at him and he holds me in his arms. "Greece agrees with you." He smiles lovingly at me.

"I know." I laugh. "It really does."

He chuckles, and a few moments later we hear the words we've been waiting for. "All clear."

"Thank you," Spencer says as they walk back out into the garage. "I'll call you in the morning. No plans, we're just here to relax."

"Okay."

He slaps Wyatt on the back as he walks past him.

"We have our phones if you need us," Anthony calls.

"Thanks."

Spencer guides me through the huge timber double front doors, and my mouth falls open as my eyes bounce around the space.

"Oh my God," I gasp.

It's all white and minimalistic. The walls are made from rendered cement, and the floor has a beautiful terracotta tile to it.

The room is glowing pink, and I've never seen anything more beautiful.

The sunset.

The entire back of the villa is made of glass that overlooks an exotic infinity pool and the most beautiful view. The sun is just

325

setting over the water. Spencer leads me out through the French doors to a balcony that is decorated with exotic daybeds and deck chairs. Beautiful cushions are scattered around the pool, and I can't help but smile as I take it all in.

"This is like some crazy movie scene," I breathe, feeling the pink glow on my face. The sea breeze blows my hair around, and I look up to see Spencer smiling at the ocean. "Thank you," I whisper.

He takes me in his arms and pushes the hair back from my face. "I'm sorry about today."

"It's not your fault." I wrap my arms around his broad neck, and his lips touch mine. "Let's go swimming."

"Okay." He immediately begins to undress, lifting his shirt over his shoulders.

"What are you doing?" I ask.

"We're skinny-dipping."

"I don't think I want that on the front page of a magazine." I hold my arm up to gesture to the villas above us on the hill. Who knows who can see us from up here?

"Didn't think of that." He kicks off his shoes, slides his jeans down, and he steps out of them. I'm rewarded with the sight of his tight, white boxer shorts. My eyes drop down his body and back to his face.

"Get your bikini on. Now." He smirks darkly. "I'm about to fuck you in this pool."

Goose bumps scatter up my arms and I giggle like a schoolgirl. I run inside and grab my bag, taking it through to the main bedroom.

This is the best weekend ever.

I stop dead in my tracks when I see the room.

Once again, I'm rendered speechless. There's a king-size bed made out of a pale timber that has beautiful white netting surrounding it. The back wall is made of glass windows, and it also has magnificent views of the ocean. Through a large mint green barn-style door is a gigantic bathroom with a triple shower and a sunken spa bath in the middle.

I put my hands over my mouth in awe. I've never been anywhere so beautiful. I scramble through my bag and find my gold bikini. I throw it on and run back out to the pool. Spencer is sitting on the step, and he smiles when he sees me.

I hold my hands out wide. "Ta-dah!" I announce.

Spencer's eyes twinkle with a certain something I haven't seen before. He stands and takes my hand, leading me into the pool.

"Look at you, you're blossoming before my eyes."

I frown in question.

"A month ago, you were self-conscious and shy, and now..." He holds his hand out to my bikini. "Sexy and confident as fuck. Exhibit A."

I giggle as I wrap my arms and legs around him in the water. "Well, I have a very good teacher."

He looks down at me, the sinking sun lighting his face. The water is still, and suddenly, it's as if the whole world stops. Our eyes are locked, our bodies snuggled up tight together, but it's his heart I'm here for. His big, beautiful, caring heart.

This is a tenderness I've never known—one that a lot of women will never know.

The closeness between us is everything.

His eyes search mine as if he feels it too, and for a long time, we just stare at each other in the twilight. Finally, he takes my face into his hands and his lips gently brush over mine.

"I love you, Charlotte," he whispers.

"I love you too." I smile softly. Oh...this is so perfect.

He is perfect.

We kiss, long and slow, and I can feel his erection up against my stomach.

"You didn't have to bring me all the way to Greece to say that." I smile down at him.

He gives me that cheeky, boyish grin I love. "I did. I fucked up the condom first, didn't I?"

"Well, if you had just asked."

"Can we not go back to that nightmare? I had visions of myself driving a minivan with five scruffy kids in the backseat."

We laugh out loud, and then quickly fall serious again. "We came to Greece because I wanted the first time I said it to be special."

I smile at him.

"This is a big fucking deal in my life, you know? I've been going on TTT therapy trips over this for years."

I laugh against his lips and squeeze him tight.

"Promise me that Edward won't come between us," he says.

"He won't, baby." I push his hair back from his forehead as I look into his big blue eyes. "I promise."

His lips take mine, and this time there's an edge to his kiss. I know the times when I'm going to get it hard, and tonight is one of them. With his hands on my hips, he guides me back and forth over his hard length. The water begins to ripple around us.

"Bring your legs up," he orders huskily, his focus shifting to my mouth.

I love it when he fixates on my mouth. I know he's imagining how I would feel around him.

I bring my legs up onto the step on either side of him, and he inhales sharply as he grinds my body down onto him. "I'm going to fuck you right here, angel."

"Hmm."

He pulls my bikini to the side and begins to rub his thick cock through my wet flesh, back and forth, back and forth. I feel myself quiver already.

Damn it, I'm hopeless.

"Hold it," he whispers. "Don't come."

I smile. "Like it's a choice."

With his hands on my behind, he guides me down onto him and we both moan at the burn as he goes a little way in.

He grabs my hand and puts it over his heart. I can feel it beating hard in his chest.

His eyes hold mine. "Every time, angel. Every time I'm with you, my heart races."

He grabs my jaw and kisses me hard and uncontrolled. He's only an inch in, but I swear I'm going to come.

"I can't get close enough to you," he whispers. "I can't get enough of you. Do you know how long I've waited to feel like this?"

My eyes fill with tears. *I'm so in love with him.*

Our kiss turns desperate, and he grabs my shoulders from behind, slamming me down onto his cock. It's so hard, the air is knocked out of my lungs.

He's thick, long, and hell, I'm blessed that the man I love is so virile and strong. His cock is rock-hard...just for me. He slowly slides my body up and down on him and circles himself deep inside.

His eyes are dark when he licks my open mouth. "I'm going to try something, okay, baby?"

His hand goes around to my behind, and he puts a finger over my back entrance.

My body instantly tenses up.

"Shh." He calms me as his dick moves in and out of my sex to its own rhythm.

"Lean forward," he whispers.

I stare at him, and I know this is it—the moment he's asking me to try something new.

And I want to, I want to be adventurous for him.

With my lips locked on his, I lean forward, and he slides a finger deep into my back entrance, slowly sliding me down onto his cock at the same time.

My eyes widen as they hold his. The look on his face is one of pure satisfaction.

"Feels good, angel, doesn't it? I'm going to fuck you here one day."

Hearing him say such filthy things does something to me, and I convulse immediately, my body spiralling into a throbbing orgasm. I moan loudly and completely lose control.

"Oh, my girls likes it," he whispers in an unrecognisable voice as he begins to let me have it hard.

The water slams into the side of the pool, and it feels like the closer he gets, the deeper his finger and cock feel. "Lift your legs!" he barks.

I'm half scared to, but I lift my legs higher. He throws his head back and holds himself deep inside of me. I feel the telling jerk of his cock as it empties.

"Fucking...hell," he moans. He continues to pump me full, and finally stills at once.

With his eyes locked on mine, his finger continues to move in and out of me. He's fascinated.

He's unable to stop.

I kneel over him, completely transfixed as he explores my body to satisfy his needs.

"Fuck, you turn me on." He bites my nipple through my bikini top, his finger slowly sliding in and out, and I know he's making the most of it while he has me like this. "Can we fuck here now?" he whispers up at me in awe.

I kiss his big, beautiful lips. "One day."

He smiles softly and continues to work me, and damn, it feels so intimate and raw.

So unexpectedly good.

Who would have ever thought that this would be a special moment?

He bites my nipple hard. It makes me wince, and I wiggle away from his over exploring finger. He's so naughty.

"You may just be the Devil himself, Mr Spencer."

He smiles mischievously and fakes a bow. "At your service, my Lady." He tips me back and bites my neck. "I look forward to our *one day*."

. . .

The sun peeks over the horizon, and I smile in awe, sucking in a slow breath.

It's early, and I'm out on the deck, watching the dawn of a new day. It's too beautiful to go unwatched. I wrap my robe around me and smile as the golden glow bounces on my face and the sea breeze swirls around me and whips my hair.

Heaven.

This place is something else. It's so exotic and gorgeous...otherworldly. I look down at all of the white villas on the cliff below us and wonder who's inside of them. Are the women down there as lucky as I am?

My beautiful Spencer is still fast asleep in bed, unaware he's missing the most perfect sunrise ever. He's also blissfully unaware of the fear that I have deep in the pit of my stomach. I don't want Spence to know I'm worried about that stupid magazine story on our weekend away. I'm acting as hard as I can, but honestly, how can I not be scared? I'm shaken to my core.

I imagine Edward and my father reading the story and what they would be saying—or screaming—and I close my eyes with regret.

This is not how I wanted to tell them about Spencer. It couldn't be further from how I wanted to tell them, but of course, that choice has been taken out of my hands now. He will be judged before they even meet him. I have a feeling he already has been.

At least by Edward.

My mind goes to him visiting Spencer at work this week and how Spencer was annoyed that Edward didn't make time to come and see me when he was in London.

If I'm honest, it did hurt my feelings, but I would never let on to Spence that it did. It would only infuriate him, and I need to try and make the two of them get along. It will make my life so much easier.

But why didn't Edward come and see me? I just don't understand.

A boat is loading down in the water, and I watch the people

board. Then, as it slowly pulls out, I watch it disappear across the water. I wonder where they are going today. What adventure are they about to have?

I feel two large hands snake around my waist from behind and lips gently dust my temple. "Good morning, beautiful," his deep voice purrs.

I smile and place my hand up on his face. "Morning," I whisper. "How did you sleep?"

"Like a log." He wraps his arms around me and holds me tight.

"God, it's so beautiful here, Spence."

He smiles as he looks out over the horizon. "It is, isn't it?"

We stand in each other's arms for a moment as we drink in our surroundings. "What are we doing today?" I ask.

"Sightseeing."

I smile broadly.

"On mopeds."

I flick around to face him. "Mopeds?" I gasp. "I've... I've never..."

Spencer laughs at my sheer terror. "Don't worry, I'll be driving. You're just being my biker bitch."

"Biker bitch?" I frown. "What the hell does a biker bitch do?"

"Me." He winks. "You sit on the back of my bike all day, and then you sit on my cock all night."

I burst out laughing. "You're an idiot."

With a huge smile, he bites at my neck and walks me backwards inside the house.

"But first you have to earn your leathers."

"I don't think this is a good idea." Wyatt frowns.

I glance over at Wyatt as Spencer puts my motorbike helmet on. I don't think this is a good idea, either, if I'm honest, but I'm trying my hardest to act braver than I really am.

Spencer frowns while he concentrates on fastening the strap under my chin.

"This makes me feel claustrophobic," I say.

He smirks, choosing not to respond verbally.

"How much experience do you actually have on motorbikes?" I ask. I look at the nippy little machine parked in our garage.

"Heaps." He knocks on my helmet three times. "I've only been to hospital three or four times. A few broken bones have been the worst of it."

"What?" My eyes widen.

"Both legs, both arms," he teases. "Fractured skull."

"Tell me you're joking."

"I swear, if you crash with her on the back of that bike..." Wyatt interrupts.

Anthony laughs as he watches on.

"Stop laughing, Ant," Wyatt warns. "This could be the last trip we ever come on."

"Or last trip we ever make," I mutter flatly.

Spencer's eyes widen with delight. "Will you all fucking relax? I'm an excellent driver, and..." He throws his leg over the bike and leans down, pretending to ride fast. "You won't be able to keep up with Charlotte and me."

Good grief, I may actually die today. "Spencer, I don't know about this."

"Get on, woman." He gestures to the back of the bike with his chin.

I put my hands on my hips and smirk at him. He's said that to me before, although the context was completely different. "Get on and wrap your legs around me."

I do as I'm told, enjoying the way he helps me onto the seat behind him.

"You boys all right with everything?" Spencer asks them. Wyatt starts up his engine, followed by Anthony. Spencer starts our bike up too.

"Go slow," Wyatt warns him. "Don't drive stupid."

Spencer rolls his eyes. "You nag me to fucking death, Wyatt."

Anthony chuckles. "Right?"

Spencer turns around and flips my little glass screen down over my eyes. "Hold on tight, angel."

He pulls out slowly, and I scrunch my eyes tight and hold on.

He begins to pick up speed, and I squeeze him so tight that I'm afraid he may pop.

We pull out into the street and down the hill.

"You okay?" he calls.

I nod, too scared to reply. We ride on the cobblestone streets for a while, and I watch the people flash by us in a blur.

He runs his hand along my thigh. Hmm, maybe this isn't so bad after all.

We pull out onto a wider road and he speeds up a little. Wyatt appears on his bike beside us out of nowhere, holding his hand up for Spencer.

"Slow down!" he calls to us.

Spencer shakes his head, flips him the bird, and accelerates away.

"Ah!" I scream as I am pushed back from the G-force.

I look behind us to see Wyatt and Anthony chasing us with a look of sheer terror on their faces. I giggle and shout out to Spencer, "Lose them."

Spencer nods and twists his wrist to send us faster.

"See you later, motherfuckers," he cries.

I hear Wyatt's horn blare to life, and I put my head down on Spencer's shoulder and laugh.

Being naughty is so much fun.

Three hours later, we pull into a beach, and I smile goofily as I take my helmet off.

That was the most fun I think I've ever had. We've seen so much of the island and had a great time doing it too.

Wyatt and Anthony pull in beside us, and Spencer laughs as soon as Wyatt takes his helmet off.

"I just aged fifty years thanks to you." Wyatt huffs. "You're a maniac driver."

Spencer holds his hand out at the beach. "But look at your reward."

We look around and see the most beautiful beach of black sand. It has deck chairs lined up in pairs with straw-thatched beach umbrellas above them. The water is bright blue and crystal clear. There's a beach bar, too, and people are sitting out the veranda, drinking cocktails.

"May I present Perissa Beach on the Aegean Sea."

"Wow." I smile. "Impressive."

"And an added attraction of this beach is the spectacular view." He gestures to the deck chairs, where there are rows of beautiful women all oiled up and topless.

"This beach is also known as Juggernauts Hangout."

We all laugh, and I roll my eyes. It's such a Spencer thing to say.

"See, boys, I have your best interests at heart." He winks mischievously.

"Excellent." Anthony smirks.

Spencer helps me off the bike and rests our helmets on the handlebars.

"Charlotte and I are going to have some lunch before we take a swim and lie around for a few hours. Do whatever you like," Spencer tells them.

"We will be close," Wyatt assures us.

"Not too close." Spencer takes my hand in his. "Take the hint and go look at some boobs or something."

I smirk at the boys. Being told to go and look at some boobs is not something I imagine that they have ever heard from their employer before.

"This way." Spencer takes off towards the restaurant. Anthony walks beside him, and Wyatt gives me a lopsided smile, as if he has something on his mind.

"What's that look?" I ask as I link my arm with his and we turn to follow the other two.

"I like seeing you like this," he says, stuffing his hands in his pockets.

"Like what?"

"Happy."

I bump my shoulder with his. "Does it really show?"

"Like a beacon."

We walk for a moment, and I see Spencer up ahead laughing out loud at something Anthony has said. His laugh is childish and carefree. "This is a lot better than suffocating in Nottingham, isn't it?"

Wyatt smiles as he looks at our surroundings. "For all concerned."

The late-afternoon sun is warm on my face, and I smile at the sky. We've been at Perissa Beach for hours. It's simply too good to leave.

The boys are up the back somewhere, and we are down by the water on our deck chairs in our swimwear.

We've eaten, swam, drank, and I even had a little nap. Spencer has gone to the bar in search of some cocktails while I lie here in my bliss.

The sound of the waves, the seagulls, the laughter, and music in the distance... I think this may just be my most favourite place I've ever been to. And I've been to a lot of amazing places, but I think it's because of who I'm here with.

Spencer is my favourite place. Anywhere with him is Heaven.

He reappears with two very pink and exotic-looking drinks in his hands. I sit up with a frown. "Wow, what are these?"

He passes my tall glass, bright pink and bubbling with fancy straws placed in it. "A Pinky Sweetheart for my pinky sweetheart."

I smile as I look at the glass suspiciously. It's probably as toxic as all heck. "How am I a pinky sweetheart?"

He sips his drink and narrows his eyes. "Well, you're my sweetheart, and your bits are a delicious shade of pink." He shrugs. "Pinky sweetheart."

I laugh and take a sip. He falls into the deck chair beside me. "This is delicious." I nod. "Good choice."

He raises his glass to me. "Not just a pretty face."

Isn't that the truth?

Spencer is so far from being just a pretty face that I don't even notice he's so good-looking anymore. It's what's inside him that I love. The two parts of him that make him so different to anyone I've ever met. He's playful, honest, and sweet, but then he has this dominant side that only ever comes out properly when we're in the bedroom. I remember how he was when he first met Wyatt and Anthony, and I know he's no pushover to people who don't know him.

Like Edward.

"Can I ask you something?"

He nods as he sucks through his straw. "This drink is lethal, by the way. Don't let us swim, we may die."

I giggle. "You said that you went on a Triple P trip. What does that mean?"

"Oh." He frowns. "Triple T?"

"Yes, that's it. What's a Triple T trip?"

"It's a time-to-think trip. You know, when things get too much and you can't handle it anymore, you have to escape life to have time to think."

"So what do you do?"

"I go away on my own for two to three weeks. Do nothing, speak to nobody, reflect."

"Where do you go?"

"The Four Seasons in Maui. It has to be the Four Seasons in Maui."

"You did this?"

"I've done it every year since I turned seventeen."

My face falls. "Every year? You can't handle things every year?" I ask. Oh, this is news... What can't he handle?

337

"The first time I went, I was a hormonal teenager and my mother was at her wit's end with me. She sent me to Maui in the hope that I would calm down." He twists his lips. "I didn't know anyone, and I didn't talk to anyone."

"Were you upset about your father?"

He shrugs. "Yeah. I would start the year off going mad and getting into trouble. My birthday is on the 31st of December, so I would spend the last day of every year waiting for him to call me." He pauses and stares into space. "And then I'd spend the first day of every new year devastated that he hadn't."

"Your birthday is on New Year's Eve?" I ask.

He smiles softly and nods. "That's how the TTT trips started. As I grew older, I would go for a different reason."

"What was the reason?" I reach over and take his hand in mine. "You can tell me. I won't judge."

"I thought I was broken. I never felt attached. I would meet all these great women and sleep with them, and then..." He shrugs. "Nothing."

"Nothing?"

"Seriously, nothing. I would be in bed with them after sex, thinking about work and watching the clock tick to see when it was acceptable to leave without looking like a prick."

I squeeze his hand and he gives me a sad smile.

"Every year it got worse. I began to beat myself up about being like him. I didn't want to be near anyone on my birthday. I hated who I was becoming, and I would pretend to my family that I was away so I didn't have to act happy."

"Spence," I whisper sadly. "So you spent every New Years alone?"

"I did for a long time, until Masters's wife died. Then Seb and I would spend it with him and the kids. He was in a darker place than I was."

I smile softly. They are such good friends to look after each other. "What did you do last year?"

He smirks. "Played board games at Masters's house. Such party animals."

I pick up his hand and kiss the back of it again. "Can we come back here to Santorini for your birthday this year? We could bring Seb, Masters, and their family, if you like?"

He reaches over and cups my face in his hand, dusting his thumb over my bottom lip. "Do you know that I love you?"

I climb beside him on his deck chair and hold him tight. I get an image of him all alone for so many years on his birthday. New Year's Eve! It makes me so sad.

"From now on, it will be different, Spence," I whisper as I hold him tight. "Now you have me, and I will never leave you alone."

He crushes me to him and holds me close. "All this time, I thought I was broken. It turns out I was just waiting for you."

My eyes fill with tears and we kiss. It's long, tender, and perfect. "You should take me home for some intimate relations," I whisper.

He smiles and his eyes widen. "Is it one day?"

"Don't push your luck."

We stumble into the bar on our last night in Santorini. It's late, and we are messy. By messy, I mean we've had way too many cocktails and we're laughing like fools.

Everything is hilarious.

I can't remember ever being this relaxed and carefree. I don't think I've looked in the mirror for three days. I don't need to. Spencer makes me feel like I'm the most beautiful woman in the world just as I am.

I'm wearing a short yellow beach dress, with my hair down and messy. I have a red flower tucked behind one ear—a flower Spencer picked from a garden for me. He's wearing a white linen shirt with the top buttons undone, and pink shorts with white hibiscus flowers on them. He's also donning a bright green dinosaur cap that he bought for his niece.

The bar is practically empty, and there's a one-man band

playing on a small stage. He has a harmonica on a stand, a set of bongos, and a guitar. His long brown dreadlocks give him the ultimate hippy vibe, and his voice is beautiful.

Spencer's eyes light up, and he drags me to the dance floor. He grabs my hands, pushes me out, and then slams me back to his body. "I love this song." He smiles down at me.

"I've never heard this before in my life."

"Me neither." He pushes me away and spins me again.

"Then how do you know you love it?"

"I love everything I do with you." He smirks down at me, and the air swirls between us. Even drunk and disorderly, he's the most perfect man in the entire world.

The song finishes, and we both clap and cheer to make up for the lack of enthusiasm from everyone else.

"What do you want me to play?" the singer asks in his thick accent.

Spencer points at him and his eyes widen. "Aussie?" he asks.

"Yeah, man." The guy laughs.

Spencer high-fives him as if they are long-lost best friends. "I fucking love Australians."

I turn to see Wyatt and Anthony snickering from the corner. They can deny it all they want, but I know they like Spencer too now. How could anyone not? He's the friendliest person I've ever known.

"What's your name?" Spencer asks the singer.

"Reg." The guy smiles.

"That's a great name!" Spencer cries, as if it's the most exciting piece of information he's ever heard.

I laugh out loud again. Oh man, we are so drunk.

"Play us a song, Reggie." He picks up my hand and kisses it, waiting for the song to start.

Reg takes a sip of his drink and picks up his guitar. "This song is called 'Dream Catch Me.'"

Spencer smiles down at me and gives me one of his swoony winks. The song starts, and he begins to move me side to side to the beat. As the words pour out of Reggie, Spencer sings them to me, but with a delay. He's listening to them first and then repeating everything clearly.

His timing is completely off.

We begin to really sway side to side as our dancing gets a bit out of control, and I'm laughing as Spencer sings the wrong words as he dances and swings his hips.

His big, beautiful smile covers his face as he sings to me, and I laugh up at him in the goofy dinosaur hat as he swings me around like a rag doll.

The chorus breaks out and Spencer lets go of me. He begins to bop, jumping up and down, having the time of his life.

"Jump." He laughs.

I find myself mirroring his dancing, bopping along with him with a huge goofy smile across my face. What must we look like? Who even cares?

This is so much fun.

The music begins to wind down. "Great song." Spencer claps. "Play it again."

"Yes." I laugh. "Again."

Reg laughs with us and begins the song from the beginning. This time, Spencer sort of knows the words and sings to me as he holds me in his arms.

His voice and the combination of the words, there is nobody else on earth tonight.

Only him.

The chorus rings out again and he begins to bop once more.

I throw my head back and laugh, unable to stop myself from joining in. He looks utterly ridiculous in that dinosaur hat, yet he's the happiest I've ever seen him. His huge smile is infectious. I glance over to see the boys are laughing out loud at the spectacle we are making of ourselves.

Spencer spins me around the entire dance floor. "Be anyone I want to be!" he sings to me. "But it is us I see...and I cannot believe

I'm falling." The song begins to wind down, and he pulls me close. Our lips touch, and he dips me back.

"You know what else I'm going to do one day, angel?" he whispers.

"What?" I smile up at him.

His eyes hold mine. "Marry you."

My heart stops.

"What?" I whisper.

The chorus kicks in again, and Spencer kisses me quickly, pulling me up to bop around once more.

"Jump!" he cries.

This isn't even a song you can jump around to. It's a ballad, and I begin to laugh so hard that I can hardly stand. He begins to dance like he's crazy, jumping from side to side with his hands in the air like he's at a rock concert. This is the funniest thing I've ever seen. I laugh so hard, I have to rest my hands on my knees to hold myself up.

The song finishes, and we both clap with our hands in the air.

"Bravo, bravo."

I laugh as I continue clapping.

"Brilliant, mate," Spencer cries in excitement. "Best fucking song ever."

Reg laughs and shakes his head at the lunatic in the bright green dinosaur cap. "You're hectic, man."

I'm laughing when Spencer drags me from the dance floor and signals to the door to the boys.

"Where are we going?" I ask.

"We need to go home." He turns and puts the dinosaur hat on my head. "That dream song made me horny."

"You're always horny."

He turns and takes me into his arms. "I'm only horny for my dreamcatcher."

I smile up at him and my heart swells. He could say the word 'potato' and I would find it romantic.

"I love you." He smiles down at me.

342

"I love you more." I run my hands through his hair.

"Oh, Jesus," Wyatt moans behind us.

"Dream catch me when I fall," Spencer sings at the top of his voice. "Or else I won't go home at all." We stumble outside the front steps and Spencer raises his hand like he's drawing a sword. "To the kebab shop!" he cries.

We're waiting in the boarding lounge, and I'm staring at the beautiful man in front of me. He's more dishevelled than I've ever seen him and hungover like nothing else. I'm dreading going home and back to reality. We've had the most beautiful weekend in paradise, and I want to stay here in our little love bubble.

Spencer rebooked the villas for two weeks over New Year's. I can't think of anything more perfect.

My phone begins to bounce around the table as it vibrates. The name Edward lights up the screen.

My stomach drops.

I stare at it as it rings for a moment, and Spencer frowns in question when he looks over at me. I know I can't avoid this call for forever.

"Hello," I answer.

"Where are you?" Edward growls.

I close my eyes, hearing the obvious anger in his voice. "Greece."

"Get your fucking arse back to Nottingham *now*!"

He hangs up, and my heart constricts. I look over at Spencer with fear running through me. I swallow the lump in my throat.

They've seen the magazine story.

"I need to go home to Nottingham," I whisper. "Tonight."

18

Charlotte

"Who was that?"

"Edward." I rearrange the napkin on my lap, trying to calm myself. "They've seen the story, I have to go home."

"We'll go this weekend," he says flatly.

I frown. *We?*

"No, that's okay, you can come up on the weekend to see me." I pull my fingers through my hair, trying to sound casual. "I'm going to head back tonight."

His eyes hold mine. "No."

"What do you mean, no?"

"You're not going on your own."

"Spence," I sigh. I need to go and see them alone first. I don't need him coming in like a bull in a china shop. He'll ruin everything.

"This is my mess, Charlotte. I'll be the one to clean it up."

"Spencer, I want to see them alone first."

"That's not happening." He clenches his jaw and stares at me. "You stay in London and I'll go alone."

"What?" Has he gone mad? "You're not going alone. We haven't even discussed this."

"We're discussing it now. I go with you, or I go alone." He stands, and without another word, he walks off to the bar.

I begin to hear my frantic heartbeat in my ears, what a mess. My worst nightmare is for him to go there and face them alone. He has no idea who he's dealing with here. I just want to keep them apart so I can live in peaceful denial for the rest of my life.

Spencer orders two drinks and returns to the table. He hands me a glass of wine, and I glance down at his.

Scotch. Gone are the cocktails and fun drinks; he's back onto the hard stuff. I exhale heavily. Unfortunately, life is back to the hard stuff.

Spencer grabs the leg of my chair and pulls me closer to him. He rests his hand on my lap under the table, and I force a smile his way.

"I don't want you to fight with them," I whisper.

"I don't want to fight with them either."

"I think it's better if I see them alone first."

He sips his scotch and then swirls it around in his glass. "And I told you the answer is no. I'm not leaving you alone to deal with this. The story is about me, let me defend myself. Why should you take all the heat alone?" He squeezes my thigh in reassurance. "Why wouldn't you want me to deal with them?"

My eyes search his. "I'm terrified that they are going to scare you away," I whisper.

He puts his drink down and takes my face in his hand. "Angel, I will not be forced from your life against my will. Not by anyone. You are the only person who can end what we have."

"Promise?"

"I don't need to, you already know it's true." He kisses me. "Don't you?"

I smile softly, knowing he's right. I do know he wouldn't cower to Edward like everyone else.

Spencer Jones may be a lot of things, but a coward isn't one of them.

"Do you love me?" he asks.

I nod.

"So trust me. Tonight, we deal with your brother, whether he likes it or not."

He makes it all seem so simple.

"Okay?" he asks.

I nod. "Okay."

I'm freshly showered and dressed back in my sensible clothes—black Capri pants and a cream woollen jumper that sits off my shoulders. My hair is in a high ponytail, and I'm wearing black ballet flats. Gone are my sundresses from Santorini, along with any relaxation I had while I was there. My father and Edward have cut their trip short by two weeks to come home, and I know they mean business. Spencer is upstairs getting ready while I am sitting at the kitchen counter of his apartment, looking at the stories on my laptop.

The more I read, the sicker I feel.

Every tabloid has reported us over the weekend. There's headline after headline about how the love rat Spencer Jones has struck again, how he will break my heart, how he is after my money, how there's a huge Prescott family divide.

How he has been pursuing me for months. It's complete rubbish. I didn't even know him months ago.

I know my family will have read all these stories, and what hurts the most is the niggling little voice in my psyche screaming at me to listen to the warnings.

What if it's all true?

It's not. I know Spencer. I love Spencer.

This is what they do. They poison your thoughts with false stories.

My mind is in overdrive. I have no idea what's going to happen

346

tonight when I walk into my father's house with Spencer in tow. I don't know whether to call my father and pre-warn him, but then they'll be ready and they'll attack him with all guns blazing.

I'm confused what way is the right way to go about this. I still think it would be better if I went alone. But Spencer won't allow it. What the heck happened in his office that day when he kicked Edward out, anyway? I want to know what was said, word for word. I pinch the bridge of my nose as I try to calm myself down.

"You ready?" Spencer asks.

I look up to see him dressed in a navy suit, white shirt, and a tie.

"You're wearing a suit?" I ask.

He smooths his tie and shoves his hand into his pocket. "I feel more comfortable in a suit."

My heart drops. What he means is that he feels more equipped to fight in a suit. "You said you didn't want to fight with them."

"And I don't."

"So why are you wearing a suit?"

"I'm not taking any shit tonight, Charlotte."

"They're my family, Spence."

"I know that. But they need to know that you're my future and you won't be kept from me. I won't stand for it."

"Promise me you won't fight with them."

He picks up his keys. "Let's go."

"Spencer, promise me."

His eyes meet mine. "I can't do that. Let's go." Without another word, he walks towards the front door. I stare at the kitchen counter for a moment with my heart hammering hard in my chest.

Please let this go well.

Two hours later, we pull up at the large stone gates of my father's estate, and Spencer punches in the security code. It was so long ago that he was here. How on earth does he even remember it?

Wyatt and Anthony are in the car behind us, and I know they are feeling my nerves right along with me.

Their heads are about to roll too.

The gates slowly open. "Main house?" he asks, keeping his eyes on the road.

"Yes." I nod and stare down at my hands in my lap. We've said two words to each other on the whole trip here. Actually, we've said five. He asked me if I needed the bathroom when he stopped for petrol. It's like he was already angry before he even got here.

I have a bad feeling about this. "Just let me do the talking," I say.

Spencer's jaw clenches as he looks through the windshield.

I watch him. "Spence? Did you hear me?"

"Yeah, I heard you. I didn't agree with you, that's all."

I roll my eyes. "Don't fight with them. In time, they'll calm down and be reasonable. If you fight with them tonight, you'll start a war and I'll be so mad with you."

His tongue comes out and trails over his bottom lip.

He's arrogance personified.

"I mean it, Spence. Please, for me. Don't fight with them."

He reaches over and picks up my hand to kiss my fingertips, his eyes still glued to the road.

"Why aren't you answering me?"

"Because I'm not promising you anything."

"Oh, for God's sake, let's turn around and go home, then. I don't even want to go in if you have this attitude. This is my family, of course they are worried. How do you expect them to react to these magazine stories?" I snap. "I'm not exactly thrilled about them myself."

He tilts his chin to the sky in defiance and gives a subtle shake of his head.

"What?" I snap.

"And there it is. You haven't even seen them yet and already you're beginning to side with them."

"I'm not," I snap angrily.

He smirks. "Whatever you say." He pulls in and parks the car. My heart begins to thump hard in my chest. I grab his hand and look over at him as panic begins to set in. Is he right? Are they going to change the way I see this?

"I love you," I whisper.

His dark eyes hold mine. "Prove it." He gets out of the car and slams the door. I close my eyes.

Fuck.

Spencer

I open Charlotte's car door and nearly rip the damn thing from its hinges.

I'm fucking furious.

Get your fucking arse back to Nottingham.

Nobody gets to speak to Charlotte like that.

Nobody.

I take her hand and drop my head. I can hardly look her in the eye.

"No fighting," she whispers again. I glance over to Wyatt and Anthony, who are parking in the bay beside us.

I inhale through my nose to try and calm myself as Charlotte walks up to the front door and slowly opens it.

"Hello!" she calls. "I'm home."

"Darling." I hear a man's voice greet her. "Edward, Lottie's home." The man comes around the corner, and the second he sees me, his face falls. He's an older man, obviously her father. He's good-looking, too—distinguished and reeking of money.

Charlotte looks between us. "Dad, this is Spencer," she whispers nervously.

I nod. "Hello." I force a smile and put my hand out. "Spencer Jones."

He shakes my hand, his face expressionless. "I know who you are," he replies flatly. "Harold Prescott."

We stare at each other.

"Dad," Charlotte whispers. "I want to speak to you alone, please."

"Not now, Charlotte."

From out in the hall, I hear someone say, "What the hell is going on, Charlotte? Have you seen the headlines?" Edward appears from around the corner, and just like his father before him, his face falls when he sees me. "What the hell are you doing here?" he snaps.

Unable to help it, I smile sarcastically. "Nice to see you again, Edward."

"Go to Hell."

"Edward, please," Charlotte whispers. "I wanted him to meet you."

"Why?"

"Because I'm in love with him." She takes my hand in hers. "We...we're...we are in love," she splutters nervously.

Harold gasps, clearly shocked, and I have to fight the urge to smile again.

Edward's features curl together in disgust. "Don't insult my intelligence now, Charlotte. You've known him for a week."

"No." She shakes her head. "I've known him for much longer."

Edward's cold eyes meet mine, filled with contempt. "I warned you to stay away from her."

"And I told you it's none of your business. The only person I will answer to is Mr Prescott." I nod at Charlotte's father in acknowledgement.

Harold raises his chin as he watches the two of us carefully.

Charlotte picks up her father's hand. "Can we have some dinner, Dad, and talk about this...please?"

My anger boils at seeing her having to beg on my behalf.

I don't want to have dinner here. I don't want her to have to beg for me to be accepted.

They don't even fucking know me.

Fuck them.

Harold's eyes hold mine, and then he turns to her. "Of course, dear." He kisses her hand. "I have missed you so much." He turns and leads her up the hallway.

Edward and I stare at each other until he takes a step forward. "You may have her fooled...but you don't fool me."

I raise my eyebrow and smile. "It's a good thing that I'm not sleeping with you, then, isn't it?"

"You fucking prick." He loses control and pushes me hard in the chest.

"Hit me." I smile. "I dare you."

He pushes me again, and I grab the lapels of his shirt. "Stay out of my fucking way," I growl into his face.

"Oh, I'm in your fucking way, all right."

"Edward!" Harold calls from the other room, as if he knows exactly what is about to happen. "Here. Now!"

Edward glares at me, and without another word, he pushes me away and walks into the other room.

I exhale heavily as adrenaline courses through my veins, and I run my hands through my hair.

My blood is boiling.

"Spencer?" Charlotte calls. "Can you come here, please?"

I turn and follow her voice, walking into a large living area. The room is filled with expensive antiques. It looks more like a museum than a home.

"Let's have something to drink." Charlotte smiles hopefully, gesturing to the dining table for us all to sit down.

My heart swells with empathy. My poor angel.

"That would be nice." I fake a smile and take a seat.

"Abigail!" Charlotte calls.

A middle-aged woman in a uniform appears immediately. "Yes, Charlotte."

"May we have some drinks, please?"

"Of course. What can I get you?"

She looks around at us, twisting her hands nervously in front of her. "Three scotch on the rocks, and a..." She frowns to herself. "Make it four scotch on the rocks."

Abigail nods. "Very well."

Edward frowns. "You don't drink scotch."

Charlotte nods nervously. "I do tonight."

"Charlotte and her guest will be staying for dinner," Harold says.

"Yes, sir." Abigail smiles, and with a graceful nod, she disappears from the room.

Harold sits at the head of the table, Charlotte next to him, and I sit beside her. Edward is opposite Charlotte. Who the other twenty-four seats are for is anyone's guess.

Who has a dining table this big?

Edward sits back in his seat, eyes fixed on me. "So, where did you two meet?"

"It was through work," Charlotte immediately fires back.

What's she doing? We didn't meet through work.

"We've known each other for a long time. We've become good friends," she says softly as our drinks arrive.

"Thank you." I take my drink from the male waiter. How many staff do they have?

"It should stay that way," Edward retorts.

I roll my lips to keep myself from getting up and hitting this fucker in the head.

"You don't even know me," I say calmly.

"I know I don't like you. That's all I need to know."

I turn my attention to Harold. "Mr Prescott, with all due respect, I would like for Charlotte and me to talk to you without Edward here."

Edward slams his hand on the table. "Go to fucking hell, this is my house."

"And you're acting irrational."

Harold pinches the bridge of his nose. "Edward, enough!" he snaps.

Charlotte slides her hand into mine on my lap.

"The stories you have read in the magazines are mostly untrue," I begin.

"Mostly." Edward huffs. "Un-fucking-believable. You were with another woman last week in Ibiza, for Christ's sake."

"No, he wasn't," Charlotte interrupts. "Those were all lies."

"Charlotte, you cannot be that gullible," Edward cries. "I've worked too damn hard to protect you from shit like this to have your reputation ruined in an instant by a cad like him."

I glare at Edward as I swirl my scotch around in my mouth. I get an image of myself diving over the table and strangling him 'til he turns blue.

Charlotte's face falls. "He's not a cad, and I'm in love with him."

Harold rolls his eyes. "You are not in love, Charlotte, you are in lust. He's your first boyfriend. There is a big difference, darling."

"You're wrong," I tell him. "We are very much in love." I reach into my inner pocket of my suit coat and take out the folded piece of paper in there, handing it over to Harold.

He narrows his eyes, opens it, and begins to read.

"What's that?" Edward whines.

"It's a prenup of sorts," I reply. "A cohabitation agreement."

Charlotte's face falls as her eyes search mine.

"*What?*" Edward roars, standing immediately. His chair falls back and hits the floor with a thud. "Over my dead fucking body are you moving in here."

"Charlotte's moving to London with me." I take a sip of my scotch. "Tonight," I add.

Edward's eyes narrow and he marches across the room and stands over me.

"Edward, stop it," Charlotte whispers. "Dad, do something."

"You're not going anywhere, Charlotte. He's a player, and he's using you," Edward seethes.

I lose my grip on my temper. "For what?" I yell. "I'm in love with her. How is that using her?"

"Her bank balance is an incredible incentive, isn't it, Mr Jones?" He sneers.

"I don't want your goddamn money. It's there in black and white in that contract." I gesture to the contract in Harold's hands.

"I'm successful all on my own, and I have enough money for both Charlotte and me to live forever without touching a penny of your inheritance." I stand angrily. "I didn't come here to justify my character. I do, however, have some serious doubts about yours. Tell me, Edward, why is it you travelled halfway across the world to see me, but not *once* did you contact your sister to see how she was?"

He narrows his eyes.

"She is not a fucking possession. She is a beautiful woman who deserves to be loved, and I will not allow you to keep her here as your trophy for one minute longer," I yell as I completely lose control.

"Wyatt!" Charlotte calls, sensing that this is about to get out of hand.

Harold frowns at what I've just said.

I turn to Harold. "She is a prisoner of your fucking bank balance!" I yell.

Edward pushes me, and I quickly grab the lapels on his shirt.

"Edward!" Harold yells, standing abruptly.

"Stop it!" Charlotte cries. "Stop it, both of you."

Wyatt and Anthony appear and run to break us up.

"You're both fucking fired!" Edward yells to them as they drag him back from me. "How did you let this happen?" He breaks free from their grip. "You were supposed to guard her from men like him."

I suck air into my lungs and glare at him. Contempt for him drips from my every pore. I don't think I've ever hated anyone as much. I step back and straighten my suit.

"Anthony and Wyatt, you work for me now," I tell them breathlessly. "You guard Charlotte for me. To hell with this Prescott bullshit. They can stick their precious money up their arses."

Harold's face falls.

"Let me tell you this," I say. "I'm in love with Charlotte. I'm marrying Charlotte, with or without your permission. Get used to it."

I turn and take Charlotte's hand. "We're leaving."

"Spencer," she whispers.

"Now," I growl.

"Don't you fucking go anywhere with him, Charlotte," Edward hisses. "I'm warning you."

I turn to Edward and point at him. "Don't you dare warn her. Nobody speaks to her like that. Do you fucking hear me? If you upset her or disrespect her in any way, I will come here and personally knock you the fuck out."

Edward's eyes blaze with anger.

I turn to Harold and nod. "Mr Prescott, you are welcome in my home any time. I'm sorry that tonight didn't go as well as Charlotte and I had hoped it would."

"Goodbye."

I take Charlotte's hand and lead her outside. Harold follows us. "Don't go," he begs her softly.

Charlotte wraps her arms around his neck. "I'm sorry, Dad, I have to."

I shake his hand. "I will hopefully see you soon."

He drops his eyes to the ground, unable to make eye contact with me.

I lead Charlotte out and open her car door for her. She hesitates and looks up at her father on the porch, silently begging him to accept me.

"Let's go, angel." I put her in the car and then drive out the gates, unable to miss the way her eyes fill with tears.

I run my hand through my hair when I see Wyatt and Anthony pull out behind me onto the road. My heart is beating so hard in my chest.

What a fucking disaster.

I grip the steering wheel with white-knuckle force. I can't believe what just happened. Why the hell do they hate me so much when they don't even know me? Fucking Alexander York is getting a visit tomorrow. What's he told them about me?

Charlotte begins to cry, and my stomach drops. I instantly feel like shit.

355

"I'm sorry that didn't go to plan, angel." I reach over and take her hand in mine.

Her face screws up in tears as she watches me. "That's it, isn't it?" She begins to really cry. "I'll never see them now, will I?" She sobs.

"What did you want me to do?"

"Be nice, Spencer. I wanted you to be nice. You said you were going to be nice."

"I was fucking nice. I should have knocked him out, that's what I should have done."

She throws up her hands in despair and begins to wail.

I roll my eyes as I drag my hand down my face. Great. Just fucking great.

Two very silence-filled hours later, and I pull into the Four Seasons. I hand the car keys to the valet. Charlotte wanted to sleep here tonight and not at my house.

She's angry with me for fighting with them, but honestly, what was I supposed to do? What would any man do if he were under attack like that?

I hold her hand as we take the lift in even more silence. I don't even know what to say to her to try and make this better.

I know more than anyone how much a parent's rejection hurts.

First mine, now hers.

They don't even know me.

We walk into the apartment, and she heads straight for the stairs. "I'm going to bed."

I roll my eyes. "I'm having a drink."

"You don't have any scotch left."

"I'll go down to the bar to get some."

"Whatever," she replies flatly.

Whatever? For fuck's sake. I'll give fucking Edward *whatever* when I see him. He's done exactly what he wanted to do by causing trouble between us.

I leave and head straight for the hotel bar.

"What will it be?" the waitress asks.

"I'll have a bottle of Black Label to take away, and a scotch on the rocks for now."

She smiles as she wipes the bar down. "Sure."

Moments later, she hands me my drink and I sip it sadly. I go over the conversation with Edward in my head.

"You're not going anywhere, Charlotte. He's a player, he's using you."

I run my hands through my hair in disgust. I hate that I'm perceived this way.

I honestly love her.

Wyatt and Anthony walk in, and I gesture to the seats beside me.

They sit and both look at me like I just killed a man. "Don't." I sigh as I sip my drink.

"Where's Charlotte?" Anthony asks.

"In bed."

My phone vibrates in my pocket, and I dig it out to see a private number flashing up on the screen.

"I'm going to the bathroom," Anthony says before standing and disappearing around the corner.

"Hello," I answer.

"You hurt her, and I'll fucking kill you," Edward snarls. I listen for a moment and then the phone goes dead.

Adrenaline surges through my body.

Fuck me, what next?

I exhale heavily and stare straight ahead.

"Can I ask you something?" Wyatt says.

"Yeah." I sip my scotch.

"Have you ever fucked a guy?"

I turn to him and wince. "What?"

19

Spencer

HE LOOKS me dead in the eye. "I mean...have you ever had sex with a man?"

My eyes widen. "Why are you asking me this?"

He shrugs and sips his beer.

I stare at him for a moment, my mind a clusterfuck of emotions. What the hell is he asking me this for? "No," I say. "I've never fucked a man."

"Ever been fucked?"

"No." I frown. "Mate, I like vaginas."

He stares at me.

"Vagina." I shake my head in disgust that I'm discussing Charlotte's body parts with him. This day is way too much. I feel like my head's about to explode. Why the hell would he ask me that now?

"I'm going back upstairs." I stand in a rush.

Anthony comes back to the bar. "What did I miss?" he asks, looking between us. "Also, can we talk about our new terms of employment?"

Wyatt stares straight ahead and sips his beer, clearly uninterested in the terms of employment.

"Tomorrow. I'm going upstairs."

"Okay."

I walk to the elevator and hit the button with force. The doors open, and I text Masters and Seb.

Breakfast at seven. I need to debrief
Day from fucking hell.

My eyes drift over the beautiful woman sleeping in my bed. Her blonde hair is splayed across her pillow, and her eyes flutter while she sleeps. I reach down and slowly bring the blanket up to cover her, and I gently kiss her face.

She tossed and turned all night.

We both did.

Her mind was on her family, my mind was on Wyatt.

Why did he ask me if I've ever fucked a man? It was so random...and the timing was weird. Has he heard something about me that's about to be released to the magazines?

Another fucking lie.

I wouldn't put it past these fuckers; they'll do anything for a story—anything that causes shock value and will make people buy their trash. I feel sick to my stomach and totally out of control of the situation.

Charlotte deserves better than this. So much better.

I pick up her phone and set her alarm to go off in an hour. She was so upset last night, she forgot to do it. I lean down and brush the hair away from her face.

"I'm going, angel," I whisper. "I love you."

She smiles sleepily with her eyes closed. "I love you too." She wraps her arms around me.

I hold her tight, and with one last look at my love, I kiss her cheek and leave her in peace.

I've got a mountain of shit to sort out today.

First on my hit list: Alexander fucking York.

. . .

I walk into the restaurant right at seven and take a seat at our table. The boys aren't here yet, so I order our coffees and regular meals. I'm on high alert, as if on a drug that makes me super aware of everything and everyone around me. The adrenaline in my system is at an all-time high, making my leg bounce under the table uncontrollably.

Have you ever fucked a guy?

I get a vision of Charlotte's face if a story ever came out saying I fucked a man. Her family...

"Hey," Masters says, falling into his seat beside me.

"Hi." I force a smile. "How's Bree?"

"Good, good. I saw you all over the tabloids. Dirty bastards."

I roll my eyes. "Don't remind me."

Seb comes into view and waves merrily.

"What's he so fucking chirpy about?" I sigh.

Masters chuckles as he watches our friend bounce in.

Seb falls into the seat. "Hello."

"What are you so happy about?" I ask him.

He grins and places his napkin on my lap. "Oh, I don't know." He raises his brow.

"Maybe because I spent the weekend in bed with Angela."

I look at him, deadpan. "Tell me you're joking..."

"Nope."

Masters pinches the bridge of his nose. "Jesus Fucking Christ."

"You fucked your ex-wife's sister?" I frown.

Seb winks. "Every which way I could."

I drag my hand down my face. "Are you fucking crazy? You know she's going to go postal and take you to the cleaners." I put my hand up for more coffee. "You can say goodbye to Bentley. Should I make this a scotch breakfast again?"

"She's already taken me to the cleaners, and besides"—Seb smirks—"it was well worth it. I've always had a thing for Angela. Felt good to finally fuck it out."

I roll my eyes. "Oh God, do not fall for Angela." I point at him. "I'm warning you."

"I'm not falling for her, just having some fun. But I can confirm that my suspicions were right and she's a lot better in bed than her witch of a sister." He smiles, obviously very happy with himself. "Anyway, what happened with you yesterday?" His eyes widen. "That's right, your weekend in Santorini. How was it?"

"Perfect." I sigh. "Should have stayed there."

"Why?" Masters asks. "Is she pregnant?"

God, I haven't even thought of that. "She says not. We were at the airport coming home yesterday and she gets a phone call from her brother demanding she get her fucking arse back to Nottingham. So we went there last night...together. The brother is a total cockhead. He and I end up fighting, and her father is completely gutless. He didn't say a fucking thing. We leave, Charlotte and I get into a fight, and she won't speak. She was crying the whole two-hour car ride home. Then she goes to bed alone. I nip down to the bar at her hotel to get some scotch, and Edward, her brother, calls me to tell me that if I hurt her, he is going to kill me."

They both wince.

"Then." I widen my eyes.

"God, so many thens." Masters smirks.

"Get this, her bodyguard asks me if I've ever fucked a guy."

They both frown and then exchange looks and then look back to me.

"What do you mean?" Seb asks.

"He asked me if I fucked a guy!" I snap. "Why the fuck would he ask me that?"

"Have you ever fucked a guy?" Masters frowns.

"No."

"Head?"

"Fuck, no! You know that."

"Anything dick related?" Seb frowns.

"No! But I lay awake all night, worrying that he'd heard something through the grapevine, and now the tabloids are going to make up even more fake news about me and splash it everywhere."

Their faces both fall as they connect the dots.

"Once you're reported as ever being with a guy, the whole fucking world believes you're gay and acting straight."

"And you think this story is going to come out, and then Edward will officially kill you?" Masters sighs.

"Or worse, I'll lose Charlotte." I put my head into my hands. "This whole thing is a disaster."

"I don't think it's that," Seb says. "I reckon he just wants you to fuck him."

"What?" I frown. "He's not gay, Sebastian."

"How do you know?"

"He's all buff and big. This is the guy that I thought liked Charlotte in the beginning. He's not a bad bloke, actually. He's definitely not gay."

"Well, my guess is that he's thinking about sucking your cock," Seb mutters into his coffee.

"He's fucking not. Eww." I scrunch up my face in disgust at the mental visual. "Don't even say that out loud."

Our breakfasts arrive, and we begin to eat in silence.

"So, what are you going to do?" Masters asks.

My email pings on my phone, and I pick it up to read it. "First thing this morning, I'm going to cave in Alexander York's skull." I open my email.

"Oh, great." Masters rolls his eyes. "That will fix everything, you'll have a great chance of keeping Charlotte from your jail cell."

———

Spencer,

I hope this finds you well.

You are required to attend a tender meeting to negotiate new contracts for Universal Steel.

The meeting will take place in the office of Sheridan Walters in NYC on the 17th of October at 4 p.m.

Speak soon.

"Are you kidding me?" I snap as I read the email.

"What?"

"Oh, this just keeps getting better. Sheridan has pulled a tender meeting in NYC on the 17th."

"That's next week." Seb frowns.

"I know her game. She wants me to go to New York in the hope that she can seduce me." I feel my heart rate begin to escalate. This is turning into a very stressful day already.

"Jesus," Seb mutters. "Diabolical."

"Yeah, like screwing your ex-wife's sister."

"No, that's just fucking stupid," Masters grumbles.

I put my hand up immediately, and the waitress comes over. "Yes, how can I help you?"

"Can I have a scotch, please?"

"I'll have one too," Seb says. "Do you want one, Masters?"

"No. I have a feeling you two are going to need legal representation very soon." He shakes his head. "Preferably from someone who's sober."

Charlotte

I scramble around in the bottom of my closet and throw everything to the side. "Where are they?" I can't find one single pair of work shoes. They must all be at Spencer's house.

Great, now I'm going to have to call in there on my way to work. I storm out of the closet and call Wyatt.

"Hello," he answers.

"Hi. I've left all of my shoes at Spencer's. We'll have to leave early and call past on our way through."

"That's fine. We'll be in the foyer."

"Okay, thanks."

I quickly finish getting ready, and twenty minutes later I'm in the back of the Mercedes and on our way. While on the journey, my phone rings. It's my father. My stomach flips.

"Hi, Dad."

"Hello, darling."

I smile at the sound of his voice.

"Where are you, sweetheart?"

The car pulls into Spencer's apartment. "I'm at Spencer's."

"Is he home?"

"No, he's at work."

"I'll be there in ten minutes."

I frown. "Where are you?"

"In London. I came in this morning. I want to talk to you."

"Is Edward with you?"

"No."

I think for a moment. Oh, who cares? I'll just have the day off work. This is more important.

"Okay, Dad."

"What's the address?"

I give him the address while the boys both get out of the car and wait for me to finish my call. When I do, Wyatt opens the door.

"My father is on his way here."

The boys exchange looks, and without another word they follow me into the elevator and up to Spencer's floor.

They know that they're supposed to stand outside my door at all times. I've always wanted the privacy, so I finish them early, and as long as they are around or close by, I don't feel I need them with me twenty-four seven.

My father is different. He has no problem with eight sets of eyes on me at any given time.

We arrive at Spencer's apartment's floor, and they take their place on either side. "I'm not going to work today," I tell them.

"Okay." Wyatt nods.

I walk in and close the door behind me. I straighten up the cushions on the sofa and fold the throw that I had left out over the back of it. I walk into the kitchen and put the coffee cups from the dryer away. I check everything is neat and tidy, and then I run upstairs to get my shoes. I walk past a mirror in the hall and stop when I see myself.

My eyes are sunken. I look terrible.

"What a mess," I whisper to the girl staring back at me. I quickly go into our bathroom and apply some makeup and lipstick. I grab my shoes and hear a knock downstairs. I quickly slip my shoes on and run downstairs to open the door in a rush.

A warm familiar face greets me. "Hi."

My father smiles softly and leans in to kiss my cheek. He's wearing his customary suit and tie. "Hello, dear."

I hold my arm out. "Please, come in."

He turns to his guards and nods. He eventually walks in and closes the door behind him, taking a good look around the expansive apartment.

I hold my hands out proudly. "This is Spencer's place."

"Very nice." He nods, impressed. "Although, I'm here to see you, not Spencer's apartment."

I exhale, knowing I'm about to be lectured. "Would you like some tea?"

"That would be lovely."

We walk out into the kitchen and he takes a seat at the kitchen counter.

"What's going on, love?" he asks softly. "I hardly slept last night."

My eyes fill with tears. "Me either." I take his hand in mine. "I love him, Dad."

He smiles softly. "I know you think you do—"

"No." I shake my head. "Dad, I do."

His eyes hold mine. "Tell me everything."

I feel my nerves rise, because I know how important it is that I get this right.

"We met a while ago and..." How much do I actually tell him? All of it. "We went on a few dates."

"How did I not know you were dating anyone?"

"Dad, you don't know anything about me. I'm alone most of the time. You and Edward are so busy with work that you would have no idea what's going on with me and my life. Not really."

His face falls with disappointment.

"Spencer's not what he seems, Dad."

"Surely you can understand my fears."

"I know, and I hate his reputation, too, but he's not like that." I shrug. "He used to be, but he's changed, and a lot of the stories about him are untrue. That story said he was in Ibiza last week when he was here with me the whole time. He doesn't even know the models named in those stories."

He raises his brow sceptically.

"I know some of it's true, and I have no doubt he was a player," I add. "I'm not stupid."

His eyes hold mine. "You are a target for someone like him. You're young and innocent. He's a lot older than you, Charlotte."

"I know, but thirteen years isn't that bad. I just don't seem to like men my own age."

"You haven't dated any. How would you know?"

I shrug. "I just know."

"I feel like he's taking advantage of your inexperience."

"Dad, he rejected me at first because of my inexperience."

He frowns. "What do you mean?"

Oh Hell, why did I say that? I hesitate.

"Go on," he urges.

"After a few dates, when we got closer, I told Spencer that I was...inexperienced...and he immediately broke it off with me. He said he didn't deserve me."

His eyes hold mine as he listens intently.

"Weeks later, I lied and told him that I wasn't a virgin anymore in the hope that he would relax and take me out. I know he didn't want me if he had to take that innocence away from me."

"Charlotte," he whispers in horror. "What on earth were you thinking?"

"Dad, don't you see? I pursued him just as much as he pursued me. It's special between us."

He exhales heavily and puts his head into his hands. "I'm just..." He pauses. "I'm just asking you to slow down. I've already lost one son to a bad relationship. I couldn't bear to lose you too."

"Dad, Penelope is different."

"Is she, Charlotte?" He shakes his head. "When William met Penelope, we were warned by numerous people what she was like."

I listen as I watch him.

"Both mine and Edward's instincts told us that she was all wrong for him, but we trusted his judgement. Edward's closest friend Alexander York came to us in the very early stages of their relationship and told us that he had seen Penelope with another man at a club."

I frown. "When was this?"

"Before William even moved in with her."

"I didn't know this."

"Edward blames himself for his brother's heartbreak. He hates the fact that she holds Harrison hostage to William."

Sadness fills me.

"Your brother cannot leave that relationship without leaving his son."

I drop my head.

"He's effectively trapped if he wants his son to grow up in the same house as him."

"I know," I whisper.

"Alexander York came to us again last week...to warn us about Spencer."

I frown as my eyes rise to his.

"Charlotte, just as you feel now is exactly how William felt in the early stages of his relationship. He fell madly in love, rushed in, and got burned badly. I just don't want the same fate for you. And to make it worse, the press are involved in this now. Spencer Jones gets attention wherever he goes."

"He didn't ask for it, Dad."

"Where there is smoke, there is fire, Charlotte. He gets attention for all of the wrong reasons."

"He's not Penelope. He's a good man."

"I'm not saying he isn't. To be honest, he impressed me last night. I like the way he stood up for himself with Edward. I like the way he had a prenup contract drawn up to protect you, and I like the way he was offended by Edward's lack of time for you. It showed me he has a backbone and that he genuinely cares."

I smile, suddenly filled with hope.

He takes my hands in his. "But I cannot, with a clear conscience, let you move in with him just yet."

I sit back in my seat.

"Charlotte." He cups my face in his hand. "If you want to move to London, that's fine, sweetheart. But get your own apartment and make an informed decision about your relationship. When he's had time to prove himself...to *all* of us."

I stare at him and exhale heavily. "Dad."

"Don't Dad me. You know I'm making sense. If you show me that you are not being led like a fool, and that you'll keep your independence, I will happily support anything you do, or any man you choose."

"What about Edward?" I ask.

"Edward will listen to me, and you must know that your brother acts out of love. He couldn't stand to see you hurt like William is—it would kill him." He smiles over at me. "You honestly can't blame him for being concerned about Spencer when he has that appalling reputation of his."

I smile softly.

"To be honest, I think he was impressed with Spencer, too, although he would never let on." He winks. "Nobody will ever be good enough for you in his eyes."

"I don't want to be a fool for anyone," I whisper. "I'm not stupid and I'm not blind."

He smiles and leans forward to kiss my forehead. "I know,

darling, and I know that deep down, you know I'm right. Step back, take your time, and breathe. If he loves you and does the right thing by you, you have my blessing. I hope that he proves Edward and me wrong in every way. I want to see you happy. More than anything, I want you to be happy."

I smile.

"It isn't a race, Charlotte. If he loves you, he will wait."

I nod. "I know."

His eyes hold mine, and I know there's more.

"What is it?" I ask.

"What have you been doing with your security while I've been away?"

"What do you mean?"

"I mean, have you been clocking them off at night?"

I drop my head.

He puts his finger under my chin and brings my face to his. "What have I told you about that, Charlotte?"

"Well, I don't need them at night when I'm at home in Nottingham," I argue.

"Our estate is completely enclosed. We have guards there at all times. They don't need to stay at your door because they are patrolling the grounds every minute. Nobody can get in. Edward watched the security tapes last night, and Wyatt and Anthony have been at the bar of your hotel on most nights."

"I told them I didn't need them anymore. It wasn't their fault. They stay close."

"Do you understand how vulnerable you are? Why would you put yourself at risk like that? I trusted you to do the right thing, and here I find out you are dismissing your guards mid-shift so they can go to a bar?"

I roll my eyes.

"Don't roll your eyes at me, young lady. You've been very irresponsible."

"No, Dad, I just fell in love."

"Love is one thing, Charlotte. Stupidity is another." He stands.

"You are a target because of me. You have four billion dollars in the bank. Take the security threat seriously. I've brought four more guards with me to leave with you. You will not be photographed with Spencer Jones at all from now on. They've been instructed to take the cameras off anyone who tries. I will not have you become a trashy tabloid heading...not under any circumstances."

I exhale heavily, knowing this is nonnegotiable. "Okay."

"Now." He smiles down at me. "Where on earth is my tea? You really are a terrible host."

It's just gone six in the evening when Spencer walks in, and my nerves tumble around in my stomach.

I'm in the kitchen, cooking dinner. His face lights up when he sees me, and he smiles broadly.

"Hello, my beautiful girl."

I practically run and jump into his arms, and we kiss slowly. "I've missed you today," I whisper.

He holds me tight. "Why are there a load of guards in the hall?"

I roll my eyes. "Long story." I pour us both a glass of wine. "My father came over today." I try to sound casual, even though I'm a nervous mess.

"Oh." He smiles. "And?"

I sip my wine and look into his eyes. "He wants me to get my own apartment."

His face falls, and then he frowns. "And what did you say?"

"I said that I would."

20

Charlotte

SPENCER'S CHIN immediately rises in annoyance. I can see he's clenching his jaw.

"It's just semantics, Spence. We'll stay at your house together or at my house together. It won't change a thing."

"Then why do it?"

"Because my father doesn't want me to rush into anything. He said that he will accept our relationship if I'm not living with you straight away."

He stares at me.

"Please try and understand, my family are so important to me, and they're just worried that I'm going to get hurt."

He licks his lips, and I know he's choosing his words carefully.

"You even said yourself that if you were me, you would get your own apartment. On some level, you know what they're saying is true."

He rolls his eyes.

"But I won't have my own apartment—not really. We'll just have two apartments between us. Six months down the line, after a little independence, I'll officially move in here."

He sits on a stool and then scratches his head, remaining silent.

"What do you think?" I ask.

"Does it matter what I think?"

"Of course it does."

He shrugs and pours a glass of wine.

Just say something...anything.

I sit down beside him. I think that at any moment he's going to go crazy, watching as he sips his wine.

"Do what you want," he eventually mutters.

I frown. "What does that mean?"

"I mean do what you want." He shrugs.

"Are you angry with me?"

"Angry, no. Disappointed...yes."

My heart drops. "You're disappointed," I whisper. I think I would prefer him to be angry.

He cups my cheek in his hand. "Yeah, I'm disappointed." He exhales heavily. "I wanted to start our life together right now, but I also understand."

I'm losing track of this conversation. "What do you understand?"

"I understand that your family comes first, and that you will always, on some level, do what they want you to do."

I frown.

"It's okay." He brushes his thumb over my bottom lip and stares at me for a moment. "I'll just have to learn to deal with it." He shrugs. "As long as they're happy, you'll be happy, right? I'm going to take a shower now." He turns and, without another word, he walks away to make his way upstairs.

I stare at the refrigerator, his words playing on repeat in my mind.

As long as they're happy, you'll be happy, right?

Is that true?

Will I only be happy if my family accept Spencer?

What if I do this for them, and then they never accept him anyway? What if I let them drive a wedge between the two of us?

372

I do want to keep my father happy. It's how I am... But should I want that at Spencer's expense?

They don't even know him. What gives them the right to judge him?

We're so happy together.

He did everything right. He got a prenup to protect me, he tried to be civil while Edward was just attacking him nonstop. What was he supposed to do? Of course he was going to fight back eventually.

I drop my head into my hands.

I'm so confused.

I'm going to have to think about this. I don't want to just push Spencer's needs aside because my family don't want to be embarrassed by the tabloids. It's what he does from here on in that matters to me. I don't care about his past; I want his future.

I finish my wine and head upstairs to find Spencer in the shower. He's washing himself when he turns to me and smiles sexily. He has no idea of the turmoil I'm in.

"You getting in?" he asks.

I give him a lopsided smile, undress, and get in under the hot water. His big arms come around me, and he holds me tight.

"I love you." I smile up at him.

"I know you do, angel." His mouth takes mine, and his tongue slowly slides through my lips.

"I don't want to disappoint you, Spence," I whisper.

"Baby, you could never truly disappoint me. I know where they're coming from, and to be honest, I would give anything to have a father who loves me as much as your father loves you. It's a blessing."

My eyes fill with tears. *My poor man.*

My heart breaks for him and the pain he has been through at the hands of his so-called father.

We kiss again, and it's long and deep and tender, and I feel my arousal burn deep inside me. His erection is up against my stomach. He motions to lift me, but I stop him.

"Spence, I can't."

"What?"

"I have my period."

His face falls and he drops my feet back to the floor. "Oh." He frowns.

I smile softly up at him as I push the hair back from his face. "I thought you couldn't wait for my period to come. Remember, you thought your life was over last week."

He chuckles. "Hmm." He holds my face and kisses me again. "After my initial freak-out, I kind of liked the idea of having my baby inside of you."

My heart stops, and my eyes search his. This is it, everything I ever wanted is here with me.

The water runs down over his face. I've never seen a more beautiful man.

"I'll give you a baby one day," I whisper.

He smiles. "Promise?"

I nod and wrap my arms around him tight. Oh, this feeling of closeness between us is so strong.

It's a tangible force...all-encompassing. We hold each other close for an extended time.

His hand eventually slides down and grabs my behind. "Is it one day today?" he asks, his playful tone returning.

I pull back and frown. "That depends on which one day you're meaning."

"The one day when I give you anal?"

I laugh out loud. "You idiot." I flick water at him. "This is a romantic moment and you're wrecking it."

His eyes blaze with mischief and he pins me to the wall. "I'm deadly serious. We need to fuck, angel. You have three choices of where you get it."

He bites my neck and I laugh as he ravages me. "Spencer Jones, you are a sex maniac."

He growls, causing goose bumps to scatter up my spine. "But I'm all yours."

. . .

I punch the code into the security gate.

1105

The large metal gates slowly open, and I feel my nerves rise. The boys are in the car behind me. I'm driving Spencer's car today. I wanted to drive myself to Nottingham this time.

Don't ask me why, because I don't even know what significance me driving myself here even has.

But it matters somehow.

Spencer doesn't know I'm here. I dropped him off at work this morning and told him I would pick him up. He didn't ask questions as to why I wanted his car, but that's Spencer for you. He's supportive of my every decision, even if he doesn't know the reason behind it.

I didn't sleep last night. I watched the beautiful man beside me instead, going over his childhood and the way he suffered at his father's lack of conviction.

The way he cares for me, the way he makes me feel, the way he's tenderly teaching me about myself and my body...

I love him.

And sometime in the middle of the night, I had an epiphany.

I will never lack conviction in my love for him. I will never put him second...not even for my family.

I'm here to move my stuff out. I'm moving in with Spencer today, and if they don't like it, they can lump it.

I will not be held responsible for their fears.

Because I have none.

He is my soul mate. He is the man I've been waiting for, and I won't cower to their demands. Not for anything.

I crawl up the driveway and park outside the front of my house. I have no idea what I'm going to take, but I just know I had to come home to make it final.

. . .

Three hours later and I'm sitting on the grass of the manicured garden in the family graveyard of my father's estate. I stare at the tombstone.

I'm with my mother, and a feeling of deep sadness fills me. I wish she could meet Spencer. I wish she were here to see how happy he makes me.

I've packed all of my things and loaded them into the back of the cars. I know my father is home, but he hasn't been down to see me. He knows.

"He's got blonde hair, Mum, and blue eyes," I whisper through a lump in my throat. "He's tall and handsome, and if you could see the way he looks at me, you would understand." Tears roll down my face. "I love him."

I just want to hear her voice, just one more time.

I want her to tell me that's it's okay—that she understands why I'm doing this.

But she can't. *She never will.*

She's gone.

Sometimes the pain of her not being here is too much.

It's like I have to fight for my next breath.

How am I supposed to live without her?

I feel a hand on my shoulder, and I jump in fright. "Are you all right, darling?" my father asks.

I stand and wrap my arms around him. "Not really," I whisper against his shoulder. "I miss her, Dad."

"I miss her too."

"I need her to tell me that this is okay." I lift my chin and his eyes search mine. "Because I'm moving in with him, Dad. I love him and I'm not waiting."

His face falls. "But you said—"

"I know what I said," I cut him off. "But I've thought about it."

"He talked you out of it, you mean."

"No." I shake my head. "Not at all. He doesn't even know I'm here. It's time for me to grow up and make my own decisions, Dad."

His eyes fall to the ground.

"I love Spencer. In time, you will come to love Spencer, too, because he's a wonderful man."

"Charlotte," he whispers. "I can't support this relationship."

"Then you won't see me."

His face falls. "Don't say that."

"Remember when you fell in love with Mum and the whole world was against you... but you knew it was right?"

He frowns.

"I know this is right. In my heart of hearts, I know this is right."

"Charlotte, you are so young and naïve. What's the rush, darling?"

"Why would I wait?" I whisper. "Why wait when he makes me happier than I've ever been?"

Dad drops his head.

"I'm moving in with him today. My things are already packed, and I would like you to come and visit me."

He stays silent.

I scowl and swallow with regret. I feel like my heart is being ripped out of my chest. "I love you, Dad."

"I love you too," he whispers.

"Will you come and visit me?"

He stares at me blankly. "No."

I blink as my vision becomes blurred.

"I cannot accept this relationship if you move in with him. I've told you that already."

I frown and step back from him, shocked, but not surprised by his coldness. "This is goodbye, then."

He stares at me, his face blank and emotionless. I wait for him to say something, but he doesn't.

I can't stand this, I need to get away.

I turn away with tears streaming down my face. I walk as fast as I can and get into my car, wasting no time in pulling out of the driveway.

I watch the property disappear in the rearview mirror, feeling the pain in my chest.

I thought he loved me more than that.

"Angel?" Spencer calls. "Are you okay, sweetheart?" he whispers as he sits down beside me.

"Huh?" I push up on my elbows. "Oh, I must have fallen asleep." I sigh as I look down at myself sprawled across the sofa. My face falls. "Oh my God, I forgot to get you from work?" I whisper in a panic. "What time is it?"

He brushes my hair back from my forehead and smiles. "That's okay, I called Wyatt when I couldn't get you and he came to pick me up. We guessed you were asleep."

I lie back down and put my forearm over my eyes. I just want this day to be over.

Spencer looks around at the boxes of my things spread everywhere. "What's all this?"

"I moved in." I give him my best attempt at jazz hands. "Surprise!"

He smirks. "I thought you were getting your own apartment."

"I wanted my own Spencer instead."

He leans down and kisses me. "I told you I didn't mind."

"I know." I wrap my arms around his shoulders. "But I minded. I'm not coming into this relationship with anyone but you as my priority."

"I love you."

"Lucky. Because my father doesn't want to see me again."

"He'll come around." He sighs as he pulls me up by the hand. "Come on, get up and get yourself ready."

"Why, where are we going?" I sigh.

"We have to celebrate. This is a big day. We just moved in together. Let's see if we can find a bar that will play our song."

I laugh. "There are no Australian one-man bands in London who know the song 'Dream Catch Me', Spence."

"Karaoke it is, then."

Five hours later, and I'm smiling up at my handsome dance partner, rearranging his tie. "Thank you." I smile.

"For what?"

"For dancing with me in a deserted bar at 1:00 a.m. on a school night. I know you're trying to take my mind off things."

He spins me around. "You're wrong about that, Prescott. I'm putting your mind on to things. This is a strategic move. I'm playing the game of champions."

I fake amazement and narrow my eyes. "Oh, really? Tell me, Mr Spencer..." I reach up and brush his hair back from his forehead and kiss him softly on the lips. "Is your brain in your dick tonight?"

"No, my brain is in my heart."

And what a beautiful heart it is.

"My erection is in my dick." He kisses my temple.

I giggle at his ridiculous answer, and we sway to the music.

"Will you love me when I'm poor, Lady Charlotte?"

"Why would you ever be poor, Mr Spencer?" I smirk.

"Sheridan wanted me to go to New York next week for a tender meeting."

I stop dancing.

"I said no."

"What does that mean?" I frown.

"It means she has the right to pull my company's contract."

"Do you think she will?"

He shrugs and starts to sway us again. "I don't think so. She's ballsy, but she's not a bitch. She isn't vindictive."

I stare at him.

"My company supplies her with good-quality steel, she knows that."

"Why don't you just go?" I say.

"Because I don't want to leave you." He kisses me again.

"It's okay, Spence, I trust you. You can go. I don't want you to lose business over us."

"Angel." He smiles down at me. "I will not be held for ransom from an old lover and risk fucking up what I have in this room. She can jam the fucking contract up her arse for all I care."

I look around at our surroundings, unable to stop myself from grinning. "We have two drunks in the corner of this room. I'm happy to sacrifice them," I offer.

He laughs as he looks around at the two old men sitting drunk at the bar. "I wouldn't even give up them."

Spencer looks over and spots Wyatt, and I see a frown crease his brow. "What's wrong?" I ask.

"How well do you know Wyatt?"

"Why?"

"Nothing." He frowns. "Just something he said to me the other night has me weirded out a bit."

"What did he say?"

"He asked me if I'd ever fucked a guy."

I stop dancing again. "What?"

He widens his eyes. "Weird, right?"

"Seems I haven't been the only thing he's been watching, then."

"What does that mean?" He frowns.

"Wyatt is into men *and* women."

"What?" he gasps.

I giggle at his surprise.

"How do you know this?" he whispers.

"We're friends, of course I know this. He was in a three-way relationship with a woman and a man for over twelve months. They broke up last year."

"You think he's checking me out?" he whispers, completely terrified.

"No, I think that was his way of trying to tell you that he's bisexual without coming out and actually saying it. When he said that to you, did you ask him the same question back? Because I know that's how he told Edward."

"What do you mean?"

"He asked Edward if he'd ever fucked a guy, and Edward said no, and then Edward asked him if he had. Of course, Wyatt said yes...that he swings both ways."

Spencer's eyes close, relief pouring out of him. "Thank fucking God. I thought there was some sinister paparazzi story being concocted about me. I was freaking the hell out."

I laugh out loud. "Spencer, why don't you just ask me these things instead of brewing on them for days?"

"Hell, woman." He rests his cheek against mine. "I've aged thirty years since I met you."

I smile up at him. "Spence?"

"Yes."

"You didn't sing our song to me."

"Hmm." He closes his eyes. "There's a place I go when I'm alone." He rocks us to his whispered song. "Do anything I want, be anyone I wanna be. But it is us I see, and I cannot believe I'm falling." He pushes me out by the hand and twirls me under his arm, slowly bringing me back to him. "Dream catch me when I fall."

"Or else I won't come back at all," I whisper.

We smile at each other, and it's like he's the only person on earth.

My person.

"I love you." He smiles as he holds me tight.

"I love you."

Our moment is interrupted when his phone vibrates in his pocket. He digs it out and reads it. His eyes light up in excitement.

"Bree's in labour."

21

Charlotte

MY PHONE VIBRATES across my desk and I answer it quickly. "Any news?" I ask Spencer.

"She's five centimetres dilated."

"Is she all right?"

"In Masters's words, she's a champion."

Excitement sweeps though me. "How many times have you spoken to him today?"

"Every hour on the hour."

I love these men, they're so close. "Were you this excited when he had his other children?"

"Yes," he gasps. "Babies are fucking exciting, Charlotte."

I smile dreamily as I imagine the day that Spencer becomes a father, and how excited he will be. *I hope it's to my children.*

"Are you going to go see them tonight?" I ask.

"If the baby is here, we will."

"We?" I frown. "I don't want to intrude."

"Don't be stupid. You're part of our gang now. Don't you want to see the baby too?"

I smile goofily. "I do."

"I also organised for us to look through that office space I found. The estate agent is meeting us there at six."

"You...did?"

"What's with the delay?"

"Spence," I whisper. "Do you really think I can do this?"

"I know you can, angel," he replies without hesitation. "You know you can too."

I nod with renewed determination. "You're right, I *can* do this."

"The building may not be what you're looking for, anyway. We're just getting a feel for it at this stage."

"Again, you're right."

"I'll pick you up from work at five."

"Can't wait, see you then."

"Bye, angel."

"Love you."

"I love you too."

He hangs up, and I stare out the window. How this beautiful, thoughtful man loves me above all other women, I'll never know.

"And through here is the kitchen." The estate agent smiles.

Spencer leads me from the office to a large kitchen area. I'm fighting the huge smile.

"And the rental terms?" Spencer asks her casually.

"We could do a five by five."

"We're only after a two by two at this point." He looks around. "We plan on expanding within three years, and this space won't be big enough for us then."

"I'll go outside and call the owner now, see what she says."

"Thank you." We walk back out into the main office area.

The door closes behind her and he turns to me. "What do you think?"

I look around at the expansive modern space on the tenth floor, right in the middle of London. There are six offices, all with glass walls and views that look out over the city. The reception area is large and modern. It has a kitchen, a conference room, and its own private bathrooms.

"Spence," I whisper. "It's perfect."

"Right?" He smiles, proud of himself for finding it.

"Are you sure I can do this?"

He kisses me softly. "You can do anything you set your mind to, angel. Stop doubting yourself."

I imagine how I could make this place look, and excitement fills me.

"Don't act interested," he says. "Play it cool while I negotiate the rental terms."

"Okay."

I walk over to the offices and start looking through them again. The agent returns.

"When would you want to consider beginning your rental agreement?"

I think for a moment. "Probably after Christmas. It would be hard for me to find suitable staff at this time of the year."

"The owner said that should be fine."

Spencer nods. "Okay, we're going to look at a few other buildings this afternoon, so I'll let you know."

My face falls and Spencer gives me the look. Oh, that's right, we're playing it cool.

"The rent is rather high," he says casually.

"Let me see what I can do about that," the agent replies.

"If we can get the rent down a little, we may be able to work something out."

I shake her hand. "Thank you for meeting us."

"My pleasure."

We follow her outside, and I take one last look at the space and fight to hold back a huge smile.

I think we just found an office for me.

. . .

I follow Spencer as he strides down the hospital corridor. He's carrying the biggest bunch of flowers I have ever seen, and I'm loaded up with gifts too. I think Spencer bought half of the store today.

"Hurry up," he whispers.

He's so excited.

I'm seeing this other part of him I never knew existed...the paternal part.

My ovaries have exploded to smithereens.

Playboy Spencer is hot, fuckable, funny, and the entire world wants a piece of him. But family Spencer, the one that only a few select people get to know, is caring and considerate, swoony and beautiful... I could go on and on.

All I know is that I'm a very lucky woman to have him love me.

The way he looks at me, the way he loves me, it's all I need.

We get to a door and he turns. "You ready?"

"I'm not the one having a baby, Spencer."

He chuckles and knocks on the door.

"Come in!" someone calls.

Spencer tentatively opens the door. Bree is in bed and Julian is sitting in a chair beside her, holding their newborn baby.

Spencer places the flowers down and rushes to Bree's side. "Are you okay, darling?" he whispers as he kisses her temple and takes her hand in his.

She laughs at him. "I'm fine, Spence." She turns to me. "Hi, Lottie."

"Hello." I bounce with excitement. "Congratulations."

"Thank you." She smiles proudly. "He's just perfect."

Spencer turns to Julian and lets out a quiet chuckle. "Congratulations, man." He shakes Julian's hand and then pulls the little blue blanket down to look at the baby.

"What's his name?" Spencer asks softly.

"Henry." Julian looks like he's about to burst with pride. I find myself getting teary watching the two men swooning over this little baby boy.

I turn back to Bree. "Was the birth okay?" I ask softly.

"God." She sighs. "It was fucking hell."

I bite my bottom lip to hold back my smile. I love Bree. She's so *normal.*

"You know how they tell you your whole life that it's bad?"

"Yeah," I answer cautiously.

"It's worse than bad. It's ten times worse." She widens her eyes. "I thought I was going to die."

I giggle and my attention goes back to Julian and Spencer, who are staring at the bundle in Julian's arms. They are utterly awestruck.

"Where are the kids?" Spencer asks.

"They've just gone home. They're coming back in a few hours," Julian tells him. "Bree hasn't even showered yet."

"Oh." My face falls as I glance between them. "I'm so sorry to intrude."

"Don't be silly. Seb was trying to come into the delivery room." Bree smiles. "He's just gone to get us some dinner."

"Can you two watch Henry while I help Bree shower?" Julian asks.

"Of course." Spencer stands and takes the baby from Julian. I watch on as he lifts him up to his face and gently kisses his little forehead, and then I melt into a puddle.

I can't deal with this. Spencer with a baby is frying my brain.

Julian helps Bree up and leads her into the bathroom. I walk over to Spencer as he holds the precious little bundle, and I pull the blanket back and stare at the perfect chubby little face.

"I can't wait to have a baby of my own one day," I whisper.

Spencer smiles, leans down, and kisses me softly. "Me too."

We both smile at little Henry, who is staring back at us.

"You're going to make a wonderful father, Spence."

"One day." His eyes rise to meet mine. "This, angel...you and me."

Emotion overwhelms me. My eyes fill with tears. "What a perfect day that will be."

We kiss. It's soft and intimate, a celebration of life and a promise of things to come. "I love you," I whisper.

"I love you too."

Edward

We're sitting in the car, watching Charlotte as she walks down the street.

"This is killing me." My father sighs.

"It's for the best." I watch Wyatt and Anthony follow her into a café. "She'll come around. She won't stay with him, I know it."

Dad exhales heavily, a mutual sadness rolling over us. We're so close yet so far away.

"Every week we've travelled to London to watch her this way. I miss her, Edward."

"Me, too, but I have no idea what this Spencer Jones wants with her, and until I know for certain, we cannot, with a clear conscience, encourage this relationship."

Ten minutes later, Charlotte reappears with a fresh juice and a brown paper bag containing her lunch. She disappears down the street. I start the car and pull out into the traffic.

"At least she's okay." I sigh.

"I'm not okay, Edward. We need to start thinking about making peace with this. She's not coming home."

"Trust me, he will hang himself...we just have to wait."

Charlotte

"Anthony called me," Beth says casually as she sips her cocktail.

I gasp and look over at him standing up against the wall with Wyatt. "Oh my God, when?"

"Last night."

"And?"

"Shh, I don't want Lars to know."

"Why not?"

"Because if she is getting it on with Edward like we suspect, she's going to tell him."

"Hmm, good thinking." We're in a cocktail bar on a girls' night out. Spencer and Sebastian are at our place, watching football. Lara is in the bathroom of the bar right now, but she's staying at our place tonight.

"What did Anthony say?" I whisper.

"He asked me if I wanted to go out some time. He told me that Spencer warned him away from me a few weeks ago—said he didn't want us to date because if we didn't work out, then he didn't want my friendship with you to suffer."

My face falls. "What?"

"Apparently, Spencer knew that Anthony had the hots for me all along."

My mouth falls open. "You're kidding, he said that?"

"You know, Spencer is more like Edward than you think." She huffs.

"God."

Lara smiles warmly, arriving back at the table. "Another round?" she asks.

"Please." I smile.

"Sure," says Beth.

We both watch as Lara saunters to the bar. "I think she's definitely sleeping with Edward," I whisper.

"But why wouldn't she tell us that? We tell each other everything. I don't get it. Why is she hiding this?"

"I don't know." I shrug. "All I know is that in the last month my family haven't talked to me, Lara has been to stay at Spencer's house five times. That's more than she's ever seen me. It's as if she's checking on me for Edward."

"But surely she can see how happy you two are together." She frowns. "He dotes on you, for fuck's sake."

Lara arrives back at the table with three drinks.

"Thank you."

"Tell me all about your new business venture." Lara smiles. "Where are you up to with it?"

"It's not a business, it's a charity." I smile proudly. "So far, I have the office space I wanted, and I hired two people who I was working with at the mailroom in my old job."

"Who?"

"Sarah and Paul."

"Isn't Sarah a loose cannon?" Lara frowns.

"No. She's smart, intelligent, and I adore her. As for Paul, well, he is just Paul. He'll be good for the place until his next trip."

"Who else is going to work there?"

"Two young lawyers straight from university—both guys. They start in February."

Beth bounces in her seat. "This is so exciting, Charlotte."

"I know."

"Don't let Sarah bonk the solicitors," Lara warns me. "Or Paul, for that matter."

I laugh. "I already warned her: no sex with the staff."

"What did she say?" Lara asks.

"She told me she was hoping for a threesome on their desk." I smirk.

"Charlotte." Lara gasps. "You're going to have pubes on your desk too."

We all burst out laughing. "How are my father and Edward?" I ask.

"Good." Her eyes meet mine as she catches herself, shrugging casually. "As far as I know."

"Have you seen them?"

"I ran into Edward the other day. He asked me how you were."

"What did you say?"

She shrugs again. "I told him you were happy."

I watch her.

"Did you tell him to fuck off from me?" Beth asks casually, lifting her drink to her mouth. "I'm so fucking annoyed with him."

She tuts. "If he took the time to get to know Spencer, he would see how wonderful he is. He pisses me off to no end."

"Edward just wants you to have your own place, Charlotte. It's not unreasonable, if you ask me."

Beth's eyes meet mine. *Always defending him.*

"I'm old enough to make my own decisions, Lara. I love Spencer. I want to live with him. My family should accept that and stop judging him like they judge Penelope. Spencer's done nothing wrong, and I won't stand for him to be treated the way that they treat him."

Lara rolls her eyes at me, clearly unimpressed.

"Have either of you ever tried bondage?" Beth asks. "I met this new guy, and he wants to tie me up."

I bite my lip to stop myself from smiling. I can't believe Beth. She's fishing for information for me.

Lara smiles darkly. "Being tied up is fucking hot. Handcuffs are a personal favourite of mine."

Beth looks at me again. I swear that was her in Edward's room that night.

"Have you ever fucked Edward, Lara?" Beth blurts out.

Lara chokes on her drink. "What?"

"Have you ever *fucked* Edward?"

My eyes widen in surprise. I've never asked because I didn't want to force her to lie to me.

"What on earth?" Lara splutters. "Why would you ask me that?"

"It's a yes or no question, Lars," Beth states.

Lara waves her hand around in the air. "Don't be ridiculous. Oh, look, there's Charlie." She stands. "Back in a minute." She takes off and nearly runs to the other side of the restaurant to get away from us.

Beth and I stare at each other.

"She's totally fucking him," Beth says.

I sip my drink. "Yep. I know."

. . .

The car slows to a stop, and I peer in at the house through the window.

I'm here to meet Spencer's family, and I'm nervous as all hell.

Family meetings haven't gone that well for us so far.

Spencer opens my door and practically drags me from my seat. "I'm nervous," I admit in a rush.

"Don't be nervous, they'll love you." He takes me by the hand, leading me towards the house.

"What if they don't?"

"Then we'll be even."

Oh God.

The house is nice, neat, and of average size, sitting out in the countryside. I smile as I look around at the neighbourhood. I get a vision of Spencer, Seb, and Julian hanging around here, riding their bikes as kids, and I smile.

"Hello!" Spencer calls as he opens the front door. The smell of something amazing cooking wafts through the house.

"Hey!" I hear a woman call from another room before she rushes in. "Spence."

I clasp my hands nervously in front of me when she comes into view. She's attractive and in good shape. She has blonde hair that sits just below her shoulders, and blue eyes that shine like Spencer's. She immediately wraps her arms around me and pulls me close. "Hello, my dear Charlotte."

"Hi," I whisper nervously.

She takes my hands in hers, smiles, and looks me up and down. "So, you're our Spencer's girlfriend? Beautiful."

"Thanks."

She turns her attention to Spencer and kisses his cheek. "Hello, sweetheart."

"Hi, Mum." He smiles. "Where's Dad?"

"Out in the garage."

He calls his stepfather his dad? I didn't know this.

Spencer takes off outside, returning only moments later with a big, burly mechanic-looking guy. Spencer presents me like a prized pig.

"And here she is. This is my Charlotte," he says proudly.

My Charlotte.

The man wipes his hands on a tea towel before he shakes my hand. "Hello, love, nice to meet you."

He looks like he has some kind of Italian or other European heritage. He has big, brown, kind eyes. He puts his arm around Spencer, and I smile at the two of them. It's obvious that they are very close.

"I hope you're hungry. I've been cooking up a storm." His mother smiles.

I nod nervously, unsure what to say.

Spencer rolls his eyes and wraps his arm around me. "She's nervous."

His mother laughs. "That makes two of us. You're the first girl Spencer has ever brought home. I'd almost given up hope."

"About time, Son," his dad interrupts. "And she's so pretty too."

I giggle, feeling a little more at ease.

His mum takes me by the hand and pulls me into the kitchen. "If Spencer loves you, we love you."

I'm in bed, staring at the television, but I'm not watching it or even listening.

My mind is in Nottingham with my father.

I miss him...*desperately.*

Spencer is reading beside me, and things couldn't be any better between us. We laugh, make love, fuck, and talk about the charity I'm creating. He's become my best friend and my partner in crime.

We're hopelessly in love.

But I have this thorn in my side that won't go away.

It was one or the other: my family or my love. Why couldn't I have both? I know if they just gave him a chance, they would love him.

Spencer reaches over and slides his hand up my thigh. "You okay?" he asks.

I nod, unable to speak past the lump in my throat.

He puts his book down and wraps his arms around me. "What is it, angel?"

I shake my head because I don't want him to know that I'm grieving the loss of my family.

"I'm just tired, baby," I whisper as I kiss him softly. I run my fingers through his two-day stubble, and I stare into his big, beautiful eyes. He kisses me slowly, his tongue sliding through my open mouth. For a long time we lie in each other's arms and kiss. It's tender, unhurried, and intimate, and when he kisses me like this, there is nobody else on earth but us.

His lips drop to my neck and he bites me with just the right amount of pressure before his hands slowly slide my panties down my legs.

He bites my nipples, kissing each one in reverence, and then he drops lower and lower. He spreads my legs and pulls me apart for his pleasure. I hold my breath as he looks at me. His lips gently kiss my inner thighs.

It always feels so intimate when he looks at me like this...the intimacy I crave from him, the entrée to perfection.

His thick tongue slides through my flesh, and I arch my back as the pleasure takes over. Spencer rests my legs over his shoulders. His hands are splayed on my lower stomach, and I watch him lick me like I'm a goddess.

His goddess.

With every swipe of his tongue, I love him just that little bit more. My hands rest on the back of his head.

"Baby, come up here," I whisper. "I want you close tonight."

He crawls up and over me. His lips glisten with my arousal. "Do you know how much I fucking love you, angel?" he whispers.

I wrap my legs around his waist. "Why don't you show me?"

In a perfectly practiced move, he slides his thick cock deep inside me, and we both moan in unison. I feel my pulse throbbing in every part of my body. Our lips crash together, and we kiss as his body withdraws and slowly slides in home once more.

"Spence..." I murmur against his big lips.

"Yeah, angel."

"I want you to roll me over and fuck me hard."

He bites my bottom lip and tugs on it with his teeth. "I've created a monster."

He flips me over and slams into me with a hard slap on my behind. He grabs my nipple and squeezes it, causing me to cry out in pain.

"Fuck me," I moan as my sex clenches around him. This is what I love—a certain kind of craziness that comes over me when he awakens the animal inside of my soul. "Fuck me *hard*."

22

Charlotte

Eight weeks later.

"HOLD the keys up to your face as if you're going to kiss them," Spencer instructs.

I roll my eyes with a smirk, secretly loving his directions. I do as I'm told and hold the keys up while he clicks away on his phone.

It's early on a Monday evening, and we're standing at the front door of my new office, having just picked up the keys. Spencer is in his element being the event's photographer.

"Okay, babe." He gestures towards the lock. "Open your new office."

I turn the key and open the big, heavy door, seeing the huge, bronzed letters on the wall hanging over the reception desk.

ALA

"Angel's Legal Assistance," Spence reads aloud, gently poking me in the stomach. "That's you."

"Oh my God, Spence. I can't believe we did it."

"*You* did this." He smiles proudly and takes me into his arms.

I smile up at the gorgeous man in front of me. "Thank you, I couldn't have done this without you."

He kisses me softly. "Yes, you could have."

"I really couldn't. You're the most supportive man I've ever met, and you've helped me every step of the way."

He wrinkles his nose. "I was aiming for the hottest lover in history, but whatever."

I giggle. "That, too."

"I think your desk arrived today. Go and take a look." He smiles.

I skip down the hallway and open the door to my office. My mouth falls open.

My desk did arrive, and on the top of it are vases and vases of beautiful flowers. "Spence," I whisper as I look around at them all and see a card is pinned to one. I open it.

To my beautiful Charlotte
Congratulations.
I am so very proud of you.
You are the light of my life.
I love you,
Spence
xox

My eyes instantly fill with tears and I turn to him.

"I love you." He smiles tenderly down at me.

"I'm the luckiest girl in the world," I whisper, overcome with emotion.

I turn back to the desk and notice a black briefcase. "What's in there?"

"That's your office supplies." He smirks with a mischievous look in his eyes.

I frown and click open the catch. All set out and strategically placed inside black foam are a large assortment of dildos and sex toys.

"What the hell?" I gasp as my eyes fly up to his. "Spencer!"

He chuckles at my shocked reaction.

"What on earth would I need this for?"

"To keep in your desk in case of an emergency."

My mouth falls open. "You think I'm going to masturbate in my office? Are you crazy?"

He shrugs. "It's a great stress reliever. Being in business is tough, babe."

"Oh my God." I roll my eyes. "You are a sex maniac." I slam the briefcase closed. "We're taking these home. There's no way in hell I'm doing *that* in *here*."

He licks his lips, arousal flickering in his eyes. "Threesome tonight, it is."

"You want to have a threesome with me and a dildo?"

"That's right."

"Spencer Jones, you are a sexual deviant."

He grabs me by the behind and sinks his teeth into my neck. "One who likes to watch."

Spencer

I'm staring at the diamond rings beneath the glass cabinet in Tiffany's.

Nothing stands out to me.

This is the fifteenth jewellery store I've been to.

How could a diamond set in gold possibly show how I feel about her?

There aren't enough words in the dictionary to describe it.

This woman, this perfect angel, has swooped into my life and changed everything I thought I knew about myself.

I thought I was happy. I thought I had life all figured out, but I was fucking miserable before I met her. I just didn't know it because I had nothing to compare it to.

I couldn't bring Masters or Seb shopping with me. This is just so deeply personal and something I never thought I would be doing.

I need to do it alone.

"Can I help you, sir?" the shop attendant asks.

"Uh." I frown, still looking at all the rings on display. "I'm just trying to get some ideas, although I've no idea what I am looking for."

"You're getting engaged?"

"Hopefully." I smirk to myself.

"Soon?"

"I plan to ask her on Christmas Eve."

"What a wonderful time of the year. Does she know?"

I shake my head. "No, it's a surprise."

"How wonderful. I'll leave you in peace, but please call me if you see anything that catches your eye. We also have a jeweller who can help you design the ring of your dreams."

"Okay, great. Thank you. If he has a moment to spare, I'd like to speak to him, please?"

"I'll see if he's around." She disappears out of sight.

I keep looking through the cabinets. I wish I could ask Sheridan for her opinion. She's always been my confidante.

I miss her.

Not the sex. I don't miss sleeping with her. I miss her friendship, but I know that one comes with the other and it's not possible to have her in my life anymore.

But at moments like this, when normally she would be the first person I would call for an opinion, her absence is all around me.

It makes me sad, if I'm honest.

Ten years is a long time.

"Hello, sir." A man smiles, appearing behind the counter. He holds his hand out to shake my hand. "I'm Cyrus, the designer."

"Hello." I smile.

"Shannon tells me that you're looking for an engagement ring."

"Yes. It has to be a perfect diamond and extremely feminine, not chunky. It can't be too big, she hates flashy. It needs to be understated and classically beautiful...just like she is."

He smiles brighter. "She sounds special."

"She is." I smirk, my heart swelling with pride. "How she loves me, I'll never know."

Six hours later, I walk out of the elevator on my floor and see the ever-present guards by my door. I passed another two on the bottom floor, and there is someone with our cars in the basement parking bay at all times now.

"Hello, Spencer," they greet me.

"How long has she been home?" I ask just to make conversation.

"She left work early today, so she's been home for a few hours now."

I frown. That's strange. "Have a good night," I say to them before I walk into my apartment.

The television is on, the lights are off, the apartment in darkness. A feeling of unease fills me.

"Angel?" I call.

No answer.

I walk out into the living room to see her sitting on the floor, tears streaming down her face. My face falls.

"What's wrong?" I crouch beside her and notice that there are boxes of Christmas decorations sitting next to the Christmas tree box I got out of storage yesterday.

I pull Charlotte onto my lap and hold her tight, listening as her quiet sadness turns to loud sobs.

"Baby?" I whisper as I rock her.

After a moment, she speaks quietly. "I just don't think I can do it."

"What?"

"Can we go to Santorini now?"

"What...why? What's happened?"

"How can it possibly be Christmas without your family?" she whispers through her tears. "Can we just skip it this year? I promise next year I'll make it up to you."

My heart drops. She can't stand the thought of having a Christmas with her family not talking to her. "What did you do today?" I ask, looking around helplessly.

"I bought Christmas decorations."

"Do you want to put the tree up?"

She shakes her head. "No."

I watch her for a moment. I remember how hard this time of year used to be for me, too. "Do you want me to put the tree up naked?" I tease. "You can drink wine and watch."

"No." She wipes her eyes. "I just don't want to have Christmas this year, Spence. Let's just leave it."

She doesn't want to have Christmas?

We remain silent, both of us lost in our own thoughts, until I can't stand the quiet a moment longer.

"Why don't you go home to Nottingham for Christmas, babe?"

She frowns up at me in question.

"Go home for Christmas and spend it with your family. I'll see you after," I offer.

"I'm not having Christmas without you." She gasps, as if shocked by the mere suggestion of it.

"There's no other way around it, Charlotte. They don't want me there, and I hate seeing you like this. I'd rather spend Christmas alone than see you hurt."

"I'm staying with you, Spencer. Don't you see?"

"See what?"

"This is a no-win situation. I can't be without you, so I have to learn to live without them."

She curls herself into my chest and holds me tight as she cries. Loud, uncontrollable sobs make her entire body shake.

All I can do is sit and hold her.

The room becomes a shady haze of red as I feel the adrenaline begin to pump through my veins.

"What can I do?" I whisper. "I'll make you some dinner."

"I'm not hungry, thanks." She kisses me as she tries to pull herself together. "I'm just going to go to bed, baby, is that okay?"

I brush her hair back from her forehead. "Of course it is."

"I'm sorry."

"Don't be." I kiss her. "I'll be up to tuck you in in a minute." I help her off my lap and watch her walk up the stairs until she disappears out of sight.

I pour myself a scotch and drink it down. Anger is coursing through my veins like wildfire. The only thing she ever did wrong was fall in love with me.

I drink my scotch with a shaky hand.

Who the fuck do they think they are?

1105

I punch in the code to the gates of the estate and drive through to the main house. I shouldn't be here, but I'm past caring what they think of me.

I hardly slept last night. I stayed awake, watching my angel cry.

I can't do it anymore. I have no patience and no fucks left to give.

I park the car, and Harold's guards appear out of nowhere. "What do you want?" one asks me.

"I want to see Harold," I announce, despite it being early morning. The earlier my arrival, the more chance I had of them being home.

"He's not here."

"Then I'll wait. Or...find him," I snap. "Better still, get Edward out here."

One of them scurries into the house, leaving me to stand at the bottom of the porch steps. It seems a lifetime ago when I was at the bottom of Charlotte's steps on that first date, begging her to let me in.

If only I knew what kind of Heaven awaited me, I would have stayed that night and saved us both a lot of time.

The front door opens, and Harold's face comes into view. I glare at him and storm up the stairs, brushing past him to enter his house.

The guard tries to stop me, but Harold holds his hand up. "He's fine."

I soon find Edward in the living room. "You fucking prick." I growl and push him hard in the chest.

"What the hell?" He staggers back before regaining his composure and pushing me in return.

"Stop it." Harold growls. "I've had enough of you both!"

"Are you happy?" I yell at Harold.

"Get the hell out." Edward sneers.

"Don't push me, cunt, or I'll fucking knock you out. Explain to me why Charlotte, a woman you're both supposed to love, spent the night crying because you two won't see her?"

Harold's face falls.

"She's fucking heartbroken!" I cry. "And why? All because neither one of you has enough guts to trust me?"

Edward glares at me. "You're no good for her."

"She doesn't want a fucking Christmas because of you. I came home from work last night to find her on the floor, sobbing over her fucked-up, selfish family."

Edward's eyes drop to the floor.

"I don't give a fuck if you don't like me," I shout. "But you will not punish her for loving me." I'm so angry, my eyes fill with unexpected tears.

Edward lifts his chin in defiance. "She needs to come home. It's where she belongs."

My temper hits an all-time high. "Nobody can love her more than I do. Nobody! I've done some fucked-up things in my life, I'll admit, but I love her and I'm marrying her whether you like it or not. If you keep going like this, the hurt you inflict on her will be way too deep for you to ever repair."

Harold watches me, and I turn to him. "Do you think your wife would be proud of the way you're treating your beloved daughter?" I whisper in contempt.

His haunted eyes hold mine.

"I wouldn't treat a fucking dog the way you've treated her. *You*, of all people, should understand how she feels." I sneer. "You fell for the hired help, for Christ's sake."

"You leave my mother the fuck out of this," Edward snaps, and throws a punch at my jaw. I stagger back, recover quickly, and then I punch him in the face as hard as I can. We grab each other, turning it into a scuffle. Punches are thrown and the table tips over in the foyer. A guard comes rushing in from outside.

We struggle on the floor until I'm dragged to my feet by my biceps.

"Get him outside!" Edward yells.

"You make this right!" I yell at Harold with hot blood trickling from my lip. "Do you hear me? You fix this."

I'm pushed out of the front door and down the stairs before I'm thrown into my car by the guards.

I'm so angry, I can't even see straight.

I take off and speed out the gates, glaring at the estate behind me disappearing quickly. I wince as I touch my eye. I think it's already black.

It's late afternoon, and I'm just tidying up for the day. I had to buy a new shirt before I could come into the office. The one I was wearing got ripped this morning in Nottingham. I have no idea how I'm going to explain this black eye and cut lip to Charlotte, either. I'll think I'll say it happened in the gym while boxing.

My phone rings and the name Angel lights up the screen.

"Hello, my beautiful girl."

"Hi," she breathes, and I can tell that she's smiling. "Thank you for being so wonderful."

I frown, wondering what she means. "How are you feeling?" I

ask. Does she know about my little psycho attack in Nottingham this morning?

She exhales heavily. "Better. You won't believe it."

"What?"

"My father just called me."

I frown. "He did?" I hesitate. Shit. "What did he say?"

"He wants to repair this rift between us. He wants to start again."

My eyebrows rise in surprise. "What?"

"He invited us to go to dinner with the family in London on Saturday night."

"He did?"

"William is coming home, too, and Dad wants to have dinner with everyone there. I'm so excited, Spence. I was hoping he would come around, and now he has," she gushes happily.

I blow air into my cheeks. To be honest, the last thing I want to do is go to dinner with those fucking pricks.

"That's okay, isn't it?" she asks with obvious hope. "You *will* come with me and try to get along with them, won't you? Start afresh."

I scratch my head. "Of course. I'll do anything for you, you know that."

"You have no idea what a relief this is to me. I feel like a weight has been lifted, and once they get to know you, I know they'll love you as much as I do."

I roll my eyes. If she only knew what had gone on this morning. Actually, I don't care. As long as she's happy, that's all that matters.

"And you'll get to meet William and his wife. They're back from Switzerland. Oh, this is going to be fantastic."

"Okay, babe," I sigh. Fantastic, another brother. I'm already dreading it. "Sounds great," I lie.

"I'll see you soon. I'm leaving work now. Let's put the tree up tonight."

I smirk. "I thought you didn't want to have Christmas this year?"

"Christmas is officially back on. I love you." She smiles.

"Lucky." I smirk as I touch my throbbing eye socket. "See you soon."

I hang up and exhale heavily, staring at the phone in my hand. I swing my chair from side to side. Maybe my little visit this morning worked, after all.

Interesting. I'm going to find out exactly what is going on here.

I dial Harold's number. He answers on the first ring. "Hello, Spencer."

"What's the catch?" I ask

"No catch. I want to move on."

"And Edward?"

"Edward wants his sister to be happy. This dinner will be a starting point."

I stay silent on the phone.

"Thank you for coming to me with your concerns for Charlotte. I appreciate it."

"Does she know I came to you?"

"No, and I don't want her to."

"I only want for her to be happy."

"As do we. Charlotte is my only concern. So, will I see you Saturday night?" he asks.

"Sure, I'll see you there."

"Don't bring up anything about the fight we had." Charlotte smiles. She's holding my free hand even though I'm driving, her eyes on me while I watch the road.

It's Saturday night and we're on our way to meet her family. Charlotte is buzzing. Me? I'm trying my hardest not to roll my eyes.

"Yes, got it."

"And ask William about his job as a doctor. He loves speaking about that. It'll break the ice."

"Okay."

"And ask Edward about work. Try to make casual conversation with him, even though he's quite abrupt at first."

No shit.

"Do you think I look okay?" She straightens out her dress.

I glance at her and then frown. "You look beautiful."

"And just—"

"Will you stop telling me what to say?" I interrupt. "I am perfectly capable of holding a civilised conversation."

"I know," she sighs. "I just really want this to work out." She leans over and kisses my cheek as I keep my eyes on the road. "It means so much to me that you're willing to forgive and forget."

I force a smile because it's kind of cute how excited she is. Honestly, I just want this night over with.

This is for her.

We soon arrive at the restaurant, and I can already see four guards at the door. I park the car and take Charlotte's hand in mine, and then we make our way inside.

Charlotte spots them quickly and waves happily. I can see Edward, Harold, and another man who I'm assuming is William... and then...

The blood drains from my face.

"Who is that woman at the table?" I whisper.

Charlotte smiles and drags me through the restaurant. "That's Penelope. William's wife."

I feel the floor move beneath me. No, it can't be.

Oh my God.

I'm the man Penelope fucked behind her husband's back.

23

Spencer

I STAND STILL, my feet frozen to the spot.

The air drains from my lungs.

William glances up and sees me as we approach the table, and his face quickly falls.

He recognises me.

"Charlotte," I whisper, coming to another stop. "I need to talk to you. Outside...now."

"This way." She keeps dragging me to the table.

"You fucking dog." William sneers as he stands.

Penelope's eyes widen in horror. "Oh my God," she whispers the second she sees me.

Charlotte's face falls in confusion as she looks between us. "William?" she asks.

"What's wrong?"

"Get the fuck outside, now!" William growls.

My jaw feels like it's on the floor. What are the chances?

I'm completely speechless. What the fuck do I say to this?

"You know each other?" Edward asks, confused by our interaction.

William glares at me. "Oh, we know each other, all right."

Charlotte glances between the two of us. "I don't understand."

"Last time I saw him, he was in my bed, balls deep inside *my wife*." William lunges for me, connecting a fist to my jaw, which forces me to fly back.

"Oh my God!" Penelope yells when the table goes flying.

I glance over to see Charlotte's hands are over her mouth as she connects the dots.

Harold holds on to the table to stop himself from falling over and, of course, Edward erupts like a madman. "What the fuck?" he yells.

"No!" Charlotte cries. "That can't be true." Her haunted eyes meet mine.

"I'm sorry," I whisper.

"No!" she whispers. Her face screws up in pain as she realises it's true.

"Charlotte," I whisper as she begins to cry hysterically. "I didn't know she was married. I swear to you."

Edward grabs me and pushes me towards the door. I see the flash of a camera hit my face.

"That's not true!" Penelope yells. "You knew exactly who I was married to, and you were after his money. You pursued me for months until you wore me down."

"What?" I cry. "You fucking liar. I didn't even know you as Penelope. You told me your name was Stephanie." I'm hit from the side by William again. The whole restaurant is watching, and the guards suddenly seem to come running from every direction.

Edward drags me towards the door to pull me away from Charlotte.

"Charlotte," I cry. "She's lying, I swear to you."

I struggle to break free, but I still see Charlotte crying hysterically in Harold's arms.

No!

This can't be happening!

More cameras flash in the distance.

I grab the doorframe to try and stop them from dragging me away from her. "Charlotte!" I cry. "Charlotte, come here. Listen to me!" I beg.

Charlotte's haunted eyes hold mine for just a second before she shakes her head and turns her back on me.

I dig my heels in to try and stop them from dragging me away from her. "Charlotte!"

"Just leave, Spencer," she yells into her father's shoulder. Harold wraps his arms around her, shielding and protecting her from me.

I'm dragged outside, and I struggle to break free. All at once, Charlotte is rushed out of the restaurant, the clicks of cameras flashing everywhere until she is put into the back of the Bentley.

"*Charlotte!*" I scream, and the car speeds off into the distance.

Edward walks up to me, his stare cold and full of hatred. "Are you happy now?"

"I swear to you, Edward, I didn't know." His guards hold me by my arms.

Edward punches me in the stomach and the wind is knocked from my lungs. I double over and fall to the ground on the cold, grey pavement.

Blood fills my mouth.

I hear footsteps, cars, and the flashes of more cameras. And then there's a cacophony of car tyres screaming in the distance. After a short while, I feel myself being lifted from the ground. I look up to see Anthony and Wyatt.

They've stayed with me.

The only ones.

I look around to see everyone else has gone.

"Come on, let's get you home." Wyatt sighs sadly.

"Charlotte," I whisper.

"She's gone, mate," Anthony says with regret.

I stammer in a panic. "We-we have to go get her."

Wyatt looks at me, his face sad and full of sympathy. "She

doesn't want to see you, Spence. She told me to keep you away from her."

I wince and drop my head.

This can't be happening.

I stare at the television on the wall of the bar I'm in.

Masters and Seb are beside me, staying silent. What is there to say?

I've fucked it. I've completely fucked it.

"She'll come around." Masters sips his beer.

"I don't think she will," Seb mutters. "Have you seen the papers today? This scandal is fucking everywhere."

"You're not helping, Seb!" Masters snaps. "Try calling her again."

I pass my phone to him. He dials Charlotte's number and, once again, it goes straight through to voice mail. Her phone has been turned off since dinner last night. She hasn't been back to our apartment. If I try to drive to Nottingham, they won't let me see her, anyway.

I'll wait here in London for her to come home.

Please come home.

"I don't understand how you didn't know this." Masters frowns. "How do you fuck a married woman and never find out who she was married to?"

"It's not something I wanted to know, all right? Fuck."

Seb smirks and stares down at the table.

"What?" I say, deadpan.

"You do have to admit it is a little bit funny. What are the chances?"

"It's not funny, Sebastian, you fucking idiot. What will be funny is when I rearrange your ugly face," I growl.

Masters chuckles. "Now that will be funny. I'd pay good money to watch you do that."

A text comes in from Bree.

Spence
I can't get a hold of her.
I'll keep trying.
Bree

I drag my hand down my face in despair.

"She's not seeing anyone or taking any calls. Beth called me this morning, and Charlotte won't even see her. I don't know how the fuck I'm supposed to fix this when she won't even speak to me."

We all fall silent.

"She'll come home." Masters sighs. "She's just in shock."

"Join the fucking club," Seb grumbles. "I'm in shock too."

I glare at him. "I swear to fucking God, your face is so punchable right now, I can't even stand it."

The both laugh at me.

"Can you two just fuck off and leave me alone?"

"Nope," Masters answers without hesitation. "We've been through tougher times than this, and we always stick together."

I pinch the bridge of my nose. A memory of Charlotte's face when she realised I'd slept with Penelope takes over, and my heart hurts.

I can't believe I slept with Penelope.

What have I done?

Charlotte

Thirty-seven hours since he held me.

Thirty-seven hours since I had my heart completely ripped from my chest.

I'm in my bed, staring at a wall.

I can't drink, I can't eat, I can't think.

I wish I couldn't feel…

I keep seeing Spencer's face as they dragged him away from me —the fear in his eyes.

He knew…he knew then, in that moment, what our future was.

We aren't a love story. We're a tragedy.

Tears roll down my face. The hysterical tears are over, replaced with numbness—a cold, dead feeling now taking over my heart.

I'm an empty vessel, broken beyond repair.

Everything I thought I knew was a lie. The life I planned with him is over.

Love with him will never be the same.

The man I fell in love with doesn't exist.

In his place there's a home-wrecker, a man who I despise, and everything he stands for.

A man with different morals than me, and one I couldn't possibly be in love with.

The pain is deep, real, and I feel like I'm grieving someone's death all over again.

It hurts.

I hear a car horn in the distance.

Beep, beep, beeeeeeeeeep.

What's that?

Beep, beep, beeeeeeeeeep.

I hear a door bang, and then footsteps as someone runs past my house down the gravel road.

What on earth is going on out there?

I drag myself to the window and peer through the sheer curtains only to see Spencer's car outside the gates. He's standing next to it, pushing on the horn through his open door.

Beep, beep, beeeeeeeeeep. "Charlotte!" he yells. "Come out here." *Beep, beep.* "CHARLOTTE!" he screams.

I wince and feel more tears fall as I watch him. He's frantic.

"Angel, please," he begs. "I promise you, I didn't know."

I slap my hands over my ears. "Stop it," I whisper. "Leave me alone."

"Charlotte?" I turn and see Edward. I crash to his chest as he wraps me in his safe arms. "It's okay, Lottie, they're taking him away now."

I howl against his chest, this pain unbearable.

The worst thing is, I know that Spencer will be hurting just as much as I am.

But what's done is done.

He can't change the past, and this will never be something I'll be able to live with.

He slept with my brother's wife. *Penelope.*

I taste bile, imagining him in William's bed with William's wife, and I cry harder and harder until I can't breathe. I can't see him.

I don't ever want to see him again.

There is nothing he can say that will take away what he's done or the hurt he's caused my beloved brother.

A new rush of pain seeps through another layer in my heart.

"Spencer," I cry. "*My love. Why?*" I howl. "Why did he do this, Edward, why?"

"Shh."

I hear the car horn again and Spencer screams my name. "Charlotte!"

"Make him go away," I cry.

"They're taking him now. Dad is at the police station taking out a restraining order against him as we speak. He won't be able to come here at all without being arrested soon."

The thought that he can't legally come here anymore breaks my heart even further, and I cry uncontrollably.

"I'm sorry I let this happen," Edward whispers against my hair. "This is all my fault."

"Charlotte!" Spencer screams again, and I slap my hands over my ears.

"Make it stop, Edward, make it stop."

"Charlotte, please... I love you," Spencer yells, his voice breaking. "I love you."

The guards begin to shout, and then there's a commotion. I know that Spencer is struggling with them to try to get to me.

I pull out of Edward's arms and roll into a ball on my bed, holding my hands over my ears as I cry hysterically.

Make.

The.

Pain.

Stop.

Spencer

I stare at my computer, looking at pictures of myself outside the restaurant.

But all I see is Charlotte's hurt face.

Every tabloid, every magazine, everyone knows I slept with Penelope—Charlotte's brother's wife. Her damn sister-in-law.

To make it worse, someone even filmed what Penelope was saying in the restaurant. It's been played over and over and over.

Everywhere.

It's not even true.

Did I sleep with her? Yes.

Did I know she was married? No.

I had no idea what her real name was. I hooked up with her a few times and she told me she was divorced. I saw her at a club one night and we went back to her house.

What I thought was her house, anyway.

Then a crazed husband burst in on us midway through sex, and he completely lost his shit. I picked up my clothes and ran. I never saw her again.

I still remember the devastation on his face when he caught us. It's something I have thought of often over the years.

It's the kind of thing you never forget.

There was no way in hell I would have been there if I'd have known the truth. I wouldn't knowingly sleep with a married woman unless she was in an open relationship. I know what Seb went through. I would never inflict that pain on someone else.

My chest constricts as I remember the only person that matters in this story.

Charlotte. My beautiful Charlotte.

I've lost her.

She won't answer my calls, she's not opening my texts. She won't see me.

She's heartbroken, and who can blame her?

I don't know what to do, I don't know what to say. How do I salvage this?

A little voice from deep inside my mind tells me that it's impossible.

I click out of the story on my screen and run my hands through my hair in disgust.

I'm sick to my stomach.

This is God punishing me. I'm being punished for being promiscuous before I met her.

My love...*gone.*

I hear my office door open and I look up and see a familiar face. Unable to help it, tears of relief fill my eyes, and I stand quickly.

"Spence," Sheridan whispers, taking me in her arms.

I cling to her as if my life depends on it. After a long time, she pulls back to look at my face, holding it in her hands.

"Are you okay, darling?" she asks softly, her eyes searching mine.

"No," I whisper. "I am not."

She takes me in her arms again and holds me tight. "It's okay. I'm here now, baby. I'll look after you. We'll get through this together."

Charlotte

I wake from my groggy sleep and lie in the darkness.

It's Christmas Day—the day I was dreading spending without my family. That pain pales into insignificance now. I get a vision of my Spencer waking up alone in his apartment and my bottom lip quivers.

Is he okay?

415

I will not cry today. I will not cry today, I chant in my head.

Penelope and William had a huge argument, and she left the estate last night.

She took Harrison with her... *it's Christmas.*

It's been ten days since I saw Spencer. Ten days without his love....his touch.

I feel like a part of me has died and I'm trying to learn how to live without a limb.

I'll get through this, I know I will.

I need to talk to Spencer, but I feel too weak to do so at the moment. I know if I see him now, he will somehow talk me around. I don't have the strength to say what I need to say without crying and begging for him to turn back time.

To be honest, I don't know if I ever will.

His love was perfect. It was something I feel I was meant to experience.

But that was before.

We were supposed to be leaving for Santorini in three days. I get a vision of us laughing and driving around on motorbikes the last time we were there, and I close my eyes, hating the way my chest constricts.

How do people do this? How do they bounce back?

I've always heard of people going through a bad breakup, but until you've actually had your heart ripped out and stomped on, you have no idea of the enormity of it.

It's like the world is ending.

William needs me today. He's spending Christmas without his son.

I know the fight they had last night was over Spencer. I heard his name called out as they yelled at each other from upstairs.

I think seeing Spencer opened a can of worms for William. How do you move on when you've seen another person making love to your wife? When that person turns up years later as your baby sister's new boyfriend? It would have to mess your mind up.

I know mine is completely scrambled.

The bitter taste of betrayal fills my mouth.

He had sex with Penelope...more than once.

I could never look at him the same again. He is forever tainted in my eyes.

I keep getting a vision of them naked together, again and again, as if I saw it with my own eyes.

It's making me sick.

"Charlotte," my father calls from the hallway of my house. He's been staying with me since this all happened. I think he's scared to leave me alone. Scared of what, I'm unsure.

"Yes, Dad."

He comes into view, peeking around the door. "Merry Christmas, my darling."

I smile and my eyes fill with tears. He's the one man I can always rely on.

"Merry Christmas, Dad."

"You know what?" Lara says. "I'm glad this happened. At least now we have proof of what Edward and your father have been saying all along."

I roll my eyes. "Not helping, Lars."

We're sitting out on the front porch of my house on December 26th.

Lara and Beth have come over to try and cheer me up... I think at Edward's insistence, although Lara is not doing a very good job of it. I had one of the worst days of my life yesterday.

Christmas without Spencer.

"Bullshit. How could you say such a thing?" Beth snaps at her.

Lara shrugs. "They thought something was off, and they were right."

Beth rolls her eyes. "Did Edward tell you that while you were sucking his dick?"

I smirk.

"Will you drop it with the Edward crap?" Lara whines.

Beth is now openly ribbing Lara about Edward, and Lara is avoiding the topic by not answering a direct question. I really do think they either are fucking or have fucked in the past. Which one, I'm not sure. It's something I don't like to imagine.

"Will you stop making Spencer out to be the evil villain in this story? Because he's not." Beth grumbles angrily. "It's fucking Penelope and her loose vagina that's caused all this heartache. Spencer wasn't married. Spencer didn't have a girlfriend. Who cares who he fucked before he met you?"

"When it was my brother's wife, I do, actually, Beth," I hit back.

She rolls her eyes at me, choosing not to respond.

"Everybody will know. For the rest of my life, everyone will know that he fucked my brother's wife. It's been in every tabloid for a week." My eyes fill with tears. "I can't be with someone who's done that, no matter how much I love them. I can't get past it."

"Then go talk to him and break up with him like a real adult."

Guilt fills me.

"Why are you hiding from him?"

"Because if I see him, he'll talk me down."

"Because you know he's fucking right!" Beth snaps.

"Oh, just shut up, Beth." Lara sighs. "She can't be with him after this. She'll be the laughingstock of society."

Beth scowls at us both and stands in an outrage. "Lara, I would expect you to bow down to society and suck their balls. But you"— she points at me—"are being fucking ridiculous. Spencer is a wonderful man, and I don't care what he's done before he met you because I see how happy he makes you *now*. If he fucked her now, it would be different. But he didn't. It was years ago. Wake up and smell the damn coffee."

I stare at her through tears.

She points at me. "You're going to lose him, and in ten years' time when Penelope is long divorced from William, and Spencer is happily married to someone else, you're going to kick yourself for throwing away the best thing that ever happened to you."

We both stare at her, and fear runs through me. What she's just said is a real possibility.

"Now, I'm going to bed, because you two and this society-shame bullshit is pissing me off." Before she leaves, Beth turns to me. "I thought you wanted to marry for love, Lottie?"

"I do."

"You're not acting like you love him. You're acting like a selfish little girl—"

"Fuck off, Beth. She is not, she's being smart, for once," Lara interrupts.

"Imagine how he's feeling right now."

Tears roll down my cheeks.

"You know what? I wish Spencer Jones had fallen in love with me, because there is no way in fucking hell I would be sitting here in this fucking prison with you."

I stare at her.

"Your father didn't talk to you for eight weeks because he didn't get his own way, Charlotte." She throws her hands in the air. "What does that tell you about this fucked-up situation? How can you not see it?"

"Stop it, you're upsetting her," Lara demands.

"Where was Spencer?" Beth snaps. "Where was Spencer when you needed him?"

I drop my head into my hands as my emotions boil over.

"That's right, Lottie, Spencer was right by your side the whole fucking time. Never once have you doubted his love for you."

Wyatt walks around the corner after hearing our raised voices. "What's going on here?" he asks.

"Nothing." Beth sighs in disgust. "I'm going to bed. These two and their lack of priorities are making me sick." The door slams behind her as she disappears.

Wyatt frowns, and his eyes flick to me in question.

"You go to bed, too, Lars. I'll be up in a minute." I sigh.

She kisses my cheek and walks inside the house.

"Are you okay?" Wyatt asks softly.

"I hardly know anymore," I whisper.

He sits on the step at my feet, and we both stare out over the property and into the darkness of the night. He doesn't say anything, and he doesn't try to talk me into his way of thinking.

He just stays, and in this moment, that's all I need.

Spencer

Bang, bang, bang!

What on earth?

It's two days after Christmas, and after possibly the most depressing Christmas I've ever had, I'm packing for Santorini.

She'll come.

I know she will. Our love was too strong. She won't forget that, no matter what's happened.

She'll come.

I have to believe that. I have to believe that she'll be able to move past this because the reality is that if she doesn't, it'll be more than I can bear.

Bang, bang, bang!

I open the door in a rush.

"Where is she?" Edward growls, looking past me and into the room.

"What?" I frown. He and Harold barge past me and walk into my apartment. "Please, do come in," I mutter with an eye roll.

Assholes.

"Where is she?"

"What are you fucking talking about?"

"Don't act dumb, you know exactly where she is."

"I haven't seen her since the restaurant, you know that."

Harold pinches the bridge of his nose. "She could be anywhere. She's taken off." He falls onto the sofa.

"Her guards aren't with her?" I ask in confusion.

"She's... Charlotte is completely alone," Harold stammers in a panic. "She snuck out in the middle of the night."

"This is all my fault." Edward groans. "Why did I...?" His voice trails off.

"What?" I frown. "What happened?"

He shakes his head and drops next to his father on the sofa. "We fought."

"You fought with her?" I snap. "She's hurt enough, why the fuck would you fight with her?"

"I don't know. I was angry with Penelope for taking off, and I..." He shakes his head at himself.

"What did she say?" I begin to freak out.

"She left a note saying she would be back soon," Harold tells me quietly.

"What note?"

He digs around in his suit pocket and pulls out a piece of paper. He hands it over.

Dad,
I'm confused and I need time alone to think.
I'm taking a TTT Trip. Don't worry, I'm safe.
I'll see you in two weeks.
I love you,
Charlotte

My heart swells with hope and pride.

That's my girl.

24

Spencer

IF SHE'S GONE for a TTT trip in its truest form, I think she's gone to Maui and will be staying at the Four Seasons. If she left in the middle of the night, she won't even be there yet.

She's at my special place.

I want her to have time to think. I want her to be able to make this decision on her own. But then... I look at the worry on Harold's face and I can't do that to him.

"Just a minute." I walk to the kitchen, grab my phone, and Google the hotel. When it pops up, I dial the number.

"Aloha, Four Seasons," the receptionist answers.

"Hello, can I be put through to Maxine, please?" I ask. "Tell her that it's Spencer Jones calling."

"Of course, sir."

I wait on the line until the phone connects to another line.

"Hello, Spencer." Maxine laughs excitedly. "It's been a long time."

"It has, and I'm due for a trip very soon." I glance up to the two men in front of me. "I have a friend arriving there tonight. Can you check if she's arrived yet for me, please?"

"Sure thing. What's her name?"

What would she have used? I think for a moment while Harold and Edward watch on.

"Lottie Preston."

"Just a minute." I hear her tapping away on the keys at her computer. "Ah, yes. She won't arrive until later tonight. Can I leave a message?"

"No, thank you. I'll call back later," I say before hanging up.

I turn to them. "I know where she's going."

They both place their hands over their chests in relief. "Thank God. Where?"

I stare at them for a moment. This is my only leverage, and I need to use it.

"I want to speak to William," I say steadily.

"Fuck off," Edward growls. "He doesn't want to speak to you."

"Fine. Then get out."

Harold's face falls. "Please, Spencer, tell us where she is. She's in danger out there on her own."

"I'll tell William where she is."

"Why would you want to speak to him?" Edward snaps. "Haven't you done enough to him already?"

"I need to apologise." I pause. "I had no idea she was married."

"Bull-fucking-shit. She told us everything."

I raise a brow. "And you believe anything that comes out of that lying bitch's mouth, right? I knew her as Stephanie, and it gets worse. She's actually contacted me a few times over the last few years and begged to see me again."

Harold's face falls.

"Every time she's in London, she tries to see me. I'm telling you, she's fucking other guys all the time."

"I knew it." Edward narrows his eyes. "I need proof."

Harold frowns as he watches me. "Have you ever...?"

"Fuck, no." I wince. "I'm mortified that she put me in the position she did that night." I drop my head in shame. "I'm not proud of it, I'm telling you." I exhale heavily. "The look on William's face will haunt me forever."

Edward glares at me.

"I love Charlotte. I would never have pursued her had I known that she knew Stephanie."

"Penelope." Harold glares at me. "Christ, you don't even know her fucking name."

"That's right, I don't. Now she's telling all these lies to protect herself at the expense of Charlotte's heart." I sigh sadly. "She makes me fucking sick. Charlotte doesn't deserve to be hurt like this. I can't stand that she is."

"It's your word against hers," Edward says. "Give me proof. I need concrete evidence that she's come to you. If I can prove that she's still sleeping around, he can divorce her and get custody of Harrison."

"I don't have any. Maybe my phone records can show the times she's contacted me?" I offer. "I don't know." I hold Edward's stare. "Bring William to me and I'll tell you where Charlotte is."

"Why should we?" Harold snaps.

"Because you both need to realise the truth. I was a player. Hell, I've fucked around for years, I'm the first to admit it. But as soon as I met Charlotte, I stopped immediately. I don't want anybody else. I have no secrets, and Charlotte knows everything about me. I haven't lied to her once, and if I knew about Stephanie, I would have told her. Do you honestly think I would want her to go through this? For Christ's sake, I don't even speak to my own fucking father because he's an adulterous prick."

They both watch me as they listen.

"I've never even been in a relationship before Charlotte because of this exact reason. I couldn't be a two-faced liar. It's not who I am."

Edward rolls his eyes.

"You know what fucking pisses me off the most about this?" I say.

"What?" Harold sighs.

"If you had just given me the time of day back when we met instead of treating me like dirty Stephanie or whatever her fucking name is, you would have seen the truth. You would have known how I feel about Charlotte."

Harold raises his chin.

"I've done nothing wrong." I hold my hands up in front of me. "I promise you, and you know I haven't. You probably have people watching me, hoping to catch me out."

Edward rolls his lips, and I know that I'm right.

"My poor Charlotte is on her own on the other side of the world with a broken heart, and you two haven't supported her at all. You're all so fucking poisoned by that bitch that you've taken her sins out on me instead. But it's Charlotte who has taken the brunt of this."

"What a mess." Harold exhales heavily. "Please, Spencer, tell us where she is."

"Not until you bring William to me." I stare at them and open my front door. "Now, please leave."

"You're kicking us out?" Edward gasps.

"Yeah, I'm kicking you out. You've kept Charlotte from me when I've wanted to try and explain. I'm sick of your power trip shit."

Harold shakes his head as he walks towards the door. "William will be here soon."

"Good."

Edward's eyes hold mine, and for the first time ever I see empathy in them. "She won't be able to take you back after this. You have no idea how much she hates Penelope."

I clench my jaw and nod. That's my biggest fear. "I know." I sigh sadly. "I understand why. I'm not sure I could if I were her."

With one last look, they both turn and leave. A wave of new sadness overwhelms me. That interaction with them seemed so final, and it felt like they knew it too...like I'll never see them again.

Maybe I won't.

It's dusk when I hear a knock at my door. I close my eyes in regret.

William.

I'll never forget the look on his face that night, the pure devastation. I felt sick about it for weeks, and what made it worse was that she kept calling me, wanting to meet up. She had absolutely no remorse.

I put myself in his shoes now and imagine how it would feel if I walked in and saw another man having sex with Charlotte.

I couldn't cope. I would completely lose my shit.

I open the door and his face comes into view. He's tall and good-looking, similar looking to Edward but with a softer edge and more refined. I don't remember much about that night, but I remember his face. How could I ever forget it?

"Spencer," he says flatly.

He doesn't want to be here either, it's obvious.

"Hi." I hold out my hand. "Please, come in."

He walks past me and into the apartment.

"Do you want a drink or anything?" I ask. "What would you like?"

He shrugs. "Whatever you're having."

I inhale deeply and pour two glasses of scotch. I hand him one.

He takes a sip. "So, you fucked my wife," he says calmly.

I nod. "Yes."

His cold eyes hold mine. "That's it? That's all you can say?"

"Nothing I can say would ever make up for that."

He inhales sharply and walks to the windows to stare out over the city, deep in thought.

I have no idea what to say, so I remain silent.

"How many times?" he asks with his back to me.

"Three occasions."

He turns back to look at me, and I know the real question he wants answered.

"Many times on those three occasions," I admit shamefully.

426

He turns back to stare out of the window.

"Can I ask you something?" I say. "Why didn't you leave her?"

"It would have been easier to."

"Why did you stay?"

"I have a son." He drains his glass. "I don't want to take him away from his mother, but then I don't want to leave him with her, either." He walks over and refills his glass. "The only way I can assure his future is to stay with her until Harrison is older."

I frown as I watch him. He seems strangely detached from all this. "Do you love her?"

"I did."

"Not anymore?"

"Love and I don't mix, Mr Jones." He looks up at me. "I learnt that lesson the hard way."

"Does she know this? Does she know you don't love her?"

"Yes."

"Then why does she stay?" I frown. "I'm confused."

He narrows his eyes as if it pains him to say it out loud. "I think we both know why she stays."

The money.

I drop my head as disappointment on his behalf fills me.

"I'm sorry. I know you don't believe me when I tell you this, but I thought she was divorced, and I knew her as Stephanie. I had no idea when I met Charlotte that she was your wife...or that you were Charlotte's brother."

He smiles as he stares out of the window.

I frown. "What's to smile about?"

"I always blamed you for our demise—blamed myself, blamed everyone but her when, deep down, I knew the truth. A month ago, another doctor at the hospital I work with told me he met a woman called Stephanie on the Ashley Madison dating site...the one for married people to have secret affairs. They'd been sleeping together for a while." He scowls lightly. "I had a sixth sense go off, and I asked to see a picture of her."

I close my eyes. Fuck.

"You can imagine my surprise when I see an image of my own wife, all messed up and just fucked, asleep in his bed. She had no idea that the image was even taken."

"Jesus Christ." I tip my head back and drain my glass. This is un-fucking-believable.

"I have lawyers tightening the prenups as we speak. She doesn't know that I know about my work colleague. He doesn't even know she's my wife. Every time we argue, she threatens to take Harrison. I can't risk that." He sips his drink. "I have to wait until all my ducks are in a row."

"And when will that be?"

"That's where I need your help."

"What?" I ask.

He turns to me. "You can testify."

I frown. "What do you mean?"

"You can testify for me in a court of law that you slept with her while she was married to me."

"Jesus Christ, you can't ask me to do that. It would kill Charlotte," I whisper. "The tabloids would go into overdrive."

"They already are, and I need proof that Penelope is an adulterer or my prenup is void."

"What do you mean?'

He smiles. "I was so stupidly in love with this woman, I waivered the prenup."

I close my eyes.

"The only stipulation that voids me giving her half of my estate is her infidelity."

I stare at him.

"I don't really fancy giving her two billion dollars, Spencer." He smirks as if amused. "It's not like she deserves it."

I pinch the bridge of my nose. "Fucking hell." I think for a moment. "Does your family know any of this?"

"Yes." He rolls his eyes. "But Edward has his own agenda. He doesn't give a fuck about my feelings. When she first slept with you, I thought it was a one-off. I blamed myself for being a workaholic and leaving her alone all the time. We went to marriage counselling and I tried...for the sake of my son. But Edward wouldn't give up. He was sure she was staying with me for the money, and he became nasty and abusive towards her. It caused a great rift between him and me. If I wanted to try and repair my marriage, it was none of his business."

I exhale. I know what a fucking cock Edward can be.

"He hated her so much and made it unbearable for her to be around my family. She and I would fight about it, and it made things so much worse. So, in the end, I just stayed away. We moved to Switzerland to try and make a new start."

"I'm sorry." I sigh.

His eyes meet mine. "Me too."

"What are you going to do?"

"Divorce her. Now, where's Charlotte?" he asks.

"I'll tell you on one condition."

"What's that?"

"You have to go to her yourself."

He frowns. "Why?"

"Because she needs you, and only you."

His eyes hold mine.

"She told me that she's closest to you."

His eyes drop to the floor. "I haven't been around for her lately."

"You had your own shit going on. She understands."

He thinks for a moment. "Okay. I'll go."

"Thank you." I force a smile. "She's at the Four Seasons in Maui."

"If you know where she is, why didn't you go to her yourself?"

"Because it was her decision to leave." I pause for a moment. "She needs to come back to me of her own free will. I would never force her into something that she doesn't want. I love her too much to try and control her. She's been controlled enough in her life already."

He exhales heavily. "You know, under different circumstances,

I'd probably think you weren't a bad bloke." He shakes his head. "This is fucked up."

"I know." I smirk.

He turns to me. "So, will you help me?"

"I'll lose Charlotte if I do. She won't deal with that kind of publicity."

His eyes hold mine. "I hate to tell you this, Spencer, but you've already lost her. She's gone, man."

I drop my head and stare at the floor. *What if he's right?*

"I'm sorry, I really am." He sighs. "But I can't stay married to this woman, and I can't lose my son." His eyes search mine. "Say you'll help me."

Charlotte

The eagle hovers over the water, watching her prey. What must it be like to be a bird? To have no responsibilities, no expectations.

No heartbreak.

I'm on the deck chair under the big umbrella, staring out at the ocean. It's nearing 4:00 p.m., and the sun is still warm on my skin. I have a cocktail beside me and have just been for a swim. Maui is beautiful—the perfect place to escape.

If only he were here with me.

I close my eyes. Stop it, stop thinking about him.

It's over.

It's been a long few days. I bought my ticket with cash at the Heathrow Airport so that they couldn't track me. I had a lot of time, and stupidly, I bought all of the magazines, just to see what they were saying about us. I don't know why, but I needed to know.

I shouldn't have. I should have listened to Spencer and stayed away. It resulted in me crying silent tears for most of the trip, London to LA with a four-hour wait for a connecting flight to Maui. Headline after headline about Spencer sleeping his way through the Prescott family assaulted me. Images of him have surfaced with every woman on Earth, and I know that they are old pictures, but it just adds to the insult.

The footage of the horrific moment has been played on TMZ too. It was uploaded by a person who was eating in the restaurant at the time. William's anger, my horror, and then my hysterical tears as Edward went ballistic...

I've never been more ashamed.

A sinking feeling of regret sits deep inside my stomach. Disappointment and sadness all rolled into one heavy lead ball rest there. I let myself fall in love with him. I knew he had earned his reputation and I didn't care. I jumped in headfirst, ignoring every warning that was given to me. I never thought his past could hurt me the way that it has. Never in a million years did I see this coming.

My boyfriend slept with my brother's wife...it doesn't get more headline-worthy than that.

I still miss him. I miss him so much, it physically hurts my chest. How am I supposed to live without his love?

But every time I get a vision of my beautiful Spencer, I see him with her. It's all I can see. A dark cloud hangs over him. It's like my memory of him isn't just him anymore. She's intertwined like a poisonous vine strangling the life out of our love. I've relived every sickening moment he spent with her, over and over in my mind. I get visions, vibrant visions of him naked...with her.

Hard...for her.

Did he fuck her the way he fucks me? What positions did they do? Penelope is beautiful, and she has an amazing body. It's a body I'm sure pleasured him immensely.

How many times did he come?

Oh God...

I blink, knowing there is no cure for this heartbreak. I can't get my head around it. I will never get my head around it.

Spencer Jones is forever tainted in my eyes; I'll never look at him the same again.

And it hurts...so much so, that it's unbearable.

My phone buzzes next to me, and I glance over to the table. An unknown number is calling.

It's him.

I blocked Spencer's number on that very first night when he was calling me nonstop. But every day he has sent me a message from a new phone number. I don't know if he's buying new phones each day or going through every one of his friends' phones.

Either way, his texts hurt.

I sip my cocktail and stare out over the water, just in time to see the eagle make her move and swoop down. She reappears a few seconds later with a large fish in her beak.

Success, I smile sadly. At least someone around here is getting what they want. I exhale heavily and open the message that's waiting for me.

Dream catch me

Tears well in my eyes.

The words are so fitting now.

I wish I could text him back, but I'm angry. I'm angry at him, angry at myself for not being able to move past this…just so angry.

He has fallen and I can't fucking catch him.

How dare he ask that I do?

I frown and stare out at the sea, and a second text arrives. Damn it, I forgot to block the number straight away like I normally do. I click it open.

Don't leave me
You said you loved me.

I hit *block caller* and I drain my glass.

"I did love you, Spencer," I whisper angrily. "But that was then and this is now."

This is not going to stop. These texts are doing my head in and are no good for me right now.

I take the SIM out of my phone and put it into the glass of iced water that sits beside me. I watch it float from side to side before it sinks to the bottom.

He can go to Hell.

I'm done.

The candlelight flickers on my face, and I sit in the warm ocean breeze. I'm alone at a table for two outside on the deck of the restaurant. My dinner was beautiful, and I've just ordered my third margarita. Under normal circumstances, this would be the perfect night.

I've been in Maui for two days, and I have to agree, it's the perfect TTT trip destination.

"Mind if I sit down?" a familiar voice asks.

I look up in surprise to see William. "What? Where... How did you...?"

He pulls the seat out and sits down. "A little birdie told me where to find you."

"How did he...?" My face falls. "The letter." I look around in a panic.

"I'm alone, don't worry." He smiles softly. "You really need to up your hiding skills, though." He takes my hand over the table. "I suggest Switzerland if you don't want to be found."

I lean over and kiss his cheek and smile. "I'm sorry about all of this."

He squeezes my hand. "Don't be."

The waiter comes over. William looks at my glass. "What are we drinking?"

"Margaritas." I smirk.

"Two margaritas, please," he tells the waiter.

"Yes, sir." The waiter disappears.

"Who sent you?" I ask.

"Spencer."

The mere mention of his name brings tears to my eyes. "Is

he..." *Okay?*

He shrugs and stares out at the ocean. "I don't really care how he is, to be honest."

I nod and am quickly reminded of who I'm talking to.

"Are *you* okay?" he asks me.

I shake my head. "No, but I will be." I get a lump in my throat. "I just need some time."

He nods as he watches me, and his drink arrives. He holds it up.

"Miserable in Maui." He smirks as a toast.

"Isn't that the truth?" I take a sip. "I mean, I wanted to spend some time with you, but this type of bonding is a bit extreme."

He chuckles, and my eyes linger on his face. The wind whips up, and the sound of the gentle waves lapping on the shore echoes in the distance.

"What?" he asks.

"You seem different." I frown.

"How so?"

"I don't know, you just do."

"I'm divorcing Penelope."

"You are?" I ask hopefully, and then my face falls as reality creeps back in as to why. "Is this because of Spencer? Has seeing him opened a can of worms for you?"

He stares out over the sea as he thinks. "No, we were always going to end." He sips his drink. "It took some time to prepare myself to walk away. Although all this has forced my hand. When you get married, you just assume..." He shrugs. "You assume that it's all going to turn out, you know?"

I nod as I listen.

"Finding out that the person you fell in love with doesn't love you back...it's a tough pill to swallow."

His words come a little too close to home, and my eyes glaze over.

"I never aspired to be a divorcé." He frowns. "She's been seeing someone else."

"What?"

"I caught her out again just recently. She doesn't know that I know."

I stare at him, my heart filled with sadness. "God, Will."

He shrugs. "I asked Spencer to testify that he was sleeping with her while she was married to me."

"What?" I frown. "What did he say?"

"He said that he didn't want to drag you through the mud any more, and his only concern was you."

My heart drops. My welfare has only ever been his concern.

We sit in silence for a while as we both stare out to sea, lost in our own sad thoughts.

"Are you going to take him back?" he eventually asks.

I bring my feet up onto my chair and tuck them under myself. "I wish it was that easy."

He raises a brow. "What do you mean?"

I run my finger along the edge of the table as I try to piece together my jumbled thoughts. "Every time I think of him, I see Penelope. He knew she was married, for sure."

He clenches his jaw. "I don't think he did, to be honest."

"He's made a fool of both of us, William. Have you seen the tabloids? We're a laughingstock," I whisper. "How am I supposed to forgive him for that?"

I wipe a stray tear and smile sadly. "I'm not sure I like this relationship thing."

"It fucking sucks. Badly."

I giggle at the irony of our situation. "Did you ever imagine sitting here in Maui and having this conversation?"

He shakes his head. "Can't say that I did."

I giggle despite my tears, and then some kind of sanity band breaks and we look at each other and both burst out laughing.

William puts his hands over his eyes. "This is the most fucking ridiculous situation I've ever heard of."

I laugh harder. "I know."

"Poor fucking Edward." He chuckles.

We suddenly fall serious as we think of the anguish our brother will be going through over this. He'll be having a conniption from the disgrace of it all.

"He knew heartbreak was imminent for me," I say.

"I know he did." He sighs sadly. "He was only trying to protect us both in his own fucked-up way."

"Maybe we should have listened when we had the chance."

Once again, we fall silent.

"Well, Charlotte," he says with renewed purpose. "There is only one thing to do in this situation."

"Please." I smirk. "Tell me what that is, because I have no idea."

"Drink all the alcohol on the island."

He raises his glass, and I smile as I lift mine to meet his. "Sounds like a plan."

"Bottoms up."

The afternoon sun shines through my sheer drapes. I'm in a sleepy daze.

William wasn't joking, and he and I did practically drink all of the alcohol on the island last night.

We've taken it very easy today. There's been swimming, eating, and now an afternoon nap.

I'm past being upset. Now I'm angry.

My hotel phone rings, and I frown.

"Hello," I answer.

"Hello, Miss Preston?" the concierge asks.

"Yes."

"You have a visitor here in reception."

"Who is it?"

"She says her name is Sheridan Myer."

25

Charlotte

"I BEG YOUR PARDON." I sit up immediately. "What did you just say?"

"A Sheridan Myer is here to see you."

My blood runs cold. What the hell does that bitch want?

"Please tell her that I'm not accepting visitors."

"Just a moment." She puts her hand over the phone, and I hear her relay my message in the background.

"What? Give me the phone." Sheridan says before I hear her voice directed at me. "Listen, princess, I've flown a long way to come and see you, so you get your arse down here right now."

"I've got nothing to say to you."

"Well, I've got plenty to say to you, and I'm not going home until I do."

"What do you want?"

"Come downstairs, for Christ's sake, and I'll tell you." She hangs up the phone before I can argue.

I slam the phone down in a fluster and stare at it for a few moments.

What the hell?

I run my hands through my hair and begin to pace as my nerves go into overdrive. What does she want? I can't deal with her right now.

What if she's been with Spencer this week and she's here to brag about it?

I feel sick to my stomach.

The phone rings again, and I stare at it before answering. "Hello?"

"Hello, it's concierge again. Miss Sheridan wants to come up to your room."

My eyes widen, and I swallow the lump in my throat. I guess that would be less of a spectacle. God knows I've had enough of those this last week.

"Miss Preston, is that okay?"

"No. I'll come down now."

I don't want that witch in my damn room. I despise her.

Another one of his harem.

I get dressed in a white linen shirt and navy shorts. I quickly brush my teeth and put my hair back into a ponytail.

I look so juvenile compared to her glamorous style, but I clearly wasn't thinking straight when I packed. I brought the most ridiculous clothes with me. Somehow, all of my winter clothes made it into the suitcase and nothing else. I even had to buy a swimming costume when I arrived. I guess that happens when you pack at two in the morning while crying hysterically like a madwoman and suffering from a frozen heart.

With one last inhale and look at myself, I make my way out into the corridor. Anthony is waiting for me, forever my trusty, loyal companion who has never disappointed me. Of course when William turned up last night, so did my security team.

"I'm going down to meet someone in the foyer," I say as I walk past him.

"Who?"

"You don't want to know."

"Who are you meeting?"

438

"A woman." And before I can stop myself, I blurt out, "She's one of Spencer's old girlfriends. God knows what she's doing here."

His face falls. "Oh... I..." He shakes his head. "I strongly advise against it, Charlotte."

"I'm only talking to her for five minutes." I sigh. "If it looks like it isn't going well, come and get me."

"Is Spencer with her?"

My eyes widen. I hadn't thought of that. But he must have told her where I was.

Damn it, is this an ambush?

Surely he couldn't be so stupid.

Before I can second-guess my decision to talk to her, we jump in the lift and travel downstairs. The elevator doors eventually open, and Sheridan comes into view with her back to me and Anthony. She's wearing black Capri pants and a black fitted top.

Still a power outfit, and worse than that, still fucking amazing.

She turns to face me, and her eyes find mine. Unable to help it, she tilts her chin in disapproval.

She holds out her hand to me. "My name is Sheridan."

"I know who you are." I look at her blankly and walk past her, through the hotel, towards the bar. I hear her huffing behind me.

That was so rude of me not to shake her hand, but she can go to Hell. I hate this woman with a passion.

We get to the terrace and she gestures to a table. "Shall we sit here?"

"That depends. Are you going to drop to your knees and try and go down on me to get your own way?"

Her eyes hold mine. "Well, well." She smirks, and I know I've surprised her. "You don't have the right equipment for me to want my own way with you." She pulls the chair out and takes a seat.

"What do you want?" I snap as I sit down.

She smiles and puts her hand up for the waitress, who immediately comes over. "I'll have a martini on the rocks." She turns her attention to me. "What do you want?"

"Same. Whatever." I'm too angry to string two words together.

"What type of martini would you like, miss?" the waiter asks me.

"I'll have mine perfect and she'll have hers dirty."

Sheridan's face falls for just a second before she throws her head back and laughs sharply.

"Oh, that's a good one. And so fitting. I do actually prefer a dirty martini."

I roll my eyes, unimpressed. "Of course you do."

The waiter leaves us in peace, and I glare at her. Her long dark hair is down, and she has the perfect bone structure. She really is beautiful. "What do you want?" I ask.

"I want to talk to you."

"Why?"

"Because someone that I love is hurting."

"I bet you've been there to mop up his tears."

She smirks and raises a brow. "I have, actually."

Our eyes are locked and suddenly we are alone in the world, the sky is suddenly red with my rage, and she is my only target. "Of course you wouldn't miss the chance to race in like a knight in shining armour and save the day."

A cold smile crosses her lips. "I'm more like Lady Godiva."

Bitch.

Our drinks arrive, and I take a sip of mine. Ugh, I hate these things. I hate her, too, so I guess the drink is fitting.

"So, you flew all the way out here to tell me that you slept with Spencer this week?" I ask.

"No." She reaches into her pocket. "I flew all the way here to give you this." She holds out her hand and holds up a memory stick.

I frown as I stare at it. "What is it?"

"Well, while you've been over here playing the pathetic damsel in distress, and Spencer has been at his sickening pity party for one, someone around here has actually been using their fucking brain."

"I don't understand."

"Spencer has a PA who needs to be fired, and I was quite sure she would try and sabotage him at some point. I wanted to catch her out and protect him."

I stare at her.

"I put security cameras in his office."

"What in the hell does this have to do with me?"

"Did you know that Penelope came to him the day before you saw her with William at dinner? Did you know that she wanted him to meet her for sex that night?"

"What?"

"Did you know that they argued, and he kicked '*Stephanie*' out of his office?"

"I don't understand."

"No, you wouldn't." She sits forward. "Because you're a selfish little bitch who won't even listen to what he has to say. You're so caught up in your own fucking agenda that you can't see the forest for the trees."

"Go to Hell. You don't even know me."

"I'll tell you what I do know," she whispers angrily. "I've watched hours and hours of footage from Spencer's office this week, trying to piece together anything that will prove his innocence."

My face falls.

"That's right, sweetie." She sneers. "I've heard his conversations with you. I've seen him defend your honour to your brother. I watched your arguments over me, and Hell, worst of all, I've watched him fuck you on his desk."

My eyes hold hers.

"And I would give anything to have him look at me the way he looks at you. To hear those three words I've so desperately wanted to hear for ten goddamn years."

My eyes fill with tears.

"Don't be a fucking idiot, Charlotte. If you leave him, it will be the biggest regret of your life."

I blink quickly, unsure what to say.

"The man I'm in love with is in Santorini as we speak, waiting for you."

I drop my chin to my chest as sadness overwhelms me. "Did you sleep with him?"

"Time to go," a voice snaps.

We both look up to see Anthony looming over us like a gorilla.

"Who the hell are you?" Sheridan sneers.

"I'm her bodyguard, and I don't appreciate you upsetting her."

"Oh, just fuck off, you idiot." She sighs with an eye roll. "We're in the middle of something here."

He looks at me and I nod. "Please go." He walks off to the other side of the pool.

Our eyes meet again, and hers are cold, while mine are full of tears.

"You love him?" she whispers.

I nod. "Yes."

"If you knew Spencer Jones at all, then you'd know damn well he wouldn't have slept with me this week. He's in love with you. He's a proud man, and if you don't go to him soon, you won't ever get the chance again. You've hurt him deeply, Charlotte. Truth is, you may already be too late."

"I don't know how to get past this. Every time I picture him, I see her."

She exhales heavily. "I can't help you with that one. If Spencer loved me, nothing else on this Earth would matter." We stare at each other. "Are you really going to let Penelope take him from you, for something that happened four years ago when he had no idea who she was or that she was even married?"

I stare at her as a clusterfuck of emotions run through me.

"Fuck the tabloids. Fuck your family. Take what's yours and hold on to it with two hands."

"Is this your motivational speech?"

"This is your 'wake up to your fucking self and get to Santorini'

442

speech." She drains her glass and stands, and without another word, Sheridan walks off into the distance.

She flicks her hair over her shoulder, and I watch her sexy little figure sashay out through the reception area.

I glance down at the memory stick in my hand.

What now?

Spencer

The sea breeze floats over my skin as I watch the reflection of the moon dance across the water. I'm on the balcony, high up above the ocean with the most beautiful view at my fingertips. The fire pit is lit, and I stare back into it.

I can hear the celebrations in the distance. There's muffled music and coloured lights sporadically strung from one property to another on the hill above me. They all twinkle in the distance. Every so often, a crowd cheers as they celebrate together.

Their giggles hang in the air with an eerie echo.

It's New Year's Eve. It's December thirty-first. It's my birthday.

I'm in Santorini, and I'm very much alone.

She didn't come.

And here I am, scrolling through photos of Charlotte on my phone, remembering the good times.

It's heaven and hell all rolled into one.

Image after image, I see her beautiful smiling face staring back at me.

It's almost like I can feel her arms around me. I remember back to when we first met and the way my heart began to beat faster whenever she looked at me. The way my stomach would flutter at her smile...

Her kiss...her perfect kiss.

I exhale heavily and pinch the bridge of my nose. I've had some bad birthdays in my life, but this one takes the biscuit.

I haven't left the villa all day, convinced if I did that, she would come while I was out. Maybe it's me. Maybe I'm destined to have the people I care about walk away from my life.

My mind goes back to a time when I would be feeling just like this—alone in my bedroom, waiting for *him* to call me on my birthday. Waiting for him to extend an olive branch, and desperate for the smallest sign that he did, in fact, love me like my friends' fathers loved them.

I drag my hand down my face. *This is fucked.*

And then the doorbell of the villa rings out.

The doorbell? What?

She's here.

I stand and run to the front door, opening it in a rush. But it's Wyatt who stands before me, not Charlotte.

"Hi." I look past him. "Where is she?"

Sympathy flares in his eyes. "Charlotte asked me to bring you this." He holds out a sealed cream envelope. I read my name written on the front in her fancy handwriting.

My eyes search his. "Where is she?" I whisper, pushing it past the lump in my throat.

He shakes his head. "I'm sorry, man, she isn't here. She wanted me to hand deliver you this."

I don't remember closing the door, getting back to my place by the fire, or opening the letter.

I hold it in shaky hands.

> *My beautiful Spencer.*
> *Happy birthday, my darling.*
> *I wish I could be with you today to celebrate.*

I frown and close it back up. I can't do it. I can't read this fucking letter. I don't want this fucking letter.

I want her.

Somehow, I force myself to read on.

444

I'm so sorry for the pain you've suffered over the last two weeks.

Please forgive me, my love. Inflicting this on you is something that I will never recover from.

We meet people at certain times of our lives for reasons unknown.

But I know exactly why I met you. You taught me how to love, and how to be loved in the most beautiful way.

I cannot thank you enough for all of the times that we have shared.

However...

"No." My heart begins to race, and I skim ahead on the letter. "No, Charlotte." My eyes fill with tears. "Don't you fucking do this to me," I whisper angrily. "Don't you dare fucking do this to me."

No matter how hard I try, I cannot move past your relationship with Penelope.

It kills me that I can't be a bigger person, and I can barely see what I'm writing through my tears right now.

My heart is completely broken, and it will never recover.

It's not fair for you to be with me when my love for you is tainted this way.

You deserve better.

Not all love stories have a happy ending, my darling.

Some are beautiful, some are fearsome, and some are tragic.

Our love story is all of those things.

I'm letting you go, Spence.

You will always be the love of my life, the man who taught me who I really was.

My soul mate and my everything.

Please remember me with love, sweetheart, and with time, I know you will understand.

Love should never be tainted, especially not one as beau-
tiful as ours.
I love you.
Dream catch me.

I screw up the letter and stare at the flames of the fire.

Dream catch me when I fall.

For some sick fucked-up reason, I need to hear it. I need to hear our song one more time. I flick through Spotify and hit play.

I sit and stare at the fire as the tantric beat of the song plays all around me, and I listen on as the lyrics tear open the last pieces of my heart.

She doesn't love me enough.

I throw her letter into the flames and watch it slowly burn as the melody comes to an end.

I dig in my pocket and take out the engagement ring that I bought her. All I can do is stare at it.

I had so much hope and so many dreams for us when I picked it.

Cheers erupt in the distance, and I look up to see the fireworks going off over the water.

It's midnight—the end of one year, the beginning of another. A celebration for most.

The end of the world for me.

I walk to the balcony's edge, and I stare at the diamond ring through tears. The lump in my throat is painful.

Anger surges through me, and I throw the ring as hard as I can over the cliff.

I watch it bounce from the rocks and disappear into the night. Emotion overtakes me, and I sob, my breath quivering with every breath I suck in.

"Happy New Year. Happy fucking New Year."

26

Charlotte

Fourteen Hours Earlier.

I LOOK up at the board and read the dreaded words.

Flight delayed.

"No." I turn to Anthony. "It's delayed."

"Fuck."

"Find us another flight, please," I say as I begin to panic. "Why did I send that damn letter with Wyatt?" I whisper angrily. "What on earth was I thinking?

"Please try and call Wyatt again. He can't deliver it. He just can't."

"He's in the air, he has no service." Anthony shakes his head, silently saying *I told you this ten times already* before he disappears to the front desk to try and organise flights.

I drop to my seat with my head in my hands. I get a vision of my beautiful Spencer alone on his birthday, waiting for me.

Why the hell did I take so long to get my shit together?

What the hell is wrong with me?

I don't have my phone because I threw my SIM in the water during my delusional tantrum. Anthony's phone isn't working here, as we are in another country, so I can only call Spencer from a payphone.

I've been trying for an hour, but he's not picking up. Presumably because he doesn't know the number.

Anthony reappears, his face solemn.

"Any luck?" I ask.

"I can get us on a flight in another hour and a half."

"Oh, great, do that."

"But it has another stopover, so it will actually get us to Santorini later than the original one."

"Oh my God. I've ruined everything," I whisper in a panic. "It's his birthday today."

"It's only early morning there. We'll make it."

"We won't get there in time. You know we won't."

Anthony exhales heavily, and I know that's his way of agreeing with me.

"Call my father. Send the jet. I need his plane urgently."

"By the time it fuels up and gets here, the flight we're on will be quicker."

"Why the hell are they delaying all the flights?"

He puts his arm around me. "Just calm down. We have three hours until we board and then a fourteen-hour flight. You'll have a heart attack before you get there at this rate."

"This is a nightmare. No wonder people complain about flying commercial. I had no idea the delays were so bad."

He smirks as he watches the flight board, and I know I just sounded like a complete spoiled brat. "I think you need a drink." He sighs.

"No, what I need is to try and call Spencer again." I march over to the public phones and get in line. This is all my fault.

Please pick up the phone, Spence. *Please pick up.*

Nineteen Hours Later.

The cab pulls into the driveway, and a heavy sense of dread rests on my shoulders as I stare at the darkened villa.

I missed his birthday. Wyatt was still in the air when we boarded, so I couldn't tell him not to give him the letter. When I wrote it and sent Wyatt before Sheridan came to me, I thought I was doing the right thing by setting him free—giving him closure to start the New Year fresh.

In hindsight, I was just so hurt at his past that I couldn't think clearly, and I will never forgive myself for putting him through that.

I squeeze Anthony's hand. "Wish me luck," I whisper.

He gives me a lopsided smile. "Good luck."

We get out of the car and I walk up to the front door. I turn the handle and realise it's open. He's here.

"Stay out here, please," I whisper.

"I don't thi—"

"Stay here," I cut him off.

I walk through the villa. The small lamps are on, but the main lights are off. It's just as I remembered it, only a lot sadder this time. He must be asleep. I walk into the bedroom but the bed is empty, still made. He hasn't been to bed yet, but his bags and things are here. I check the other bedrooms and then walk out into the living area.

He's on the balcony. My heart begins to race as I make my way out there. It's 4:40 a.m. local time, and the sky is just starting to brighten.

It's eerily quiet. The fire pit has glowing red embers as the last of the fire dies out, and a bottle of scotch is empty on the table.

Spencer's not here.

I walk over to the balcony rail and look down at the view over

449

the cliff. All I can see is darkness as the sea breeze whips my hair around. For a long time, I stand and peer over the cliff.

I get a vision of him spending his birthday alone, and my heart hurts.

Wyatt.

I hope he's with Wyatt. Yes. My hope returns. Hopefully Wyatt and he went out.

I hope they painted the town red.

I'm exhausted, so maybe I'll just go to bed. *He'll be back soon,* I try to comfort myself.

Yes, shower and bed.

I turn to walk inside, and I stop dead in my tracks.

Spencer is sitting in the dark up against the wall, his cold eyes fixed firmly on me.

He has a glass of scotch in his hand.

"Spence," I whisper.

He glares at me as he sips his drink.

"Spencer." I smile hopefully. "I'm here, baby. I'm sorry."

"Get out." He sneers.

My face falls. "What?"

"I said get the fuck out." His voice is gravelly and distorted. He's really drunk.

I step back, affronted by his tone. "I understand why you're angry," I whisper through tears.

He sips his drink, the look on his face murderous.

"Spence, we can work through this," I whisper.

He sips his drink again but remains silent.

"I love you."

"Don't!" he snaps. "Don't. Don't you dare fucking say that to me."

"It's true."

He steps forward and leans in so that his face is only an inch away from mine.

"Get out of my fucking face," he growls.

Fear runs through me. I've never seen him like this.

"Spencer."

"Get out!" he screams at the top of his voice.

My eyes fill with tears.

I go to wrap my arms around him, but he pulls away.

"Don't fucking touch me." He throws his glass at the wall, and it smashes into a thousand pieces.

I put my hands on my head in shock.

From my peripheral vision, I see Anthony sneaking around inside, watching...waiting to see what happens. Spencer is too drunk and way too furious.

"When you're feeling better, we need to talk, please," I whisper through tears.

"I've got nothing to fucking say to you." He storms inside and trips on the step, nearly falling over. Thankfully, he doesn't see Anthony, and he disappears into his bedroom. The door slams hard.

I close my eyes as my heart races wildly.

What the hell was that?

Adrenaline is coursing through my body, and Anthony comes out. "You can go," I tell him, embarrassed by what he just saw.

"I'm not leaving you here with him in that state."

I sit down at the fire pit and stare at the red embers. The sun is coming over the horizon now. I pick up a blanket and wrap it around me. It's cold and chilly...just like my welcome.

How hurt must he be to be acting like that? That is as far from his personality as he could possibly be.

What have I done?

For half an hour, I stare at the fire, my mind in overdrive. Eventually, as exhaustion begins to take over, I can't fight my eyelids any longer. I go inside to the bedroom to find Spencer naked and fast asleep on his back.

I walk back out to Anthony, who is on the sofa. "He's asleep. You can go sleep in the spare room at the end of the hall. I'll sleep in the other one."

"You sure?" He frowns.

I nod and take his hand. "Thank you for looking after me so well."

He smiles sadly and then smirks as if remembering something. "Where the fuck is Wyatt?"

"Hopefully, he's having more fun than we are."

He chuckles. "This is one fucked-up New Year's Eve."

I smile. "Right?"

He gets up and walks in to check on Spencer before he walks around and locks everything up.

"Good night, Charlotte," he says.

"Good night." I sit for a long time and watch the sun slowly rise through the windows. It's like the world has gone into slow motion, and I know more than anything that I need to make this right. I walk into Spencer's bedroom and take a long hot shower. Once clean and naked, I crawl into bed beside him.

He smells like he's tipped a bottle of scotch over his body. I could get drunk from the fumes alone, but I don't care. I wrap my arm around him and put my head on his shoulder, throwing my top leg over his. I gently kiss his chest, and with the familiarity of his warm body up against mine, I drift into an exhausted slumber.

I wake to the light beaming through the window. My eyes flutter to fight against it.

Spencer is still fast asleep, flat on his back, and I roll onto my side to watch him.

His large arms are up behind his head. My eyes drop down over his broad chest and ripped stomach, and then lower down over the well-kept pubic hair onto my favourite body part of his.

His cock is standing to attention up against his stomach. It's big, beautiful, and ready to fuck. I smile at the sight of it. Even in deep sleep, he is the perfect specimen.

Unable to help it, I kiss his chest, and then his bicep as my fingers trail down his abdomen and keep moving lower. I feel my arousal creep in as my fingers run through his pubic hair.

452

God, he's beautiful. *I've missed him so much.*

My fingers wrap around his thick length, and his lips part as he sleeps. "Oh, I could make you feel so good, baby," I whisper to myself.

I stroke him, and he inhales and spreads his legs as if granting me permission. I stroke him again and pre-ejaculate beads on the end of his head. "Do you need me, baby?" I murmur against his chest. "Because I need you."

His legs spread wider and I begin to feel my pulse between my own legs. It's been a long time since we touched each other. I felt like a part of me was missing. I slowly kiss down his abdomen and over his hip bones. I kiss his cock, and it flexes under my lips. I smile as I lick up the thick length of it.

He moans as he stirs, his knees parting and falling to the mattress.

Oh, I need him. I know he's angry with me, but what a great way to make up. I take him into my mouth and my tongue swirls around the tip. He inhales sharply in his sleep, and I smile around him.

"You like that, baby?" I take him deeper and deeper, building a rhythm, and my mouth becomes flooded with pre-ejaculate.

I begin to lose control and take him deeper, when he suddenly jumps awake with a start.

His eyes meet mine and I stop what I'm doing, waiting for his reaction.

Is he going to push me away?

I smile softly around his cock, and he clenches his jaw as he watches me, his hands still above his head.

Okay, he didn't push me away. I'll keep going. I take him deeper, and my hand begins to stroke him as it follows my lips.

He inhales sharply, and I can tell he's close. I can feel his cock quivering under my tongue.

"I missed you," I whisper around him.

His dark eyes hold mine. I begin to flick my tongue over the end of him, something I know forces him to either come or fuck. He has nowhere to go when I do this. He can't hide.

His body convulses. He grabs two handfuls of my hair to hold me in place and he begins to fuck my mouth with deep pumps. I gag at how rough he's being and pull off him. Saliva streams from my lips to his cock.

"Fuck." He moans at the sight of it. "Fucking hell."

Before I know what's happening, he flips me and has me pinned to my back, my legs spread wide.

His dark eyes hold mine as he slides in deep with one hard thrust.

My body convulses, and he pulls out only to slam back into me even harder. "Ouch, Spence," I whisper. "Don't hurt me."

He flips me onto my knees. "Famous last words," he growls as he slaps me hard on the behind and slams in deep, driving me into the mattress.

Oh shit!

He has a handful of my hair in one hand, while the other is holding my shoulder as he slams my body back onto his.

I can feel him so deep inside of me, and he's so thick. He's getting faster and faster, and, oh God, I can't deal with how rough he's being. The sound of our skin slapping together is echoing around the room.

"Spence," I moan as the air is knocked from me. "Oh God."

He grabs my shoulder and pushes me down to the mattress. His cock reaches a new, deeper place. A guttural moan leaves my body, and he slaps me on the behind again.

"Take it." He hisses. "Take it."

I clench and scream into the pillow as I see stars, my body thumping as an orgasm tears through me. He keeps working me at such a fast pace. I can only grip the sheets beneath me and feel the stretching burn of his possession. He holds himself deep and throws his head back, and I feel the jerk of his cock deep inside of me.

But instead of the tender strokes he usually empties himself with, this time is different. He continues to fuck me hard, banging pumps, as if my body is only a tool that he's using to empty his pleasure into.

There is no emotion in his touch.

It's as cold as ice.

With each hit, my tears form. This is foreign to me—so different to how we usually make love.

It's like he's a stranger.

He slaps me on the behind once more, and then he pulls out. Without a word, he gets up and walks into the bathroom, slamming the door behind him.

I lie in shock, my body still quivering from the orgasm I just had. My breathing is ragged as I gasp for air.

Dear God, *what the hell was that?*

I roll over onto my back and stare at the ceiling through my blurred vision.

Fuck this.

I get up and storm into the bathroom. He's in the shower, soaping up.

"What the hell was that?" I demand.

He glares at me. "I'd like to fucking know too."

I scowl in confusion. "What do you mean? You just fucked me like you don't even know me."

"That's because I don't fucking know you."

My face falls. "Spence."

"You're too late," he barks, and my heart drops. He's so hurt.

"Baby." I step under the water and wrap my arms around him. "I love you. I'm so sorry. I had to work this out by myself, and it took longer than I thought it would. I couldn't get a flight, and then I spent all day calling you. Why didn't you answer your damn phone?" I blurt out.

He stands rigid, his hands down by his sides.

My eyes search his and I cup his cheeks. "Can we talk and work this out together?"

"The time for talking was last week, Charlotte. You've put me though fucking Hell."

"I know," I whisper. "I've been to Hell and back myself."

He gets out of the shower in a rush. "I don't want to fucking see you."

"Don't say that," I plead as I reach for him. "I missed you."

He stares at me.

I stand on my tiptoes and softly kiss his lips. I take his arms and wrap them around me. "I love you, Spencer Jones. I'm going to spend the rest of my life making this up to you."

"How could you do this to me?" he asks quietly, his voice breaking. "I didn't know she was married. I swore that to you."

"I know." My eyes fill with tears. "You have no idea how hard this has been on me, Spence. I'm so devastated at how things turned out."

"You think I fucking liked it?" he cries.

"I know that too. I don't know how to get over this, but I do know that I can't live without you. I tried and I couldn't."

He stares at me.

"Let me stay, spend the week with you, and we will try and..." I pause as I articulate my feelings. "We'll try and work through this together."

"No."

"No pressure to get back together. I just need time with you," I plead, and I try to pull us back under the water.

He frowns, as if remembering something.

"What?" I ask.

"I think I threw your engagement ring over the cliff."

"What?" I frown. "You had an engagement ring?" My heart free-falls from my chest as I imagine him waiting with it, and my eyes fill with tears. "Oh my God, Spence, I've ruined everything."

"Yes. You did. In spectacular fashion."

I feel a tiny bit of his resistance begin to cave, and I lean up and kiss him softly. Our lips linger over each other's and my tongue gently slips through his open mouth.

"I love you so much," I breathe.

Our kiss deepens, and I feel the emotion run back through us like a lifeline.

"Spence." The bathroom door opens, and Julian comes into view. His face falls when he sees me.

"What the fuck, Masters?" Spence yells.

"Oh, shit." He turns his back immediately, although too late. He's already seen everything. "Sorry." He winces. "I thought you were alone." He hunches his shoulders as if excited. "Hi, Charlotte."

I smile as I look up at my beautiful man and cup his face. "Hi, Jules."

"I was just coming to see if you...well, both of you now, wanted to come to the beach. But I can see you're busy."

Spencer's eyes hold mine. "We'll meet you there."

I can't stop kissing him, even though Julian is still in the room.

"Although Charlotte may be in a body bag by the time I've finished with her," Spencer adds dryly.

Julian chuckles. "Okay, well, just make sure that her body-guards don't see you kill her. I'm not sure I could get you off that one, and you're way too pretty to go to prison."

I smile softly, and in that moment, I know it's going to be okay.

We *are* going to make it through this together. His friends, my friends, and our families combined will make it work...whatever it takes.

"See you later," Julian says as he walks out.

I frown, confused. "Where's Julian staying?"

"He, Bree, and the kids are three doors up, and Seb is in town. They wouldn't let me come alone in case you didn't show up."

"Why weren't they with you yesterday?"

"I wanted to be alone. I was waiting for you."

I stare up at the beautiful man in front of me. "Can you ask me to marry you now?"

"No." He kisses my lips.

My face falls, and I think for a moment. "Fine. Then, Spencer Jones...will you marry me?"

"Again, no."

"Spencer," I whine. "You're supposed to say yes."

"And you were supposed to stay by my side when things got rough."

My heart drops. I hate that I let him down.

"I will now. I promise." I pause and smile. "Do you know what this is, Spence? It's a new beginning for us."

He exhales heavily and hangs his head. "The last two weeks..." His voice trails off.

I stare into his big blue eyes, and the hurt in them breaks my heart wide open. "Baby," I whisper. He wraps his arms around me and holds me tight. We stay in each other's arms for a long time, and it's like the longer our bodies touch skin to skin, the more I can feel the emotions run between us.

"Let's go back to bed," I suggest quietly.

He nods, and we step out of the shower. I dry us both off, and then he leads us into the bedroom. I lie down beside him.

"I love you, Spence."

His eyes close as if hearing me say that pains him, and then he kisses me. He really kisses me with his heart on his sleeve and without holding back.

It's long and slow and deep and everything I've missed about us.

He rises above me and slowly slides in deep. Our mouths fall open in the overwhelming pleasure of each other's bodies. I've missed this. *I've missed him.*

"I love you."

His eyes search mine.

"Spence...?"

"I love you too, angel."

Our lips crash and we cling to each other as tight as we can as we try desperately to banish the fear of losing one another ever again. I don't know what kind of Hell we've just been through, but now I can see a glimmer of light at the end of the dark tunnel.

If we hold each other tight enough, we might just make it through.

"Are you ready to do this?" I ask him.

Spencer shrugs, and I take his hand in mine. We've just landed at Heathrow Airport and we're just about to walk out into the arrivals lounge. I already know that the paparazzi are waiting for us. Security have called the boys to let them know, so I take my mother's ring off my right hand and slip it onto my wedding finger.

"What are you doing?" He frowns.

"Giving them something to talk about. If they think we're already married, they won't notice when we do actually get engaged. And besides, from now on I plan on giving them as much bogus material to publish as possible. I want the world to know that they can't trust what they read in this trash."

He rolls his eyes. "We're not getting engaged, Charlotte. That ship well and truly sailed when I threw a quarter of a million pounds over a fucking cliff."

I smile up at him. Anthony, Wyatt, and I searched that damn cliff for two days, looking for my ring...with no such luck. Spencer wouldn't help us, of course. He stayed on the deck by the pool, drinking cocktails. He said that the ring was bad luck and a sign that he should never get married. I plan on proving him wrong if it's the last thing that I ever do.

"Have you got a ring you can put on your ring finger?" I ask.

He looks at me, deadpan. "No, because I'm not getting married."

We've had a good week in Santorini—a wonderful week—and even though I know he's still holding a grudge against me, we're together, we still love each other, and every day we get a little bit closer to where we used to be. I really messed things up between us, and every time he tells me we are never getting married, I silently freak out.

"Okay."

"I fucking mean it," he whispers as we come into view of the photographers.

"Charlotte!" the photographers all cry. "Over here, over here." I smile at the cameras as I grip Spencer's hand with my right hand and wave with my left. He keeps his head down and concentrates on moving us forward.

"The car is out the front," Wyatt says as he ushers us forward towards the doors.

"She's wearing a ring!" someone calls out, and they all push forward.

"Charlotte, did you marry Spencer Jones? What does your father think about this? What about William? Have you seen your lover Penelope Prescott, Spencer? Were you on your honeymoon?"

The black Mercedes wagon comes into view and pulls up by the kerb. Spencer opens the door, and then hesitates when he sees my father and Edward already in the car.

"Get in," I urge as the cameras are clicking away.

Spencer gets in and slams the door shut, and I hold my breath. The car pulls away to escape the madness.

"Hello, Spencer," Edward says.

"Fuck off," Spencer mutters. "Drop me home now."

Edward and my father exchange looks. "We want to talk to you."

"Yeah, well, I've got nothing to say." He keeps his eyes cast out the window.

I take Spencer's hand in mine, resting it in my lap, and I remain silent.

"We need your help," my father says.

Spencer's eyes rise to theirs, and he smirks. "You've made it quite clear where you and I stand. Don't come to me when you need help to get rid of her." He shakes his head in disgust. "I won't be used."

460

I grip his hand tightly.

"Charlotte, talk some sense into him," Edward says.

"No. I won't, and he's completely right. Leave us alone. I'm telling you right now that if you don't accept Spencer into our family, you will not see me either."

They both glare at me.

"Spencer and I are getting married. Whether you come to our wedding or not is up to you."

Edward clenches his jaw.

The car pulls up at Spencer's building, and he gets out in a rush. My father and Edward jump out behind me.

"What are you doing?" my father asks.

"I'm going home, Dad."

"Your home is in Nottingham."

"My home is with Spencer. Wherever he is is home to me."

Tenderness fills Spencer's eyes as he watches on, not saying a word.

"Now, if you would both like to come to London next weekend and have dinner with us, then that would be great. If not, I'll see you around." I rise up to kiss Spencer, and I take his hand in mine.

Edward inhales deeply, clearly trying to hold his tongue.

My father smirks and glances between us. He knows that this is it. I won't back down again.

"Dinner would be lovely, darling. See you both next weekend. I'll look forward to it." He kisses my cheek and holds his hand out to shake Spencer's. For a moment, Spencer just stares at him. I hold my breath as I watch on. There's so much history, so much heartache...

Please just shake his hand.

Eventually, good manners prevail, and Spencer gives in and shakes his hand.

"Look after her," my father whispers.

Spencer gives him a curt nod and turns, leading me into the building. We get into the lift and the doors shut behind us.

461

I smile at the beautiful man in front of me, grateful that he is willing to move on from all of this.

"I love you," I whisper.

He wraps his arms around me. "You can show me how much in a minute."

I giggle. "Swoony Spencer Jones at his romantic best."

He gives me a sexy wink and we kiss as the elevator takes us higher and higher.

It doesn't matter what happens from here, because I know everything is going to be okay.

He loves me and I love him.

He is my everything.

EPILOGUE

Spencer

Two Years Later.

BEYONCÉ'S VOICE pours out the lyrics to "*Naughty Girl.*"

I stand on the side of the dance floor with Masters and Seb as we watch the girls. Bree, Beth, and Charlotte are solid friends now. They laugh and giggle at a private joke as they dance. Charlotte's business is booming. She now has six lawyers working for her, and they just won an award for best charity of the year. Sarah and Paul are still there for Charlotte's moral support, supplying her with plenty of laughs.

Apparently, Hot Dick City is a real place. Who knew?

Life is good. We still live in my apartment in London. We're also still madly in love, and nothing much has changed. Actually, nothing has changed. Things between us have only gone from strength to strength.

Charlotte got a grey and white kitten and we called him Greyson. That cat is the most adored thing on Earth, and he runs rings around the both of us. He rules our apartment.

I testified in a private court hearing against Penelope twelve months ago, and William and her now share custody of Harrison. Strangely enough, Edward and I now get along well. He's not a bad bloke underneath all the power-tripping bullshit he has going on. Harold is insisting on teaching me parts of the business so that I could help Edward if anything were to ever happen to him.

William and I are...complicated. He's a great guy, and I respect him immensely, but he will never forgive me, and I don't blame him after what he walked in on. It's a guilt I have had to learn to live with. We are amicable, and I know he's happy that Charlotte is happy, but that's about it. He lives in London now and Charlotte sees him regularly. I see him at family events only.

I watch Charlotte's sexy little arse move to the music, and arousal sweeps over me.

This woman, this beautiful woman, came into my life and changed everything about who I thought I was. I smile softly as I watch her laugh with her friends.

She's perfect. Inside and out.

"Is Charlotte still on your case about getting married?" Masters asks.

"She hasn't mentioned it for a while. Hopefully she's given up."

"You're fucking mad." Seb scoffs in disgust.

I roll my eyes and sip my beer.

"Every time you're in a room with her, you watch her like an awestruck little schoolboy."

"Yeah, well, we know what happened last time I tried to propose. Getting married is fucking bad luck for me."

"Bullshit." Masters huffs. "You're just scared."

I sigh and continue to watch my angel's behind. *I'm going to fuck that beautiful ass tonight.*

"How much did you pay for that ring you threw off the cliff like a madman?" Masters frowns.

"Way too much." I smirk. I was going mad that night, without a doubt.

"You know she wants a baby," Masters says casually as he sips his beer.

"What?"

"I heard her tell Bree the other day when they were in my kitchen. She was holding Henry and she said that she would love a baby."

I frown. "She's not mentioned anything to me." Fear swirls in my stomach. The thought of changing the dynamics between us terrifies the fuck out of me.

"Why would she?" Seb snaps. "You won't even fucking marry her."

"You know why I won't marry her. It has nothing to do with how I feel about her."

"Does she know that?"

"She does know that."

I watch her dance as my stomach clenches.

Marriage and babies...with Charlotte.

My biggest dream.

My greatest fear.

My true destiny?

Charlotte

Six Weeks Later.

I wake to the feeling of Spencer curled around me from behind, and I turn my head as he kisses my temple.

"Good morning, Mr Spencer."

I feel him smile against my skin. "Good morning, Miss Prescott."

"It's Saturday." I smile sleepily.

He pulls me closer to his body and I feel his erection up against my hip. "My favourite day of the week. I get you all to myself." His lips drop to my neck.

I look around the room. "Where's Greyson?"

"Hmm. Who cares? Probably ripping up the sofa downstairs."

I giggle.

We hear his little bell, and then something smashes downstairs. "Fucking cat," Spencer mutters under his breath.

I laugh and climb out of bed. I throw my robe on and go downstairs to investigate. A potted plant has been tipped over, and there is dirt everywhere.

"What are you doing?" I whisper to the naughty kitten as he rubs against my legs as if proud of himself.

"Greyson," I sigh, assessing the damage. Spencer pretends to hate our cat, but I know he secretly loves him. Every time I come in, they are snuggled up together on the sofa. I clean up the dirt, make us both a cup of coffee, and then head upstairs. I walk into my room to find Spencer in the bathroom at the sink. I place the coffees down on the bedside and walk in to put my arms around him. I glance down his body in the reflection of the mirror, and I see he has an erection.

The man always has an erection.

I smile and reach around to stroke him, and I feel something. "What's that?"

He turns to me and I look down. He has a red ribbon tied in a bow around his hard dick. "What in the world?" I laugh. This man kills me.

He smirks with that mischievous look that he does so well. "You better unwrap your present."

I giggle and bend to take him into my mouth. I begin to untie the bow, when I notice a ring on the ribbon.

I frown as I stare at it. It's a huge solitaire diamond sitting on a rose gold band. My eyes meet his.

"Marry me."

"W-what?" I breathe.

"Marry me, Charlotte." He smiles.

"You tied my engagement ring to your dick and asked me to marry you with your dick in my mouth? Spencer Jones!"

"It was either tied to that or to your butt plug." He shrugs casually. "And I wanted a story to tell our grandkids."

I laugh out loud as he pulls me to my feet. "You are the craziest man I know."

Our lips meet in a kiss. "Marry me, angel."

Our foreheads touch. "That depends…"

"On what?"

"Oh, I don't know." I stroke his dick and widen my eyes. "Things."

His eyes dance with delight, and he grabs me roughly and slides the ring onto my finger. "I'm asking one more time before I fuck you unconscious. Will you marry me, Charlotte Prescott?"

I kiss his lips with a huge smile. "I love you."

"I love you too. Now answer the damn question."

"Yes, I'll marry you." I grin.

We smile broadly at each other. This proposal is just so Spencer.

"Good. Now get on your knees and finish what you started."

Five Years Later.

It's 11:00 p.m. and I'm watching my beautiful man walking around the living room with our daughter in his arms as he tries to console her. Amelia is eighteen months old, teething, and in a world of pain.

"It's okay, baby. It's okay, daddy's here."

If you thought Spencer Jones was swoony before, you should see him with a daughter. He worships the ground she walks upon.

I'm heavily pregnant with our second child, sprawled on the sofa, defeated by exhaustion. It's been a long week.

This teething thing is tough. We've had no more than three hours of sleep on any given night…and it's about to get tougher.

"Babe," I whisper.

"Yeah, angel." He sits down on the couch at my feet. "Look how tired mummy is," he says to Amelia as he rubs my feet.

"I'm having contractions."

His face falls. "What?"

I nod.

"Now?"

"Uh-huh."

He looks at me, deadpan, and he rushes to sit on the floor beside me, watching me for a moment.

"Lie to me," he whispers. "Give me something to hang on to here."

I smile softly. It's such a Spencer thing to say. I reach up and run my fingers through his stubble. "We are on a yacht, sailing around the Caribbean."

He smirks. "Yes."

"And I'm wearing nothing but a gold string bikini."

He leans forward and runs his fingers through my hair. "God, this sounds so good."

"We've been having crazy sex all day," I whisper.

"Yeah, I like it. What am I doing now?"

"Sleeping uninterrupted."

He smiles and then bursts out laughing. "You're right—sleep is my ultimate fantasy at the moment."

Amelia struggles in his hold and breaks out crying again. He scoops her up into his arms. "Come on, baby, we've got to take mummy to the hospital. You can have a sleepover at Grandma's." He begins to take her upstairs to get her ready.

"Spence!" I call.

He turns back to look at me.

"One day, we'll go to the Caribbean just so you can have your fantasy. I promise."

He walks back over to me and kisses me softly, his hand resting tenderly on my huge stomach.

"Every day with you is my fantasy, angel. Every single day."

Read on for an excerpt of Mr Garcia...

MR GARCIA - EXCERPT

FULL BOOK AVAILABLE NOW

April

The whirl of the traffic spins past at a deafening speed.

People, like ants, conform as they rush along the congested sidewalk.

Morning rush hour in London is always hectic. A fast-paced mecca filled with the busiest of the busy people, and I'm no different, rushing to get to my job at a coffee house.

I'm late, as usual, after studying into the early hours of this morning.

I really need to get a High Distinction on my test this afternoon. Getting a full scholarship for my law degree was amazing, but living on the other side of the world from my family and friends now is not.

If I get enough HDs, I'm hoping to transfer back to the United States and study there. At least then I'll have my family, and being a broke student won't be so fucking lonely.

I stride up to a busy four-way intersection. It's packed, and a lot of people are waiting for the lights to change to cross the street. I stand up against the row of shops, waiting, only to glance over and see a man on his knees, dishevelled and shoeless. He sits on his knees, holding a cup out, asking for spare change from those around him. I take out my purse. Damn it, I don't have any cash on me.

My heart constricts as everyone pretends not to see him, like he doesn't exist or matter—a stain on society.

How did we become so numb to the homeless and poor? It's just assumed he's an addict. That's how these people justify ignoring him. They think that if they react, then they will be feeding his addiction. They think you have to be cruel to be kind.

I don't get it, I really don't.

I exhale at the thought of our depressing reality. One filled with brand names and social media. Everything this poor man is not.

From the corner of my eye, I see a man stop in front of him.

He's tall, wearing an expensive suit. He looks cultured and wealthy, with black hair and a handsome face.

He stands and looks down at the man.

Oh no, what's he going to do? Is he going to kick him off the street for begging?

Is he going to call the police? Or worse...

He drops to one knee in front of the homeless man, and my heart constricts.

The lights change, but I'm too worried to walk across the street. I need to see what this guy is going to do. He'd better not drag him to his feet, or I'll lose my shit.

He's harmless. Leave him alone.

I get a vision of me kicking the handsome man in the balls in the beggar's defence.

Stupid rich twat.

The man in the suit says something, and the homeless man nods. I watch as he reaches into the inside pocket of his suit jacket to retrieve his wallet, pulls out a fifty-pound note, and hands it over.

What?

He asks the homeless man a question, and the beggar smiles

up at him as though God himself has just bestowed a sacred gift. The homeless man puts his hand out to shake the handsome man's hand, and he shakes it with no hesitation.

With a kind nod, the rich guy stands, completely oblivious to anyone around him, and he bids him goodbye before he turns and crosses the street.

I watch him walking away, and I smile to myself, my faith in the human race restored.

Wow, that was unexpected. I continue on my way with a spring in my step. I finally cross the street and make my journey via two streets before I walk two blocks, and I catch sight of the man in the suit up ahead again. I crane my neck to look ahead to see him. He disinfects his hands with a small bottle of hand sanitizer that he has pulled out from his pocket.

My heart swells. He waited until he was out of the homeless man's sight to clean his hands.

Thoughtful, too.

I stop still and watch him; he's handsome and possibly in his midthirties.

I wonder who his wife is, the lucky bitch. I bet his kids are kind, too.

He disappears around the corner, and I turn and walk into my coffee shop, listening to the bell over the door ringing out.

Monica looks up from her place on the register. "Hey."

"Hi." I smile and walk past her, out the back to put my bag in a locker.

The café is packed, with every seat occupied. Damn it, I was hoping for a slow morning. I need to save my energy for my exam this afternoon.

"Hey, chick," Lance says as he carries a box of cups out the back door.

"I thought you were working tonight." I frown.

"I got called in." He sighs. "*So* not in the mood for this fucking shithole today."

"Join the club." I put my black and white apron on and tie it at the back before I walk to my place at the cash register. "I'll take over."

I bump Monica out of the way with my hip, and she stumbles to the side.

"Good," she mumbles, "I'm dying of Bourbon-itis."

"Bourbon is bad. That shit will kill you," I whisper.

The next person in line steps forward.

"Hello. How can I help you?"

"Do you have goat's milk?" the trendy-looking woman asks.

"Umm." I glance behind me to ask Monica, but she's disappeared. I've never heard of goat's milk before.

"I want a goat's milk turmeric latte, thank you," the customer says.

"Let me go check." I quickly dart out the back to find someone to ask. Lance is cutting up boxes. "Do we serve goat's milk turmeric lattes?"

Lance screws up his face. "Who the fuck would want to drink that shit?"

"This nut out there."

"Fuck's sake," he mutters dryly. "People are trying too hard to be trendy. Goat's milk turmeric. Now I've heard it all."

"So that's a no?"

"Hard no." He smashes a box up. "This is a goat-free milking zone."

I giggle. Monica walks past us, out the back door and into the ally. "Going to the bathroom. I feel sick."

"You okay?" I call, watching as she runs for the door.

"What's wrong with her?" Lance asks.

"Hungover. Bourbon."

Lance winces. "Nasty."

"Cover the coffee machine for me, will you?" Monica says as the door bangs shut behind her.

I go back to the front of the shop to see I now have a huge line waiting. Great. "I'm sorry, we don't have any goat's milk turmeric."

"Why not?" the customer asks.

"Because we don't stock it. I'm sorry." I fake a smile. "This is a goat-milk-free coffee house."

"That's not good enough. I want to see the manager."

Oh, fuck off, bitch. I'm not in the mood for you today. There isn't even a manager on duty.

"Now!" she demands.

I fake another smile. "I'll just go get him." I march out the back to Lance. "She wants to see the manager."

"Who does?"

"The goat chick."

"What about?"

"I don't know. Fucking goats! Get out there." I march back out to the register. "He won't be a moment." I smile. "Can you please step aside so I can serve the next person?"

She glares at me and crosses her arms, then steps to the side and waits.

"Can I help you?" I ask the next man.

"Hi." He grins. Oh God...*not you*. "It's me, Michael."

"Yes." I cringe. "I remember. Hi, Michael. What can I get you?"

"I'll have the usual." He winks.

I take his order and the bell rings over the door to tell me someone else has entered. "That will be four pounds ninety-five," I say coldly.

I take Michael's card and swipe it through the card machine. I can't make casual conversation with Michael because he's way too flirty.

"I want goat's milk," I hear the woman demanding.

"Well, we don't have any," Lance replies. I can tell by the tone of his voice that he isn't in the mood for this crap today, either.

"I want you to put it on the menu immediately."

I glance over to Lance. His face is murderous, and I bite my lip to hide my smile.

"Look, lady, if you want goat's milk, you're going to have to go somewhere else. We are not into milking goats."

"You'd rather milk a cow?"

"Or kick them out of my coffee shop," Lance mutters dryly. "Either, or."

Jeez... I drop my head to hide my smile.

"Did you just call me a cow?" the woman gasps.

Shit, buzz off, bitch. Enough with the dramatics. Just leave already.

"Can I help you?" I ask the next customer, and look up at the queue.

Big brown eyes stare back at me, and I step back in surprise.

It's him.

The guy from the street.

"Hi." I smile bashfully and tuck a piece of hair behind my ear.

He's wearing a perfectly fitted dark navy suit and a crisp white shirt. He looks like he might be European or something.

"Hello." His voice is deep and husky.

I feel my cheeks blush, and I smile nervously. "Hi."

We stare at each other. *Fuck me.* This guy is completely gorgeous.

A trace of a smile crosses his face, as if he's reading my mind.

I smile goofily over at him and hunch my shoulders.

He raises his brows. "Do you want to know my order?"

"Oh." I pause. "I was waiting for you," I lie. Fuck, I'm acting like a starstruck teenager. *Get it together, stupid.* "What would you like?"

"I'll have a double macchiato, please."

I twist my lips to hide my smile. Even his coffee is hot.

"Would you like anything else?" I ask.

He raises his eyebrow. "Such as?"

I open my mouth to say something, but no words come out.

He smirks, realizing he has me completely flustered.

Oh, hell, act fucking cool, will you?

"A muffin?" I reply. "They're delicious."

"All right." His eyes hold mine. "Why don't you surprise me, April?"

I stare at him as my brain misfires. "How do you know my name?"

"It's on your apron."

474

I scrunch my eyes shut. "Oh...right." *Please, Mother Earth, swallow me whole. Way to bimbo it out.* "Ah, excuse me. I'm not with it today," I stammer.

"You look completely with it to me." He gives me his first genuine smile, and I feel it to my toes.

It's official: *this man is delicious.*

"And your name?" I ask, holding my pen to his cup.

"Sebastian."

"Mr. Sebastian?"

"Mr. Garcia."

Sebastian Garcia. Even his name is hot. "Would you like another coffee for your wife?"

"There's no wife."

"Girlfriend?"

"No girlfriend." A smile crosses his face once more. He knows I'm fishing for information.

Our eyes are locked, and the air crackles between us.

The man behind him in the line sighs heavily. "I'm in a rush, you know."

Oh, get lost. I'm trying to flirt here.

Dickhead.

Mr. Garcia steps to the side, and I bring my attention to the man behind him. "Can I help you?"

"I want a toasted ham and cheese sandwich, and you'd better make it quick," he barks.

"Of course, sir." Fuck, why is every asshole in London in my café today?

"Excuse me," I hear from the side.

The man and I look up to see Mr. Garcia has taken a step towards us.

"What?" the asshole snaps.

"What did you just say?" Mr. Garcia raises an eyebrow, clearly annoyed.

The man shrivels, taken aback. "I'm in a rush."

"No need to be rude." Mr. Garcia's eyes hold his. "Apologize."

The man rolls his eyes.

"Now."

"Sorry," the man mumbles to me.

I press my lips together to hide my smile.

Mr. Garcia steps back to his place by the wall.

I feel my cheeks flush with excitement.

Saw-oon.

"That won't be a minute," I say, and the man nods, not saying another word.

I glance around, wondering who is making the coffees.

Oh, shit, I'm supposed to be.

Wait, how do you make a double macchiato again?

I have never done this before, although I have watched the others do it a million times. I concentrate and do what I think they do. I turn back to the customers.

"Mr. Garcia," I call, and he steps forward. "Here you go."

His eyes hold mine as he takes it from me. "Thank you." He nods and then turns, and I watch him walk towards the door. Shit...that's it?

Turn around and ask me out, damn it.

He stops on the spot and I hold my breath. He turns back. "April, I'll see you tomorrow."

I smile. "I hope so."

He dips his head, and with one more breathtaking smile, he turns and walks out onto the street. Like a little kid, I pick up a cloth and practically run to the front of the café so I can watch which direction he takes.

I pretend to wipe a table near the window so I can spy.

Sebastian walks past a few shops, and I see him take a sip of his coffee and wince. He screws up his face, and with a shake of his head, he throws it in a trash can.

What? After all that, he didn't even drink it!

My mouth falls open.

"Am I going to get served here or what?" the rude man calls from the counter.

"Yes, of course, sir." I fake another smile and make my way back to the coffee machine.

You're going to get the worst fucking coffee I've ever made, asshole.

And judging by Mr. Garcia's reaction, that's pretty bad.

I walk down the corridor of Holmes Court, my dormitory accommodation at university.

I think I flunked my exam, damn it.

The sound of laughter echoes through the hall, and a faint techno beat can be heard in the distance. Coming home to this place is a living hell.

I have never hated living somewhere as much as I hate it here. I mean, everyone is nice enough, but I feel like their grandmother. At the age of twenty-five, I'm considered a mature student, yet for some unknown reason, my scholarship houses me with the freshmen, all of which are eighteen and on their first leave of absence from home.

Everyone is either blind drunk or having sex, and I don't really care what they do, but do they have to make so much fucking noise when they do it?

This place is like a twenty-four-seven nightclub. They party all night and sleep all day.

How they are actually passing any of their subjects is beyond me.

I exhale heavily as I trudge up the stairs. The music is getting louder now. Of course it is.

Penelope Wittcom: my neighbour and archenemy. We share a common wall, and on my side of it, I try to study, sleep, and be a respectable student. On her side, it's party and orgy central. Her bedroom is known around campus as the 'Rave Cave'.

Open all fucking night.

She even has a disco ball in there.

People come and go at all hours, slamming doors, partying, and yahooing. To be honest, I think she might be dealing drugs.

477

She has to be. Nobody can be that popular and have so many visitors.

And that's not the worst of it by far.

I've never heard so much screaming during sex in my life!

I've lost count of how many men she has gone through. I mean, good for her—at least one of us is getting it—but does she have to howl every time she comes?

I've put in complaints. I've requested to move buildings. I've done everything possible. But it's pretty hard to be heard when Penelope is sleeping with the floor manager.

And besides, I'm on a scholarship. I'm not paying to live here, so I have to suck it up.

I just have to get through the rest of this year, and hopefully my grades will be good enough to get a scholarship to return to the States.

When I left my cheating, douchebag ex-husband Roy, I walked out with nothing. Every cent I had earned is in the house that he still lives in, and until he agrees to sell it, I have to live with the fallout.

I'm in my second year of law school, which I'm so proud of, but I also need to live while I study. I've applied for every job under the sun, but my course hours are intense, and nothing ever seems to fit in with my schedule. I'm grateful for my job at the café, but with only three shifts a week, it just doesn't pay enough for me to get an apartment of my own. So, for now, this is my life.

The music is really pumping when I walk past Penelope's room. Her door is propped open. Four or five guys are sitting on her floor, and the distinct smell of cigarette smoke invades the corridor.

I walk past them without so much as a smile and close my door behind me. The loud music only softens a little, so I put my head-phones on. Who knew I would need noise-cancelling headphones just to get through my day?

I flick the television on, which is connected by Bluetooth to my headphones. I grab a mineral water from the fridge, flop onto the couch, and I begin to scroll through my phone. I open an email.

Subject: Application
From: Club Exotic
To: April Bennet

Congratulations, April.
You have been successful in securing an interview with Club Exotic.
We look forward to meeting you at 290 High Street, London East, at 11:00 a.m. on the 22nd of next month.
We pay above National Minimum Wage, have an excellent career development pathway plan, and we are recruiting ten team members to join our beloved crew.
Please RSVP within seven days of receiving your invitation.

Club Exotic.

I sit up instantly.

I applied for this job *months* ago. A girl who used to work at the café worked at Club Exotic one night a week at the bar, and it covered her entire rent.

I jump off the couch in excitement.

I mean, I know it's not ideal. It's a gentlemen's club, but it *is* only behind the bar.

How hard can it be to pour drinks?

Plus, I've had to listen to Penelope having sex every night for free, anyway. I'm pretty sure my pure eyes and ears can handle anything these days.

If I don't find something beforehand, this could work out okay. I speed-read the email again. Gosh, that's five weeks away, though.

Damn it, five weeks is a long time.

My phone begins to vibrate.

"Hello."

"Hello, April?"

"Yes." I don't recognize the voice.

"This is Anika from Club Exotic."

"Oh." I frown. "I actually just opened an email from you."

"Yes, that's why I'm calling. We've just had somebody leave without notice, and you were the first person on our interview list who has answered."

"Okay..."

"Do you want to come in tomorrow for an interview? I know it's last-minute, but otherwise your interview isn't until next month."

I quickly run through my schedule for tomorrow. I guess I can skip my lecture. "Yeah, sure. That would be great. What time?"

"Can you be here at eleven?"

I don't finish my shift at the café till 10.30 a.m., though I could get ready before my shift. "Okay, that sounds great, thank you." I smile, excited. "I'll see you then."

"Can I help you, sir?"

"I'll have a toasted cheese on rye and a flat white, please."

"Sure." I smile as I tap his order into the computer. It's another day at the café, another few pounds. "That will be nine pounds ninety-five, thanks."

He hands over his money, and I hear the distant bell over the door as someone new enters the building.

This is the longest shift I've ever done at the café. I'm nervous about my interview this morning. After thinking on it all night, I've decided that I really want that job.

If I could just work two shifts a week, then I could move out of the dorm and into my own studio apartment.

Imagine that!

Don't get excited. You haven't gotten it yet, I remind myself.

"Can I help you?" I ask as I glance up and stare straight into the eyes of Mr. Garcia.

He came back.

"Hello," he says in his deep voice.

The air between us is doing that thing again...electricity and butterflies all rolled into one.

"You back for more of my great coffee?" I smirk.

He gives me a slow, sexy smile. "I am."

To continue reading the paperback version of Mr. Garcia, find it in your favorite bookstores from September 2024.

AFTERWORD

Thank you so much for reading and
for your ongoing support.
I have the most beautiful readers in the whole world!

Keep up to date with all the latest news and online discussions
by joining the Swan Squad VIP Facebook group and
discuss your favourite books with other readers.
@tlswanauthor

Visit my website for updates and new release information.
www.tlswanauthor.com

ABOUT THE AUTHOR

T L Swan is a Wall Street Journal and #1 Amazon Best Selling author. With millions of books sold, her titles are currently translated in twenty languages and have hit #1 on Amazon in the USA, UK, Canada, Australia and Germany. Tee resides on the South Coast of NSW, Australia with her husband and their three children where she is living her own happy ever after with her first true love.